THE
LAST
SUMMER
IN IRELAND

D0869725

BOOKS BY NOELLE HARRISON

The Island Girls

The Boatman's Wife

The Gravity of Love

The Adulteress

The Secret Loves of Julia Caesar

I Remember

A Small Part Of Me

Beatrice

Noelle Harrison

THE
LAST
SUMMER
IN IRELAND

bookouture

Published by Bookouture in 2022

An imprint of Storyfire Ltd.
Carmelite House
50 Victoria Embankment
London EC4Y 0DZ

www.bookouture.com

Copyright © Noelle Harrison, 2022

Noelle Harrison has asserted her right to be identified as the author of this work.

All rights reserved. No part of this publication may be reproduced, stored in any retrieval system, or transmitted, in any form or by any means, electronic, mechanical, photocopying, recording or otherwise, without the prior written permission of the publishers.

ISBN: 978-1-80314-259-3
eBook ISBN: 978-1-80314-258-6

This book is a work of fiction. Names, characters, businesses, organizations, places and events other than those clearly in the public domain, are either the product of the author's imagination or are used fictitiously. Any resemblance to actual persons, living or dead, events or locales is entirely coincidental.

*For Lizzie for shining so bright
And for Kate and Donna for sharing their light.*

The Song of Fionnuala

Silent, oh Moyle, be the roar of thy water,
Break not, ye breezes, your chain of repose,
While, murmuring mournfully, Lir's lonely
    daughter
Tells to the night-star her tale of woes.
When shall the swan, her death-note singing,
Sleep, with wings in darkness furl'd?
When will heav'n, its sweet bell ringing,
Call my spirit from this stormy world?

— FROM THE POEM BY THOMAS
MOORE (1779–1852)

CHAPTER ONE

IRIS

ROSCOMMON, IRELAND

Iris sat in the garda car in stunned silence. She stared at the back of Ruairi's head, noticing a whorl of dark hair which had escaped when he had taken off his hat to drive. He was no longer her friend because Ruairi was one of the guards who had just arrested her. Next to him sat the other guard, Eamon. On Christmas Eve in the pub, Eamon had been jovial and laughing, not at all how the cops were back in New York. But what she had done had wiped the smile off Eamon's face.

She just couldn't believe it. It didn't seem real. Less than one week ago, Iris had been on the top of Queen Maeve's Cairn with Ruairi by her side, her heart soaring. She had stood with her arms spread wide and felt the wind behind her, lifting her up, as if nudging her to take flight. The rolling green land of County Sligo with the majestic tier of Ben Bulben mountain had been to her right, while the sweep of the Atlantic Ocean had lain ahead. The sea had appeared turquoise, glittering in the fragmented sunlight which had shot through the cloud strata as white crests of waves had crashed upon the golden strand. It had been a perfect first date.

She remembered dropping her arms and smiling at Ruairi.

'It's a great view, right?' he had shouted above the sound of the wind, his cheeks ruddy in the elements, and his eyes bright.

'Yes, it sure is,' she had shouted back.

He had taken her hand in his and their fingers had naturally intertwined. She imagined the heat of his heart in the warmth of his body passing through his skin into her own. Her heart had raced, fuelled by his touch. She had never felt this way before with a boy. That day on Queen Maeve's Cairn, Iris had thought of her home back in New York City, all the way west further than her eye could see, but there all the same. At the time, she had been glad to be in Ireland, but now she had seen another side of the country and she wanted to leave, desperately. She wanted her mom, but of course she could never have her back.

Ruairi was driving her in the wrong direction. Every second she was getting further and further away from her freedom. The garda car sped down the narrow lanes, bumping over potholes and making her stomach lurch. She was feeling sick anyway, and the jolting of the car made her want to throw up. She clamped her mouth shut. The situation was mortifying as it was, and she was determined not to vomit in the back of a cop car. She turned to look out the window as the landscape flashed by. It was early morning, and mist snaked across the old bog road, while the spruce woods on either side were so dark night still clung to their tight contours. As they cleared the woods, the sky appeared the blankest white, the sun hidden behind thick mist. Flashes of green fields emerged amid vaporous wreaths, the land drenched in a heavy fall of dew. Her shock felt like the white sky. Blank and glaring, pulsing in every part of her.

Iris had been just about to leave, all packed up and ready to hit the road, when the gardaí had turned up. She hadn't even realised they were there for her until Eamon had informed her she was under arrest.

'What for?' she'd asked him, turning to look at Ruairi, but he had dropped his eyes to the ground, cheeks crimson.

Eamon had informed her of her offence and before she could stop herself, she had barked out a laugh, though there was no joy in it.

'This is no laughing matter, Miss Kelly,' Eamon had said, narrowing his eyes. 'This is murder we're talking about here.'

Iris had stared at the guard in disbelief as the seriousness of her situation had begun to dawn on her. But the question which had surfaced in her mind, which was haunting her still, as she sped towards the garda station in Carrick-on-Shannon, was: how did they know? She licked her dry lips, fear beginning to make her legs shake although she was seated. Her family had betrayed her. The treachery swept through her body, and now she understood about her mother, and why it was she had left Ireland all those years ago and never come back.

'Mom,' she whispered, as tears threatened to fall. She needed her so badly because she had never been so scared in her life. What was going to happen to her now?

CHAPTER TWO

AISLING

BROOKLYN, NEW YORK

Aisling staggered up the steps of the stoop, clutching the brown paper bag from the grocery store. She felt the sun on the back of her head, burning a patch of exposed neck beneath her pony-tail. She stopped at the top, took a breath. The heat was suffo-cating. New York was one giant furnace, and they were all its kindling. The tops of her thighs were stuck together and sweat trickled down her breasts onto her swollen stomach. Inside was her baby. Cocooned from the sudden soaring spring tempera-tures of the city and protected from all the hustle of the crowded streets. In this noisy hot place, Aisling felt more at home than she ever had back in Ireland, where there had been so much space, and silence abounded.

When she had left Ireland, it had been pouring with rain, and she had shivered in her wet coat all the way up to Dublin on the bus, praying her father wasn't following in his car. But when she had eventually got to Dublin airport, his Ford Cortina had been nowhere to be seen. She had got on the Aer Lingus flight to New York clutching one small suitcase in her hand, the terror of being caught consuming her. As they'd taken off, she had peered out of the rain-streaked window, not quite believing she had managed to escape. But the horror of what she had left behind was not something she could fly away from so easily. Every time she closed her eyes, she could see the censorious face of the priest and hear his advice to her father.

'Gabriel, if you don't wish to see the place, I will take Aisling myself to the home,' Father Francis had said.

'I'm not going into a mother and baby home, Daddy,' Aisling said.

'You're a holy disgrace,' her father said to her. 'After all we've been through and then this...' He shook his head.

'Daddy, please,' she begged him.

But her father wouldn't look her in the face. His cheeks were flushed from the whiskey he had shared with Father Francis. The priest had spoken and it was as good as if God himself had ordained her fate.

'I am truly sorry, Gabriel, the tribulations you have endured with your daughters,' Father Francis said. 'I will think of you in my prayers.' The priest rose from his seat and put a hand on Aisling's shoulder that made her skin crawl.

Aisling thought of her sister with a lurch. If Maeve were there, she would be able to influence her father's thinking in a way Aisling never could. She was three years younger, and their father's favourite. But Aisling never wanted to speak to Maeve again, not after what she had done.

'I shall collect you at eight in the morning, Aisling,' Father Francis said to her. 'Do not look so frightened, child; it is the best for you and your family, so there is no shame.' He gave her a thin smile. 'And when it is all over, and the baby is adopted, you can return here and carry on as before in your job. Nobody will be any the wiser.'

Aisling felt a wave of nausea assault her. Her cheeks burned with fury. How could this priest speak so blithely of giving away her child, whose life pulsed within her? But she said nothing because the outcome of the conversation had made her mind up. She was going to run away to America.

Aisling pushed open the door of the apartment building in Brooklyn and began climbing up the stairs. Trina's apartment was on the top floor and there was no elevator. But it was a small complaint because Trina had saved her. The summer before, Trina had left Ireland – the church state, as she called it. Already she was set up with a rent-controlled apartment in Brooklyn Heights and work in her brother's bar. Trina was younger than Aisling and had been several years behind her in school. Her mother had worked for Aisling's father sometimes, and Trina used to hang out with Aisling's sister. Aisling and Trina had not been close, but she was the only person Aisling knew from the locality who lived in America. Because Aisling had decided that if she was going to escape, London wasn't far enough away from Ireland. In her desperation, Aisling had written a letter to Trina not long after she had discovered she was pregnant.

Dear Trina,

I got your address from your mam. I am sure you must be surprised to hear from me, especially after what happened this summer. I can't even begin to put into words how I am feeling about all of that, and how you must be feeling.

I know we've never been close, and always you've been my sister's friend rather than mine, but Trina, I don't have anyone else to turn to. It's really hard for me to tell you this, but from what I know of you, I believe that you are not judgemental. I haven't told anyone, not even Maeve. The thing is, I am pregnant. If I stay in Ireland, I just know Daddy will send me off to a mother and baby home and force the baby to be adopted. But I have decided I want to keep her. (I don't know why I feel so certain the baby is a her, but I do.)

I have some money saved and if I come to New York, could you put me up for a while until I find my feet? It's a lot to ask. I don't deserve your help. But Trina, I am desperate. Can I come?

I hope to hear from you soon. I am about two months gone, but you wouldn't know.

Love,

Aisling

P.S. Please don't even ask about the father.

It had been a long shot, but Trina had written back to Aisling telling her to come to New York. During their weeks of communication, it had been autumn and she had managed to hide her pregnancy under baggy jumpers and rain jackets.

You can decide when you get here what to do, Trina had written.

But Aisling had held on for a few more weeks hoping for a miracle, and days had gone by in Ireland when she'd pretended this wasn't happening to her. She'd kept thinking she would wake in the morning and discover it had all been a dream and she wasn't pregnant. And then she'd kept hoping the father of her child would come to her, tell her it would be all right. But he didn't even know she was carrying his child, so how could he give her comfort?

She was all alone.

But not quite, because Trina wrote again.

You've got to get out of there, Aisling. You know what they'll do to you.

Trina Finlay knew all about small-town gossip. She had been castigated by Father Francis from the pulpit for joining the Irish Women's Liberation Movement and taking part in the Contraceptive Train the May before last. Trina's mam had been mortified by her having hurled a packet of pills at the priest in response to his sermonising, in front of the shocked congregation. (They had in fact been aspirin, but it was the point which had counted.) Aisling had always viewed Trina as too confrontational and damning of the old traditions, but now she was glad she had an ally.

Trina's letter felt like being plunged in cold water, and Aisling broke out of her stupor. She had the money saved up for the ticket hidden in her room, but she'd been frightened of leaving home and going so far away. There was a part of her that didn't want to abandon her sister Maeve, and a small hope the crisis of an unplanned pregnancy might bring the family back together again. In her heart, though, Aisling knew her family was too broken to fix, and she did her best to avoid Maeve. But one morning, as she was on her way to work, Maeve accosted Aisling as she was getting into her car.

'Why are you avoiding me?' she accused her.

'I'm going to work!'

'You're always sneaking off, even when you don't have to work,' Maeve said. 'You don't care about anyone else but yourself.'

'I've been working, earning money.'

'Yeah, you've made it clear that money means more to you than family.'

There was a frozen silence then, because Aisling understood perfectly well what Maeve's subtext was. She bit her lip. She wasn't going to rise to it. At the end of the day, it was clear Maeve felt guilty about what had happened that summer. She was lashing out at Aisling to alleviate her own conscience.

'That's not true, as well you know,' Aisling said.

'But why are you so secretive, always acting as if you're so much more important than us?'

'I don't—'

'It's hard you know, working the farm, but someone has to help Daddy.'

Maeve stood with her hands on her hips. She was taller than Aisling, the musculature on her arms well-defined, her skin golden from the summer outside. Freckles littered her cheeks and brought out the sea-green of her eyes, while her chestnut hair had gleams of copper in it. Maeve always complained about the fact she was the sister with the boring brown hair, but Aisling thought Maeve's hair looked magnificent, streaked with pure red in the morning sun. She appeared as fearless and strong as her Celtic warrior queen namesake: Maeve of Connacht.

'That's because it's your farm,' Aisling countered. 'Daddy's made it plain he's leaving it all to you.'

Maeve had the decency to blush. 'You could try a bit harder with him, Ash. Underneath it all he is a good man—'

'When he's not drinking,' Aisling interjected.

To her surprise, Maeve took a step forward and placed a hand awkwardly on her shoulder. It was hard to imagine that once they had been so close. As little girls, they had shared baths, combed and braided each other's wet hair, but now her sister's touch felt heavy and unwanted upon her. And yet Aisling ached to confide in Maeve. Was her only choice to run away to New York and land herself on Trina? Surely if anyone could help her, it would be her own sister?

'What's wrong, Ash?' Maeve asked.

Aisling looked into her sister's eyes. Could she trust her? Did she really know who Maeve was? They might be flesh and blood, yet Maeve had been someone else this summer. There had been times Aisling had not known what to make of her behaviour.

'I can tell there's something up,' Maeve pushed.

Aisling was overwhelmed with the need to share her secret and the words came tumbling out in a rush.

'I'm pregnant...'

Maeve's eyes opened wide in shock. 'Oh no!'

Aisling felt a lump in her throat. She pushed back the tears.

'Who's the father?' Maeve asked, her voice a panicked staccato.

Aisling shook her head. She couldn't share that information, not yet. 'You can't tell Daddy,' she said, immediately regretting her confession.

'But he'll find out soon enough,' Maeve said, glancing down to Aisling's belly.

'I'm going away,' Aisling said in a shaky voice.

'No, no, you can't, Aisling, don't do that, please.'

'I'm keeping the baby...'

'Oh.'

'But that means I can't stay here.'

'Maybe Daddy will be okay.'

'Come on, Maeve!'

Maeve frowned, chewed her lip. 'But where are you going?'

'I don't know yet,' Aisling said, thinking of Trina in New York and sensing she needed to keep it secret. 'Promise you won't tell anyone.'

'Okay, but Aisling, you can't run away. Where will you live? How will you survive?'

Her sister's questions made Aisling feel frightened and panicked. Maybe she should take the boat to London and get an abortion, like so many other girls in her position. But she had lost so much already, and somehow, despite the circumstances, and the horror of that summer, there was a tiny part of her which felt this baby was a gift. It was stupid, impractical, but she felt so alone. She craved someone to love.

'You can't leave me...'

Maeve's plaintive whine broke through Aisling's thoughts. Typical of her sister to think of herself first. How did she always manage to say the one thing to ensure Aisling would get annoyed?

'Maeve, this isn't about you.'

'Whose baby is it?' Maeve challenged her again. 'Is it Conrad's? Are you going to ruin everything?'

'I think you've managed that all on your own,' Aisling said tartly, before opening her car door and getting into the driving seat. Maeve said no more, but she gave her such a look of resentment, before turning on her heel and stomping away across the yard. Aisling started up her car and took off as fast as she could, bumping down the boreen as the tears she had been holding back trailed down her cheeks.

She should never have confided in Maeve. Just three days later she returned home to the fury of her father, and his demand she meet with Father Francis the next morning. She had no doubt how the encounter would go with the priest, the overlord of their village, who held sway over all their mortal souls. He would want to lock her up and take away her baby. Aisling wasn't sure what had hurt more: the slap across her face her father had given her, or the betrayal by her sister.

Get yourself out of Ireland. You know what happens to unmarried mothers! Trina had written at the bottom of her letter.

Trina had taken the place of a sister. Aisling would be lost without her. She unlocked the door and staggered inside the hot apartment, walking down the narrow hall to place the grocery bag on the table under her loft bed in the kitchen. It was a three-roomed apartment. Trina had the main bedroom, also with a loft bed. They had a big lounge with views of Brooklyn Bridge, and a small kitchen, with Aisling's loft bed by the window. There was also a bathroom with a big old bathtub. It had become a bit of an effort climbing up and down the ladder to her bed now she was so heavily pregnant, but once she was up there Aisling would lie for hours looking out of the window at the lights of New York City. She had escaped her past. But what would her future bring?

She could hear Trina talking in the other room, and guessed it was with her current love, Sam. She could smell the pot emerging from under the door. She busied herself unpacking the groceries and filling a bowl with oranges. They were heavy to carry, but she had been craving them for the past three months. She took out a knife and cut one of the oranges in half, sucking on its juicy innards. She could hear Trina laughing, then Sam. They were both so good to her, but sometimes it hurt to be around them. She had no one who looked at her the way Sam looked at Trina.

Trina emerged, a wide smile upon her face, clearly stoned.

'Ash, guess what? I'm going to meet Sam's parents!' she said, opening the fridge and pulling out a jug of iced tea.

'But don't they live in Trinidad?'

'They sure do,' Trina said, grinning. 'It's going to be wild!'

'But how are you going to afford the trip?' Aisling was fully aware that Trina's waitressing work was not the best paid.

'It's Sam's treat! The family sent the tickets.'

'That's great,' Aisling said, already feeling a little anxious about being in the apartment on her own. 'When are you going?'

'Don't worry – not until September and long after the baby's born. Sure it's any day now; you're already a week late.' Trina took a swig of her iced tea.

Aisling bit her lip. 'I'm so scared,' she whispered. 'I don't think I can do this—'

'You're going to be a great mother!' Trina said. 'And Sam and I will help you.'

Trina put her arms around Aisling. Their embrace was a little awkward with the bump between them, but just to feel Trina's touch calmed Aisling down. Things had been tough since she'd been in New York, but Trina had always been by her side. First off, getting her a waitressing job, and then going with her to all the hospital appointments.

'I won't go if you don't want me to,' Trina offered.

'No!' Aisling said. 'I'll be grand by September.'

Trina did a little dance around the kitchen. 'I can't wait!' Aisling couldn't help feeling a little envious about her friend's life of freedom.

That night while Trina and Sam were out clubbing, Aisling found herself missing Maeve more than ever. In the end, she wrote her a letter, and put her address and the telephone number of the apartment at the top.

Dear Maeve,

I am writing to let you know that I am well and living in New York with Trina. She's really helped me out and I have a job, and a good place to live. I am sorry I haven't written to you before now but I felt very betrayed by you. I don't understand why you told Daddy I was pregnant. But that's done with now, and it's not why I am writing.

I miss you, Maeve. I wonder about you. How are things back home? Are you still working on the farm? Sometimes I dream about home and when I wake up I can almost smell it – the rich scent of the earth in the woods – and feel the soft veil of drizzly rain upon my skin. This longing for home is one I will always have to live with because I can never come back.

I know you feel guilty about what happened at the end of last summer. So do I! But you shouldn't have tried to blame me, Maeve. That wasn't fair. It wasn't my fault, and you know it. However, you are my sister and I want you to know I forgive you – for what happened at home last summer, and for telling Daddy I was pregnant. The baby is due any day and I would love for you to meet her (I am sure it's a girl!). Please come any time you want to.

Love,

Aisling

Two months after Iris was born, the reply came. Two short sentences written in pencil on a piece of paper torn out of a jotter. Written with such force that the words broke off as if the pencil had snapped, and Maeve had had to get another, blunter, one:

Do not write to me again. I will never forgive you!

Her words had felt like a punch in the stomach. Aisling had gasped in shock, and felt her baby murmur in response as she nestled her against her breast. It could never be fixed, the rift between her and Maeve. They would never see each other again. Her sister would never meet her daughter, Iris. And although she was so angry with Maeve, she burst into tears. Memories of the summer before came rushing back. Those long, hot days lazing by the lake. It had been idyllic. But so fragile, because in the space of a few minutes, everything had changed, and she had lost her sister.

CHAPTER THREE

IRIS

BROOKLYN, NEW YORK

It was snowing. Iris curled up on her mother's bed in the apartment in Brooklyn. She was cocooned in the quilt, nestled in the scent of The Body Shop's White Musk, her mother's favourite perfume. She stared out the window from the loft bed at the digital time on the Watchtower building blinking through the cascading white. Today was Thanksgiving, and though her college roommate, Riley, had invited her to her family home in Washington out of pity, Iris had said no. To be with another family would hurt too much. It was bad enough alone. Every day when she first woke up, there was one second of freedom from her sorrow. But then her reality would slam into her, and she would begin to cry. Her mom was dead. She had been gone for over a month now. Her last day on this earth had been 21 October 1991. It was all wrong. She had been supposed to live for decades more. They had joked about her living to over a hundred and wowing all the octogenarians in the old people's home. But her mom hadn't even made it to forty.

For the first time in her life, Iris wished she had a sibling. Someone else who knew exactly how bad it felt. But it has always been just her and her mom. Sometimes her godmother, Trina, would show up and the three of them would go on a road trip. The best had been when they'd taken Route 66 all the way to the Grand Canyon last summer – her mom and Trina like Thelma and Louise from the new movie, sassy and outspoken as they wound their way across the States, not taking shit from any men. Just eighteen, Iris had wanted to be like them so badly. Not caring what boys thought of her. But somehow, she never had been. That much was evident. When her mom had found out about how her high school boyfriend, Freddie, had been treating her, she'd gone wild.

'You deserve better, Iris,' she'd said. 'I didn't bring you up to be walked all over by a little punk like Freddie.'

Her mom had been a warrior. A fierce and proud single mom, who had worked so hard to make sure her daughter had all the opportunities she hadn't had. Her mom had worked two jobs all during Iris's years at school – cleaning houses during the day and waiting at night – so she could afford to pay for Iris to go to college. She had paid for private tutors and Iris had done so well at school she'd been put up a grade. Iris had got a scholarship for Berkeley even though it meant they would be on opposite sides of the country from each other.

'It'll get you away from Freddie, too,' her Mom had said.

Her mom had been so proud when Iris had got into Berkeley at the age of seventeen. They'd dressed up and gone out for a fancy meal in the city. Her mom had got a little tipsy on the wine, saying it was the best day of her life.

'But Mom, what about you? Didn't you have dreams when you were young?'

Her mom's face had clouded. 'When I was young, I had

you, Iris. I didn't have the privilege of dreaming. I just needed to provide.'

Iris knew her mom didn't mean to make her feel guilty, but she did. Her mom had high expectations of her. The whole of her first year at college, Iris felt the weight of them. She dutifully went to all the lectures, spent hours in the library, and yet, when it came down to writing her papers, she would stare at the blank sheet for hours as if hypnotised by its white emptiness. Finally, in the small hours of the morning she'd cobble something together and scrape through the assessment. Whenever her mom asked, she said it was all going great, but she missed New York. She missed their neighbourhood – Joe's Diner on the corner where she and her mom got breakfast on Sundays, the little cinema where they went to watch movies on her mom's nights off, walking across the Brooklyn Bridge with a steaming cup of takeout coffee in her hand. She missed the smoky, edgy world of New York City. California wasn't the same. The skies were bigger and brighter, and the roads wider. Though she liked San Francisco, it wasn't New York. She felt exposed and insignificant, in a way she never did at home in Brooklyn.

If she had been back in Brooklyn, maybe it might not have happened. Maybe her mom would have been home with her, watching *Cheers* together, and eating chips. Her mom wouldn't have taken the evening shift at the bar, nor would she have stepped out in front of the yellow cab because she was cold and tired and wanted to get five hours' sleep before she had to be up for her cleaning job at five thirty in the morning.

Her mom had been killed just round the corner on Pierrepont Street and Iris hadn't been able to walk to their favourite deli since, because it was on the same street. The phone call had come from the hospital just as she and her roommate, Riley, had been planning to go to a classmate's party. Instead, Riley had driven her to the airport, Iris white-faced, unable to speak, Riley trying to tell her it would be okay. But it hadn't been.

She had arrived too late. She had never got to say goodbye to her mom.

Iris buried her head in her mom's pillow now and began to sob again. She would have to wash the sheets soon, but not yet. She needed to absorb every last part of her mom.

Iris had had her mom cremated on her own because she hated the idea of everyone looking at her in the crematorium. She had been in shock and just wanted it done fast. The funeral had been a week later the day before Hallowe'en, in the apartment. It had been small: a few of her mom's workmates, a couple of Iris's old friends from high school, and Riley had come with her mom from Washington. She had hoped Freddie would turn up, or at least call her, but he was a no-show. And of course, her godmother, Trina, had flown in from Mexico, a torrent of tears and emotion. Iris had made a big barm brack but it hadn't turned out like her mom's. Even so, the small gathering had politely eaten the dried-out fruit loaf and drunk tea and coffee, before making a hasty exit as fast as they could. Afterwards, Iris and Trina had collected her mom's ashes from the crematorium before bringing them to Central Park. It had been her mom's favourite place to sit on her rare days off. Iris had scattered half of the ashes onto the golden October leaves which were spread thickly upon the ground. Watched them wisp away on the breeze. Something had stopped her from scattering them all, and she'd carried the heavy box in a brown paper bag all the way with her back to the apartment.

The sky was darkening by the time Trina and Iris had returned to the Brooklyn apartment.

'Let's have a drink,' Trina said.

Iris shook her head. 'I just want to go to bed,' she said.

'Come on,' Trina said, scooping her arm under her god-daughter's elbow. 'You need a strong drink. It's been a hell of a day.'

'I'm underage!'

'Screw that,' Trina said.

They walked in the opposite direction from the bar where her mom had worked. Past houses decorated with giant jack-o-lanterns on their stoops, and windows filled with flying witches on broomsticks with black cats. Iris loved dressing up for Hallowe'en but this year she had no interest. The world of ghosts and dead spirits felt too real. The night was mild for late October, and the wind was gentle and warm upon Iris's cheeks. She felt as if she was barely walking, Trina almost lifting her off her feet as she whisked her into a bar.

They took a table in the corner, by the jukebox, and Trina ordered them two Scotches on the rocks. No one asked for Iris's ID, as if they sensed not to bother the two mourning women. They sat in silence for a while, and Iris was grateful her godmother was not trying to make her feel better with platitudes, because it would be pointless. She took a sip of the Scotch. She had drunk it plenty of times at college parties, and with her mom at home. This one she could tell was expensive, and strong: it burned her throat, curling down into her belly. She shivered, as if the Scotch had made her more aware of how frozen she was inside.

'Let's play some music,' Trina said, getting up and perusing the jukebox. 'Ah, here's one Aisling used to love playing for you.'

Trina put some coins in the jukebox, and Candi Staton singing 'Young Hearts Run Free' came on. Iris was transported back to the living room in the Brooklyn apartment and dancing with her mom. She would have been about five, but she still remembered her mom in a pair of white bell-bottoms and a crochet poncho, holding her hand and twirling her around.

'I remember dancing to this with Mom,' Iris said, tears welling in her eyes.

Trina leaned forward and put her hand on Iris's. 'It's important to remember these happy times,' she said. 'And it's important to let yourself grieve.'

Iris nodded, but her heart was so raw; it hurt too much. Trina handed her a tissue and they held hands for the rest of the song.

'When are you heading back to college, honey?' Trina asked her when the song ended.

'Oh, I don't know, I—'

'Go back as soon as you can,' Trina said. 'I can sort everything out for you here. I'll make sure you don't lose the apartment.'

Iris looked wildly at her godmother. 'I hadn't even thought of that.'

'It's okay, the original lease is in my name – I'll get it put in yours.'

There was a pause as they both took another sip of their drinks.

'I'm not ready to go back to college,' Iris said. 'I just want to stay home – here. I need to be here.'

'Okay,' Trina said, nodding. 'I'll stick around for a couple of weeks. I can fly back to San Francisco with you too, if that helps.'

Trina sat back in her seat, looking at Iris as if she was going to say more.

'What is it?'

'Have you been in contact with the family back in Ireland?' Trina asked. 'Do you think your mother's sister Maeve should know?'

'Oh!' Iris said in surprise. 'I hadn't even thought of it. Mom never talked about her.'

'I think your mam would want Maeve to know. I sensed she really missed her, especially when you were a baby.'

'But why did they never see each other? What happened?'

Trina shook her head. 'I'm not completely sure, and I guess it would be better for you to hear it from Maeve.'

Iris had never seen her godmother look so uncomfortable. 'Why can't you tell me about them?'

'It's, well... I just think it best you talk to Maeve first because your mam promised me not to speak about any of them and it would be better coming from your aunt...'

Iris was confused by Trina's obtuse manner. It was so unlike her godmother, who was normally so upfront about everything.

Iris stared down into the golden liquid and the slowly melting ice cubes in her glass.

'And my father?' she whispered. 'Do you know who he is?'

'Did your mam never tell you about him?' Trina turned to her in surprise.

'When I was younger, she said she didn't know where he was. She said we didn't need him. It was always about me and her. But when I started college, she came to visit me, and she was going to tell me who he was... but I told her I didn't want to know.' Iris raised her head and looked into Trina's brown eyes.

'Ah,' Trina said. 'I'm sorry, honey, I really don't know anything about him. Your mam was very private.'

'It's okay. He may as well be dead, as far as I'm concerned.'

Trina nodded in agreement. 'But what about your Aunt Maeve?'

The mysterious figure of Aunt Maeve had no face in Iris's mind. Her mom had sometimes spoken about the west of Ireland with nostalgia, but it was always about places, never people. She'd talked about the wild Atlantic Ocean, and the little windy roads, and the green fields and stone walls. She'd talked about a forest she'd liked to walk in and sometimes she'd mentioned a lake, although when she did so her voice shook and she often changed the subject abruptly. Her mom had never talked about people from her home country, even when Iris had pushed.

'Why won't you tell me about your family?' Iris would ask.

'Because they're not nice people,' her mom had retorted. 'And I am *never* going back home.'

Iris looked at her godmother, Trina, again, and although she suspected her mom would tell her to leave it, to never dig into the past, she craved to know more.

'Yes,' Iris said, 'tell her. Tell Maeve.'

'I can give you her address if you want to write to her,' Trina offered.

Iris shook her head. She wouldn't know where to begin if she had to write a letter to her mystery aunt. Most likely, she would never write the letter. 'Please can you reach out to her?' Iris asked. 'You know her.'

'Okay,' Trina said, shrugging, although Iris detected discomfort in her eyes. 'I'll do it for you.'

That had been a couple of weeks ago now and Iris had had no word back from her mother's family in Ireland. Iris guessed her mother had been right. They weren't nice people.

Trina had left, offering to bring Iris with her on her travels. But Iris had told her no, she was ready to go back to Berkeley, and Trina had looked relieved.

———

Iris's stomach rattled. She couldn't remember the last time she had eaten something. She slowly emerged out of her mom's quilt. On the windowsill by her mother's bed was the little glass swan which had sat there for as long as Iris could remember. Her mom had brought it all the way from Ireland. She reached out and held the swan in her palm, tracing its contours with her finger. The sweep of its curved neck and the undulations of its body: blue, purple and green, like swathes of water. Iris clasped the little swan tight as she slid down the ladder to land on the floor of her mom's bedroom. She padded down the hall, wearing the same pyjamas she'd been wearing for at least a week. She needed to wash badly, but it just felt like too much effort. She picked up a hair tie from the hall table and pulled up her lank greasy hair into a tight bun.

Inside the kitchen, there was nothing to eat. The fridge was empty apart from a bag of coffee and a tub of margarine.

Iris placed the little glass swan on top of the refrigerator and flicked through the takeout leaflets tacked onto the noticeboard. Her heart gave a jolt to see her mother's handwriting on the board. She had written out two quotes and stuck them there. Something she had begun as a habit to encourage Iris when she was studying for exams. Little quotes and sayings, designed to spur her daughter on to greatness.

Dance like nobody's watching; love like you've never been hurt. Sing like nobody's listening; live like it's heaven on earth.

The words hurt her because Iris couldn't imagine ever dancing or singing again. She couldn't imagine experiencing the joy her mom demanded of her through these words. The second quote was by Robert Frost, one of her mom's favourite poets.

In three words I can sum up everything I've learned about life: it goes on.

Those three words cut her – *it goes on.* But she didn't want to go on. She couldn't be the daughter her mom had deserved. It was too much to live up to.

On an impulse, Iris dialled Freddie's number rather than the pizza place. It rang for a long time, and she was just about to give up, when it was picked up.

'Hey,' she said.

'Irish,' Freddie said back, his name for her because of her heritage.

Why had she rung him? He hadn't shown up for her mom's funeral, hadn't even sent a card. She was about to hang up when he spoke again.

'I'm sorry, babe,' he said. 'I heard.'

She couldn't reply because her whole body was shaking. Just to hear his voice made her feel so vulnerable, and all the emotions she'd been trying to suppress were beginning to overwhelm her.

'Why didn't you call me?' he asked.

'I couldn't...' she managed to choke out.

'Are you okay?'

'No,' she whispered. 'I need you.'

As soon as Freddie arrived, he was kissing her and she was kissing him back. Despite the fact he'd cheated on her and broken her heart, and she'd spent nearly a year trying to get over him, none of that mattered now. Because her mom was dead, and Freddie was the only other person she had loved as much.

Freddie had never been a big talker; he said what he needed to through his body. And as he held her in his arms, and kissed her naked skin all over, she felt as if he was speaking words of comfort to her. He was consoling her as he twisted his legs around hers and she felt the bones of his hips upon her own. She felt his sympathy as he entered her, and for a few seconds she forgot about her mom, and let Freddie carry her on a wave of release.

Afterwards, she sobbed in his arms, but she felt a little better. As if by making love with Freddie, he had lifted a little of the weight of her grief off her.

Freddie stayed in the apartment with her. They ate takeout and fucked. They slept and fucked. They smoked pot, lots of it, and drank Scotch and fucked some more. Freddie helped her not feel her loss and it was the only way she could survive. She had told Trina she was going back to Berkeley, but the idea of returning to Berkeley felt impossible. When Riley called her up, asking when she was coming back, she told her to find a new roommate.

'Are you sure, Iris?' Riley asked, shocked. 'Are you okay?'

'I just need more time,' Iris explained.

'Get compassionate leave, don't fuck it up,' Riley had said.

She had meant to sort it out but it had all felt too much. Two weeks had gone by and she still hadn't contacted anyone at Berkeley. It made her feel wretched. Her mom had sacrificed so much and she was throwing it away. But her mom shouldn't have died. She should have watched where she was going when she stepped out. She shouldn't have left her.

Iris existed in a twilight world of sex and being stoned. She took out a bunch of money from her savings and gave it to Freddie to buy pot and whatever he wanted as long as he stayed with her. As long as he didn't leave her alone.

The Thanksgiving snow had thawed into sleet and icy winds. Iris and Freddie hibernated in their den, one day merging into the next. It was a watery Friday morning, the sleet turned to violent rain, when the phone rang. It was Iris's mom's old boss, Dan, explaining that there had been a collection at the bar from regulars and co-workers. They wanted to give it to Iris to help her out.

'Come on over, Iris, honey, have some food too,' Dan told her.

She didn't want to go, but Freddie insisted. 'Take a break, and I'll clean up,' he offered, before kissing her on the cheek. 'Besides, it would be rude not to go by and thank them. And say, we need the money, right?'

She shrugged her shoulders, finally let him persuade her to

take a shower and get dressed in her jeans. Despite all the take-outs, they hung off her.

'I'll be back in a couple of hours.'

'Don't rush, Irish,' Freddie said, pecking her on the cheek again, but refusing to catch her eye.

Outside in the falling rain, she felt as if she had awoken from a big sleep. What the hell was she doing? Her mom would be furious to know she'd taken up with Freddie again. In her heart, she knew he was no good for her. But she hadn't wanted to be alone, and he was just there.

On the way to the bar, she had to pass the spot where her mom had been knocked down. She stood on the street corner, staring at the road as if examining it for remnants of her mother. Was that a spot of blood she could see against its hard black? She shook her head. Course not. Breaking out of her reverie, she pushed open the bar doors.

They were all crowding around her with words of sympathy and how great her mom had been.

'Why are you crying?' she wanted to scream at one of the waitresses. 'She's not your mom!'

Dan insisted she eat a pizza he'd made with all her favourite toppings.

'I remember your mom bringing you in here when you were only little,' he said, his eyes glistening with tears.

It was late in the day by the time Iris managed to escape, her bag weighed down with the four hundred dollars they'd collected. It had been awkward and painful to accept it, and to receive all the pity and sympathy of people who'd loved her mom.

Her earlier realisation that Freddie was no good for her didn't matter any more. She needed to get back to the apartment, get stoned and fuck Freddie. It was the only way to numb the grief which her mom's old workmates had stirred up inside her.

But when she pushed open the door and walked down the hall calling his name, Freddie didn't reply.

She took a beer out of the fridge and popped off its cap. As she took a big slug, her eye caught the little glass swan on top of the fridge, where it had sat since the day she had grabbed the phone and called Freddie. She picked it up and put it in her jeans pocket before trailing down to the lounge and collapsing on the couch. She stared out of the window as the light seeped from the sky and rain battered the windows. She shivered and pulled one of the cushions onto her lap. As she did so, an earring clattered to the floor. She picked it up, frowning. It was a big gold hoop. Not her mom's kind of earring at all, and certainly not one of hers. Maybe, maybe her mom had changed her style while she'd been in college... but Iris knew, instinctively, the earring hadn't been there earlier today. She laid it on her palm in disbelief, stunned by Freddie's audacity to have another girl in her apartment when she was just round the corner. And where was he now? She closed her eyes and sighed. What did she expect? Freddie was a cheater, always would be. Surprisingly, she wasn't angry, nor did she cry. Because the loss of her mom was far worse than anything Freddie could do to her now. Besides, he'd be back, to spend the money her mom's co-workers had just given her.

The phone rang for the second time that day. It wasn't Freddie, because he never called – just showed up, sometimes staying for weeks, other times disappearing within the day. Maybe it was Riley or Trina checking in on her. She picked it up.

'Hey,' she said.

'Who am I speaking to?' said an unfamiliar voice.

'Who are you?' Iris whispered. There was something about

the accent, a cadence to it, which reminded her of her mother's voice, though the Irish accent was stronger.

'My name is Maeve Maguire, and I am looking to talk to Iris Kelly.'

'That's me,' Iris said in a small voice, shock washing through her.

'I'm your mother's sister,' the woman said. 'I'm sorry...' the woman stumbled. 'I should have rung sooner, but it was difficult.' She paused. 'I'm sorry about Aisling.'

There was a long silence. What could Iris possibly say to her? She couldn't say thank you or it was okay, because it wasn't.

'I can't come and see you because I don't fly,' Maeve continued. 'And, well, I was going to send a card – but then I thought – well, Iris – would you come visit us in Ireland? Come for Christmas. I'll pay for your ticket.'

Iris was speechless. The aunt she had never met or known had the audacity to invite her for a family Christmas in Ireland, after ostracising Iris and her mom for the whole of her life? She was about to lash out at the woman, fling the phone down, but then something stopped her. She saw the quotes her mom had pinned on the noticeboard again – the call to dance, sing, and love again, and then the simplicity of Robert Frost's declaration.

> In three words I can sum up everything I've learned about life: it goes on.

It felt like a message. Besides, she needed to break away from Freddie. He dimmed her light and made her sad. She needed to go on, as life inevitably did. Iris pulled the little glass swan out of her pocket. This had come all the way from Ireland and it meant something to her mother. She wanted to know more.

'Okay,' she heard herself saying. 'I'll come to Ireland.'

CHAPTER FOUR

AISLING

7 APRIL 1984

BROOKLYN, NEW YORK

Aisling had called her daughter Iris because of the yellow and purple irises which grew around the edges of Lough Bawn, right by her family home. Iris was a part of her, but she was also a part of her past. She had been conceived during the last long summer Aisling had spent back home in Ireland under the purest blue sky, the only sound the lap of the lake shore at the bottom of their garden and the wind through the trees. Aisling remembered the sound as if it were a distant sea and there were times in New York City when her longing for her childhood lake was so intense it made her feel sick. She would stand stock still on the sidewalk, and people would stream past her as if she were a boulder in the middle of it, the watery city rippling around her. But then she would come back to her senses. She could never return – in fact she didn't want to, not in her heart. She belonged now with all the other Irish diaspora making fresh starts in new worlds.

The winter before Iris turned eleven, Aisling got a cleaning job on Saturday mornings for Leonardo Monetti, a Wall Street banker, in the parquet-floored apartment in which he lived with his wife and children on Fifth Avenue. They were often away at their house in the Hamptons, and it was on these days that Aisling was able to bring Iris with her rather than leave her with a neighbour. How Aisling missed Trina's support, not just with childcare but in every part of her life. But her best friend had been travelling for nearly five years now, committed to her humanitarian work. She was currently in Ethiopia, working for an NGO as famine ravaged the country and its people. Aisling used to worry about Trina but she appeared to have nine lives and would always turn up for Christmas with jaw-dropping tales of her latest travels.

The last time they'd spoken had been the phone call from Italy, back in February. Trina had told her about the Ann Lovett case.

'It's a fucking disgrace, so it is,' Trina had ranted. 'Don't tell me nobody noticed she was pregnant! Giving birth all alone in the freezing cold in Our Lady's Grotto of all places.'

'I wonder if she was making a point,' Aisling had said.

'More like, she hoped Our Lady would appear to her, and help the poor love,' Trina sighed. 'That girl should never have died. The Church has her blood on their hands.'

They had dropped into silence for a moment. It wasn't hard for Aisling to imagine the desperation, the fear and shame, that poor Ann Lovett had experienced. It could have been her.

'Aren't you glad you left Ireland now?' Trina had echoed her thoughts.

'Of course,' Aisling had admitted, for without a doubt Iris would have been taken from her had she stayed. The idea of life without her daughter was inconceivable. But it was so lonely, being a mother on her own. 'But I miss my family.'

'Aisling, you're well out of it, you know it.'

'I know,' she had replied. Trina was right, and yet she possessed such a deep ache for her kin. Would it ever fade away?

The first Saturday in April, Aisling and Iris took the elevator to the Monetti apartment. Iris was carrying her own bucket and mop, not quite the teenager yet, still young enough that she was keen to help her mom make the apartment sparkle.

They tackled the kitchen and bathrooms first. Aisling didn't want Iris to handle the bleach and other chemical products, and so she set her daughter the task of polishing all the taps with a soft cloth until they gleamed, catching the spring sunshine as it spilled through the windows. The last big job was polishing the parquet floor in the huge lounge with its panoramic views of Central Park. Iris plumped the cushions on the couches while Aisling worked away on her knees. The smell of the wood polish reminded her of the smell of the confessional in the old church back home in Ireland. The memory made her shiver. She'd not been to confession since she'd landed in New York. Sure, she'd had Iris christened, because she wanted to make it official that Trina was her godmother, but she'd managed to avoid Iris's First Communion and any other Catholic rituals by sending her daughter to a secular school. The scent of the polished floor brought her back to emotions of guilt and shame, despite her firm rejection of her childhood faith even before she had left her home country.

A lone note from the grand piano plucked Aisling out of her reverie. She swivelled around on her knees to see Iris sitting at the Monettis' grand piano, the lid open and her fingers touching the ivory keys.

'Iris, what are you doing? You know you're not allowed to touch,' Aisling said, getting up off her knees.

'I just wanted to see how it sounded. Sorry, Mom,' Iris said, closing the lid and sliding off the piano stool.

Aisling looked at the Steinway grand piano properly. She had always tried to ignore the sight of it because her longing to touch it every time she came into the room to clean was so strong. Now she found herself walking over to the piano and stroking its gleaming dark wood.

'Oh, it's a beauty,' she whispered, looking at the Steinway and admiring the shimmering Canadian maple and Alaskan spruce.

'Can you play it, Mom?' Iris asked, looking at her with mild interest.

'Yes I can, Iris,' Aisling said, opening the lid again.

The ivory and ebony keys beckoned to her. Before she could stop herself, she sat down on the piano stool and hovered her hands above them, spreading her fingers and landing them gently upon the keys. She closed her eyes and took a deep breath. Then her fingers began moving as if beyond the control of her mind. Music flooded through her body. Music she had silenced for twelve years. She was playing only her part – the dancing melody of the piano – but in her head it intertwined with other instruments – fiddle, drum, harp, flute and voice. It was a song they had written themselves, together, inspired by the Children of Lir. The words came trembling back to her in the lost, heart-wrenching diction of her sister.

In her mind's eye she saw Lough Bawn, smooth and calm beneath a blooming full moon, and gliding upon its surface, two white swans. Their necks arched in intimacy in the shape of a heart. Her sister was standing upon the shoreline, singing with her back to her as her younger self. So real, Aisling ached to reach out and touch her. The words floated from her as if mist rising off the lake, and became enchanted music which had the ability to comfort, to forget bad things that had happened.

When Aisling opened her eyes again, Iris was dancing. Her

hair fallen out of its ponytail, her feet free of their shoes. Her quiet, serious child had transformed as the music cast a spell on her. Aisling looked at Iris in wonder. For upon her daughter's face, she saw the expression of another she had once loved. She jerked her hands off the piano keys, breathless, shocked, but Iris kept on dancing, spinning, and wheeling her arms as if she were one of those folktale birds, soaring and sweeping, shedding feathers as if they were secrets.

CHAPTER FIVE

IRIS

23 DECEMBER 1991

ROSCOMMON, IRELAND

Iris first saw the sign with her name on it as she walked through customs into the arrivals hall at Dublin airport.

IRIS KELLY

It was being held by a man with a thick crown of red hair, his brown eyes searching the crowd. Iris approached him, blushing and self-conscious as she squashed the doubting voice in her head. *Why is my Aunt Maeve not meeting me? Who is this man? What am I doing all on my own in Ireland? These people are strangers!*

As soon as the man caught sight of Iris, he went white in the face and recoiled as if he'd been punched.

'Hi, I'm Iris Kelly,' Iris introduced herself timidly, trying not to be put off by the man's reaction.

'Oh, oh,' he said, gathering himself up. 'Oh, hello there, Iris, isn't it? I'm your Uncle Conrad.'

The man was still staring at her. He had dropped his sign and his hand hovered by his side as if he wished to touch Iris. Not knowing what else to do, Iris bent down and picked up the sign, handing it to Conrad.

'Thank you, yes, welcome, welcome to Ireland,' Conrad said. 'I was up in Dublin for the day so I told Maeve I'd pick you up, drive you home.'

'Okay, well, thanks,' Iris said. She had been expecting to meet her Aunt Maeve at the airport and it was an anti-climax to be met by her uncle. She felt self-conscious by the man's startled reaction to her appearance. Did she look that much like her mother?

'Let me help you with your bag.' Conrad offered a shaking hand.

'I'm fine, thank you,' Iris responded, picking up her suitcase.

They walked out to the car park. Conrad appeared to have regained some of his composure, asking her whether she'd been to Ireland before and what she was studying at college. As they got into the car, he turned to her. 'I am sorry about your mother,' he said gently.

'Thank you,' Iris mumbled, then, looking up at Conrad, 'Did you know her?'

'Yes, yes.' He nodded. 'We all hung out together as teenagers...'

He broke off then, cheeks reddening.

'It was a long time ago,' he said, sounding sad. 'I can see a little of her in you, around the eyes.'

'So, I look like her when she was my age?' she asked.

Granted, their eye shape was similar, but her mom's eyes had been blue; Iris's were green. They both had fair hair too, but while her mom had been narrow-hipped and tall, Iris was shorter and more curvy. But she had never seen any photos of her mom in Ireland, simply because her mom had never possessed any. Nor had Trina.

'The past needs to remain right there in Ireland,' Trina had told her firmly, as her mom had nodded in agreement.

Thinking of her mom gave Iris a pain in her chest. All of a sudden, she wanted so badly to be curled up in her mom's bed back in the apartment in Brooklyn. She wanted to hide away from the world and burrow into her grief, but it was too late. Here she was, exposed and alone in Ireland. Being driven to her mother's old family home by a stranger.

'No, that's not who you look like, not your mom,' Conrad said quietly. Before expanding, he turned on the car radio. Then whom? Iris thought as she looked out of the car window. Had her Uncle Conrad known her father? She wished she had the courage to ask.

Soon the city gave way to fields the deepest shade of green she had ever seen. They drove through squalls of rain, brilliant sunshine, arcing rainbows and back into rain again, the weather shifting as her emotions leapt and fell. She had done it. She was finally back in her mother's ancestral land and she was going to meet her mom's sister – and yet would her mom have wanted her to be here? Why had she never brought Iris here before?

Lulled by the radio and the sound of the windscreen wipers, Iris found her eyes dropping closed. She had missed a whole night's sleep, being so nervous she'd been unable to rest on the plane. Unable to prevent herself, she drifted into sleep.

When she awoke again, the sky was darkening. She glanced at her watch, but it was still on American time.

'What time is it?' she said, shifting in her seat.

'You're awake!' Conrad said in a bright voice. 'It's nearly four in the afternoon. We're nearly there.'

Iris looked anxiously out of the car window. In the early winter dusk, she saw a rural landscape. Lumpy fields with cattle grazing, framed by tight woods of spruce trees, interspersed by long, low bungalows or stone farmhouses. There was hardly any other traffic on the road – the odd car or tractor – which Conrad waved to as they drove past.

Her uncle indicated to the right and they drove between two stone pillars with sculptures of swans on them. The car bumped along a narrow laneway through a canopy of shadowy trees, and as the drive emerged from the trees it swept in a circle in front of a big stone house with three storeys of windows reflecting the cloud-filled sky. In the centre of the house was a big green door, with pillars on either side and a stone staircase leading down to the drive; above it was a semi-circular window which made Iris think of an eye looking at her. Despite its grandeur, there was something about the house which made Iris feel uneasy. It looked empty to her, although she could see a twist of smoke emerging from one of its big chimneys.

Conrad drove past the front of the house and through a stone archway in a wall. The car bumped onto the uneven surface of a yard. Down one side of the yard were stables; on the other was the back of the house, even more austere than the front, the grey stone of its exterior punctuated with three storeys of shuttered windows. But in front of Iris was a large garden, trailing all the way down to a lake, its smooth surface splashed by pink, orange, and gold from the setting sun. The beauty of the spectacle almost took her breath away.

Was she meeting her aunt in a hotel? Did she not want her in her house? She turned to Conrad in confusion. 'Where are we?'

'Why, we're home,' Conrad said, unfastening his seatbelt. 'Swan Hall.'

'Swan Hall?' Iris repeated, incredulous.

'This is your family house,' Conrad explained, noticing the look on Iris's face. 'Did your mother never tell you about Swan Hall?'

Iris shook her head. 'She never spoke about where she grew

up,' she said. 'I just thought it was a regular house, you know, normal... but not this!'

'The Kellys of Swan Hall are far from normal,' Conrad said, eyebrows raised. 'This house has been in your family for generations. They were one of the few Catholic families to own land and property – your great-great-great-great-grandfather was involved in the Land League with Parnell.'

Iris had no idea what Conrad was talking about. She knew next to nothing about Irish history. But this giant house belonged to her mom's family and she had never told her! Iris thought of all the years they had scrimped and saved in their little apartment in Brooklyn. Night after night eating spaghetti, because her mom couldn't afford groceries the week before rent was due. All this time, her mom had come from a posh family in a big house and she'd never told her. Iris felt a surge of anger. Why had her mom hidden all this from her? Made them suffer needlessly if she'd come from such wealth?

'It looks grand on the outside, but believe me, it's falling apart on the inside,' Conrad told her, hoisting Iris's case out of the trunk.

As they approached the back door, Iris could hear a cacophony of barking.

'Don't mind the dogs,' Conrad said, turning to her.

But the sound was so fierce, Iris couldn't help tensing. She had always been a little afraid of big dogs. As Conrad unlatched the wooden door, three large black Labradors came bounding towards her. She froze, unable to move as they leapt up at her.

'Oh, get them off!' she said, shaking with fear.

'They're harmless, just give them a shove,' Conrad said.

But Iris was rooted to the spot as the dogs grouped around her, sniffing her and jumping up at her. One of them was so big his paws landed on her shoulders. She was close to tears as Conrad gave a long low whistle.

'Get down, Fiacra, Conn, Aed! Get down,' he boomed.

She recognised those names. They were the boy swans in the story of the Children of Lir that her mom had told her time and again as a little girl.

The dogs calmed down as Iris looked up to see a woman emerge from the house. She was tall, with wavy brown hair. As her gaze fell on Iris, her reaction was even more visceral than Conrad's had been at the airport. She brought a hand to her mouth and gasped loudly.

'I know, Maeve!' Conrad exclaimed, seeing his wife's reaction. 'It's *her.*'

Iris stood awkwardly, confused by her aunt's response to her arrival.

'Hello, Aunt Maeve?'

Maeve pulled herself together and reached out her hand, a deep flush of embarrassment on her face.

'Welcome to Swan Hall, Iris,' she said. Her manner was cooler than Conrad's, and her fingers felt icy cold as she shook Iris's hand. She stared intently at her face. 'Remarkable,' Iris heard her whisper under her breath.

'Shall we go into the house, have some tea?' Conrad interjected. 'Iris has had a very long journey.'

'Yes, yes, it's so good to meet you at long last,' her Aunt Maeve said. 'Excuse my bad manners. It's just you're the image of Nuala. I thought it was her for a moment!'

'It's uncanny, isn't it, Maeve?' Conrad said, before turning to Iris. 'You nearly gave me a heart attack, young lady, when I first saw you in arrivals.' His face broke into a reassuring smile as he clearly detected Iris's unease. 'Well, what a pleasure it is, though, that you've finally made it for a visit. Quite astonishing you look so like Nuala – my goodness, did your mother never remark upon it?'

Iris shook her head. 'Who's Nuala?'

Conrad's eyes widened. 'Did Aisling never tell you about Nuala?'

Iris shook her head as Conrad stared at her, lost for words.

'Well, before we talk about it, come in out of the cold, have some tea,' Maeve said, her manner brisk.

Iris followed her Aunt Maeve into the house, aware of her uncle behind her and the three big black dogs padding beside them. They entered a large kitchen with a circular oak table in the centre, an old cooking range on one side of the room and a white porcelain sink under the window. Iris looked out through the glass. Evening darkness was gathering in and she could see the watery shadows of the lake.

Conrad pulled out a chair for her before sitting himself down opposite, while Maeve put a big kettle onto the stove. Conrad took out a packet of cigarettes and lit one, observing Iris as he did so. Maeve handed her a mug of tea and Iris wrapped her hands around the mug, letting the warmth of it comfort her palms.

'You've her hands, too,' Conrad said in a soft voice. 'Nuala's hands,' he clarified.

'But who is Nuala?' Iris demanded. Maeve pushed over a jug of milk and a bowl of sugar, while Conrad continued to observe her.

'Your mother never sent us any pictures of you,' her Aunt Maeve said, sitting down opposite her and nursing her own mug of tea. 'We had no idea of the similarity.'

'How old are you now, Iris?' Conrad asked her.

'Eighteen.'

Aunt Maeve sighed. 'Nuala never got to be eighteen,' she said in a sad voice.

'There were three Kelly sisters,' Conrad explained. 'Aisling, your mother, was the eldest, then Maeve in the middle, and Nuala the baby, a beauty...' He paused, glancing over at his wife, but Maeve was staring into her mug of tea.

Iris sat back in her chair in astonishment, her eyes fixed on her aunt's face.

'I have another aunt?' she whispered.

'Not any more,' Maeve said, her voice sharp. She got up from the table suddenly and stood at the kitchen window, looking out at the darkness, her back to Iris and Conrad. 'We lost Nuala the last summer your mother was in Ireland.'

CHAPTER SIX

NUALA

17 JUNE 1972

No more school! I am never going back. Daddy thinks I will, but no way. The day of our last exam – Higher Maths, the worst one of the lot – I decided, that's it. Dear diary, I am leaving and never coming back. I swear it!

Me and Trina pulled our shirts out of our school skirts and graffitied them. Trina drew a picture of a swan on mine because of my home, and then I wrote a song on hers all about a girl with red hair just like her. Then all the girls started writing on their shirts and we sent each other good luck messages, like in a year-book but on our bodies. The nuns went mental, especially Sister Ignatius, but they couldn't stop us because it was THE LAST DAY! And they couldn't put us in detention or throw black-board rubbers at us any more. We were FREE FREE FREE!

Me and Trina just marched out of the front gates of that bloody convent and into town. We sat in the Golden Egg café, eating chips and drinking tea. Not caring that we missed the school bus back home. (Hitching was better fun anyway.) We were enjoying the disapproving stares of all the old ones too much. Bet they were thinking – *Just like her mother.* But so what if I am! Rather be a crazy dancer than a dried-up old biddy fawning all over the parish priest like he's some kind of god.

I hate this place. Sometimes I just can't breathe, and I feel like I understand what my mother went through. I don't blame her. No, I don't.

Me and Trina are getting out of here as soon as we can. We're saving up all the money from waitressing and when our summer jobs are done, we're booking tickets to New York. We're going to America! Trina's brother Johnny is already there, working in a bar. He says there's loads of jobs and we can stay with him and his mates until we get sorted out. Johnny didn't stay on at school either. I wish I had a cool brother rather than my sisters. Maeve's so bossy you'd think she was the eldest, though she's only two years older than me. But at least she talks to me. Aisling is weird. She looks right through me sometimes, as if I'm not there. She thinks she's so much better than me, being nearly twenty-one and able to drive her own car. I hate being the youngest, and the smallest – Aisling and Maeve are so tall and skinny, it's not fair – but now I'm sixteen I've a chance to GET OUT OF HERE! The only time Aisling includes me is when we make music and that's only because she can show off to Conrad Maguire.

I hate it when they make me sing those religious songs. Daddy driving the three of us off to some gathering in a church in the bog hole of nowhere with his best pal Peadar Maguire, and his son Conrad, who thinks he's God's gift to all the girls. (Okay, sure he is hot, but what an ego!) Both Aisling and Maeve panting around him. Christ, they're pathetic. Even I know that boys don't like desperate girls. What does Trina say all the time? Act mean and keep them keen!

We're all dressed up in hickey clothes. Long white socks and pleated kilts worse than our school skirts, and white shirts with the buttons done up all the way so I can hardly breathe. When I undo the button, Maeve tells me off.

'Do it up, Nuala!'

'I can't sing properly if I do,' I complain.

'Don't bother telling her what to do, Maeve,' Aisling says. 'Sure, Nuala always does what she wants anyways.'

And then she whispers something to Maeve, and they both giggle and look at me. I try not to be hurt. It's always been this way. The two of them so close, and me the one left out, left behind, not as important. But the tables turn when we get to our destination, and our little musical group takes the stage in front of the altar, with the parish priest hovering over us, and the pews filled with the special select super-religious – mostly men, I note, as their wives are too busy slaving over the dinners.

Anyhoo, Conrad goes and sits down with his guitar first. Thinks he's like Bob Dylan – what an idiot – but he's just okay. Maeve picks up her fiddle – she's not bad, I guess, and Aisling is at the piano. But they are all in position to accompany ME. Yeah, like, I'm the star. Everyone knows it. I carry my harp as if it were my new-born baby – honestly I think I do care for it more than my family. And once I'm sat down in the middle of them all, they wait for me. I'm the natural and they follow my lead. I play the harp well, yes I do, but it's my voice which everyone says is my BIG talent.

'Your Nuala sings like an angel, Gabriel,' Peadar Maguire congratulates my father. 'You can see the hand of Our Lord working through her when she sings.'

When the old bastard says things like that (and I am not being unfair when I call him a bastard because he talks to his son as if he is worth less than one of his prized cattle) I want to scream like a banshee into his face. I want to stop singing about Our Lord, and Jesus his son who died on the cross for us, and I wanted to screech and howl and frighten the living *bejesus* out of him. I try to bring an edge to my voice, and sometimes I change the words.

This amuses me greatly. No one seems to notice apart from Aisling, who gives me a sharp look but never says anything about it.

I can't wait until this summer is over and me and Trina can get away from the whole lot of them. My sisters always do what Daddy says. I don't know why they're still here in this big old draughty house where you can never get warm indoors, even in the summer. Well, Maeve's just finished her Leaving and she says she wants to help Daddy run the farm. What a sap! I don't know why Aisling's stuck around. She could have gone to college in Dublin – she had a place and everything – English Literature and History – but Daddy was raging with her for applying and she just gave the place up because he said she should. Now she works in the shop all the time at Lough Bawn Forest Park. What a loser!

Daddy's favourite is Maeve. The way he carries on makes me sick. And she takes advantage of it all the time. He gives her extra money because she's 'working' on the farm and she gets to buy new clothes. I have to wear Aisling's cast-offs, which were someone else's cast-offs before. When Daddy shouts at Aisling because she's done something wrong – like let his dinner get cold or something like that – she just ignores him. I don't know how she does that because I can't help shouting back. Sure, he wants a fight I know. Last night he yelled at me to look at him, and then I could see the drink-fuelled glaze in his eyes, and he said:

'You're to go out with Maeve, and help spread the slurry.'

'I'm not touching any of that shit!'

'Don't be giving me cheek, young lady. You think you're too good for that?' he rampaged. 'You think you're better than your sister?'

'Yeah,' I taunted him.

Sure the hand went out then and he gave me a slap on my arm, but I didn't care. Not a bit of it. He's hit me enough times.

Aisling stepped in then. 'Calm down, Daddy.' And turning to me, 'Why do you have to wind him up, Nuala?' As if it's my fault our father is a brute and a drunk.

Maeve just watched, all smug, because he never hits her.

'You're a monster,' I hissed at our father, ignoring Aisling's warning. 'No wonder Mammy drowned herself.'

There was a terrible shocked silence because no one ever *ever* talks about Mammy and especially not what happened to her. Even our father looked stunned. I turned on my heel and fled before he had a chance to attack me again.

I ran out the door into the hot June evening, the ground so parched and dry as I fled to the lough. It hadn't rained for days and as I gazed at the water it felt as if the lough were shrinking. Sometimes in my head I call it the Lake of Birds, after the Children of Lir story, because there's swans nesting on it. But its real name is Lough Bawn, and I like the sound of that because it sounds as raw as my feelings when I come down here. I sat down on the hard ground, and I gathered my knees to me. Hugged them tight, forcing myself not to cry. I thought about Mammy somewhere at the bottom of the lake. She has been stuck there for so long. All the water has bloated her and turned her hair green and it waves in the current like algae. Mammy stares up from the bottom of the lake, and all she can see is an eternity of blue, or sometimes the bottom of a boat and a fishing line dropping in the small lead weight like a bullet shooting past her eyes, or sometimes the strong limbs of the two swans and their cygnets gliding above. She's stuck there and all she can see is blue, but she can hear me. That's what I like to think. So I sang to my mammy down by the lake. I made up a song and sang to her.

Then the swans came. As if they belonged to my mother, were her emissaries of calm. They soothed my fury, and I unfurled my fists. Just a few more weeks, I promised myself, and then I would be free. I looked up and saw Trina walking towards me through the sun-parched reeds, and I felt better already.

'Let's swim,' she said. 'It was so hot today.'

I didn't tell her about Daddy hitting me and she didn't ask. We took off our clothes, and got into the chill water and it was a balm. We swam out into the lake, and I dived into the water and swam beneath the surface. I am the best swimmer of all of us, and I like to go down deep, holding my breath for as long as I can. When I came up to the surface again Trina was waiting for me, paddling in the rippling water. I thought of Mammy beneath me, watching us as we splashed about and laughed. I could hear her in my head. *Fly free, fly free for me.*

CHAPTER SEVEN

IRIS

23 DECEMBER 1991

It was dark outside. After a traditional Irish dinner of potatoes, bacon and cabbage, they moved from the kitchen into the drawing room, passing by the front door and through the hallway where a grandfather clock ticked loudly next to a sweeping staircase. The drawing room appeared immense to Iris, as if their whole apartment in Brooklyn could fit within it. It was a long rectangular room with windows on either side – two facing onto the front drive, and two onto the garden and lake. Down the side of one wall were bookcases crammed with dust-covered books. The walls were papered in dark red, and sun-bleached green drapes hung at the windows. On the walls hung three paintings of a lake in different weather: one under a blue sky, calm and serene; one choppy, with stormy clouds; and one at night with a full moon and glinting stars. In all the pictures, two swans were on the water. The fading grandeur of the room reminded Iris of the house in *Gone with the Wind* – abandoned of family, empty, yet filled with sad memories. Iris shivered, although a fire blazed in the grate as the three black Labradors sprawled in front of it.

Iris sat down on a big lumpy couch upholstered in the same velvet as the curtains, with her Aunt Maeve next to her. Conrad was in a leather armchair by the fire, staring into the flames. Conrad replaced her tea with a tumbler of Irish whiskey. Clearly it hadn't occurred to him that Iris was officially underage in the States. The burn of the bitter liquid gave her strength. She was weak with shock and emotion, because her Aunt Maeve was showing her an old photograph album, and for the first time in her life Iris was looking at pictures of her mom when she was a little girl.

'So that's the three of us, the Kelly sisters,' Maeve said, pointing at a black and white photograph, its edges curling slightly in the old album. 'Daddy took that before one of our concerts.'

Iris stared at the photograph of her mom dressed in a pleated skirt and buttoned-up shirt, with long socks up to her knees. Her hair hung in two fair plaits, and she was wearing glasses. Tears welled in Iris's eyes to see the familiar look in her mother's eyes which hadn't changed since she was child.

'Aisling was about fifteen in that picture, I would have been thirteen and Nuala was eleven.' As Maeve spoke, she pointed first to Iris's mom, then to herself, the tallest of the three, with a violin case in her hand, and then to Nuala, carrying a small Celtic harp.

Iris couldn't speak. She hadn't prepared herself at all for this journey into her mother's past and now she wished she hadn't come at all. Her Aunt Maeve and Uncle Conrad felt little more than acquaintances to her, and yet they were blood. Iris let her gaze fall on Nuala. Yes, she could see that she looked a little like her, which felt very strange. Why had her mother never told her about Nuala? From what her Aunt Maeve had said in the kitchen, it was clear Nuala had died, but how? She was desperate to ask, but not sure whether she should. She turned the page in the album. On it were more pictures of her Aunt Maeve. One on a horse, and two more with a collie dog and a terrier.

'Yes, I'm afraid there's a lot of pictures of me,' Maeve said, hastily turning the page again.

'Well, you were your father's favourite,' Conrad interjected.

'Not at all!' Maeve argued. Conrad rolled his eyes at Iris, and she looked away, embarrassed by his familiarity.

'Where's the pictures of Nuala by the lake – remember the ones we took that summer?' Conrad said.

'Yes, here we are.' Maeve turned the page. Iris looked down at the album on her aunt's lap, and the face looking back at her made her start in surprise.

'Oh, wow!'

Conrad got up out of his chair and came over.

'See you look just like Nuala, it's uncanny,' he said, looking down at the photograph. He was standing over her, and Iris could hear the heaviness of his breath behind her, making her shift forward on her seat. She looked at the image of the dead sister, Nuala. Staring back at her was herself but with a different hairstyle. Nuala's hair was long and unkempt, whereas Iris kept hers shorter – but apart from that, they were almost identical. It made Iris shiver with unease. How could her mom not have told her? Iris and Nuala had the same shape face, lips, eyes. They looked to be the same physique: medium height, curvy hips, small hands. Nuala was standing by the water in her swimsuit and waving her hand at the camera as if shooing it away. Her mouth was open as if she was in the middle of saying something. Her expression – well, it was one Iris had seen upon herself too in pictures, when she was trying to be scathing. The picture was black and white, but its bleached-out quality gave Iris a sense of the sunlight spilling into the photograph.

'We had some very hot days that summer; I'll never forget it,' Maeve said in a soft voice.

'How old was she when she died?' Iris ventured.

Maeve slammed the photo album shut, making Iris jump, while Conrad stepped back.

'That was the last photograph ever taken of her,' Maeve gave her as an answer, sighing deeply.

'Well now,' Conrad said, walking over to the sideboard, and helping himself to a large whiskey. 'The evening has taken a very macabre turn. Apologies, Iris. But we did assume Aisling would have told you about Nuala.'

'It makes sense that she didn't, though,' Maeve added mysteriously.

Iris felt uneasy. She hadn't warmed to her aunt. It had been foolish to come all this way when she could hear the hostility in Maeve's voice when she spoke about her mother. Now she was stuck here for Christmas.

'Do you really need another?' Maeve watched Conrad pouring more whiskey into his glass. Her husband ignored her, and Iris could feel a tension in the room between the couple.

'You must be tired, Iris.' Maeve turned to her abruptly, putting down the photograph album. 'Shall I show you to your room?'

It was more like an order than a question, but Iris was happy to nod yes because the whole situation felt overwhelming. She longed to hide in her bed and pull the covers over her head.

Iris collected her suitcase from the kitchen and followed Maeve back into the hall up the staircase. The wood of each stair was bare in the centre where there had once been a stair carpet, and on either side there was chipped white paint. With each step Iris took, the stairs creaked and she looked down, nervous they were so old they might collapse. Unlike the luxurious, though ancient, wallpaper in the drawing room, these walls were painted ochre and bare of any paintings, although Iris could see squares of more intense ochre where paintings had once hung.

Maeve paused on the landing of the first floor rather than continuing up the rickety stairs to the next floor. Here the ochre paint was replaced by green wallpaper with a pattern of red berries and blue birds. Iris realised with a jolt they had had similar wallpaper in the apartment in Brooklyn when she was a little girl. Had that been intentional on her mom's part?

She followed Maeve down the first-floor corridor. Hung along its length was a series of hunting prints. Hectic images of men in red coats on big horses with packs of hounds by their sides, chasing the elusive red fox into the woods. Iris hated any kind of hunting, and these pictures didn't make her feel good at all. They seemed in complete contrast to the serene paintings of swans in the drawing room.

They passed two doors with peeling white paint and big brass doorknobs, the second of which Maeve paused at, placing her hand upon it.

'This is my bedroom if you need anything,' she said. 'Please don't hesitate to knock.'

Despite her offer, it was said with little warmth.

The next door opened onto the bathroom. It was vast, with an iron-claw bath, a toilet with a wooden seat and a cistern above it, a large wash basin, and a shower in the corner. The floor was tiled black and white and there was a big window with tatty net curtains. Although it was now completely dark outside, Iris could hear the scratching of tree branches against the glass.

'If you want a bath, you'll need to turn on the immersion heater, which is in the press just here.' Maeve opened a large airing cupboard opposite the bathroom. It was stacked with linens and towels which looked as old as the house itself.

Finally, Maeve led her to the end of the corridor and a third door. It too was cracked white, with a large brass doorknob.

'And this is your room,' she said, pausing for a moment on the threshold. 'It used to be Aisling's bedroom.'

Iris's heart tightened as she stepped after her aunt into her mom's old bedroom. The first thing that hit her as she put down her suitcase was the musty smell: a mixture of damp and a faint hint of lavender. The room was a little chilly and Iris hugged herself as she walked over to the window. With the moon full, the view was of a tangled, overgrown garden and the lake glinting silvery and choppy. She turned around again to face her mom's childhood bedroom. The walls were cream, in places yellowed with age, and she could see cracks in the wall by a big mahogany wardrobe. There was a dressing table with a stool covered in golden velvet, and a mirror in a wooden frame with a drawer beneath it. There was only one picture on the wall, of a painting of irises – purple and yellow. Iris felt a lump in her throat at the thought of her mom lying in bed and looking at the picture of irises. She had named her after the flower, as if marking her daughter with a part of her past Iris had never known about.

'I gave the room a bit of a clean,' Maeve said, walking over to the bed. 'These are new sheets,' she added. 'I hope you like them.'

Iris glanced at the high bed with the iron frame. It looked like a bed out of an old movie, but the bedsheets were pristine white with little purple sprigs of violets on them. Her aunt was standing awkwardly by the bed, needlessly plumping the pillows, a tiny blush on her cheeks.

'Oh, they're nice, thanks,' Iris said.

'Purple was Aisling's favourite colour, so I hoped it was yours, too.'

Iris didn't want to contradict her aunt, but her mom's favourite colour had always been green. But maybe she'd changed even that when she came to live in New York.

'Do you want to close the curtains?' Maeve asked. 'Keep in

the heat.'

Iris was tempted to ask what heat, but she didn't want to appear rude.

'Sure,' she said, turning around, intending to close the heavy curtains, which were the same gold velvet as the stool seat. Again, the lake beckoned to her, its ruffled surface catching threads of moonbeams. Beyond it, she could see closely knit trees swaying in the wind. Was this the lake her mother had sometimes talked about?

'What lake is that?' she said. 'Do you own it?'

Her aunt came to stand next to her, and Iris realised the smell of lavender was coming from her. Even though she was younger than her mom, her Aunt Maeve felt older. She was dressed in old jeans and a big shapeless sweater, whereas her mom had always taken care of her appearance, even if she wore clothes from resale shops. Her Aunt Maeve's face was more lined and gaunt, with dark shadows under her eyes, while her brown hair was frizzy and streaked with grey. She clearly didn't believe in make-up, either, which was a shame because Iris thought with a bit of attention she could look good.

'Oh yes, well, we don't own the lough, but it's on our land,' Maeve replied, which made little sense to Iris.

'Does it have a name?'

'Lough Bawn, although sometimes Nuala would call it the Lake of Birds after the Children of Lir story,' Maeve said. 'She loved all those old legends – well, we all did.'

'Aunt Maeve, what happened to your sister Nuala?' Iris asked in a tentative voice.

The clock ticked in the hall below and the house creaked around them as the wind picked up outside, the trees waving to her from across the ethereal lake. Iris thought for a moment Maeve hadn't heard her or wasn't going to answer, but then she spoke.

'She drowned in that lough, just like our mam.'

CHAPTER EIGHT

NUALA

25 JUNE 1972

It's so hot today! It doesn't feel like Ireland. The reed bed is cracked, and the green shoots of the reeds themselves are browning while the irises are drooping, their petals sad flops of yellow and purple. The heat has made the air hazy and thick so that you can't move fast. You have to take each breath carefully. You have to walk slow.

It feels like Trina and I are the only two souls out. It's nearly dinnertime and the sun's still bouncing off the land, and everyone who can retreats to the shady side of their gardens. Daddy has even brought the cows into the sheds like he does when it's too cold for them. It's so hot I keep my sandals on, and don't walk barefoot as usual, because the hot earth feels as if it could burn my soles.

We have to go swimming because it's too much to bear. The moment the cool blue water touches my skin, I can feel her fingers on me. Mammy. I look down and see my toes sinking into the soft sandy bed, and the reeds swirl around my ankles like locks of her hair. And the whispering begins all over again.

We wade into the water until it is up to our shoulders. I look back at our house, Swan Hall, all three storeys. It appears even higher in the sky from my viewpoint in the lake. The windows blink back at me in the sunlight and it feels as if the house is watching my every move. The silent witness censoring my past, haunted by God knows how many forlorn ancestors. Was Swan Hall my mother's last sight as she dropped beneath the surface of Lough Bawn? Did she imagine her three daughters tucked into the corners of the old house, innocent to the horror of what the day would bring? No. It's impossible to think she would have gone ahead if she'd done so. Surely not? What was she thinking of, then? Or had her mind been so shattered, from years of abuse, she needed to put it out of its misery? All the little broken pieces of her are scattered upon the lake bed like treasure to be retrieved.

Trina sees my suffering. But she doesn't understand because she still has a mother. She flicks some water at me to make me laugh and I splash back. We submerge our bodies under the surface of the cool lake and we swim as far as we dare, going underwater while mindful of the warnings of riptides ingrained upon us since we were little. When we come up for air, the late afternoon sun still beats relentlessly down upon us, and I turn my face to it, feeling it evaporate the lake water upon my skin, drying my hair which tumbles over my face. The gold of it even brighter in the sunlight.

I flip onto my back and I float, bobbing upon the smooth water. I surrender to the buoyancy of the water, to not knowing where I might drift.

'Come back,' I hear Trina call. 'You're too far out.'

I open my eyes, and flip onto my stomach again. She has swum back to the shore, and is drying herself with a towel, her red hair springing in wet curls around her head like a wild halo. I push my hands through the silken water and look down, and I cannot see the bottom of the lake. I am out deep. But I am not afraid. I am not alone because I can see the two swans, side by side, gliding upon the water. Have their cygnets already left the nest?

I am on the cusp of another life, just like those cygnets, and I wish I could tell my mother about it. I think she would be excited for me. Where would she tell me to go? Spain. Yes, not America, Nuala, head for Spain. My mother, Áine Kelly née Lynch, was a dancer. She was as tall as Maeve, and as fair as me, and she had Aisling's searing blue eyes. When I was little, sometimes Mammy would take me with her up on the train to Dublin. Just me on my own and I loved those days. Maeve didn't want to come anyway because she wanted to stay with Daddy and help him on the farm, but Aisling would moan that she wanted to go with us.

'Aisling, you're too big now,' Mammy would tell her.

Aisling's face crumpled, but she didn't cry. Instead, she gave me a look of resentment for usurping her place as favourite, before stomping back upstairs to her bedroom.

When would I be too big to go with Mammy? It seemed like I never was.

We stayed with friends of my mam's, Kate and Donna, in a house in Dublin by the canal. There were lots and lots of swans there, and ducks too. We'd go out to feed them. Kate and Donna were married to Spanish men, and together with my mam they all made a lot of noise, laughing and talking in a mixture of English, Irish and Spanish, but I loved being part of it. I remember seeing them all dance together. Flamenco. Whirring round and round clickety clackety clickety clackety, and my mother's yellow hair was piled on her head, her eyes flashing and her neck so long. She held her arms out wide, a violet shawl hanging from them, her chest forward. In her hands were her castanets, her fingers pressed against them as she played them expertly. She looked like fire when she danced; all the women did. Whirling their skirts and stamping their feet, while one of the husbands played the guitar and another sang in Spanish. When it was over, my mother would come and embrace me. The heat of her body merged with my cool skin and I licked her damp cheek, and felt myself part of the dance.

When I pull myself out of the lake, I want to dance. Now my body has cooled from the water, I have energy. The hot evening feels good now. We place Trina's sunflower yellow radio on a rock and tune it into Radio One – we can pick up the English stations and the music is so much better. Carole King is singing 'I Feel the Earth Move'. It's OUR SONG! We know all the words; it's our anthem. We jump around, towels wrapped around us until they fall down and our damp skin dries in the warm air. I shake my tangled hair and belt out every word. The song makes me believe I will run free and unchain my mind from the heavy yoke of my childhood, the church, school and my family. I can taste the liberty on my lips and it is thrilling! Just a few more weeks, we promise each other, holding hands.

Returning home, we slip through the back door and check downstairs. The house is quiet and sounds empty; it's likely Trina's mam and Aisling are in the kitchen preparing dinner while my father is having a beer in the garden, and Maeve is probably out grooming the horses. We creep up the stairs to my bedroom. I don't want to break the spell of dancing by the lake. I drag out the record case from under my bed and select one of Mammy's old records – *Chants Flamencos*, Angelillo de Valladolid, Juan Soto. I pull on one of Mammy's old dresses, which hangs off me, but to feel it rustle against my skin makes me stand tall and erect. I take her castanets and slip them on. I am her now. Trina sits on the bed and watches me, her expression beaming with admiration.

I place the needle carefully on the first track. The music is hurried like a prayer, rhythmed like a heartbeat, and my body is fiercely cold now like a stalagmite. My arms begin to flow, birds wheeling above the lake; I fling my hand, a cry above the water, and the castanets begin to breathe. They are apart from the dance, an instrument as subtle as a voice. See how they are. Evolving like words, like poetry with a power of their own. My feet become the blood beat, battering the ground, punishing it, and my body is now the throat of the song. My eyes, all is contained in my eyes, as I look at Trina. If I were to close them, she would see nothing.

The door of my bedroom is suddenly pushed open but I don't stop, because I can't, I just can't. Aisling pushes past me and pulls the needle off the record, with a terrible screech.

'You've scratched it!' I yell at her, in fury at the interruption. But she is shaking white with rage.

'How dare you?' she spits at me.

'Mammy gave me her things; I can do with them what I want!' I say haughtily. Trina gets off the bed and stands between us.

'We're sorry, Aisling,' she says gently. 'We thought no one was in.'

'I am NOT sorry,' I declare. Then for the first time, I catch sight of Conrad Maguire standing behind Aisling and looking on in wide-eyed fascination. 'What's Conrad doing here?' I ask Aisling.

She blushes.

'Oh I see, my dancing was interrupting the two of you—'

'No, we're just about to practise music together downstairs, and you're making such a racket, we couldn't...'

She stumbles, but she's given herself away.

'We never saw you downstairs at the piano, and where's his guitar or his bodhrán?' I sneer, turning to Conrad. 'Are you taking advantage of my sister, Conrad Maguire? Well good luck to you, because she's a frigid cow!'

'Nuala!' Trina admonishes me. But she doesn't understand,

because she doesn't have sisters. Aisling has never said a kind word to me my whole life. I tried for years to make her love me, but she's always resented me because Mammy loved me best.

'Shut up, Nuala,' Aisling snaps. 'It's none of your business.'

But I ignore Aisling and continue to hold Conrad's gaze. Now he's colouring, and it is good to feel the reaction I have on him. He's staring at me as if he's in the desert and I am a big drink of water. For all his pretence of liking my sister, I know he likes me better. His eyes drop as he takes in the dress clinging to my body, my chest still heaving from the dancing.

'What will Daddy say, Aisling, to find out you and Conrad have been canoodling in your bedroom?' I mock.

'That's not true,' she says in a shaky voice, and then crosses her arms. I can tell she is lying, because she won't meet my eyes, and Conrad has gone as red as a tomato. I cock my head and flutter my eyelashes at Conrad. I am so angry with Aisling that I consider stealing him from my sister. But then I remember Trina is still there, and I don't want her to think I am a bitch, so I flick my hand at my sister and her boyfriend dismissively.

'Well, let's say I don't tell Daddy about you two, and you don't let on I've been dancing to Mammy's record.'

Aisling says nothing, but I can see she is furious.

'So get out! To be clear,' I say.

'It's not fair,' she hisses. 'Why do you have all of her things?'

'You know why, Aisling, because she loved me the best.' I can't help the cruel words spilling from my mouth, and for a second I feel bad because Aisling flinches as if I'd hit her.

'Oh, Nuala,' Trina says and I can hear her disappointment. I bite my lip. It isn't a lie. Because I loved Mammy best too. So it was worse for me, way worse for me, when she went and drowned herself. Why wasn't I enough for her?

'Sorry.' I turn to Trina, once Aisling and Conrad leave the bedroom.

'It's not me you should apologise to,' Trina says.

I shake my head.

'No, she's always been so mean to me, Trina,' I defend myself. Now my anger has left me, I feel weak and very sad. I can sense tears welling up. 'I still miss my mam so much. Why did she do it, Trina? Why?'

CHAPTER NINE

IRIS

Iris couldn't sleep. She lay in the bed which used to be her mother's, her heart racing. It was all too much to take in. Her mother had grown up in this grand house and she had had two sisters, not one. The second sister, Nuala, looked just like her and she had drowned in the lake. Why had her mother never spoken about any of this to her before?

Iris pressed her palms over her eyes and moaned. She missed her mom so much. Everything was confusing and unstable, and her mom had always made her feel so secure, even though she'd never had a father. But now her mom was the reason for her distress and she couldn't help feeling betrayed by her. Why had she hidden who she really was? Her mother's past was clearly complicated. She should never have come here. Iris pulled her hands off her eyes and took a deep breath. She had to get herself together. Although her Aunt Maeve was a little aloof, Conrad seemed friendly and kind. All she had to do was get through the next week. Christmas in Brooklyn on her own would have been worse. At least all the mystery surrounding her dead Aunt Nuala was distracting her from the gaping hole of loss in her life back home.

She tried to slow and deepen her breathing like they did in the yoga classes she sometimes went to with her mom. But her mind kept flying all over the place. It was so quiet. She wasn't used to it. Back home in Brooklyn she slept to the sounds of people shouting on the streets, and sirens blaring by. But in Swan Hall the eerie silence was broken by strange, unidentifiable creaks. She shivered, pulling her duvet up to her chin and squeezing shut her eyes. The next moment it felt as if something passed before her in a rush of cool air. She opened her eyes and sat up with a jolt.

'Who's there?'

But the room was empty and dark.

She switched on the bedside lamp and got out of the bed. She opened up her handbag and rummaged around until she found the little glass swan. She placed it on the bedside table and sat on the bed looking at it. The swan was her talisman, a part of her mother to protect her, but she still felt unsettled. Hugging her sides, Iris got up again and walked around the room, pausing in front of the big mahogany wardrobe. She pulled open the door, which screeched on its stiff hinges. The part of her that had watched too many horror movies with Freddie was a little afraid someone might jump out, but that was stupid. However, she was surprised to find the wardrobe wasn't empty. Far from it. It was jammed with clothes. As she leafed through them it was clear they were vintage, from the Seventies – an apple-green flowery maxi dress, a suede mini skirt with a fringe, red bell bottoms and frayed jeans. There was so much colour crowding inside the wardrobe: pink, yellow, baby blue, peach and purple – so much purple – making her feel drab in her heather grey sweatpants. She fingered a purple paisley blouse and then snatched back her hand in fright. This was the shirt her mom had been wearing in one of the photographs Maeve had shown her. These were her mother's clothes. Had no one else occupied this bedroom since her mother had left almost twenty years ago? She reached back into the wardrobe again and pulled out item after item, throwing them onto her bed. Purple leapt out at her among the rainbow colours – shirts, pants, sweaters. Iris had never seen her mom wear purple back home. In the corner of the wardrobe, on the floor, was a pair of vintage go-go boots. Iris couldn't help but give a squeak of excitement. She never dressed up. She lived in the college 'uniform' of rolled-up jeans, turtlenecks, and sweatshirts, but a part of her longed to wear something a little different. And she loved boots. They were too big – her mom's size – but that didn't put her off putting them on and clopping around the bedroom. Where had her mom gone in these boots? And why had she left them behind?

As Iris put the boots back inside the wardrobe, she spied an old cassette player. She pulled it out and clicked it open. Inside was a tape – Diana Ross, *Surrender*. She swallowed hard: she remembered how much her mom had loved Diana Ross. They'd had that album back home and her mom had played it to death. Iris placed the tape deck on the bed, and then poked around in the bottom of the wardrobe again. Her fingers landed on a purple plastic square case. She pulled it out and opened it. Inside were neatly stacked tape cassettes. All the music was real old. She knew most of the bands, such as the Bee Gees and the Supremes, and singers like Carole King and Nina Simone, but some of the stuff she'd never heard of. There were other tapes, with her mother's handwriting on the spines of some of them: *Christmas '70 Mix Tape*, *School is Out Mix*, *Summer '71 Sounds*. *Christmas '71*. *Holidays '72*. She read the list of the songs: Marvin Gaye, 'What's Going On'; Aretha Franklin, 'Bridge over Troubled Water'; Diana Ross, 'Remember Me'; the Temptations, 'Just My Imagination'. Her mom's love for Soul had clearly begun before she came to America, but there were lots of folk and rock music tapes too – Bob Dylan, the Rolling Stones, Janis Joplin and Led Zeppelin. Her mom had just loved music. At the bottom of the box, one tape was blank and its case had no writing on it. Intrigued, Iris plugged the cassette recorder in by her bed, put the tape in and pressed play.

'Testing, testing.' Her mother's voice leapt out at her and Iris pressed stop quickly. She wasn't ready to hear her speak.

She placed her hand on her heart and walked towards the window, away from the bed piled with her mother's old clothes and the cassette recorder with all the tapes. The curtains weren't quite drawn and moonlight spilled into the bedroom through the gap. She pulled them back a little and looked outside. Her mother's bedroom was at the back of the house. She could see the shadowy outline of the garden, a little unkempt and wild, and beyond that the glitter of the lake. The wind had dropped. It was a cold, stark night and the still water mirrored the night sky, reflecting the moon and stars upon its surface. She saw movement in the garden beneath her – a fox flitting beneath her window. When she looked back at the lake again, there was a figure standing by it. Pressing her face to the window, Iris thought it might her Aunt Maeve. The figure was as tall as her aunt, but wearing a big shapeless coat, their hands thrust in the pockets. As if they sensed they were being watched, the person turned and looked back up at the house. Instinctively, Iris stepped back from the window, but not before she had seen her aunt's expression lit up by the moon. It wasn't one of sorrow as she had expected, no: her face was contorted by anger.

Iris woke under a mound of her mother's old clothes. It felt as if she had just fallen asleep and that it should still be the middle of the night, but weak light leaked into the room through the curtains. She gently pushed the clothes aside. The whole room smelt musty from age, and she went and opened the window. Damp air streamed into the room and she shivered, grabbing her sweater and pulling it on over her sweatpants and t-shirt. She looked out at swathes of mist rising from the damp lawn. The lake was concealed by fog, but she could hear it lapping and the sounds of birds calling. She had no idea which ones, because she'd never taken much notice of birds back home in Brooklyn. How lonely this place felt! No wonder her mom had run away. She remembered one of the few times her mom had spoken about Ireland. She'd come to see her at college, on her way to meet Trina for a holiday in Mexico. She had sat on Iris's bed in her dorm and asked her if she was being safe with boys. Iris had wanted to laugh out loud at her mom, because it had been a little late for that talk. She'd lost her virginity with Freddie back in high school when she was fifteen. Surely her mom had realised that?

'Of course, Mom, I'm not going to get pregnant,' she had said, irritated. 'I'm not that dumb!'

Her mother had blushed, and Iris had felt bad immediately. How insensitive she had been.

'I don't want you to be taken advantage of,' her mom had said softly. 'That's all.'

There had been an awkward pause. Her mom had been studying her with an almost haunted expression and Iris wondered now if she had been thinking how much her daughter looked like her lost sister, Nuala.

'Would you like me to tell you about your father now?' her mother had asked, looking down at Iris's quilt.

'No, Mom,' Iris said, shocked by the mention of her father. Her mom never talked about him, but she wasn't ready. All she knew was he was some boy her mom had met in Ireland. The last thing she wanted was heavy stuff about who her father was. She had enough to deal with at college.

'I don't want to know anything about him right now. I keep telling you. He means nothing to me.'

'But—' her mother began.

'Listen, we've managed just fine, me and you,' Iris said. 'I don't want to know, right?'

Her mother sighed. 'Okay,' she said. 'But you should know the truth one day, Iris.'

'But what about your family, Mom?' Iris had asked.

'My mother was already dead when I got pregnant, and my father was a very strict Catholic,' her mom had told her. 'He made it clear my only option was to go into a mother and baby home. That's why I left Ireland. It was no place for a single mother.'

'And what about your sister?'

Her mom had looked away, shaking her head, clearly getting upset.

Iris had reached out and put her hand on her mom's arm.

'I'm real glad you didn't give me up, Mom.'

Her mother had turned back to her, eyes swimming in tears.

'Never!' she said with vehemence. 'But it was tough. Trina was my saviour. She wrote to me and invited me to New York.'

Iris couldn't help wondering now what would have happened if her mother's father had let her keep the baby. Would Iris have grown up in this big house in Ireland in the middle of nowhere? The idea made her shiver. Despite its splendour, the place was spooky. She clasped her hands, so grateful her mom had been brave and run away to America. But there was something in the way her mom had sometimes spoken about Ireland which had made Iris think her mom missed it, too. Was this why Iris had agreed to visit her family? Was she her mom's emissary, here to heal the rift between sisters?

But there was only one sister left. Maeve, who was distant, cold, and angry. It was too late.

Downstairs, Iris could smell fresh bread and coffee. She followed the sound of voices along the hallway. In full daylight, she could see that for all its size, the house was even more rundown than it had first appeared, and dirty, too. The paint was faded or splattered with unknown stains, the wallpaper peeling, the window ledges were thick with dust and the floorboards uneven and cracked, with bald patches where rugs had once been. She pushed open a green door, the paint flaking, into the kitchen. Maeve and Conrad were sitting at the round wooden table drinking coffee.

'Good morning.' Conrad gave her big smile. 'How did you sleep?'

'Okay,' she said, not wanting to go into the details of her restless night.

'You look tired,' Maeve said, getting up and putting the kettle on a cooking range. 'Sit down and have some breakfast. I've just taken bread out of the Aga.'

'Is an Aga the stove?' Iris asked.

'Yes, that's right. I suppose you didn't have one in New York.'

'Oh no, our kitchen is real small,' Iris said, thinking of the tiny two-ring hob which she and her Mom often didn't even bother cooking on. Takeout was so much easier, and often cheaper than buying food and cooking it.

The bread was still hot from the oven, and Iris spread butter on it, and then a spoon of jam which Maeve said was made from raspberries collected in the woods. She gobbled it down, helping herself to another slice.

Maeve handed her a steaming mug of coffee. 'You like the soda bread?'

'It's delicious,' she said, her mouth full.

'My mother's recipe,' Maeve said. 'It's the buttermilk that makes the difference, and we've always made raspberry jam.'

'Remember we went out collecting them when we were kids, Maeve?' Conrad said.

Maeve's eyes flickered towards Conrad. 'Yes,' she replied softly, but didn't expand.

'Aisling, your mam, always collected the most, she was so competitive!' Conrad said to Iris. 'Then Maeve, but me and Nuala were a disaster. Sure we ate most of what we collected.' Conrad chuckled, despite the unamused expression on his wife's face.

'Well, it's the wrong time of year for collecting raspberries,' he said, finishing off his coffee as Iris heard a car pull up outside, beeping its horn. 'That'll be Donovan and the lads,' he added.

'Where are you off to with that lot?' Maeve asked her husband, a look of displeasure on her face.

'Never you mind, dear wife,' Conrad said lightly, picking up his jacket.

'Conrad, please don't go with them,' Maeve said tightly.

Conrad paused on the threshold, looking past his wife to Iris as she wolfed down more bread and jam.

'You even eat like Nuala,' he said to Iris, ignoring his wife's request. 'Honestly, it's as if she's back here with us.'

Iris stopped eating, feeling self-conscious.

'Conrad, don't say that to Iris!' Maeve admonished him.

'But you know Nuala was special.' He shrugged as the car outside blew its horn again. Maeve narrowed her eyes at him as he made his way to the kitchen door. 'You'll see me when you see me!' he said. The three Labradors stirred from where they had been lying under the table, following him to the door. 'No, lads, stay here with the women, no room in the car for hounds today.'

Maeve got up as soon as he left the room, and stood leaning on the sink and shaking her head as she watched her husband being driven off. Iris wondered who this Donovan and the lads were, because her aunt clearly disapproved of them. She helped herself to another slice of bread since Conrad was no longer there to comment on it.

Her aunt turned around from her position at the kitchen sink and forced a smile on her face. 'So, what would you like to do? We could go to Lough Bawn Forest Park? There's a ruin of a castle, the lough, and walks in the forests, as well as a restaurant and shop. We could have lunch there.'

Iris looked out of the kitchen window as she munched on her bread. The mist had cleared and the day was brightening up.

'It's not actually raining, so we should take advantage of it!' Maeve said, her voice falsely cheerful.

Lough Bawn Forest Park was a ten-minute drive away. Maeve explained to Iris on the way that her mother had worked in the shop there the summer before she left Ireland.

'Nuala waitressed in the restaurant at the park that summer too,' Maeve said as she pulled into a parking spot, her voice shaking a little.

'I am so sorry she died,' Iris said, not knowing how to fill the silence.

'Don't be,' Maeve said, her tone brisk. 'It was a long time ago. What you've had to go through recently is far worse.' Her Aunt Maeve's voice turned gentle as she looked at her niece. 'We lost our mother too when we were still young – I was twelve – and I remember how tough it was.'

'Mom never talked about her mom, either,' Iris said.

Maeve nodded. 'It was devastating,' she said. 'I think Aisling took the brunt of it. She had to take over running the house after Mammy died.' She gripped the steering wheel with both hands and turned to look out of the windscreen at the bare branches of the trees surrounding the car park. 'I was very angry,' she said. 'It felt as if our mother had betrayed us all.' She turned to Iris again, and said softly, 'Sometimes I wonder, is there a curse on our family? Because our mother drowned herself in the lake at the house, just like Nuala.'

Iris felt a chill creeping down her spine. 'I don't believe in curses,' she said stoutly, pulling open her door to get out, as the three black Labradors tumbled out around her. She needed to get away from the tension in the car.

They followed a path leading into the forest. The low winter sun cast a pale ethereal light as they walked through the tall trees, intertwined bare branches above them creating a lattice through which the sunlight filtered. The woods were strangely quiet, and Iris imagined all the little creatures hibernating in its depths. They passed into a darker part of the forest with rows of tight spruce trees, the scent of pine in the chill air. So this was a place her mother would have gone walking as a girl? Maybe even now, Iris was stepping on the places her mother's feet had been. Maybe in this very wood she had secretly met Iris's father. Iris wanted to believe it had been romantic, and that she had been created through love.

'Aunt Maeve, do you have any idea who my father might be?' Iris said, shoving her cold hands into her jacket pockets. She was comforted to feel her mom's little glass swan in one of them, where she'd put it earlier.

Aunt Maeve hesitated. 'Did your mother never tell you?'

'No,' Iris said, curling her fingers around the familiar contours of the swan.

'Maybe you've been better off not knowing, then,' Maeve said, side-stepping the question.

'What do you mean?'

'Not all fathers are the best,' Maeve elaborated. 'I loved my father, of course, but he was a difficult man. He expected a lot of his girls and it put us under pressure.'

Iris didn't want to know about her grandfather, because he had been mean not to help her mom when she was in trouble. She wanted answers about her own father, but Maeve continued to speak.

'Of course, Daddy only wanted what was best for us.'

'Is that why he threw my mom out when she was pregnant?' Iris couldn't help saying. She had no love for such a grandfather.

Maeve stopped walking. 'He didn't throw Aisling out. She chose to leave,' she said emphatically.

'Because he was going to shut her up in a mother and baby home!'

'Well, I wouldn't have let him do that, no,' Maeve said defensively. 'But Aisling just ran off and let me to deal with Daddy.'

'How can you blame her?' Iris felt heat rising in her chest.

'There's more to it than that,' Maeve countered. 'You don't understand...'

'Explain it to me, then,' Iris said surprised by her own audacity.

Maeve didn't speak for a moment, but kept on walking as the three dogs fanned out around them. They climbed up a small rise of land through the trees, and when they came to the top there was a different view of Lough Bawn from the other side of Swan Hall. The lake appeared to have two parts, and this side was the larger half with rippling deep blue water and an island with a ruined castle on it. Iris waited for Maeve to speak. She felt anger burning at the back of her throat over the injustice of what had happened to her mother, and she didn't know how to express it. And why wouldn't Maeve tell her who her father was? She sensed she was hiding so much from her.

'When Aisling left, that was the final straw,' Maeve finally said. 'It broke Daddy. First my mother, then Nuala, then Aisling. All he had left was me. He hit the bottle hard, and I was left to keep things going. To look after *your* heritage, Iris.'

'I didn't ask you to—' Iris began to say, but her aunt interrupted her.

'I've been here all the time,' she said, her voice bitter. 'Stuck in the past. Your mother got to escape. She got you. I had to look after our father until the end of his days.' She blew out a long breath. 'God, it went on forever; he only passed away four years ago.'

Maeve turned around from their viewpoint and began marching back down the rise of land. Iris followed her. Had she been too rude? Her mom always told her off for her bluntness. But she'd had to speak up. Maeve hadn't been the victim; it had been her mom, right?

They entered back into the heart of the woods, and Iris breathed in deeply. The air felt so clean, and she could smell the earth. It was so strange and different to be walking along the muddy path in her sneakers rather than back home on the sidewalk. What would Freddie think? She had a feeling he would hate it. There was something about the quiet which made her even more on edge. Her sneakers squelched into a muddy puddle.

'Oh, do you not have boots?' Maeve said, suddenly noticing Iris's footwear as if they hadn't just been arguing. 'I could have lent you some wellies.'

'It's okay,' Iris lied, remembering the fuss she had made over the fact she needed Keds sneakers and nothing else would do. Her poor mom had paid way too much money for them.

They went deeper into the woods, and while Maeve was taking deep breaths and commenting on how beautiful it all was, Iris felt the place was dark and foreboding, the ground beneath her sticky with mud. It was cold too, real damp, and she longed to be back inside the warm apartment in New York, with her mom, watching TV together and smoking pot. Her mom could be so cool sometimes. It was boring here. What was she going to do all week long?

'So, you're studying at Berkeley?' Maeve asked her.

'Yeah,' Iris said tightly, thinking about the fact she hadn't gone back since her mom had died at the end of October.

'Well, that's very impressive. Conrad told me you're doing literature and history. What period of history interests you?' Maeve asked enthusiastically.

Iris shrugged. College felt so far away now. She had got very behind and the task of catching up felt insurmountable.

'Maybe Celtic,' she said.

'Are you musical?' Maeve asked, sensing her reluctance to talk about college. 'Do you play the piano like your mom? Do you sing?'

'No,' Iris said. 'I never got to learn. And I can't sing at all.'

'Nuala had the most beautiful voice,' Maeve said, a twinge of longing in her tone.

'Right,' Iris said.

Maeve talked on about how talented Nuala was, and how she had been the best singer in the whole county. Well, Iris guessed she might look like her dead aunt but she definitely didn't have her talents. She wished Maeve would shut up now. The sudden existence of another aunt bothered her. She didn't even know who her Aunt Maeve was, for a start.

As they continued to walk, she felt a little shiver, as if someone was watching them, but when she looked behind her they were all alone on the path. Even the dogs had run down to the lough to splash in the water and chase ducks. Again, she heard a rustling. It was just some animal probably – whatever kind of creature lived in these woods – squirrels, but weren't they hibernating? But as she was thinking on this, she saw a flash of movement out of the corner of her eye. Turning her head in the same direction, she caught sight of a girl standing by a tree and staring at her and Maeve. By her side was a small white dog. The girl smiled and waved at her as if she knew who she was, and then turned on her heel and ran away into the woods, followed by her scampering dog.

'Hey!' Iris found herself calling out.

Maeve stopped talking.

'Did you see that girl?'

'No,' Maeve said, looking to where Iris was pointing.

'She was standing by that tree and just staring at us.'

'What did she look like?'

'Long blond hair, big eyes, very pretty.'

'Oh, that sounds like Lizzie,' Maeve said. 'She lives with her father in a cottage the other side of Swan Hall.'

'But why was she waving at us?'

'Oh, everyone does that round here,' Maeve said. 'We all know each other. I would imagine it's very different in New York.'

Iris thought of her neighbours in the apartment building in Brooklyn, and how they had clubbed together to get her flowers when her mom died. She thought about her mom's restaurant where she worked, the kindness of her boss, Dan, and the tears of the waitresses when Iris had called in. Memories came from her childhood: Mikey, the owner of Joe's Diner, who always gave her an extra pancake when she went there with her mom on Sundays, and Pashel, who ran the deli, telling her about his family in India.

'We've community too,' she said. 'It's just weird she's on her own. Isn't it dangerous?' Iris would no sooner wander in these woods all by herself than go into Hell's Kitchen after midnight.

Maeve stopped walking and looked at her in astonishment. 'What do you mean, dangerous?'

'To be in the woods, on her own.'

Maeve gave a laugh. 'This is rural Ireland, not the Bronx, Iris,' she said, her tone slightly patronising. 'Besides, Lizzie's always been a bit of a loner. Her dad is away a lot, and her mam died when she was a toddler. She's used to her own company.'

So this girl Lizzie didn't have a mother either. Iris couldn't help finding her intriguing.

'Sometimes she helps me out with the milking, and I let her walk in the woods at Swan Hall by the lake,' Maeve said, whistling for the dogs as they came panting, wet and unruly from their lakeside splashing. 'Lizzie likes to paint by the lough sometimes. I think she's hoping to go to art college.'

Lizzie had smiled at her, and waved, as if she knew Iris. That was a bit freaky, despite the fact her aunt said it was normal. Iris pushed her hands in her pockets. Everything was so strange right now. She had travelled back not just to her mother's home, but to her past. She realised now she hadn't come to visit her family to be spared a lonely Christmas; she was here to get some answers. Who was her mother? And did she really want to find out?

CHAPTER TEN

NUALA

15 JULY 1972

We're practising for the Fleadh at the end of August. It's in Listowel this year. I can't wait. Not just because of all the music, but because we're away from the farm and from Daddy. He can't leave his precious cows (thanks be to God). Last year the Fleadh wasn't on, but the year before, Trina's mam came along with us to make sure we 'behaved'. We brought tents and camped in a big field with all the other musicians. It was great because she didn't care what we got up to as long as she could be left in peace. Truth is, Trina's mam loves to sit on the beach, her toes pushed into the sand, and have a big sleep. She's no interest in all the musical shenanigans, though of course she came to our performances, and Trina's dancing. Most of the time, though, she left us to wander while she drove off to Bally-bunion beach for the afternoon. We all split up. Me and Trina, Maeve, Aisling and Conrad.

The best bit was listening to all the impromptu music on the streets: way better than the official competition. Me and Trina buying ice cream cones and wandering around the town.

Only turning up to see the others at the competition. We did well, too. Me, Aisling and Maeve came fourth in the trio section with our rendition of 'Maeve's Reel' and I came second in the singing with 'Mná na hÉireann', 'Women of Ireland'. Honestly, I saw grown men crying. Of course, it's a rebel song about Ireland being like a woman whom the English pillaged, but I think of my mother when I sing it, and the wrongs my father did her. His ranting and raging like a bull when he had the drink in him. He drove her to her death. That's what I believe. I don't bother talking to my sisters about it because the only time I said what I thought, Aisling walked away saying nothing, and Maeve got angry and defended Daddy.

'It's not his fault, Nuala,' she said. 'Mammy was sick. He didn't make her that way.'

'Do you not remember him drunk and roaring and shouting at her?' I pushed.

Maeve's face clammed up. 'You're remembering wrong. You were too young,' she said. 'Mammy wasn't right in the head.'

I was ten when Mammy drowned in the lake right in front of our house, not so young to not remember. But I didn't push it, because when Maeve believes something there is no point arguing with her.

Today we played in the best room at Swan Hall for the priest, Father Francis, whom I like to call Father Fuck Off inside my head. Daddy fawning all over him as if he was God Almighty himself. Yes, Father. No, Father. Three bags full, Father. How can Daddy have him in the house when he said my mam committed a mortal sin by drowning herself? I hate him. But still, there's no point making an enemy of the local priest, like Aisling does by refusing to go to Mass. I'm all for an easy life and getting out of here as soon as possible, so I just play along.

Father Fuck Off was sitting in Daddy's armchair, with his

cup of tea, a splash of whiskey in it from Daddy, and listening to me, Maeve and Aisling playing a reel. I was on the flute today, Maeve on the fiddle, and Aisling on the box accordion. I think the only time we get on is when we play music together. We let our instruments join us together and I feel part of something with my sisters, however fleeting.

'Ah wonderful, Gabriel,' Father Fuck Off said when we'd finished our rendition. I saw his eyes resting on Aisling, dropping to her chest, tight in her summer blouse. It was so hot, even inside the house, and the exertion of playing her box accordion had glazed the top of her breasts, just visible at the low collar of her blouse, with a light film of sweat.

'How blessed you are to have three fine girls with such talent,' he continued, leering at Aisling. I could sense Aisling's discomfort at the way the priest was openly appraising her body. She's the womanliest of the three of us, a figure like our mam, with her eyes too, and they all say I have Mammy's mannerisms, which I think is why I incense Daddy so much. Maeve's tall and angular, like Daddy. She's definitely not as pretty as Aisling.

'Thank you, Father Francis,' Daddy said, pouring another drop of whiskey into the priest's teacup. 'We're hopeful this year the girls might do even better at the Fleadh.'

'It's in Listowel again?' Father Fuck Off asked.

'Yes, Aisling is twenty now, Father, and has her provisional licence; she's driving the three of them along with Conrad Maguire,' Daddy told the priest.

At the mention of Conrad Maguire, Aisling tensed. They went out for all of two weeks before he broke up with her. The whole town knows about the big row between Conrad and Aisling in the woods at Lough Bawn Forest Park. Apparently, Conrad had been flirting with some girl from Dublin he took out on the boat to see Church Island. Aisling's stupid to think she could ever possess a boy like Conrad Maguire. He's a big flirt, but you can't pin him down. I used to be like that, so that's how I know. I mean, it's hard not to be a flirt when everyone has been telling you how beautiful you are since you can remember. It's hard not be vain. I've probably led on every boy in the town at some time or another, but let me tell you a secret, dear diary, I have never been smitten with any of those boys, though plenty have tried to steal my heart. Sure, Conrad himself looks at me as if he literally wants to eat me every time I see him, and that makes me want to laugh out loud because he'll never have me!

'Are you not going along to keep an eye on the young people, Gabriel?' Father Fuck Off frowned in response to my father's admission that we'd be travelling unaccompanied by a parent to Listowel.

'Well now, I have the farm to mind, I can't get away, 'twill be hard enough without the help of the girls.'

'Sure I've a mind to go along myself, and I'd be happy to escort the young people,' Father Fuck Off said.

Oh no. No. No. I caught eyes with Aisling and saw she was equally unhappy. The last thing we wanted was the bloody priest stopping us from having the craic, making sure we're in our sleeping bags by 9 p.m. no doubt and up at first light for Mass.

'There's no room in the car, Daddy,' Maeve said. The only one of us confident enough to speak up against our father. 'Sure we're bringing Trina too as she's dancing, so we're jam packed, so we are.'

'Oh yes, right so,' my father said.

'Sure, I might take a spin to Listowel in my own car for one of the days,' Father Francis said, beaming at us. 'I shall make a point of going to see your girls play, Gabriel.'

'Well, I'm very grateful to you, Father,' my father grovelled.

I gave a sigh of relief. At least the priest wouldn't be camping with us, the idea of which made me want to giggle. Does he sleep in his big black cassock? Father Francis isn't old.

In fact, he is probably younger than Daddy but he dresses as if he lives in the previous century. For some reason, I started to think of his mickey beneath his cassock and that made me want to laugh out loud like a donkey. I am a true sinner, with a filthy mind, but that's your and my secret, dear diary, as is the secret of the one I desire, who will remain nameless! Or maybe I can just give them a codename: C. When I write about my beloved in day-to-day life, well then, in the pages of this diary I will use their real name, but when they transform and become all mine, then they're 'C'! And, dear diary, seeing as you are my body, heart, and soul, you'll know who C is!

After being cooped up in the house with the priest, and playing those tight reels, the rise and fall of our ancestral music guilting me, all I wanted was put on some Soul music SO LOUD, and sway my hips, and see the look on Father Fuck Off's face. But if I went upstairs and put on a record I was sure to be told to take it off again. Instead, I legged it out the house, before my sisters could tell me to help Trina's mam start on the dinner. Maeve had gone off to feed the horses, and Aisling God knows where. Ah, the sun was still blazing and I ran through waves of heat, the air wobbling all around me, blasting my face as if it were a hot fan. After a week of unbroken sunshine, Ireland was unbearably hot. Gasping, I was, for some cool relief. I ran all the way to the lake, and I pulled off my blouse and skirt. Unsnapped my bra and wriggled out of my knickers. Terrible girl! If someone saw me and told Daddy, I'd be locked up in my room, hit with the strap for sure. But I wanted to wash off the formality of our tea with Father Fuck Off and forget the way he was looking at my sister. I wanted to put my head under the water and silence the echo of my father's fawning voice. Pandering to the man who denied my mother eternal peace.

I waded out into the lake and dipped under the water. Cool, blessed relief. I pushed out, swam underwater for a while, and then came up for air, my hair fanning upon the surface of the lake. I spun in the water as if I were a spinning top. Around and around, water rippling around me, the air whizzing by, and the sound and splash of my speed filling me up. It was only when I stopped that I saw C standing on the shore, watching me. I beckoned as I did so, bobbing in the water as I waved my hands above me. C stripped off – just down to underwear – and walked into the rippling lake, before launching into the water all of a sudden, like an ungainly duck. The awkwardness of it made it all the more sexy to me, for some reason!

Ah yes, C is my lover. My lover. Sounds so exotic. We are not going out because we can't. It's a BIG SECRET AND NO ONE MUST KNOW! I have promised never to ever tell a living soul. It's a shame, because I want to shout it from the tree-tops – I AM FUCKING... But C won't allow it. Think of the scandal, I'm warned. We shouldn't be doing this.

But that's what makes it so irresistible. C reached me in the water, and I turned and began to swim to the other side. We swam together until we were hidden on the far side shore, where weeping willows trail into the lake, creating a hideaway. C held me by the waist as we bobbed in the water. We looked into each other's eyes, and then we kissed, and curled around each other. Water lapped my naked body, and I was filled with longing for the taste of C, for C to be part of me, in our rapture. I was in lust, brimming with it. I wondered – the thought idled through my mind – if my sisters are still virgins. Maeve, for sure. But Aisling? I thought of asking C, but I didn't want to break our moment. I came back to this precious, special time, for just us. It felt so right, even though Daddy, and Father Fuck Off, and every adult I know would have a conniption if they knew. But how can making love be bad? We sank under the surface of the lake, and looked at each other underwater, and I could see every detail now of C's body, underwear clinging, and I wanted to lick every part of it!

We are going to run away. Yes, we are because I AM

SPECIAL. That's what C has told me. We will be runaway lovers, and we'll disappear forever and never come back.

As we swam back towards Swan Hall, to my annoyance I saw Maeve standing on the shoreline. Arms crossed, frowning.

'Nuala, don't go out too far,' she called. Then she pulled off her summer dress to reveal a swimsuit and I realised she was planning to join us. Maeve is so annoying, always getting in the way, or turning up when I really want to be left alone. Is she so thick she can't see what's going on? But apparently, my virgin sister is an idiot and came paddling out to me and C. Our entwined legs unlinked, and I wondered how I was going to explain to Maeve that I was naked under the water. I'd just have to wait until she got out first. I pushed off away from C, away from my sister, and began to swim back again to the other side of the lake. I could hear Maeve's panicked splash, and her call to be careful, but I just wanted to get away from her. My body hummed with frustration.

Tonight, after I write my diary, I will lie on top of my single sheet, so hot I can't bear to wear my nightie, and I will touch myself thinking of C. I will do all this, thinking of the next time we can be together, and of how to find a safe place no one will find us. I will stroke myself, and imagine my finger belongs to C. My orgasm will bring me to the edge, over and away from this long hot summer of my life before it begins for real.

CHAPTER ELEVEN

IRIS

24 DECEMBER 1991

The gears crunched uncomfortably as Iris used the shift stick to change into third, and then up into fourth gear. The laneway leading down to Swan Hall felt tiny compared to the streets she'd learned to drive on, but when her Aunt Maeve had asked her if she could drive on the way back from Lough Bawn Forest Park and did she want to borrow Conrad's VW Golf which he hardly used, Iris had said yes without thinking. She'd only been in Swan Hall one night and not even a whole day and already she was feeling a little stir crazy. It was also Christmas Eve, and her last chance to do some Christmas shopping. It hadn't occurred to her to bring a present for her family from New York, but of course she should have. Iris couldn't help thinking her mom would be pleased she was being thoughtful.

She drove back down the long drive, the trees towering either side. The afternoon was gloomy, with a persistent light rain which had misted her hair before she'd got into the car. She turned on the windscreen wipers and the lights on the car as she drove out of the entrance gates of Swan Hall and onto the main road. If it could be called a main road – it was barely bigger than the drive she'd just exited. Black-faced sheep stared at her from viridian green fields behind grey stone walls. The dregs of last autumn were visible in the red russet of old land, and she could see a choppy lough ruffled with white, while undulating blue mountains appeared to fold in upon each other in the distance. She took a breath, feeling her body relax a little. It felt good to be moving along the road, exploring this place where her mom had grown up. She was driving down the same roads her mom had driven down not much older than she was now. The land was hillocky, and so very green even though it was midwinter that it didn't seem real. It stopped raining and the sun came out weakly, then it began to rain again, and Iris saw a rainbow arching over the road in front of her. She was so impressed by the splendour that for a split second she took her eyes off the road. When she looked back down, she was horrified to see what look like a cop car heading straight for her. It swerved to her left, flashing its lights and blaring its horn. Iris swerved across the left-hand side of the road, realising with horror she had been driving on the wrong side of the road for Ireland. She pulled in and turned off the engine.

'Oh crap.'

If she got into trouble on her first day driving, she wouldn't blame her Aunt Maeve if she banned her from getting behind the wheel again.

She looked in her rear-view mirror, watching as the cop car turned and pulled up behind her. She noted the word 'Garda' on the side of the car. Irish for 'police', she guessed. The door of the cop car opened, and a guard in uniform emerged. As he walked towards her, Iris couldn't help thinking he was very tall, and quite good-looking in a rustic sort of way. He wasn't clean-shaven like Freddie and his hair was long for a cop.

She opened her window as he bent down, staring at her with a very serious expression on his face.

'Officer, I am so sorry, I've just arrived from the States and I've probably still got a bit of jet lag—'

'Well, Miss, you shouldn't be behind the wheel of a vehicle then,' he said. 'You could have killed someone.'

'Yes, I know, it's very serious. I'm real sorry,' she gushed, nervously.

He scrutinised her and she could feel herself blushing.

'Are you Aisling Kelly's daughter?' he asked eventually.

She nodded, biting her lip and not meeting his eye again.

'My colleague knew her,' he said. 'I'm sorry for your loss.'

'Thank you,' she mumbled, mortified.

'Well look, I'll make an exception this one time,' he said, to her surprise. 'But stay alert, remember to drive on the left, and if you're tired, don't get into the car!'

She looked up at him gratefully, noticing the rich brown of his eyes, and a little scar through one of his eyebrows like a tiny white Z.

'Oh, thank you so much... Officer?'

'My name's Garda Ruairi Caffrey,' he said.

'Iris Kelly.'

'I know,' he said, nodding. 'You'll see it's a small enough place so everyone knows everyone here.' He straightened up, patting the roof of the car. 'Merry Christmas to you, so,' he said.

He walked back to his car and got in, and she willed him to turn around and drive away, but he seemed to be writing some kind of report. She took a breath, turned on the ignition, and doing her best not to crunch the gears again, took off in shuddering first gear, before screeching into second. Her cheeks burned with embarrassment. Thankfully, she saw Garda Ruairi Caffrey turn his police car and drive off in the opposite direction before she drove around the bend. At least he wasn't tailing her into town. After that, she drove past a sign with the name 'Bawn', and crawled like a granny into the local town, reminding herself every second she should be on the left. She couldn't parallel park at all, so it took a while to find a little car park she could pull into.

Ruairi Caffrey hadn't been exaggerating when he'd told her the town was small. It took her less than fifteen minutes to walk around the main street. She noticed a small supermarket, a newsagent, a dress shop which looked like the clothes on the window dummies hadn't been changed since the Seventies, and a large hardware store which also had a display of Christmas toys. Bawn made up for its lack of exciting shops with lots of pubs, which seemed a bit weird to Iris. She went inside the hardware store, thinking it was the most likely place to find a Christmas gift for her aunt and uncle. As soon as she stepped inside, it felt as if the two women behind the till stopped talking and stared at her as if she was something exotic. She shuffled along the aisles, looking at nails and screws and hammers, along with large dolls and jigsaw puzzles. Just as she was giving up hope, she saw a section selling candles. She selected two big scented candles – one smelling of lavender, and one of white musk – before going up to pay. She had changed some dollars into Irish pounds in the airport, but still she was shocked by how much the candles were when she changed the figure into dollars in her head.

'So are you Aisling Kelly's young one?' one of the women behind the till asked her outright.

'Yes,' Iris said, feeling self-conscious. It seemed the cop was right and everyone knew each other in this small Irish town.

'Ah God, so sorry to hear about what happened to her.' The other woman spoke up. 'We were all at school together. She was a few years below me.'

'Oh, did you know her well?'

'No, not really, sure the Kelly sisters of Swan Hall were famous and all for their music,' she said. 'But they kept themselves to themselves, especially after...' The woman paused and looked nervous.

'Well now, would you like a bag with that?' The other woman spoke up brightly.

Outside it was raining heavily again, and the wind had picked up. Iris bent her head down as she walked towards the car. As she made her way back, she felt a tap on her shoulder. She turned around, and to her surprise her Uncle Conrad was standing behind her, a big smile plastered on his face.

'Fancy seeing you here!' he said. 'Last-minute Christmas shopping?'

'Oh yes,' Iris said awkwardly.

'Fancy joining me for a Christmas pint in the pub?'

'I can't, I'm driving.'

'Sure you could leave the car here, and we can get it tomorrow,' Conrad suggested. 'We'll get Maeve to pick us up later. She just dropped me into town.'

'But isn't she joining us?'

'Ah, Maeve doesn't like pubs,' Conrad said. 'Besides, she's gone visiting friends.'

'Right,' Iris said.

'Yes, surprising I know, that your Aunt Maeve might have some friends!' Conrad joked. 'So are you up for a pint of Guinness?'

The idea of going back to cold, draughty Swan Hall, especially if she was going to be on her own, was not appealing, and so Iris found herself saying yes. Besides, it felt cool to be able to drink legally rather than back home, when she had to use fake ID.

Conrad took her to a little pub at the top of town. When they walked in the door, much to her surprise it was a grocery shop, and they had to go through a second door into the back of the pub. The place was full of chat and laughter, and the air thick with cigarette smoke. So this was where everyone was! They sat down on stools at a small round table.

'What'll you have?' he asked her.

'A Coke?'

He frowned. 'Come on now, it's Christmas Eve. I'll be getting you a glass of Guinness and I won't be hearing anything of it.'

Uncle Conrad made her laugh. It was like he knew she was sad and lonely, so he told her funny stories about some of the old men in the bar and she found herself giggling. It felt so good to relax a little. By her third glass of Guinness, Iris was feeling tipsy, but the happiest since she'd been since she had arrived. Conrad asked her questions about her life in New York and told her he had gone there once with his cousin to play music.

'Did you see my mom?'

He shook his head, looking mournful.

'I had no idea where she was,' he said. 'As far as I know she never contacted us in all these years, I couldn't even let her know when your grandfather died.'

Iris wished so much she'd asked her mom more questions about her past, but it was too late now.

'Shame you never got to meet him. He was a great story-teller, but...' Conrad paused. 'He and Aisling had a big falling-out and she must have never wanted to make peace with him.'

'And did you know my granny?' Iris ventured.

'I never knew her, or more correctly, I don't remember her too well. I mean I saw her in church and everything, but, well... she was a little strange. She was from Dublin.' Uncle Conrad took another swig of his pint of Guinness. 'Nuala got her looks from her mother, and Iris, you're a dead cert for Nuala; it's still confusing me a bit.' He grinned. 'I keep thinking I've gone back in time, but no, I'm a middle-aged man getting all nostalgic for the past.'

'I wish my mom had told me about my Aunt Nuala,' Iris said wistfully.

'She'd have had her reasons,' Conrad said, turning away and waving to a group of men setting up a table on the other side of the bar. Iris could see one of them had a fiddle and another a tin whistle. 'Well now, what do you say to a bit of music? Sure, I thought Seamus and the lads might show up. It's just as well as I left my bodhrán behind the bar.'

'What's a bodhrán?'

Conrad looked at her in surprise. 'Did your mam turn away from Irish culture altogether, then? I can't believe she never told you about our music.'

Iris shook her head.

'Sure, your mam was expert on the box accordion. The three girls won loads of competitions.'

'I knew she played the piano, but no, she never spoke about it.'

Conrad sighed. 'Ah God, well I guess she wanted to forget all about what happened. Let's get a little bit of a session going, so.'

He got up and went over to the other men. Iris took a sip of her pint of Guinness. It was a little bitter for her taste, but it also felt fortifying. The alcohol was making her want to ring up Freddie and tell him what a bastard he was. She had let him use her twice now and she wished she'd freaked out at him. But of course, she never had, just took it like the pathetic idiot she was. Well, she was the other side of the world now, so she had no way of telling him what she thought of him.

She looked across the small bar, waiting for her uncle to return, but Conrad had abandoned her. He was sitting now with the other men and had what she guessed was the bodhrán – a small round drum with a stick – on his lap. Without any kind of announcement, the men all started playing at the same time. It was a jaunty tune, a jig. More and more folk came through from the grocery store out the front and the bar filled up, everyone attentive and tapping their feet in time with the music. Iris felt as if she were part of something special. Maybe it was in her head, but it felt as if she was connected to all these strangers, she guessed by her Irish heritage. The music lifted her spirits, and she found herself tapping her feet too. After three tunes, the men took a pause, and people started chatting again. But her Uncle Conrad didn't return to the table. She watched him as he got up and walked over to the other side of the pub, where three men sat around a table in a nook under the TV. One of them had put a fresh pint down and her Uncle Conrad took a seat. Iris frowned. Had he forgotten about her already? She got up from her stool and weaved through the crowd towards him. He was deep in conversation as the men had their heads bent down, plumes of cigarette smoke wafting above as they spoke in fast whispers. She couldn't make out any of what they were saying.

'Make yourself scarce, girl.' One of the men had noticed her. He looked at her with piercing blue eyes.

Uncle Conrad twisted on his stool. 'Sure, that's my niece Iris, over from the States.'

'An American, eh?' one of the other men said.

'Off you go now, Iris, I'll be back shortly.' Her Uncle Conrad looked a little flustered as he pulled a five-pound note out of his pocket. 'Get yourself another drink.'

'But—'

'Do as your uncle tells you, girl, and keep your nose out of our business here,' the cold blue-eyed man snapped at her.

Iris stepped back in surprise, looking to her uncle for support, but he merely turned his back on her. She left his fiver on the table and stalked back to where she had been sitting, feeling confused and hurt. Who were those horrible men?

Not sure what to do, she sat back down at her table, when she heard a voice at her shoulder.

'Hello there again, Iris, is it?'

She looked up to see a familiar face. The brown eyes of Garda Ruairi Caffrey were gazing down at her.

'Hi,' she said.

He was no longer in uniform and looked the better for it, in blue jeans and a deep green sweater. He was holding a pint in his hand and appeared to be alone.

'Would you like a drink?' he asked, indicating her empty pint glass.

'Sure,' Iris said, spirits immediately lifting. Now it didn't matter that her uncle had abandoned her, because Ruairi joining her for a Christmas drink presented a more attractive turn of events.

While Ruairi went up to the bar, Iris watched the men in the corner with her uncle. They seemed very out of place, with their grim expressions and heads bent in conference, and yet also invisible, because no one in the pub went near them. Quite suddenly they all got up, including her uncle, who shook hands with the blue-eyed man before he headed back to the small troupe of musicians as they started up again. This time Conrad was singing and the music took a sadder tone, more like a ballad. Ruairi returned with two pints of Guinness, removing Iris's empty glass from the table, and placing the fresh one down in front of her on a beer mat. He sat down on Conrad's empty stool.

'Your uncle has a great voice, has he not?' he whispered to her.

'Yes, I guess, it's the first time I've heard him sing,' she said, watching her Uncle Conrad as he closed his eyes, as if lost in the music. He was singing in Gaelic. She didn't understand the words, but the tone of it was very moving.

Ruairi took a packet of cigarettes out of his shirt pocket and offered her one. She took it, not that she smoked much, but anything to calm her nerves. Talking with Ruairi made her nervous, and not just because he was police.

The song finished and everyone cheered before Conrad took up his bodhrán again and the group broke into a reel.

'Are you off duty now?' Iris asked Ruairi.

'Course,' Ruairi said, smiling. 'How's the driving going?' He winked at her.

'I'm leaving the car in town tonight,' she said, flustered. 'I mean, I'm not driving...'

'Glad to hear it,' he said. 'You might need to be fully present every time you get behind the wheel until you get used to our roads.'

'Yes, sure, sorry, and well, thank you.'

'I reckoned you needed a break,' he said gently. 'I lost my mam a year ago so I feel for you.'

'Oh,' Iris said, turning to him in astonishment. She didn't know anyone else young who had lost a parent, apart from the girl Lizzie whom Maeve had told her about, and she was a stranger. It felt like a sort of connection between her and Ruairi. 'I'm sorry. What happened?'

'Cancer's what happened,' Ruairi said, sighing, before taking another drag on his cigarette. 'Anyhow, I had days when I just blanked out after the funeral. It felt like it happened so fast, even though we knew she was dying. But it must have been worse for you – I heard what happened.'

Iris felt a lump rising in her throat.

'It must have been so sudden for you, with an accident like that,' he continued.

'It was shocking,' she said in a hoarse voice. She could tell he was being kind, inviting her to open up and talk about what had happened to her mom. But she could barely speak about it because it still didn't feel real. 'Yeah,' she said, swallowing down the lump in her throat. 'Yeah, it was tough.'

As if sensing she was getting upset, Ruairi began talking again. 'Tell me, Iris, is it your first time in Ireland?'

'Yes, first time, though it feels kind of familiar, maybe because my mom talked about the countryside a lot.'

'You can take the Irishman out of Ireland, but not Ireland out of the Irishman,' Ruairi said. 'I went travelling to Australia after I finished school. Loved it, but I always wanted to come home, so.'

'Why did you become a policeman?'

'A garda,' Ruairi corrected her. 'My dad's one, and it's always been in our family. Just felt like the way my life was supposed to go.'

Iris took another sip of her Guinness and felt herself relaxing. She was enjoying Ruairi's company. He was easy to talk to, and she found him very attractive. She wondered what he thought of her. God, what did she even look like? She'd been rained on walking through town and must look bedraggled. She excused herself, going to the restrooms, and did her best to fix her unruly hair and replenish her lip gloss. When she came back to her seat, there was an older man chatting with Ruairi.

'This is my colleague and fellow guard, Eamon,' Ruairi introduced Iris. 'Iris Kelly.'

Eamon looked at her, and his eyes widened. 'My goodness, you're a dead ringer for Nuala Kelly,' he blurted out. 'Astonishing.'

Iris blushed, feeling deeply uncomfortable.

'Well, I wouldn't know, Eamon,' Ruairi said, picking up on Iris's discomfort. 'Go on now and join your cronies, leave us young ones alone.' He shooed Eamon away to join the older men on high stools at the bar.

'Sorry about that,' he said. 'Eamon can be very insensitive.'

'It's okay,' Iris said. 'Just a bit weird. Because I never knew her. Nuala, that is.'

She paused, glancing over at her Uncle Conrad, who was

now chatting away with his musical pals, a fresh pint of Guinness in front of him. The need to confide in someone was overwhelming her. Maybe it was the drink, but before she could stop herself, she continued talking. 'Actually, I never even knew about Nuala until yesterday, when I arrived. My mom never told me about her.'

'You're joking me?' Ruairi looked her in surprise. 'Sure, what happened to Nuala is like a legend around here.'

'All I know is I look like her and she drowned in the lake at Swan Hall, that's it.'

Ruairi gave a low whistle. The music began again, so it was harder to talk, and Iris's heart was racing in time with the beat of it, but she was desperate to find out more. She leaned over and whispered into Ruairi's ear: 'What happened? Was it an accident?'

Ruairi looked at her carefully, through narrowed eyes. 'That's what some say, but others think she drowned herself like her mam.'

'Oh, like suicide?' Iris whispered, in shock.

Ruairi nodded. 'Her mother was unstable, that's what I heard – took her own life when the older girls were in their teens. Some think Nuala never got over it, being the youngest, and that it touched her in the head, you know. But...' He paused.

'But what?' Iris pushed.

'Well, Eamon doesn't agree. He says Nuala was a joyful sort of girl. She wasn't like her mam nor the other sisters. He said that out of the three of them it was hard to imagine her doing such a thing.'

'Sometimes the people who look the happiest are in fact the saddest,' Iris said, thinking of her godmother, Trina, for some reason. Intuitively, she had always known that Trina's big personality – all the jokes and laughter – hid a deep sadness.

'True,' agreed Ruairi, 'but Eamon was adamant she wasn't the type.'

'So, he thinks it was an accident?'

Ruairi offered her another cigarette. 'Nuala was a strong swimmer. She was always in the lakes. She knew where the strong underwater currents could pull you down, that's what Eamon said. So it made no sense. Besides, she wasn't alone.'

Iris looked at Ruairi in astonishment.

'The story goes that all three sisters were together at the Lough Bawn that morning. It had been a particularly hot summer, that's what Eamon told me. He was a young guard at the time and it was up to him to take everyone's statements.'

Ruairi paused to light her cigarette.

'According to Eamon, Aisling and Maeve had been with Nuala at the lake. But Nuala had swum off from them. Your mam, Aisling, said she did it a lot to annoy them because it would freak them out because of what happened to their mother. Maeve said she called to her and warned Nuala it was dangerous to go too far, but she ignored them. Apparently, Nuala was a good swimmer and often went off for few hours on her own swimming across the lake to the woods on the other side. Your mam, Aisling, had to go to work, and so she left, but Maeve said she stayed and looked for her sister. She raised the alarm a few hours later when Nuala didn't return.'

'You know a lot of details about all of this,' Iris commented.

Ruairi blushed. 'Yes, well, I always thought it a bit odd, and so did Eamon.'

Iris felt her whole body going still. The music was leaping around the room, but it felt as if she was in the eye of the storm, as if her whole world had narrowed down to this conversation between her and Ruairi. 'Why? Why did he think it odd?'

Ruairi sighed. 'I don't know what's got into me. This is your mam and her sisters we're talking about here. It's not my place to gossip...'

'Please,' Iris begged. 'My aunt and uncle won't talk about it to me, and my mom is dead, so you know it doesn't hurt her if you tell me what you think.'

'Sure, but it might hurt you, Iris.'

'I'm hurt already. My mom kept so much from me as it is. You've got to tell me what you think,' she demanded.

Ruairi took a gulp of his Guinness. 'Okay, so,' he said. 'Well, Eamon told me the Kelly sisters of Swan Hall weren't just famous for playing music together. No, it was said when they performed their music it was the only time the three girls could abide each other. The rest of the time they fought like wildcats. Got worse and worse as they got older.' Ruairi glanced at Conrad playing his bodhrán. 'And Conrad Maguire hanging around with them didn't help matters. Not a bit. Eamon said he was a bit of lad, and one week you'd see him in town with your mam, the next with Nuala, and then sure he ends up with Maeve.'

Iris's mouth hung open. 'My mam went out with my Uncle Conrad?'

'I believe so,' Ruairi said. 'I think I've said too much.'

'No, no,' Iris said, gathering up all the information. 'It's okay.'

All the mystery surrounding her mother's sisters was helping her. It was as if the heavy weight of her loss was shifting slightly by the distraction of the intrigue.

'The question Eamon always asked was: why would these three sisters, who acted as if they hated being in the same room with each other, go swimming together? Just them, on their own, and first thing in the morning. It didn't make sense. And there's something else,' Ruairi continued, looking into Iris's eyes. She felt herself pulled into their rich warm hues, gripped by his words. 'Nuala's body was never found. Just like her mam.'

CHAPTER TWELVE

NUALA

I don't believe in the Catholic God. I really don't. I know some of the girls at school pretend they don't believe in God to be cool, and to piss off the nuns, but in my heart I absolutely know God does not exist for me. That's not to say God's not real for others, like Maeve. Though I think she prays more to the Virgin Mary than the man himself. Another reason why she's Daddy's favourite, because she's always helping out at the church, and licking up to Father Fuck Off. But right from when I was little, I didn't like God. Oh here, I thought, another big man telling us all what to do. I think or I feel Mammy believed the same as me. Sure, she followed the rules like we all do. Went to Mass and all that. Did her confession, but her eyes had a mocking look to them when she came out of the priest's confessional. God didn't help her, that's for sure.

I believe in the magic in the land. I think Mammy did too. I can feel the spirits of the trees when I walk through the woods, and the divinity of water when I float upon it. Think about it. Doesn't it make more sense that what is holy is in the nature all around us? If we're going to worship anything then it should be the earth we walk on, and the sky we look up at, the rain which nourishes the land, and the sun which nurtures abundance.

Aisling is an atheist, which is better than being all holier than thou like Maeve, but I can't help thinking it's a bit sad, too. Because when Aisling looks at a flower she sees it biologically. She believes it has one brief life, one summer to bloom, and then it's gone, and then I suppose its progeny continues its line. So like, we are the seeds and our daughters or sons will be our seeds, and on we go. Aisling says we live one life and when we die, that's the end of it all. We're just flesh, bone and blood. Oh, Maeve can't bear it when Aisling says that and she goes mad, saying she's wrong. There's heaven and hell and we have to make our confessions so we get through those pearly gates. But here's the thing: if she's right, Mammy won't be there anyway. She's stuck somewhere in purgatory because when she drowned herself it was a sin. I can't believe it. I won't.

I walk down to the lake, and feel my mammy's presence there. I think she's living in the land all around me. Her spirit has become part of the landscape. I wonder if the fey people took her, and that's where she's hiding out. When we were little, Mammy would read the old Irish stories to us. We loved the story of the Children of Lir, because of the swans on our lake and the name of our house, of course. We were scared of their witchy stepmother who turned the four children into swans out of jealousy. My favourite part of the story was how the Children of Lir soothed their heartbroken father and his people with the comfort of their singing. Mammy said I was named Nuala after Fionnuala, the only sister. I'd love three brothers like Fionnuala had. 'Twould be great to look after them like she did. But I've two big sisters and they're always treating me like a baby. Well, they'll get a right shock when I head off to New York at the end of the summer.

I've nearly enough saved for the flight ticket. I get good tips in the restaurant because the customers love me, so I squirrel it all away, along with what I can from my wages, hiding it in an old handbag of Mam's in the bottom of my wardrobe. We all have to give Daddy something. You'd think with all the money and land he has that he'd be giving us allowances. Not at all. That's why I hide my money, because if he knew how much I have he'd take the lot off me.

I was on the day shift today in the restaurant at Lough Bawn Forest Park and Jaysus it was brutal hot. We have fans going all the time, but the kitchen is like a furnace. The chef, Frank, is like a raging bull with the abuse, and poor Stefan his assistant gets it in the neck, though he seems to take it in his stride. Maybe because he's German, but he doesn't shout back, just nods, and says, *Ja, ja, I hear you, Frank.* I was trying not to drop the plates, my hands were so sweaty and slippery. I can't imagine why anyone would want a full Irish breakfast during a heatwave, but there's always plenty. Then it was straight into lunches – chips and burgers being the biggest sellers – and me and Trina were the only ones on. Rushed off our feet, we were, though we always had time to leave each other big glasses of Coke, filled with ice. Sugar, caffeine and ice kept us going.

Finally, we got our break, and we went to sit by the lough and watch the boat boys taking out all the tourists onto the water. The sun beating down on us, we tried to get some shade under a tree. I could see Aisling on her own in the shop and a big queue of kids lining up for their ice creams. Poor old Stefan, on his break trying to buy a packet of cigarettes, ended up helping her out. Well, I was sure not coming to Aisling's rescue. She wouldn't do it for me.

We lay back down on the dry, brittle grass in silence, let our hot, sweaty limbs melt into the earth.

'Jaysus, that was a mental shift,' I said. 'The tips were rubbish too. The heat makes people mean.'

'It'll be hot like this in the summer in New York all the time,' Trina said.

'Yeah, but at least it's New York,' I countered.

I closed my eyes and tried to make a picture of what New York would be like in my head. It was a big city full of strangers and new places. I would miss the lake, but nothing else. I wasn't scared. I just wanted to be free.

'Nuala, I need to tell you something,' Trina said quietly, by my side.

'What is it?'

'You know Johnny's in New York, right?'

'Well yes, because that's who we're staying with when we get there, right?'

'He's had a bit of a windfall, and well, he's sent me the money for a ticket.'

'That's amazing!' I said, although I felt a twinge of jealousy. My father could easily pay for my ticket but I can't ask him, of course, because he wants me to stay on at school and then probably stay for the rest of my life on our farm.

'And he's also got me a job, at the bar where he works,' Trina said. 'He's got fake ID for me and all.'

'Oh wow!' I sat up and looked down at Trina. She was shielding her eyes from the sun with her hand and it was hard to see her expression. 'Can he get me a job, too?'

'He'll try, but the thing is...' Trina broke off. 'The thing is, I have to start on 13th August.'

'But that's in two weeks' time!' I stared at her in astonishment. 'I don't have enough money yet for the flight, and I'm still to go up to Dublin for my passport. Can you not get them to wait?'

'I can't, Nuala, I'll lose the job. He's going out on a limb for me.'

My heart sank. I should have been happy for Trina, but all I felt was let down.

She sat up now and took hold of my hands. Our fingers were hot and sticky as they touched. 'I can be our scout! It's only a few weeks. And if you're struggling to get the money for the ticket, I'll help you out. You can make great money on tips in New York.'

'Promise you won't leave me behind, Trina.'

Trina looked at me, her eyes serious. 'I promise, Nuala. You'll be right behind me. It's only a month.'

'But what about the Fleadh in Listowel? You'll miss the dance competition.'

'Ah God, this is more important than winning an Irish dancing contest. It's my future.'

'Right.' I nodded, disappointed. 'But I have to go to the Fleadh. I want to win.'

'I know, I know,' she said. 'But as soon as it's over...'

'Have you told your mam?'

'Yeah, Mam's pretty upset, but she's still pleased, too. She's driving me to the airport.'

'So your flight is booked and all?'

'Yes,' she said, looking away. 'Tuesday 13th.'

'Jaysus, Trina,' I said, feeling stung. 'When were you going to tell me?'

'I only just booked it yesterday.'

'That's why you weren't in work, then? Sneaking off to the travel agent's.'

'I wasn't sneaking off,' she said defensively. 'Don't be a bitch, Nuala.'

She was right. If I really cared about Trina then I should be happy for her.

'Sorry, you're right, it's great,' I said. 'And as you say, it's only a few weeks before I'll be with you. God, we'll have the craic, so we will!'

'We'll be able to do what we want without anyone minding us,' Trina said, grinning at me.

'Exactly,' I agreed.

Back home, after I had taken a cold bath and washed all the stink of grease from the restaurant off my body, I put on my shorts and a cotton shirt, and went down to the lake. I walked through the reeds, which most years were lush and green, but the summer had turned them the colour of my hair, and dry stalks stuck in cracked mud. It seemed to me as if the lake was shrinking, drawing back from its edges, still and unmoving. Swarms of flies buzzed around me, and I swiped them away. I couldn't shake off a feeling of dread. I should be happy and excited Trina is going to New York. It means our dream is becoming real. She will be all set up and ready to welcome me when I get my arse out of here. But somehow, it feels as if she is leaving me behind. I'd imagined us travelling up to the airport together on the bus and sitting next to each other on the plane. Holding hands as it took off, because it would be both of our first times on a plane. But now I'll have to do all those things on my own.

I felt the pull of my mother in the lake and part of me wanted to stay right here, because I am going to have to be very brave to do the whole journey on my own. That's a lot to face. But then I thought about what she'd want for me. I feels like I know who she was, and her dreams. You can say she died when I was ten, but she is inside me, and she is saying: *Go, go, go, Nuala*.

I crouched down by the lake and watched the bright blue damselflies hovering above its surface, and I dipped my hand and felt the weight of water trickling through my fingers. When I turned around, C was there, watching me.

Wordlessly, we walked around the edge of the lake together, to the other side where the forest grew densest. We went into its shade, C taking me by the hand and leading me. We found a place to hide together, and there I opened up my body. I didn't want to talk about my plans, or the end of this thing we were doing together in the lake, in the woods. C was mercurial and didn't belong to me. When C and I were together, it was like that sacred thing in nature. What our bodies did together made me feel less lonely.

When we had finished our lovemaking, I sang for C. It was my favourite song, 'Mná na hÉireann', 'Women of Ireland', and despite myself I couldn't help thinking of how it would be for my sisters when I was gone. What would they do without me? Celebrate?

Later, when the sun was setting, and it must have been very late, we came out of the woods together. The land was ticking with the heat from the day, slowly cooling down like a car engine. To my surprise, there was Aisling, standing by the lake. She rarely came this way. Hated the lake which had taken our mother away. But there she was, surrounded by midges, staring into its deep blue. She looked up at the sound of us, and saw us, hand in hand. It was too late for me to hide the obvious connection between my love and I. She raised her eyebrows, though her face had no expression. I let go of C's hand and then I ran away. Because she made me feel ashamed. And that was wrong of her.

CHAPTER THIRTEEN

IRIS

24 DECEMBER 1991

The session wound down, Uncle Conrad beginning to flag as the empty pint glasses lined up in front of him. People began to gather their things and the barman collected up empties. Iris glanced at her watch – it was a quarter to midnight. The night had flown by and she realised she'd enjoyed chatting with Ruairi and sometimes sitting in silence together, watching the music. Despite his inebriated state, her Uncle Conrad had given a great show with his friends, moving between guitar, bodhrán, tin whistle and his voice.

'Well, so,' Ruairi said getting up. 'Are you coming to Mass?'

'Mass?' Iris asked in surprise. 'It's the middle of the night!'

'Yes, but it's also Christmas Eve,' Ruairi said. 'Everyone goes to Midnight Mass.'

'Even after drinking in the pub?'

'Especially after drinking in the pub!'

The last thing Iris wanted to do was go to church. It was something she and her mom had never done at Christmas, but she didn't want to make a fuss. She was unsure exactly how she was getting back to Swan Hall – she'd had too much to drink to drive – but she thought her Aunt Maeve would most likely come and collect them, seeing as she'd dropped Conrad off. Iris began to feel a little prick of guilt. She hadn't thought about her aunt all evening. Dinnertime had long passed. Would her aunt be angry with her, or was Maeve used to her husband spending the whole night in the pub? Would she be glad her niece was with him and out of her hair? Iris had no idea as she watched her uncle staggering over to their table.

'Thanks for keeping an eye on Nuala, but you can bugger off now,' he said to Ruairi, all joviality gone, his chin jutting out and a hard look on his face.

'I believe her name is Iris, Conrad,' Ruairi said coolly. 'Are you all right, Iris?' he continued. 'Would you like to come to Mass with me?'

Iris felt her Uncle Conrad bristling next to her. 'She'll be joining me and her aunt at Mass, Garda Caffrey. Maeve will already be there keeping a pew for us.' Conrad said 'Garda' as if it were a dirty word. 'Iris is one of us and won't be hanging around with your sort.'

Ruairi's eyes darkened, but he ignored Conrad. 'Are you sure, Iris?'

'Yes, yes, I'm okay, thanks,' she replied, embarrassed by the incident.

'I'll see you in there,' Ruairi said, moving away to join Eamon, who was looking over at Conrad, hands on hips and frowning. Clearly her uncle was no friend of the local gardaí.

Uncle Conrad took a comb out of his top pocket and attempted to tame his wild hair. His cheeks were flushed from the drink, and his eyes were bright. He carried his drum under his elbow as they followed everyone out of the bar and into the cold night.

A sheen of icy rain fell upon Iris's shoulders as they turned the corner and crossed over a narrow river. Though it wasn't half as cold as a New York winter, she was shivering in her coat as if the wet chill had sunk into her bones. Her Uncle Conrad took her elbow, and already he appeared to have sobered up as they walked down the main street of the town. Iris saw the silhouette of a church tower, but as they approached she realised it had no roof, despite its beautiful empty arcades of stone glimmering in the streetlights.

'Bawn Abbey, our twelfth-century treasure.' Conrad waved towards the stone ruin. 'And not where we're heading.'

As they continued down the road, along with all the others from the pub, a bell was pealing. Iris stared ahead and caught sight of a modern circular stone building, very low to the ground, with a domed roof. It was not the kind of church she had been expecting, and despite the fact it was Christmas, something to be celebrated, Iris felt a sense of doom as she walked inside it. After their dark walk, the interior of the church was glaringly bright. Candles blazed in standing candelabra while moonlight streamed down from glass windows around the whole circumference of the dome. Iris felt as if she had entered a spaceship rather than the house of God. She followed Conrad up the aisle to a front pew, where she could see her Aunt Maeve sitting straight-backed and evidently waiting for them to arrive.

'Where have you been?' Maeve hissed at Iris as soon as she caught sight of her.

'I went to the pub with Uncle Conrad...'

'We had a grand old session, Maeve,' Conrad said, his words slurring a little.

Maeve tsked and shook her head at them both.

Iris wanted to tell her aunt that she wasn't her mom and had no right to act so disapproving, but they were in church and everyone was falling silent, waiting for the priest to begin.

. . .

After Mass, Maeve drove them back to Swan Hall. By the time they sat down in the kitchen for a cup of tea before bed, it was almost two.

'You must be tired,' Maeve said to Iris, her earlier annoyance appearing to have passed.

Although the Mass had been boring, Iris hadn't felt sleepy. She'd watched the stony-faced priest as he'd intoned the Mass. All the noisy, jolly people from the pub had been on their knees silently praying, or demurely singing 'Away in a Manger'. The whole experience had been alien to her. Even when she had looked over at Ruairi, he'd appeared completely different from in the pub. Distant from her as he knelt down, closed his eyes and prayed. Now back at Swan Hall, the whole experience had left Iris feeling more awake than she had all day.

'No, not at all,' she said.

'Probably jet lag,' Conrad said, pulling a bottle of whiskey out of the cupboard and unscrewing the lid. 'Want a night cap, ladies?'

'No, Conrad,' Maeve said, tight-lipped. 'You know I don't drink, not since Daddy...'

'His deathbed promise. Jaysus, that was cruel of the old man making you swear never to drink again. Thank God he didn't ask me!' Conrad sighed. 'I wonder if it wasn't a joke of some sort, for the some of the best nights I've had in this house was sharing a drop or two of whiskey with our fathers!'

Maeve huffed but didn't reply.

'How about it, Nuala, want a drop?'

'Her name is Iris, Conrad,' Maeve said in a cold voice.

'But she's the image of Nuala,' Conrad said.

'It's totally inappropriate,' Maeve looked at her husband with cold eyes.

Iris shifted uncomfortably on her chair. The hostility between her aunt and her uncle was palpable. She had never been around couples that much. Both her mom and Trina had been mostly single. Now she thought how lucky she'd been.

'Come on, Maeve, you can't blame me for getting mixed up, just look at the girl,' Conrad said.

'That's enough, Conrad,' Maeve said icily. 'We've a guest.'

'Oh yes, Aisling's girl, Iris, the spit of your other sister, Nuala. It must have seemed like a nightmare when she turned up!' He laughed cruelly.

'I invited her!' Maeve said, as if Iris wasn't there.

'Only because you felt guilty – but too late to be forgiven now, right?'

Iris stood up. 'I think I'll go to bed.'

Maeve had gone white in the face, apart from two bright spots of colour on her cheeks. Conrad was rocking back on his chair and grinning broadly. Iris sidled out of the room, but not before she heard Maeve hiss, 'Shut up, Conrad.'

'You'll never get over it, will you, Maeve? That your sister was the love of my life!'

Iris dashed up the stairs before she could hear any more. She ran down the corridor and into her mother's old bedroom before shutting the door behind her. The curtains hadn't been drawn and the moon was reflecting silver upon the still lake. Already, it wasn't as full as the night before, and the shadows from those lakeside trees seemed to stretch even darker and deeper. She pressed her forehead to the cold glass and took in a deep breath. Her head ached, and not just from drinking. Ruairi had told her that Conrad had dated her mom. Conrad had just announced that her mom was the love of his life to her Aunt Maeve moments ago. Was that why the sisters had fallen out? Over a man? Iris couldn't help feeling a little pinch of disappointment in her mom. Why had she let her sister steal Conrad from her?

Iris returned to her bed and sat cross-legged on it, looking around her mother's bedroom. She had piled all of her mother's clothes back in the wardrobe that morning, and the room felt bare of any personality. It was Christmas Day in Ireland, but still Christmas Eve back home. This time last year, she and her mom would have been putting the finishing touches to the Christmas tree while drinking her mom's homemade eggnog. They would have wrapped up their presents and put them under the tree. There'd always be one for Trina because some years she just showed up, although last year she'd been in Mexico.

Here Iris was back in her mom's childhood home, and she wished she could rewind time. She wished her mom hadn't been rushing to get home on that fateful night, 21 October. She wished her last words to her mom hadn't been Iris telling her she didn't want to come home for Thanksgiving. She wished her mom had looked where she was going. She wished the taxi driver had seen her step out and braked earlier. It wasn't fair. She'd never had a dad, and now she didn't have a mom, either.

Conrad's words kept going over and over in her mind: *your sister was the love of my life!*

It was strange to think of her mother's life before she had existed. Had her mother loved Conrad back? She didn't know what to make of her uncle, although she preferred him to her austere and holier-than-thou aunt.

Iris's eyes fell upon the tape cassette machine still plugged in on the floor next to her bed. She hadn't touched it since the night before. She took a breath. The ache to hear her mother's voice overwhelmed her and she pressed play.

'Testing, testing, testing.'

'Is it working, Aisling?' Iris recognised this voice – it was Maeve.

'I'm going to replay to check.' Click. Click. 'Yes, it's working.'

Iris pressed her hands to heart and took in every word her mother said as if they were spoons of pure golden honey.

'Okay, well, what are we going to play?' Maeve again.

'I'm going to sing first.' Another girl's voice.

'Oh course, it's always about you!' Her mom sounded annoyed.

'Sure let her sing, Aisling, I've to tune my fiddle anyway.'

There was a pause.

'Go on then, Nuala.'

'My name is Nuala Kelly.' The voice was suddenly crystal clear, right by the microphone. 'I am going to sing the "Binnorie".'

'Isn't that Scottish?'

'Yes, but it's a folk song which belongs everywhere.' Clearing of throat, and then a voice at once light, sweet and girl-ish, while also rich with meaning.

'There were two sisters in a bower
Binnorie O Binnorie
There came a knight to be their wooer
By the bonny mill-dams of Binnorie.'

Iris lay back on the bed, closed her eyes and let the words wash over her.

'He courted the eldest with glove and ring,
But loved the youngest above all things.
The eldest was vexed so sore
And much she envied her sister fair.'

In Iris's mind's eye she imagined her mother, Aisling, with blond hair, and her Aunt Maeve, with her dark brown hair. So was her mom the fair sister, and Maeve the dark? But then her mom was the eldest. So who was who? Had they both wanted her Uncle Conrad? And then what about Nuala? She was fair too, and the youngest. Iris couldn't sing, but as the voice of her lost aunt swirled around her, she imagined the words came from her. There was something about the ghostly voice of her Aunt Nuala which merged with her own whispering voice.

> *'She took her sister by the hand*
> *And led her down to the wide sea strand*
> *The youngest stood upon a stone*
> *And the eldest came and pushed her in.*
> *Oh sister, sister, take my hand.'*

Iris felt a cool breeze upon her face and sat up suddenly, opening her eyes. The door of her bedroom was open, and her Uncle Conrad stood in the doorway. His eyes were shining with tears.

'Where did you find that?' he croaked, coming towards the bed and pointing towards the old tape machine.

'It was in the bottom of the wardrobe.'

'Please turn it off.'

Iris clicked stop, cutting Nuala's voice off midstream.

'Oh God.' Uncle Conrad sat down heavily on the end of Iris's bed. 'It hurts so much to hear Nuala singing.' He sighed.

Suddenly it dawned on Iris: when her Uncle Conrad had said to her Aunt Maeve, *your sister was the love of my life*, he hadn't meant her mother. He had been talking about Nuala.

'I've never gotten over it,' Uncle Conrad said in a shaky voice. His confessional tone made it clear he was still really drunk. He was so close to her she could smell the whiskey on his breath. She felt a little uncomfortable that he was sitting on her bed too, but she didn't know what to say. Conrad reached his hand out and stroked the side of her face. Iris flinched in shock.

'Every time I look at you,' he said, 'all I see is Nuala.' Tears trailed down his cheeks and Iris was frozen, unable to know what to do or say. 'You're so beautiful, just like Nuala.' He withdrew his hand and clasped the cross hanging around his neck, shaking his head. 'No, no,' he said. 'But you're not Nuala, you're not.'

'Conrad!'

Aunt Maeve came barging into Iris's bedroom, taking in the scene of Iris seated on the bed so close to her uncle. Iris sprang up as if she were the guilty party. But nothing had happened, and she'd done nothing wrong. In fact, her flesh was crawling from where her uncle had stroked her face. The look in his eyes when he had done it had made her feel a mixture of revulsion and pity.

'What are you doing in here?'

Conrad didn't answer but buried his face in his hands.

'What's going on?' She turned to Iris.

'Nothing!' Iris said, indignant. 'He came in because—'

'She was playing a tape of Nuala singing,' Conrad said, looking up, his face wet with tears.

Maeve stared at Iris, her eyes widening, and it felt to Iris as if her aunt were looking through her, as if she were gazing off into a vast distance – back into the past, maybe.

'I was overwhelmed, I had to come in and listen...'

Maeve appeared to almost shake herself awake.

'Get up, for God's sake,' she said. 'Leave the poor girl alone.'

Conrad got up shakily to his feet. 'You were always jealous of Nuala,' he hissed, before stomping out.

Maeve and Iris were left staring at each other in uncomfortable silence.

'Please refrain from poking around and taking things out which don't belong to you,' Maeve said in a cold voice before leaving the room.

Iris felt as if she'd been slapped. Her aunt's hostility was more upsetting than any of Conrad's behaviour. She felt as if she had done something wrong. But she hadn't invited him into her room, and the cassette machine had been sitting in the wardrobe in her bedroom. She'd hardly been poking about.

She got into her sweatpants and pulled back the cold covers of the bed, shivering as she climbed beneath them. It had to be the worst Christmas of her whole life. She was dreading the next day, and she was here for another week. It had been a big mistake coming here. In Ireland, she was even more alone than in New York.

CHAPTER FOURTEEN

NUALA

1 AUGUST 1972

I dreamed about C last night. I dreamed we were swimming in Lough Bawn and we were under the water. We didn't need to come up for air; we could breathe quite easily beneath the surface of the lake. The water rippled around our limbs as we moved through it, as if we were parting folds of thick silk. Light showered down from the full moon, lighting a pathway for us in the depths of the lake. We were among freshwater birds – some familiar, such as herons and ducks, and others mysterious and unknown in the human realm.

We swam with each other like two otters playing, swirling our bodies and weaving in and out of each other. And when we were tired, we rested upon the bottom of the lough, gazing up through the deep blue.

When it was time to come to the surface we swam fast towards the light, as if we were two tiny rockets taking off. We splashed through the lake's surface, bobbing in the rippling moonlight. In each other's eyes we could see the galaxy above and our tiny part within it. And yet, yet, our love for each other was limitless.

Dear diary, when I woke up this morning I cried because I wanted the dream back. It was a fantasy dream, impossible, but the feelings in it were real. This is a huge love C and I share. I am so frustrated, because why does it have to be a big secret? I don't care what everyone thinks of us, but C does. Makes me promise not to tell. I want to write our names out big and bold in my diary connected by a heart, but I don't trust my sisters. I wouldn't put it past Maeve to read my diary and snitch on me. She's such a sneak.

Now Aisling can drive, she's disappearing all the time, and Maeve is even more irritating because all she has left is me to annoy. She keeps trying to boss me around, insisting she needs my help to cut the summer grasses so she can make it into silage for the winter feeding. When I refuse, saying we only have five cows and can't she manage those, she tells on me to Daddy. Of course, any excuse for him to take his belt out and give me a slap with it. I laugh in his face, although it hurts a lot, and then he says I'm a mad bitch like my mother.

I am proud to be like my mam. She was wild and untamed and in the end she chose her own destiny. I don't see her as tragic any more. I get it. If I were stuck with Daddy, I'd want to take any way out I could.

13 AUGUST 1972

Trina has gone to New York. I feel like I've been hit by a truck. It was all so quick. I didn't have a chance to prepare and there's so many things I wanted to say like she's the BEST and how she keeps me SANE. Dear diary, I feel so lonely now she's gone and it's only been two hours! Last night we got drunk down by the lake and I begged her not to go yet, not to leave me behind. It wasn't fair of me to do it, but without Trina, my protector has gone. Work won't be the same. No more dancing around the tables together in the restaurant or cycling home, looping from side to side of the road, whooping to the moon if we're coming back from the late shift.

I said, 'Please, Trina, call your brother, ask him to hang onto the job for you until the end of the summer.'

'You know I can't do that, Nuala. It'll be gone,' Trina said, looking sorrowful. 'Come now, it's only a matter of weeks and you'll be on your way. You've just to do the Fleadh and you'll be off too.'

I threw a stone into the lake. 'I want to go NOW.'

'You can't let Maeve and Aisling down, not now, so close to the competition.'

'Why not? They're always letting me down.'

Trina shook her head. 'I've always wanted sisters,' she said. 'I don't understand why you can't all get on.'

'I've tried for years. Aisling thinks she's so much better than me, and Maeve is a daddy's girl. Honestly, sometimes I really hate them.'

'It's sad,' Trina said.

'It doesn't bother me,' I said. 'Not any more, because I am going to be out of here very soon.'

'You need to tell your family you're going, Nuala.'

'Are you joking? Daddy would probably lock me up. And I can't trust Maeve not to tell him. As for Aisling, she's never around to tell. I don't feel close to my sisters, not like I do with you.'

Trina sighed. 'You'd never know it,' she said. 'When I watch the three of you playing music together you seem at ease with each other, and in such perfect harmony.'

'Well, it's the only time I can tolerate the two of them,' I admitted.

I told Trina about the tape the three of us had made and promised I would make a tape for her of just me singing, but when I got home I'd drunk too much beer, and then this morning I forgot.

It was only as I was waving goodbye as her mam drove her away that I remembered. I was so angry with myself for forgetting, which was stupid because I'm going to see her in a few weeks and will be able to sing to her in the flesh.

I was so upset after Trina left, I ran upstairs to the bathroom. I wanted to lock myself in and cry, but the door was locked. Aisling was in there ages. Eventually she came out and she was so pale.

'What's wrong with you?' I asked.

'None of your business,' she snapped. But her eyes looked rimmed with red, as if she'd been crying. She was holding something in her curled-up palm.

'What's that?' I asked her.

'Nothing,' she said, trying to get by, but I was curious so I tugged on her hand, and that was when it fell out onto the carpet. She gave a little cry and then growled my name as she bent down to pick the object up. As she cradled it in her hands, I could see it was a little glass swan.

'Where'd you get that from?' I asked her.

'You nearly broke it,' she fumed, not answering me.

'No, I didn't, you let it slip,' I defended myself.

Aisling pushed past me. 'Just get away from me,' she said, her voice raw, and I wondered: what has she got to be upset about? She's got a car, and therefore the means to get out of here because she's over eighteen. And what about the little glass swan? Where had that come from? It was very pretty, and clearly a treasured gift. I felt a twinge of jealousy because C has never given me a love-gift. *But you have C's heart, Nuala!* I reminded myself, dear diary.

But that's over too. Well, for now at least. Last night C and I parted company. Here I was again, begging this person I adore not to abandon me. C said those awful words right after we had made love in the shelter of the woods. We were sharing a cigarette while looking at the sunset over the lough. Splashes of red, pink, and gold fanned into the late evening sky.

'We need to take a break,' C told me, finishing off our cigarette.

I was afraid 'a break' would be forever.

'I don't know if I can live without you,' I said.

It was a bad thing to say, because it sounded like a threat. But C was having none of it.

'Yes, you can. You're a survivor, Nuala Kelly, just like all those little creatures.' C pointed at all the life humming above the surface of the lake – the mayflies, the whirligig beetles, and the bright blue damselflies. 'You know who you are and exactly what you want, and, my darling, that is the dream. Some of us don't know yet, and some of us will never know.'

C got up, brushing off grass from their clothes.

'What about you? What do you want?'

'I want you,' C said. 'But not now. We have to wait.'

Before I could protest, C walked away into the wood, and after a while all I could see was a tiny flash of red.

I stared into the dense foliage of the trees, imagining C swallowed up within them. Those dark woods give me the creeps. Sometimes on a still night, I've heard voices echoing across the lake, and when I get up and look out of my window I can see lights in the woods. In the morning, when I tell my father there's people on our land, he says it's just him and Peadar Maguire and his terrier after badger baiting. He knows saying that will drive me mad.

'Don't even think of telling the guards on me, girl,' he threatens.

But I think he's lying, because the badger sett is way over the other side of the woods, nowhere near where I saw the lights. I am not going to tell him that, though, now am I?

So yeah, today was a bad day. Trina left and it's over with C. Everyone I love leaves me.

CHAPTER FIFTEEN

IRIS

CHRISTMAS DAY 1991

Iris walked through the wet grass in the old wellington boots. She had found them in the back hall and they were a bit big for her, but it was better than ruining her Keds sneakers. She had woken early when it was still dark, and lain awake watching the pale wintry light slowly seep into the sky. She should have stayed in bed, tried to go back to sleep after the late night, but she felt compelled to get up.

Outside, she was pulled towards the lake. The dogs were with her, having run outside as soon as she opened the back door, but she felt removed from their rambunctious energy. Her eyes were upon Lough Bawn as wraiths of mist swirled above its still surface. It was freezing cold, and she shivered in her jacket and jeans. As she got closer to the lake, she realised that it was covered in ice. In places, it was so thin she could see the clear water beneath; in others it was thicker and more opaque. She teetered on the edge of the lake, longing to step onto the ice, while knowing for sure it wouldn't be able to hold her weight. But she just wanted to be on the lake so bad. She imagined her mom, and her mom's two sisters when they had been just a little younger than her, and how they had felt about the loss of their own mom, her grandmother. She had drowned herself in this very lake. Was that what Nuala had done, too? Iris shivered, the hairs on her arms prickling. Something bad had happened here, she could sense it. Iris raised her foot and hovered it over the icy lake.

She dug her nails into her frozen hands and pulled herself back from the edge. Turning abruptly away from the lake and its draw, she ran towards the woods, dogs at her heels, to its furthest perimeter, diving into its dark sanctuary. The air was even stiller in the woods, but she slowed down and breathed in the comforting scent of pine, listening to birds as the dogs bounded into the undergrowth.

She followed a narrow pathway, winding through the trees until she came to a small clearing. There was a circle of thick frost beneath the opening in the branches overhead – a perfect silvery circle, as if the moon had landed upon the ground. She made her way towards it. Slipping her hand into her pocket, her fingers wrapped around the cold glass of the little swan. The one memento from her past her mother had possessed, which Iris had brought with her. She took it out, placing it on her palm. Her breath plumed as if smoke in the frozen air, and she puffed upon the swan, rubbing it with her coat sleeve to make it shine. She had brought this little part of her mother back home. Despite all the lies and secrets, she had come to Ireland for her mom because Aisling had never got to return to Ireland herself. Iris bit her lip. But why had her mom not come back? Because she'd been in love with Conrad and he had dumped her for Nuala? And how had Maeve ended up with Conrad? Had her mom had anything to do with Nuala's death – was that why she'd run away? No, that was a crazy thought. But then something else occurred to her.

'Oh... oh no,' she gasped, dropping the little glass swan as she lurched forward, dizzy and nauseous.

Was it possible her father was her Uncle Conrad? It would explain why her mom had never told her the truth.

'No way.' She shook her head in denial as she composed herself, taking slow breaths. She bent down to pick up the glass swan, which glinted at her feet like a piece of polished ice.

'Oh crap!' she swore as she picked it up. She could see a crack in one of the polished curves of its body. Her mom had kept that little glass swan safe for nearly twenty years, and Iris had only had it a matter of weeks and she'd nearly broken it. Without warning, she burst out crying as grief swept through her. She squatted in the cold woods and bawled for her mom. The little swan pressed tight into her palm so that the sharpness of the crack scratched her skin.

Eventually, her sobs began to subside and she wiped her wet face with her scarf. It felt shiny, and tight with cold. Straightening up again, she heard the snap of a twig behind her. Turning around, there was the same girl, Lizzie, that she'd seen in Lough Bawn Forest Park with her Aunt Maeve the other day. This time, Lizzie was so close Iris could see the hue of her big eyes, forest green and earthy brown.

They stared at each other, and Iris thought she must look a state with her tear-stained cheeks and red-rimmed eyes. But Lizzie didn't seem to notice. She was staring at her with big eyes, and a broad smile spread across her face, revealing a tiny overbite.

'Happy Christmas,' she said, as a white terrier went bounding past her.

Aed, Conn and Fiacra, the three black Labradors, ran over to the little white dog and they all intermingled.

'Merry Christmas,' Iris said, eyeing Lizzie curiously.

'It's okay, I'm allowed to be here. Maeve said I could walk Rascal in the woods,' Lizzie said, in response to Iris's cautiousness.

'That's cool.' Iris wished Lizzie would go away. She was mortified by her outburst. Surely Lizzie had heard her crying?

'You're Iris, aren't you? Maeve Kelly's niece? I've heard about you,' Lizzie said, looking a little excited. 'I'm Lizzie. I live the other side of the woods in Bramble Cottage with my dad, though he's away. I'm on my own for Christmas.'

'Oh, that sucks,' Iris said, thinking of the story Maeve had told her about Lizzie's mother.

Lizzie shrugged. 'I have Rascal. I don't mind that much – better than being in the middle of a feuding family!' Lizzie's gaze dropped to the glass swan in Iris's hands. 'Where did you get that?'

'It was my mom's. I don't know where she got it.'

Lizzie gazed at the glass swan. 'Your mam just died, didn't she?'

Iris nodded, a lump rising in her throat again. Lizzie raised her eyes to Iris's. Her gaze was searching, and Iris felt herself blushing a little with discomfort.

'I'm really sorry,' Lizzie said, still staring at Iris. Iris waited for Lizzie to say goodbye and walk away, but she didn't. She had a sense Lizzie wanted to say something else to her. The girl took a step towards her.

'Want to see something?' Lizzie asked, her tone light changing the mood of their meeting instantly. 'We'll have to tie the dogs up for a few minutes for their own protection, but it's worth it.'

'I don't think I can get them to come to me,' Iris said, producing a tangle of leads from her other coat pocket.

'No worries, I'm good with dogs.' Lizzie gave her a cheeky smile, before producing a packet of doggie treats from her pocket and calling out to the dogs. Getting a whiff of their rewards, all four dogs ran directly towards her.

'Magic!' she said, winking at Iris as they gathered up the dogs.

. . .

Lizzie took her to the lakeside edge of the woods, following the shoreline of the water away from Swan Hall. With the interlacing of branches overhead sheltering the ground from rain and ice, it became softer and springy under Iris's feet. Closer and closer to the water Lizzie brought her, so soon Iris was wading into shallow pools in her wellies. They entered an area filled with tall stalks of wintering reeds like golden rods emerging from the glittering lake. The low winter sun gleamed through the frosty haze and all was quiet apart from the lap of water upon the shore. Lizzie stopped walking and turned to Iris, putting her finger to her lips to indicate she should be quiet. Then, squatting, she pointed ahead. Iris crouched down as well and peered through the legions of reeds towards a mound of old grasses, browned and dry.

'That's the swans' nest,' Lizzie said. 'They come back every year and rebuild it.'

'They use the same nest?' Iris asked her.

'Yes, our swans do,' Lizzie said. 'You know swans mate for life, right?'

'No, I didn't,' Iris said in surprise. She remembered the summer her mom had rented a house on Long Island and how she'd seen so many mute swans. The big birds had frightened her a little, especially when they'd hissed at her when she came too close to the water.

Lizzie straightened up. 'Want to visit the swans?'

'Oh, aren't they dangerous?' Iris said hesitantly, remembering her mom telling her about a man who'd had his arm broken by a swan.

'Only if you frighten them,' Lizzie said. 'That's why we can't bring the dogs.'

Before she could protest further, Lizzie took off, wading through the reeds. They passed the big swans' nest and round a corner to discover a tiny cove. When she looked back, Iris could no longer see Swan Hall. They were hidden from view. As she moved forward, there floating serenely on the water were three swans.

'That's the mother and father,' Lizzie whispered, pointing at the two bigger swans. 'And that's the last cygnet.' She pointed at a slighter swan with patches of soft downy grey upon its white feathers. 'The others have already left, but this one isn't ready yet.'

Iris watched the three swans as they glided upon the still lake with the mist swirling around them. It felt like the most beautiful thing she'd ever seen.

'Their elegance and grace look so effortless,' Lizzie said. 'But underneath the water they're paddling away, working hard to stay balanced upon the surface.'

Something about the swans reminded Iris of her mom. When she had been alive, people had always been commenting on how poised she was. Her mom's bosses, Iris's friends, their neighbours. Her mom had always worn her fair hair up, which made her neck appear longer, and she had very pale skin which she highlighted by wearing lots of white. In New York, her mom had been swan-like: gentle and reserved, with no evidence of the rainbow wardrobe and hippie garb of her youth.

Iris had taken her mother's unruffled presence for granted, but she knew deep down her mom had been far from at peace. Inside had been all these suppressed secrets and emotions.

As Iris watched the swans, another swell of emotion assaulted her. She wished so badly her mom had brought her to Ireland and told her about all the parts of herself. But she was gone, and now Iris had to uncover them on her own.

By the time Iris had said goodbye to Lizzie and walked back up to the house, it was after ten in the morning. There could be nothing quiet about her entrance into the back hall with the dogs bounding in ahead of her and noisily drinking out of their water bowls.

Iris took off the wet wellies and made her way to the kitchen, the dogs running before her. Aed pushed the door open and Iris followed. Conrad was at the kitchen table, head bent over a steaming mug of coffee. As he looked up, Iris thought he hadn't slept at all: his hair an unruly mess and dark shadows under his eyes. A cigarette was resting in an ashtray as smoke wafted up towards the ceiling.

'Morning,' he mumbled, not looking at her. 'Help yourself to coffee.'

Iris felt her own cheeks blush with embarrassment for him. Did he not remember what he had done last night? Her skin crawled at the memory of him stroking her face. She crossed the kitchen stiffly and filled the kettle with water before placing it on the stove.

'I'm so sorry, Iris,' Conrad said in weak voice. She turned around to see her uncle looking at her sheepishly. 'Apparently I was completely out of order last night...' He shrugged. 'What can I say? I'm a mess!'

Iris didn't quite know how to respond and was saved by the entrance of her Aunt Maeve.

'Merry Christmas!' Maeve said, a bright smile on her face.

'Oh yes, merry Christmas,' Iris said for the second time that day, although she didn't feel remotely festive.

'How are we getting on?' Maeve asked, looking between her husband and niece. Her voice was more gentle than last night.

'Ah, sure I'm wasted, Maeve,' Conrad said, giving her a crooked smile. Iris scrutinised his face. Was this man her father? And if he was, did he even know? Did her Aunt Maeve know?

'Well, I'm going to have a few hours' sleep,' he said, getting up. 'I'll see you both at dinner time.'

'Right so,' Maeve said, too chirpy for it to sound authentic.

Her aunt was clearly embarrassed Iris had witnessed such hostility between herself and her husband the night before.

After Conrad had left, Maeve insisted that she was going to make Iris a full Irish breakfast, as the turkey was going to take hours to cook.

As her aunt bustled around the kitchen, Iris noticed the room had been decorated. There was holly on the window ledges, and tinsel trailed along the dresser shelves. The table-cloth on the kitchen table had been changed to one with festive colours of red and green with a pattern of holly leaves and red berries. Now her uncle had left the room, the atmosphere was warm and surprisingly comforting.

Maeve placed a plate stacked with eggs, bacon and toast in front of Iris, before sitting down opposite her with her own breakfast.

'I met Lizzie again,' Iris said as she bit into her slice of toast.

'That's nice,' her aunt said. 'She walks here a lot, and I've no problem with it. Although Daddy wouldn't allow it. He didn't like her father.'

'Why?'

'My father called him a blow-in. Lizzie's father is German and an artist, which my father also disapproved of. We've a lot of artists from Germany and Holland living around here because property is so cheap. I think they like how underpopulated the west of Ireland is.'

'Yeah, it's real quiet.'

'Are you missing New York?' Maeve said the words 'New York' as if she were talking about a far-off planet.

Iris shrugged. 'More my mom than New York.'

'Yes, of course,' Maeve said. 'It must be so hard for you.'

'Yeah, it doesn't seem real.'

'You're still in shock,' Maeve said, placing a hand on Iris's arm. The unexpected kindness of the action brought Iris close to tears again.

'I don't know what to do,' Iris said, her voice breaking. 'I don't know how to get over it.'

'Ah, dear, all you can do is your best, carry on as Aisling would have wanted,' Maeve said. 'I believe that when we lose a loved one, well, we don't so much as get over it, as learn to live with it. That's how it was when my mother died.'

Iris nodded, unable to speak. Her aunt was so different this morning from last night with her harsh telling-off. Iris wanted so badly to ask what had happened between her mother and Maeve, but she didn't know how to bring it up. It was nice to share this moment of comfort with her aunt and she didn't want to ruin it.

After breakfast, they went into the sitting room with cups of coffee. The Christmas tree sparkled with all its bright baubles and ornaments. It was the biggest tree she had ever had because they could only fit little ones in their apartment. And yet she preferred their little tree, weighed down by ornaments she and her mom had made together, and the angel at the top which they'd created out of popsicle sticks and crêpe paper. This Christmas tree appeared staged. Every bauble evenly spaced, with a pristine star at the top. Iris eyed the small pile of gifts underneath the tree. She'd forgotten the candles she'd bought Maeve and Conrad. They were upstairs, jammed into her bag on her bedroom floor.

'Oh, I forgot to wrap my gift up,' she said. 'I'll go get it.'

'You bought me a present?' Maeve asked, flushing with pleasure.

'Sure,' Iris said.

When she returned to the sitting room, Maeve was sitting in the armchair expectantly. She got up as soon as Iris entered.

'Well, shall we exchange presents?' she asked, a sparkle coming into her eyes.

'What about Uncle Conrad?'

'He won't be up for hours,' her aunt said. 'And besides, he

doesn't buy presents because he says it's all capitalist, consumerist, and I am sure he throws colonialist in there somewhere.' Maeve rolled her eyes. 'Though I believe it's more to do with him being tight with money!'

'Oh,' Iris said, a little unsure what to make of her aunt's outspoken criticism of her husband.

Her Aunt Maeve thrust a small box into Iris's hand, while Iris handed over the candles which she had wrapped badly with the paper from the hardware store.

'It's ages since I received a Christmas gift,' Maeve told her. 'Thank you, Iris.'

She removed the candles from the packaging.

'How thoughtful,' she said, bringing them up to smell. 'Well, go on, open your gift.'

Iris unwrapped the box, and then clicked it open. Inside was a small blue medallion on a silver chain. It had an image of the Virgin Mary on it. She took it out and held it between her fingers, not knowing what to think. It was pretty – but the Virgin Mary?

'Look at the back,' Maeve said, her voice a little high-pitched with anticipation.

Iris turned the medallion over and on the back was an etching of a swan. She knew immediately this would be the side she'd wear. This, she loved.

'It's beautiful,' she said, feeling touched by how personal the gift clearly was. The medallion felt like a symbol of acceptance by her mother's family.

'We all got one when we did our First Communion,' Maeve said. 'Did you never see your mother's?'

'No, I don't think she ever wore it.'

'Ah,' Maeve sighed, a sad look on her face. Maeve brought her hand up to her neck and placed it on a small blue medallion of a Virgin Mary, just like the one she had given Iris.

'I never did my First Communion,' Iris explained. 'We

didn't go to church.'

'Never?' Maeve asked, looking a little shocked.

'No, apart from weddings and funerals.'

'I suppose I remember Aisling not wanting to take part in the church even before she left,' Maeve said with a heavy voice. 'I was always sad she had no faith, but I believed she would eventually come back to the church, especially when she had children.'

Iris felt a little defensive. Just because her mother hadn't believed in God, it didn't mean she hadn't been spiritual. 'My mom practised yoga and meditated every day, which is like praying, right?'

'Yoga?' Maeve looked surprised. 'Well, sounds like she changed a lot.'

What happened? Iris wanted to scream at her aunt. *Why did you fall out?* And yet she didn't, because she was a little afraid of the answer.

'Well,' Maeve said. 'Are you going to put it on?'

'Sure,' Iris said, putting the chain around her neck.

'That's the wrong way around. The swan side goes against your skin. Here, let me help you.' Her Aunt Maeve took over fastening the necklace so that the blue medallion of the Virgin Mary faced outwards.

Iris clasped the necklace awkwardly.

'Our faith can help us through times of loss, Iris,' her Aunt Maeve said gently. 'When Daddy passed away it was a great comfort to me.'

Iris didn't respond because she didn't believe in God, but she didn't want to insult her aunt by telling her so. She appreciated that she was trying to help her.

Her aunt stood up all of a sudden. 'Well, let's do something fun together,' she offered. 'Would you like to go for a ride on the horses before we get the dinner? Everything's in the oven and all we have to do is wait.'

'I've only been horse-riding once...'

'Ah, but it's in your blood: you're my niece!' Maeve declared, beaming at her. 'I'll put you on Pixie, our pony. You'll be grand.'

Aunt Maeve looked different on a horse. She had pulled her brown hair into a neat braid beneath her hat and sat straight-backed on a large black stallion named Merlin. She'd had to give Iris a leg up as she'd got onto the grey pony, Pixie, which wasn't as small as its name sounded. Even so, her aunt towered above her, as she clicked her tongue and encouraged her horse to move forwards. Iris followed, feeling like a sack of potatoes as soon as the pony started to trot. She was bumping all over the place.

'Up, down, up, down,' Maeve barked at her.

Iris had only been on a horse once in her life. It had been when she, her mom and Trina had gone pony trekking on a trip to New Mexico. The horses had been very docile, and they'd ambled along the dusty trail in a big group. But this was different. Maeve set off at a brisk trot on Merlin, and Pixie was keen to keep pace. Their hooves clattered on the cobbled stable yard before they headed down the drive, and then took a sharp left into a field where the gate was left open. Ahead of her, Merlin broke into a canter, and before she knew it Pixie was following suit. Iris clung onto the reins, her body tense with fear as her aunt's figure bobbed in front of her. The chill damp air of the winter day slapped her face as they went faster and faster, but she wasn't cold. Her body was building up heat under the jacket with the exertion of staying on the pony. Maeve looked behind her and gave Iris an encouraging smile. She wasn't so bad. This morning had shown her that. Her aunt had seemed genuinely thrilled with her Christmas gift from Iris.

On the other side of the field was a trail, and Maeve pulled on her reins to slow down to a trot. Iris followed suit and to her relief, Pixie slowed down too.

'How did you find that?' Maeve asked Iris, as Pixie came to trot beside Merlin.

'Great,' Iris lied, not wanting to disappoint her aunt, but still shaking a little from the fear she had felt when the horse had been cantering.

Maeve laughed, clearly seeing through her lie.

'Your mam didn't like riding either,' she said. 'She turned out more of a city girl, I guess.'

'And what about Nuala?' Iris asked, curious to learn more of the youngest sister.

'Yes, she'd come out sometimes, but she had no control over the horses.' Maeve paused. 'Or maybe she liked to let them run a bit wild. Though after she was responsible for Duke getting hurt and going lame, Daddy banned her from riding. Not that that stopped her.'

There was an edge to Maeve's voice, but at least she was forthcoming about Nuala.

'What was Nuala like?

Maeve sighed. 'She had a very strong personality – you couldn't help but notice her. But she could be selfish too, and she was always aggravating Daddy...'

'Oh,' Iris said, a little shocked by Maeve's honesty.

'My little sister was a very talented singer – I mean, you heard the tape, her voice is beautiful, right? But she was also a precocious show-off.' Maeve's voice was tinged with sadness. 'It made it hard to love her sometimes, but I did love her, of course.'

'And my mom?' Iris asked tentatively. 'What happened – why did you fall out?' Iris's heart was beating fast with anticipation, because what would Maeve tell her about her mother now?

'We fell out,' Maeve said in such a quiet voice, Iris could barely hear her. 'Oh, over many things, but mostly over what happened to Nuala.'

Iris said nothing, not knowing what to say in response, waiting for more information.

'It's hard to explain,' Maeve continued, her voice hardening. 'Aisling was the eldest and she should have been in charge the day Nuala disappeared. I blamed her for what happened. But...'

Iris waited for Maeve to expand, but instead her aunt clicked her tongue and gave her horse a little tap with her ankles to move on. Frustration swept through Iris. Why couldn't her aunt be straight with her and just tell her the whole story? Wasn't it her right as her mom's daughter to know? Now they were moving off again, but Iris wanted to get off the pony. She'd only gone along with her aunt to please her, but she was nervous of horses, and she was sure Pixie could sense her fear as he gathered speed, following the cantering Merlin down the narrow trail. This was even more frightening than cantering across the field, because she kept having to look out for low-hanging branches and duck beneath them. Sleet began falling on them, and she looked up at the sky to see it tumbling down from above. One second later a branch slammed into her stomach, and she was pushed out of the saddle. She tried to hang on, but she'd lost her balance and landed with a thud on the hard ground, calling out as she did so.

She sat on the muddy path, feeling as if the carpet had been swept out from under her feet. Tears began to trail down her face, and then she heard a sound, a deep, guttural moan. It was coming from her. She was making this noise herself. The sleet was drenching her, mixing with her tears, and she wailed with longing and loss.

'Are you hurt?' Maeve was crouching down, and her eyes were full of concern.

'No, no.' Iris wiped the tears away, trying to get herself together. Her aunt paused and appeared to take a breath in relief.

'Well, get up, Iris,' Maeve said brusquely, standing up again.

'You'll catch your death.'

Her aunt's harsh tone set Iris off again. She didn't like this cold woman. She was nothing like her warm, caring mother.

'Iris, stop it!' Maeve said, her voice rising. Iris couldn't see her face clearly through her tears, but she could sense her irritation.

'Just leave me alone,' she sobbed. 'Go away.'

There was a long pause, but Maeve didn't leave. Instead, she knelt down next to Iris.

'I'm sorry,' she said, her tone different. 'When I'm frightened I can sound angry, but I was scared you'd been hurt.' She reached out her hands.

Shaking with cold and distress, Iris grabbed hold of her aunt's chilled fingers and let her haul her up out of the mud. Maeve handed her a handkerchief to wipe her face with.

'Do you want to walk back to the house?' she asked Iris gently.

Iris nodded.

Maeve gave Iris Pixie's reins, who now meekly trotted behind her, almost as if the pony was as shocked by her fall as she was.

'You know, the feelings between three sisters can be very complicated,' Maeve said in a quiet voice as they made their way back towards Swan Hall.

Iris didn't understand. She was an only child, but she'd always dreamed of having a sister. Someone to share confidences with, to look out for her. She thought it was very sad that her mom and her sisters hadn't got on.

'Maybe it began when we were young, because I will admit it, I was a bit of a tomboy and Daddy's favourite,' Maeve said. 'But we did get on when we were children. I remember Daddy used to take the three of us fishing. We loved being on the lake in his boat. And we played hide and seek in the woods with our mam. Most of all, I remember practising our instruments together so that we could get better and better. Music always united us.'

Maeve paused before continuing.

'But after my mother drowned in the lake, everything changed,' she said. 'It was as if the family split. Nuala was Mammy's favourite, and she was so little too when she passed away. Only ten years old. We dealt with our grief in different ways. Mammy's death tore us apart.'

Her aunt took her riding hat off and pulled her braid free. Her dark hair fell in waves over her shoulders, and Iris could see strands of silver caught out in the winter sun.

'Aisling was the last person to see Mammy the day she died,' Maeve said, looking at Iris with sorrowful eyes. 'Maybe she blamed herself for not saying something that might stop her, or maybe she felt that we blamed her.' Maeve's voice dropped even lower, so that Iris almost couldn't hear her. 'And maybe we did a little.'

Aunt Maeve continued to walk on, and Iris followed her, feeling Pixie's tug as he clopped behind her.

'Your mother was fifteen when Mammy died, and it was as if she grew up overnight,' Maeve told her. 'She had to take on all the chores Mammy had done – cooking, cleaning, washing clothes. Trina's mam came in to help sometimes, but it wasn't enough. All the time Aisling spent on household chores affected her grades, because sometimes she'd have to miss days off school. It wasn't fair, but we didn't see it that way at the time. We just thought she was too bossy.'

Iris imagined her mom as a young girl, trying to play mother to her sisters. She remembered the photographs she'd seen of her mom with knee-high socks, pleated skirt and glasses. Such a serious expression on her face.

'Nuala would run wild, and I refused to help, saying I had more important things to be doing on the farm with Daddy. I mean, I did work hard too, but I suppose the difference was I loved the farm and I loved driving the tractor and helping Daddy with animals. Aisling felt trapped.'

It had been a long speech and Iris was taking it all in. She pictured her mother at the age of fifteen, stuck in this isolated part of Ireland, and desperate to get away. But she had run away a few years later because she was pregnant, that much was clear. While her aunt was opening up, Iris took her opportunity to ask the question which was haunting her.

'I heard that Uncle Conrad was going out with my mam first,' she said in a whisper.

Maeve's whole body jolted. 'Where did you hear that?'

'In the pub,' Iris said, not wanting to betray Ruairi for some reason. 'Is it true?'

'Well, yes it is,' Maeve said. 'I guess Conrad orbited around all of us; we were sort of dazzled by him.'

'How did you know him?'

'Conrad's father, Peadar Maguire, worked for my father on the farm, and we were neighbours,' Maeve told her. 'We used to play together as children. Conrad didn't have a mother either. It was all a bit of a scandal because when Conrad was about five his mam ran off with an English writer who was renting a cottage nearby for a few months. It was the biggest insult, since his father was such a staunch Republican. My mam used to make a bit of a fuss over Conrad after that, and he was at our house every afternoon for tea.'

'Oh wow!' Iris said.

'Yeah, Conrad's always saying what happened to him is worse than our mam drowning. He tells me at least I know where my mother is, and she didn't reject me,' Maeve said, sounding tired. 'But of course she rejected me. When she walked into the lake and never came back out again, she let all of us girls down, and Daddy...'

Iris was tempted to say that wasn't how it was with the suicidal. She'd talked to her roommate Riley about it plenty, because one of Riley's cousins had died by suicide just before she began college. But the need to get answers out of her aunt was more pressing. She was desperate to know the full story about Conrad Maguire. Was his heritage of abandonment by his own mother part of hers, too?

'But is Conrad... is he my father?' Iris finally spat it out.

Maeve stopped walking and looked at Iris in astonishment.

'Goodness, no!' Maeve said. 'I can assure you your father isn't Conrad. Trust me, it's not him.'

'Are you sure it's not possible?' Iris pushed.

Maeve gave a bitter laugh.

'Conrad can't have children,' she confided. 'We tried for years. I got checked out and all was fine, so it was him.'

'Oh, I'm very sorry,' Iris said, embarrassed by the personal information but also feeling a huge sense of relief that her Uncle Conrad wasn't her father. But if he wasn't, then who was? Why oh why hadn't she let her mom tell her? She had been so defiant about not needing a father, but now it would be something to know she had one parent left at least, even if he didn't know of her existence or want to know.

They walked into the stable yard, the horses clattering behind them.

'Once we've sorted out Merlin and Pixie, let's get you inside all warmed up with a hot cup of sweet tea.'

Her Aunt Maeve placed her gloved hand on Iris's arm.

'I am sorry, Iris,' she said. 'Truly. I wish I had reached out to your mother years ago.'

Iris looked into her Aunt Maeve's eyes and she believed her.

'But, you see, I was angry she left me all alone here with our father. It felt like a betrayal and, besides, people were talking about us, saying things about what happened to Nuala...'

She turned away quickly, leaving Iris with a deep sense of unease. Had Ruairi been right? Was there more to Nuala's death than a tragic accident?

CHAPTER SIXTEEN

NUALA

19 AUGUST 1972

I am raging. I hate my father. I loathe the summer. And our house and my stinking family. I want to get out of here but my dreams are all ruined now.

I want to be in New York in autumn, crunching golden leaves beneath my feet and feeling the chilled air on my skin. But I am stuck here and I can't get away from the endless summer days. Hot and sticky night and day and then it rains feeling as if you are being drowned from above as the skies open up with non-stop deluge. Wet and warm and so much mud and flies. I hate this place!

It's not fair, dear diary, because I am not meant for rural Ireland. I can see my whole life mapped out for me and it's not here! When I think about this, everything around me is heightened. The blue of the lake more intense and the call of the birds more urgent. The reeds whisper to me, and I feel the roll of the whole earth beneath my bare feet as I run through them. *Get out, get out.* My mother is screaming at me.

I just can't believe it. How did it happen? How did all my dreams come crashing down?

Only a few hours ago I was flitting around the garden, in and out of the woods, unable to be still. When I am like this it's best I'm in work because I can carry three plates on both arms, and whizz around serving all the customers with astounding efficiency. But I wasn't on shift today and my boundless energy needed some other place to go.

What made me do it? Was it all the times I'd watched Maeve up in the tractor's cab, driving it around all serious and self-important? There it was parked in the yard, with the key still in the ignition, and I just didn't think. I climbed up into the cab, sat myself in the driver's seat, and switched it on. I know how to drive! We all do – and how hard could it be to drive a tractor if my sister could do it? I put my hands on the gear stick and pushed it into first and then pressed my foot down on the accelerator. The tractor took off faster than I expected, and it made me laugh as I bumped through the yard towards the gate. It wasn't my fault what happened next! A rabbit ran out in front of me and I swerved so as not to hit it. One of the tractor's wheels bounced onto the edge of the drive, and then before I knew it I was heading towards the new fencing Daddy and Maeve had just put up. I slammed my foot down on the brake, but it was the accelerator! You can guess what happened next! Oh my God, I went crashing through the fencing and landed up in the field. Lucky it's been so dry as I could have got stuck in mud. It was all so funny that I burst out laughing. Big mistake. Next thing I knew, Daddy was hauling me out of the tractor cab, yelling at me, while Maeve stood behind him, arms crossed, looking on in silent disapproval.

'What the hell have you done, you stupid little cow?'

'Ah Jaysus, calm down, Daddy, it's just a bit of fencing, sure I could have been hurt...'

'Just a bit of fencing, is it? Well, if that's the case then you can pay for it to be fixed, my girl.'

That wiped the smile off my face.

'I don't have any money,' I lied.

'Don't be telling me your lies, child. Where'd you be putting your wages from the restaurant, eh?'

'It's gone, I gave it to Trina,' I said, the first thing I could think.

'Now why would you do that when she's not even family?' my father fumed, shaking me by the shoulders. 'That Trina has turned you into an insolent girl too big for your boots. Tell her you want the money back.'

'I can't, she's in America,' I said smugly, not caring that my father's hands were hurting my arms as his fingers dug into the flesh.

'Good riddance to the *cute hoor*,' he said. 'She's turned you into a sly one, that's for sure.'

I made to get away, but my father pulled me back, hitting me across the cheek. I bit my lip, determined not to cry out, although it hurt, and my face was stinging where he had touched my skin.

'Daddy, she's lying.' Maeve's voice came out high-pitched and strained.

My father let me go, and I stepped back shakily.

'Shut up, Maeve,' I growled.

But Maeve, the snitch, betrayed me. 'Nuala's got savings. She's hiding it in one of Mammy's old handbags.'

My father stormed into the house and went rampaging in my room, pulling everything out of my wardrobe, opening up all the bags he could find. It felt as if he were assaulting me; in fact, I think I would have rather he beat me than go through my things. He found the bag, of course, and took out every single penny I had saved for America.

'Just enough to fix the fence,' he said with satisfaction. But who was he kidding? Half of it was going to be drunk. Half of it would fuel his rage further.

'Give it back,' I screamed, catching hold of his arm and trying to reach the hand filled with pound notes. 'That's my money. Mine!'

'Nothing in this house is yours, child,' he bellowed, pushing me backwards so that I fell onto my knees.

'I hate you, I hate you,' I screeched. 'No wonder Mammy killed herself to get away from you.'

I heard Maeve gasp. As she watched on, white faced, Daddy turned on me, his face almost purple with fury.

'Your mother killed herself because she didn't love *you*, Nuala – you've always been too much for us all and it was you that drove her over the edge.'

I bounded forward and tried to hit my father, but he caught my hand, twisting my arm. I yelped in pain.

'Daddy, stop!' Aisling appeared in the doorway to my bedroom, and pushing past Maeve, she pulled on our father's arm.

'Keep out of this, girl,' he snarled at Aisling, but she wouldn't let go until he turned on her. My father was a monster – one none of us could defeat.

'Leave Nuala be,' Aisling said.

'The girl is a menace and needs to be taught a lesson.'

'And you're a bully and a brute—' Aisling began bravely, but was unable to continue as my father hit her in the face. She staggered backwards, blood streaking from her nose. Maeve began to cry, but I was looking for something to hit him with. I wanted to kill him.

'Daddy, Daddy,' Maeve sobbed. 'Please, Daddy, don't.'

My father heard his middle daughter's pleas, and the rage within him began to calm. Still clasping my money, he stormed down the stairs, and then out the house. We all knew where he was going – to Flanagan's pub where he'd meet up with Peadar Maguire and they'd give out about how bad women were. He'd be gone a good long while, maybe even to the next day, to drown his guilt in pints. The three of us were left in the wake of his rage, my bedroom torn apart as if a hurricane had passed through it.

'How could you?' I turned on Maeve. 'That was all my savings...'

'I thought it would make him stop hitting you,' Maeve tried to explain.

'Just leave her, Nuala,' Aisling said in a tired voice, holding a tissue to her bleeding nose. 'Why do you wind him up so much?'

I had wanted to thank my big sister for stepping in and saving me, but her words made me feel defensive.

'I didn't ask you to get involved,' I said haughtily. 'It's not my fault our father is a complete bastard.'

I knelt down and picked up Mammy's bag. My father had ripped the seam in his haste to get his money.

'I can sew it up,' Maeve offered.

'Just get out,' I snarled. 'Both of you. Leave me alone.'

I sat on the edge of the bed, clutching the bag and holding it to my chest. I wanted my mother back so badly. Years, she'd been gone, and I was still waiting for her to return. My high from driving the tractor had completely dissipated, and now all I wanted to do was crawl into bed and pull the covers over me.

I must have fallen asleep because I woke in darkness, still in my shorts and t-shirt, the damp sheets sticking to me with sweat. I felt a sense of utter hopelessness. No one loved me. No one cared about me. Okay, yes, Trina. But she'd left and now I had no money to go and join her. I was going to be stuck in Swan

Hall with my violent father and mean sisters for the rest of my life. No, no – I would rather die.

I got out of bed and opened the door. Crept down the stairs, trying to be as quiet as possible. The last thing I wanted was to come across Daddy after he'd had a belly full of Guinness. Lough Bawn was calling to me. I ran across the lawn, the air still humid from the hot day, and the ground warm beneath my bare feet. When I got to the lake, the water was softly lapping against its shore. It invited me in, and tonight I wanted to go right to its centre. The place we were told never to swim. I took off my shorts and my t-shirt and waded in. The cold water was bliss against my hot limbs, and I dipped my head underwater, soothing my face where it still burned from my father's slap.

Let go. Let everything go. Come with me.

It could have been so easy to have done just that, and I let my limbs relax. For the moment I was floating, but if I began to drop beneath the surface of the water, I wasn't going to fight it.

'Nuala!'

A voice called from the shore. A figure waving to me.

'Nuala, come back!'

It was Conrad. What was he doing here so late at night?

He began to wade into the water, and then launched himself in, swimming towards me. I couldn't be responsible for his end too. I knew he wasn't a strong swimmer, so I began to swim back. We met a short distance from the shore.

'Are you all right?' he asked, knee deep in water. It was hard to make out his expression in the darkness, but I could hear the concern in his voice.

I said nothing in reply because I wasn't okay, but if I paused to speak, if I didn't keep on wading back to land, I might give up.

He followed, making a lot of splashing but not moving very fast.

I climbed out, water dripping off me, not caring how I

looked. I heard Conrad get out, coughing and spluttering. I collapsed on the bank and lay back, arms across my eyes.

'Nuala, what's wrong?' Conrad sat down next to me.

'I'm okay,' I murmured. 'It's fine.'

'You don't look fine,' he commented.

His words annoyed me. I hadn't asked for his opinion or his interference.

'What are you doing out here in the middle of the night?' I turned on him. 'Are you some sad loser, stalking me and my sisters?'

'Course not,' Conrad said, licking his lips. 'Can you keep a secret?'

I shrugged. 'Depends what it is.'

'I was meeting Patrick Donovan and his cousin, Jimmy,' he said.

'The Ra heads?' I looked at him in surprise. 'On our land?'

Conrad nodded. 'Yeah, sure our fathers know all about it,' he said. 'But I can't tell you any more. I'm sworn to secrecy.'

I didn't believe him for a minute. I could see the measure of Conrad Maguire. He was all full of it, but when it came to it he didn't have convictions like Trina did. I sighed, because if it was true, he was a big eejit for sure.

'Be careful, Conrad,' I warned him. 'Those fellas don't joke around.'

'I know what I'm doing.' He coughed nervously.

I stayed where I was, listening to the night sounds. The lapping of the lake, the hoot of an owl, the creaking wood, and the humming land cooling down from the hot day. For a moment, I thought Conrad had gone, and I was back on my own.

'You're very beautiful, Nuala,' Conrad whispered out of the blue. 'In fact, I think you're the prettiest girl I have ever seen.'

'I bet you said the same thing to my sister Aisling,' I joked.

'Come on, that was nothing, ended weeks ago. Aisling's not interested in me.'

I sat up and looked at Conrad. He was gazing at me in such a way, dear diary, in admiration, as if – I don't know – as if I were a goddess.

'I love you, Nuala Kelly,' he said. 'And one day I'm going to marry you.'

CHAPTER SEVENTEEN

IRIS

Iris was getting used to Swan Hall. The first few days all she'd wanted was to get home to New York, hide away in the apartment, but now she was exploring. She discovered a dining room behind the staircase in the front hall. Inside, everything was shrouded in dusty white sheets, and the curtains were drawn. She pulled them back a little to bring in the light, and walked around the shrouded dining table, looking at the old paintings on the walls. They were nearly all landscapes, she realised as she studied them – woods, lakes, and distant mountains. Heavy clouds hung over the earthy vistas. There were no seascapes or big skies depicted on the walls of this room, or in fact anywhere in the house. The clock in the hall ticked relentlessly on, and the dark corridors of the old house lured Iris into its depths. Up on the first floor, there was a door at the end of the corridor her bedroom was on, and when she opened it she found a narrow staircase caked in dust. She climbed it and came to a tiny landing with two doors. To her disappointment, they were both locked. She hunted around for the keys. Remembering her mom used to sometimes leave their key on the ledge above the door, she stood on her tippy toes, reaching up and trailing her fingers along the dusty lintel above one of the doors. To her delight, her fingers touched something metal. She grabbed it, feeling the contours of a key against her palm. The key fit into the first door she tried. She turned it slowly, taking a breath before opening up the door.

The interior reminded her of the wardrobe in her mother's room – stepping back in time. But this was a whole bedroom in the past. She gasped in shock and horror to see the bed still made up, a dressing table littered with objects covered in thick dust, and old posters curling off the walls. One was a Diana Ross album cover, *Surrender*, with a headshot of the singer's face. What was the song her mom used to sing to her? Of course: 'Remember Me'. She swallowed a lump in her throat, pushing away the memory.

There was another big poster which was just like the pictures her mom had of Celtic goddesses and legends on the walls in their apartment. It was by the same artist, Jim Fitz-Patrick – she could see his name written on the bottom of the picture. The image was silvery black and white of a beautiful young woman, staring with confidence at the viewer, her long hair and dress mirroring the intricacy of Celtic patterning. At the bottom was written the name 'Macha', and text beneath informed the viewer that she was the Queen of Ireland from whom the mystical Tuatha Dé Danann were descended. Iris remembered her mom talking about the gods and goddesses of ancient Ireland, and naming them the Tuatha Dé Danann. The picture was so beautiful, it took her breath away. She knelt on the lumpy bed, the blanket full of holes and coarse beneath her jeans, and touched the old print with her fingertips, trailing away the cobwebs. She traced the outline of Queen Macha's face. Her head was cocked on one side, and she seemed to be asking Iris a question. She didn't look like a queen, but more like a girl of the Seventies. Iris wanted the picture more than anything, and before she could think about it she began to peel it off the wall, very carefully, so it wouldn't tear.

Placing the rolled-up poster on the bed, Iris looked around the room. She didn't need to be told: this must have been Nuala's room. It was tucked under the eaves of the old house, and she could hear birds scratching around in the roof above her. There was one window, with a narrow window seat. She walked over and knelt on the seat, looking out at the view. Below was the unkempt garden, and then beyond was the lake. It was the same view as her mother's old bedroom, but higher up, so that she could see further. She could see a tiny part of the cove where Lizzie had shown her the swans' nest. Beyond the lake was the woods: a jumble of old trees, gradually dominated by more regular rows of tight dark spruce. In the far distance she could see low mountains, blue against the pale winter sky. She imagined herself as Nuala, at the age of sixteen, the last Christmas she had spent in this house, staring out of the window and dreaming of – what? The lake would have always been there before her. Reminding her that her own mother had drowned in it, as if it were a cut which never healed, itching to be picked.

Iris faced the interior of the room again. Dust motes spun in the weak wintry sunlight, and the room smelled musty, reeking of abandonment. She walked over to the dressing table and sat down on the old stool. She couldn't believe that no one had even cleared away any of the things on the dressing table. She picked up an old bottle of dark blue nail varnish – exactly the sort of colour she would go for – and tried to unscrew the lid, but it was stuck fast. There were bits and bobs of ancient make-up, and an old stinky bottle of violet eau de toilette. There was also a bowl full of trinkets – chains, bracelets, rings. Iris picked up a big ring with a moonstone in it and put it on her finger. It was the perfect size. There was one necklace which appealed to her – a silver necklace with Celtic spirals. The silver was a little tarnished, and she gave it a good rub before putting it on. The silver glimmered and it looked good against her skin as its chain twisted around the Virgin Mary medallion Maeve had given her.

She got up and wandered around the room, opening the wardrobe up just as she had in her mom's old room. Her eyes were drawn to a long green dress with billowing sleeves, as if it had stepped out of a medieval romance. She kicked off her sneakers before pulling it off its hanger, and taking off her turtleneck sweater and jeans. Iris wriggled into the dress, the fabric soft with age with a faint musty smell wafting from it.

There was a mirror in the door of the wardrobe and Iris started at her reflection. If her hair had been longer the dress would have looked better, but even so it fit her perfectly. She glanced down at the bottom of the wardrobe and saw a pair of suede platform boots in dark brown. She grabbed them and pushed her feet into them. Of course, Nuala's boots were the perfect fit. Now when she looked back at herself in the mirror, she did see a different kind of girl than she was used to being. She strutted around Nuala's bedroom, humming to herself, the long skirts of the green dress swishing around her. Her eyes caught sight of a suitcase under the bed. She knelt down to pull it out and opened it up. Inside were neatly packed clothes, and on top of them a hardback notebook with the word *Diary* written on the outside and *PRIVATE NO PRYING* in big letters.

'Oh man,' she whispered to herself.

She opened it, and the pages were crammed with writing – a wild, slanted script – all the way to 2 September, when the entries stopped abruptly. That must have been because she had drowned.

Iris sat on Nuala's bed and flicked through the diary. Would she find the answer in these pages to what had happened to her?

She saw the name *Aisling* and her stomach clenched. Did she really want to find out who her mother had been before she was born? She thought back to her aunt's words on Christmas Day. Had her mom had something to do with Nuala's death? Had she been jealous over Conrad's affections for Nuala? She shook her head. How could she think such a thing about her mom? But then, one thing she had learned since she had arrived at Swan Hall was that her mom had not been who Iris had thought she was. Aisling had been filled with secrets, none of which she had shared with Iris. It hurt a lot. Because if she didn't know who her mom was, who was she?

It was nearly dark by the time Iris was forced to put the diary down. The bulb had gone in the overhead light and she couldn't see to read. She closed the case and slid it under the bed, but kept hold of the diary for 1972. She was hooked and needed to get as far as September. Nuala's voice was clear as a bell in her head, and Iris liked her. She was so rebellious and confident. But, hungry for mention of her mother, Iris had been disappointed by how little Nuala and Aisling had hung out that year. What had been surprising, though, was the fact that Trina had been Nuala's best friend first. Why had neither her godmother nor her mother ever told her that before? It was clear Trina and Nuala had been very close. And who was the mysterious C? She tucked the diary into the pocket of the green dress and gathered up her jeans, sweater and sneakers. It must be dinnertime, because her stomach gave a low growl of hunger.

She carried the things down to her bedroom, seeing no one on the way. She wanted to keep the dress on but decided it might attract further attention from her uncle, who already kept calling her Nuala. Also, her Aunt Maeve would ask how she'd found it, which would mean she'd have to admit she'd been snooping around the house. Reluctantly, she pulled it off and put on her regular clothes again.

Her uncle was in the sitting room, watching the TV and lolling on the sofa, drinking a whiskey. She glanced at the screen; it looked like he was watching a documentary about something that had happened in the past.

'Murdering bastards,' her uncle hissed, before looking over at her and continuing to rant. 'Twenty years ago today, three bombs went off in the Republic, planted by the loyalist paramilitaries and killing innocent civilians,' he said. 'But all we hear about is the IRA on the British news!'

'Right,' Iris responded. She knew next to nothing about the Troubles. Her mom never talked about what was happening in Ireland, apart from to say it had had nothing to do with her own life.

'Do you think there'll be a united Ireland one day?' Iris asked Uncle Conrad.

'Of course,' he said fiercely. 'You've got to believe it.' He took a sip of his whiskey. 'But we can't let Sinn Féin and the IRA sell out. Irish nationalism is about tradition, that's what. It's about being a great Catholic country with strong morals.'

'Okay,' Iris said uneasily, seeing a new side to her uncle.

What was it her godmother, Trina, had once commented on about women's rights and nationalist Ireland? That was it – she'd once said that one of the downsides of independence for Ireland was that the Catholic Church wanted control over women's lives. Her mother had loved Ireland, missed it with all her heart, and yet she'd known as a single mother she couldn't stay. *What a strange, split place this country is*, Iris thought, as she left Conrad to his documentary.

In the kitchen, Maeve was finishing the preparations for dinner. Iris could smell some kind of roasting meat in the oven.

'Ah, there you are, Iris,' she said. 'Do you want to lay the table?'

The radio was on in the kitchen, blaring out traditional Irish music. Iris found herself humming again as she laid the table. She thought about her mother and Nuala sitting at this same table, bickering like most teenage girls, and the longing to go back in time to see them together was almost overwhelming.

'Are you all right?' Maeve asked her. 'Where were you all afternoon? I went to look for you in your bedroom, but you weren't there.'

'I went for a walk,' Iris lied.

Maeve looked at her sideways. 'I never heard you go out,' she commented, but left it there.

Iris wasn't sure why she didn't just tell Maeve that she'd found Nuala's bedroom. She wanted to ask why it appeared exactly as it would have been left twenty years ago. But she didn't, because she needed to finish reading Nuala's diary first – then she would ask her questions.

'So would you like to come to Mass with me and Conrad in the morning?' Maeve asked.

'Oh, okay,' Iris said unenthusiastically.

'I was going to ask Father Francis if he'd hold a remembrance service for your mother on the 31st.'

'Right.' Iris swallowed tightly, not wanting anything of the sort.

Maeve turned to face Iris, dusting flour off her hands. 'I am sorry I didn't come to see you after the funeral in New York. I was shocked and I've never been on a plane.'

'Never?' Iris asked, incredulous.

'No,' Maeve said. 'I mean I've been to England and France on the boat, but I've always been afraid of flying.' She turned back to the apple pie she was making, lifting up the lid of pastry and placing it on top of the apples before trimming the edges with a knife. 'But I will come, Iris, I promise. I'll come and visit the grave.'

Iris didn't know what to say. She stared at her aunt as she brushed egg yolk on the top of the pie.

'Um, Aunt Maeve?'

'Yes,' Maeve said, turning to her, hands on hips.

'There is no grave.'

'What?' Her aunt looked at her, aghast.

'We had a service and spread ashes, but there's no grave.'

'But I don't understand... Are you telling me that my sister was cremated?'

Iris nodded.

'But she didn't like fire! She should have been buried. How can she not have a gravestone?'

'I couldn't afford a burial,' Iris snapped. 'And I couldn't pay for a gravestone. I didn't have the money.'

'Oh,' Maeve said, looking chastised.

'Besides, what's the point? My mom is gone; a gravestone makes no difference.'

'Oh, but it does,' Maeve said softly. 'It helps. I visit Nuala's, my mother's and my father's all the time in the graveyard in Bawn. And I mean, we never found Nuala's body, nor my mother's, but we still had funerals and gravestones, so to speak.'

'I spread some of my mom's ashes off the Brooklyn Bridge, and in Central Park,' Iris shared. 'She loved walking across it. And I brought some with me, too. I thought I should bring some to Ireland. Where do you think she'd like me to spread them?'

'In the lake,' Maeve said without hesitation. 'That way, a part of her is with Mammy and Nuala always.'

Iris wasn't so sure Maeve was right. The lake was deep and dark, and not a place she wished to surrender her mother to.

It was barely light when Maeve came into Iris's bedroom the next morning to wake her for Mass. Iris was exhausted, having read Nuala's diary until she'd fallen asleep. It was still tucked beside her under the covers, but luckily Maeve didn't see it.

The bathroom was freezing. She quickly splashed water on her face and brushed her teeth before going downstairs in a big sweatshirt over a turtleneck sweater and jeans. The whole house felt like a refrigerator and she was shaking with the cold. She hoped it would be warmer in the church.

She was surprised to see her Uncle Conrad waiting in the passenger seat of the car. He was dressed in a suit, and his wild hair had been greased down into submission. Maeve drove them in silence into the town, but for once the atmosphere between the couple seemed benign. Iris yawned. Why had she agreed to this church charade? She was an adult; she could have said no. But she felt she had to be polite.

Being a modern building, the church was well heated, and Iris began to thaw as they sat down in the pew. The place was packed too, and she could feel eyes upon her. The older generation staring openly, no doubt because she looked just like Nuala. She had an urge to run away, but she stayed put. In a few days, she'd be gone. Both her Aunt Maeve and Uncle Conrad had taken rosaries out and were twirling them between their fingers, muttering to themselves as they waited for Mass to begin. Iris clasped her own hands in her lap, not knowing how to behave. Should she kneel and pretend to pray like they were? She felt a tap on her shoulder, and turned to see Ruairi sitting behind her. He gave her a warm smile and she instantly felt better.

The Mass was longer than on Christmas Eve, and Iris didn't know any of the ceremony. She knew none of the things to say when the congregation was supposed to respond. Maeve was sharing her missal with her, but Iris's eyes kept wandering off the page because the words meant very little to her. Maybe it was because when the congregation spoke it was leaden and flat, as if they weren't thinking about what they were saying. Iris felt Ruairi's presence behind her and was a little self-conscious that he could be looking at her without her knowing. She let her gaze sweep around the church at the people from her mother's hometown. Families together: whole tribes of children in a row with the same rosy cheeks as their parents. There was the odd elderly man or woman alone, but in the main, everybody was in a family of some sort. She didn't belong in this place of family and religion. The priest's sermon was so boring, Iris let her mind wander. She was nearly at the end of Nuala's diary. She had just read how her mom had protected Nuala from their father, and Iris was proud of her mother for standing up to him, furious with her dead grandfather, and a little shocked at Maeve's lack of backbone. But most of all, she was sad that Nuala and her mom had not been closer. It seemed to her that they were two sisters that had belonged together. Maeve was the odd one out, and yet she'd got Conrad – the boy they were all after, so to speak – she'd got the farm; in fact, she'd got to live.

Iris glanced at her aunt, who had her eyes closed, fervently praying, and remembered again Conrad's words from Christmas Eve about how it was too late for Maeve to be forgiven now. Maybe she'd been thinking about things the wrong way round. Maybe it wasn't her mom who had done something terrible, but Maeve. Her mom had had to run away because she was pregnant, that's all.

Everyone got up to go to communion, and before Iris could protest that she didn't want to, Aunt Maeve was chivvying her along out of the pew to queue up along the length of the nave. The priest doling out the communion was the Father Francis Maeve had talked about, who might be persuaded to do a special Mass for her mother. God, Iris hoped not. As she neared the top of the queue, she anxiously watched what other people were doing – some were offering up their hands and giving themselves communion, and others were opening up their mouths and sticking out their tongues. She really didn't want to do this and, besides, she'd never done her First Communion. She shouldn't be taking communion! But she was locked in a line, sandwiched between Maeve and Conrad. She looked at Father Francis in his green, white, and gold-trimmed robe. He looked so grand, although his face was sunken, and he possessed hardly any hair. It was clear he was weary, as he intoned the same words to each recipient:

'The Body of Christ.'

It was her turn. Iris looked up at him, realising she was doing the wrong thing because everyone else had their heads bowed. But then the priest saw her face and flinched, the ciborium of communion wafers wobbling in his hand. For a second, he was speechless, and then the professional he was, he put his hand on her head, forcing her to look down as he intoned the words.

She offered up her cupped palms, and he put the communion wafer upon them. She put it in her mouth as she'd seen the others do. Chew? Swallow? Suck? She let the wafer dissolve on her tongue as she walked back down to her pew. Everyone was on their knees, heads in their hands, praying, and she tried to do the same. Think about her mom. But it wasn't the right place for her mom. She had read in Nuala's diary that her mom didn't believe in God. All of a sudden, she wished she'd spat out the communion wafer – that would have pleased her mom and Trina!

She raised her head and found herself looking up at the wooden dome of the church ceiling and the light gleaming through the circular glass windows which ringed its base. She caught the sight of the pale wintry blue sky and tufts of clouds, and more than anything she wished to be outside in nature and away from the stultifying atmosphere inside the church.

At last Mass was over and they were released outside. By now the sun was pushing through the clouds, and spilling light over the sodden graveyard. While Maeve and Conrad chatted to neighbours, Iris ambled over to the gravestones, glancing at the names and dates.

'There you are, so!'

Ruairi was standing beside her.

'Hello,' she said. 'Did you have a nice Christmas?'

'Yes, very, too much food eaten.' He patted his jumper, and Iris couldn't help imagining his taut stomach beneath the green wool. 'And how about you?'

'Yes, it was nice, different you know, but it was never going to be easy.'

'Of course,' Ruairi said kindly. 'The first Christmas is always the worst.' He took out his cigarettes and offered her one. 'So, how long are you staying for?' he asked, bending down to light her cigarette.

'A few more days,' she said. She wanted to go home, yes, sure she did, but then she was pretty sure she'd screwed up Berkeley and she'd no idea what to do about her future.

'Would you like to go for a walk tomorrow?' he asked. 'It's my day off.'

'Oh, yes, okay,' Iris said, taken by surprise.

'I'll pick you up around ten in the morning?' he said, taking a last drag on his cigarette before flicking it away into the wet grass.

She watched him walk away, hands in his pockets, and felt her stomach fluttering nervously. He was very good-looking, and she liked him. But she was going back to New York, and he lived in Ireland, so what was the point? Even so, she couldn't help but look forward to their date – a day away from Maeve and Conrad, and the weight of their company.

'Iris!' Maeve called to her. She was talking to the priest and was waving her over.

'Oh crap,' Iris said under her breath. She had hoped her aunt had forgotten about her promise to organise the memorial for her mom.

'Father, this is Iris, Aisling's daughter,' Maeve introduced them.

The priest clasped his hands and shifted from foot to foot uneasily. 'Blessings, child,' he said in a quavering voice.

'Hello,' Iris said, refusing to say 'Father' like her aunt had. He wasn't *her* father, just a man who pretended he was better than everyone else.

Maeve coughed uneasily, finally noticing Iris's reticence.

'The likeness is uncanny, is it not, Maeve?' Father Francis spoke up. 'She is the absolute image of poor Nuala, God rest her soul.'

'Yes, she is indeed, Father,' Maeve said.

'And so sad about your poor wretched mother,' Father Francis carried on to Iris. 'Your aunt has asked me to say a special Mass for her on Tuesday. Are there any particular readings you think your mother might have liked?'

Iris stared back at the priest. She shook her head. *Say something, Iris*, a voice in her head screamed at her. *Say your mom would not want a special Mass. Tell him she was not a poor wretched woman, but a survivor. A fierce single mother warrior!* But Iris didn't want to hurt Maeve's feelings and she guessed this would allow her aunt to grieve her sister.

'How about Matthew 11: verses 28–29 in particular?' Maeve suggested. '"Come to me, all you who are weary and burdened, and I will give you rest. Take my yoke upon you and learn from me, for I am gentle and humble in heart, and you will find rest for your souls."'

'Ah yes, very apt.' Father Francis nodded. 'Well now, you'll have to excuse me, girls,' he said, moving away to join a group of men including her Uncle Conrad, who stood together talking in low voices, heads bent, in the church porch.

Girls! Her aunt was hardly a girl. Everything about the priest made Iris's flesh crawl. And as her godmother, Trina, said, *always trust your instincts*: well, if that was the case, this man was a creep.

But her Aunt Maeve was pleased. She took Iris's arm and began walking through the graves, before coming to stop in front of a small grey headstone.

Nuala Kelly
1956–1972
Beloved daughter and sister

Beneath the script was a small carving of a swan with its wings spread as if to take flight.

'Nuala loved the swans on the lake,' Maeve said. 'I asked Daddy to have one carved on her stone. There's one on my mother's grave too.'

She indicated the gravestone next to Nuala's. Iris read the simple script:

Áine Kelly
1932–1966
Beloved mother and wife

Below the carving was another swan, more serene than Nuala's, with its wings closed as if floating on an invisible lake.

'My mother was obsessed with the lake, and the swans. She also loved all the old Irish legends and stories. Nuala was named after Fionnuala, one of the Children of Lir – do you know the story about the children turned into swans by their evil stepmother?'

'Yes, my mom used to read it to me when I was little.'

'I was named after Maeve, the Celtic warrior goddess,' Maeve said. 'My mam was called Áine after the Irish goddess of the summer, so she wanted to carry on the tradition of using mythological names.'

'Who was Mom named after?'

'I believe Aisling means a dream or vision in Irish.'

'She wasn't a goddess?'

'No.'

Iris felt a little disappointed for her mom. 'And who was... Macha?' Iris struggled to pronounce the name.

'There are several different Machas in ancient Irish mythology,' Maeve said. 'The most famous of them was one of the three sisters known as the Morrígan, or the triple goddess of war.'

'I've heard of the one who's a queen,' Iris said, thinking of the poster she'd taken from Nuala's room.

'Ah, wife of King Nemed! Where did you find out about her?' Maeve asked, giving her a searching look.

'I can't remember,' Iris said, pulling up her hood as it started to rain.

'Sometimes Nuala would call our mam Macha.' Maeve closed her eyes and took a breath. 'She could be a silly little girl, making up songs about how our mam was the mother of all Ireland.'

Maeve opened her eyes. Iris thought she had never seen anyone look so sad before.

'But in the end, our mam couldn't even manage to mother three daughters,' she said, as rain trickled down her face.

The downpour was sudden and violent as it swept through the graveyard. Crows which had been roosting in the yew trees above them took off in squawking alarm. Iris and her aunt hurried back through the graves towards the car. They passed the priest and the group of smoking men standing in the porch of the church, her Uncle Conrad among them, and as they did so Iris heard one of the men say, 'What we need is a strong church,' before she was out of earshot again.

Back at the car, her aunt indicated for her to get in the front.

'What about Uncle Conrad?'

'He's busy, with his pal Donovan and one of his meetings,' Maeve said, before getting in the other side.

'What kind of meetings?' Iris asked, once they were seated inside the car with the windscreen wipers on.

'The kind where women aren't welcome,' her aunt said tartly, as she attempted to dry her face with a handkerchief. 'Even though women are the bedrock of the church. But people like my husband don't understand that.'

'But the Catholic Church believes that women are more sinful than men, right? That they're worth less?'

'Oh no, Iris, it's not that simple at all,' Maeve said. 'At its essence, the rules don't matter. They were created by men after Jesus died. What matters is the true message of Christ: one of love and the mystic nature of the divine.'

Iris had no idea how to respond, because she didn't understand the mystic divine that her aunt was talking about. The yoga practices she had shared with her mom back home in New York made more sense to her than the Irish Catholicism of her aunt, which to Iris seemed to be clearly about the submission of women. But she didn't want to get into an argument about it.

How she wished she'd given her mom a big hug the last time they'd gone to yoga together. She longed to feel her arms around her, to smell her scent, and feel her protection. But her mom was gone, just like her Grandmother Áine, just like her Aunt Nuala. None of them were ever coming back. She owed it to her mom to protect her memory now and to find out the truth of why she became an exile from her own family. Could she be her mother's champion, as her mom had been for her all her life?

CHAPTER EIGHTEEN

NUALA

24 AUGUST 1972

We're here in Listowel and the craic is MIGHTY! It feels so good to be away from home and for once, we're all getting on. Probably because Conrad is with us, so my sisters are on their best behaviour. It was a bit of a job cramming all our stuff into the car – our instruments and the tents and all the food Trina's mam had made for us. She looked a bit teary, and I felt it too, remembering the year before last when Trina had been with us. It's hard to think about Trina over in America, and how it's going to take me even longer to get there now. But I WILL, dear diary, I'll find a way, so I will.

Because I get carsick in the back, Aisling said I was to sit up front, which Maeve whined about but could do nothing to change because last time she made me sit in the back I threw up all over the seat. Anyhow, she seemed pleased enough when she realised that meant she got to sit next to charming Conrad for the whole trip.

We had a great old banter on the way up, and then Aisling turned on the radio to listen to the latest hits. We sang along, belting out 'Baba O'Riley', 'Wild Horses' and 'Here Comes the Sun' together. Then we took turns – Aisling sang along to Aretha Franklin's 'Bridge Over Troubled Water', Maeve sang along to Carole King's 'It's Too Late' and Conrad sang 'Maggie May' with Rod Stewart. When the Carpenters came on, that was my turn and I joined in with Karen's 'For All We Know'. All me and my sisters wanted was to have fun, so every time the news came on telling us about some more bombings and killings up North or in the border counties, Aisling changed channel, despite Conrad telling her not to. Us girls didn't want to know anything about the Troubles. No way. We are sick of all the violence getting worse and worse all summer long. Well, that's how *I* feel about it, and I think my sisters do, too.

'Hey, I was listening to that,' Conrad complained when yet again Aisling changed the channel after the latest news about the Newry bombings came on. 'It's important to know what's going on.'

'We already know what's going on. The Provos botched a bombing at the Newry customs on Tuesday, killing themselves and innocent civilians,' Aisling said tightly. 'We don't need any more details, Conrad.'

'Don't you care about our country?' Conrad's face flushed. 'Don't you want the Brits out?'

'It's not that simple,' Aisling countered.

I turned around in my seat to look at Conrad. His expression had darkened.

'There's been an official IRA ceasefire since the end of May, Conrad,' I said. 'Even they're sick of it.'

'But that didn't stop British snipers shooting innocent civilians, did it? All summer long they've been doing it in Belfast.'

I guess his passion for his country could be attractive for some girls, say, like my sister Maeve, who was looking at him with wide-eyed interest, but not for me. To think he had declared his love and told me he wanted to marry me, dear diary, ten days ago! Well, what a stupid notion that was.

'Ah God, Conrad, you're a real bore,' I said, turning back to face the front.

I caught Aisling giving me a sideways look, a smile playing on her lips, and it felt good to know she liked what I'd just said. T. Rex came on the radio and I leaned forward to turn it up, cutting off Conrad, who was warming up to another lecture. Instead, he began banging on to Maeve about the injustices of Northern Ireland, poor thing, which me and Aisling couldn't hear, thank God, especially as we began singing 'Hot Love' together.

Honestly, dear diary, it was the best of road trips. Away from home, we were different. Aisling was in charge, not my father, and she seemed more carefree than I had seen her in weeks. Maeve wasn't telling me to shut up and stop showing off when I sang, probably because she didn't want to appear a bitch in front of Conrad. She always acts different around him. Maeve's one of those girls that wants men to like her, even if it means throwing one of her own under the bus. Well, we are who we are, but that doesn't mean I don't love my sisters.

Aisling drove us along the winding country roads through the counties of Galway and Clare, and into Limerick before we hit the northern coast of Kerry. As soon as I saw the sea, I was reminded of good times with my sisters. A trip to the seaside with Daddy, and Mammy when she was still alive. I remembered making sandcastles on the beach, and Maeve helping me, and Aisling – too old for such childish pursuits – reading one of her books. Daddy and Mammy had gone off to get us chips, while Aisling was left to mind us. In the end she had helped me and Maeve collect shells together, no fighting, but happily giving each other the prettiest ones to decorate our castles with. When a boy had come and kicked my castle over, Aisling had gone and kicked his down before pushing him over in the sand

and making him cry. Me and Maeve had clapped our hands in delight. Our big sister was our protector!

It was late afternoon by the time we arrived in Listowel, and the town was jammers. We followed the signs to the campsite, and Aisling pulled into a field filled with other campers. I couldn't stop thinking about Trina and the fun we'd had the year before last. I was desperate for word from her. I'd sent her a letter telling her my father had stolen all my money, but I hadn't heard back from her yet.

As we pitched the tent, Conrad's eyes were on me. I felt a twinge of wickedness and decided to tease him a little, flicking my hair and sticking up my shorts-clad backside as I knelt down to hammer in the tent pegs. I had rebuked his ridiculous marriage proposal (well, it was hardly a proposal, as he hadn't actually asked me but told me he was going to marry me!) but still that didn't mean I couldn't have a little fun tormenting him. I know I am *not* a good girl, dear diary, but how boring life would be if I was! I caught a disapproving glance from Aisling and felt a little bad. Surely, she doesn't have feelings for Conrad any more? The way she spoke to him in the car was evidence of that, and he had said it was all over and done with weeks ago. Besides, Aisling is always off somewhere in the evenings. I am sure she has another boyfriend by now. But then, who knew she was so secretive?

We got the tent up and then we went into the town to find something to eat. Locals had put up signs and had stacks of pies and sandwiches on their windowsills, but we wanted chips so we joined the big queue outside the chipper.

'We've to be at the town hall at 9 a.m. sharp,' Aisling warned us. 'Will we run through "Maeve's Reel" again?'

'Ah God, please no, we've done it so many times, sure I can practically do it in my sleep,' I groaned.

'And what about your singing? Are you ready, Nuala?' Aisling persevered.

'Yes, yes,' I sighed.

'I thought you wanted to win,' Aisling said, looking surprised at my lack of enthusiasm.

She was right. I had been so passionate about winning, but the last few weeks, hurt over the end of my affair with C, well... I've lost my hunger to win a bit. It feels as if I am going through the motions. Because my heart and soul are no longer in Ireland. They're already across the sea in America and only my body is left behind now. I just have to physically remove myself. Easier said than done when I am penniless.

Maeve cut in. 'I want to make Daddy proud of us.'

I snorted in derision.

'I don't care one fuck about Daddy,' I said.

'Don't swear, Nuala,' Aisling said, softly though, as I saw a little twist of a smile at the corner of her mouth.

'I fucking will if I want,' I gave out. 'Anyway, I bet you feel the same way after the battering he gave you.'

Aisling's smile fell away, and she folded her arms across her chest with an expression on her face as if she wished to murder me. Conrad looked at me questioningly.

'Does your father hit you girls?' he asked.

'Only me and Aisling. Sure he wouldn't touch Maeve, because he loves her so.' I could hear the nasty tone to my voice and I wished I could stop. Why did I want to hurt my sisters so much?

'Stop it, Nuala,' Maeve said, blushing crimson.

'My da has a belt.' Conrad grimaced. Then he pulled up the back of his shirt to show us a welt on his back.

'Jaysus,' I exclaimed, feeling a little sorry for Conrad now. 'What brought that on?'

'Giving him cheek, he said like my mam used to,' he said.

'I don't want to talk about all this stuff now,' Aisling said. 'We have the whole weekend to do what we want – no fathers watching over us – so let's make the most of it!'

We had reached the top of the queue and Aisling ordered our chips. She knows exactly how me and Maeve like them. No vinegar on mine, just salt, whereas Maeve likes hers slathered in vinegar. For the first time I noticed how Aisling likes her chips with equal portions of salt and vinegar. She also got some for Conrad and he asked for ketchup.

We wandered down the main street eating our chips. It was still bright and lots of musicians were on the streets playing. I stopped to listen to a virtuoso flute player, with wild red hair and a freckled face. He winked at me as he caught sight of me, and I laughed in delight, shaking my head in response although I couldn't help giving him a bit of a look. There were loads of people milling around, and when I had finished my flirt with the flautist I realised I had lost the others. Well, I didn't care too much because I knew where the tent was, and I was happy to be on my own and not having to deal with my bossy sisters.

The next musician I came across was a fiddle player. He was playing a jig and most of the crowd were dancing in time. I finished my last chip, and, licking my fingers, joined in. We whirled around in our impromptu céilí and it was just the best craic. My heart still ached for Trina to be there with me, but it was the next best thing to be enjoying the dancing.

When I dance, I am full of joy and love, yes love, for the whole wide world. My mind flicked to how low I had felt just ten days ago, and I was ashamed of myself. Conrad had saved my life that night although he didn't know it. But what he had said to me was so out of place and weird. There is a part of me that keeps thinking he only said it to distract me, because what had he been doing in our woods in the middle of the night with the likes of Patrick Donovan and his cousin Jimmy? That's not to say I don't want to experience earth-shattering love, and I have already – yes, I have – felt heaven and earth move when I make love with C. But, but... I don't want it to be real. And I don't want to settle down and give birth and look after a man. That's what killed my mam.

It was getting dark now, and most of the musicians had left the streets. I began to make my way back to the campsite. The moon was half full, and its light pooled on the street ahead. The air was still warm from the hot day and it didn't feel like Ireland at all. It felt as if I were in Spain, though how would I know, to be honest, because I have never been there. But my mam talked about it. I remember that. She described how she'd met our father at a fiesta in northern Spain. We three sisters loved to hear the story of the serendipitous meeting of the Dublin girl and the Roscommon boy in the middle of the procession of Virgen de la Guía.

'Tell us of how you met Daddy,' Maeve would be the first to ask.

'But you've heard the story so many times,' our mother would say, though her eyes would be shining with the promise of it.

'Please,' we all begged in unison.

And so my mother would sit down at the kitchen table with a pot of tea, and a plate of biscuits for us to share, to tell us her love story, and we lapped it up.

'I was on holidays in Spain with two of my friends, Kate and Donna. We were all dancers and we had come there to take part and learn about some of the regional dances. We were staying a village called Llanes, on the foothills of the Cantabrian Mountains, halfway between Basque Country and Santiago de Compostela.

'It was the night of the procession when the women of the village, dressed in their Spanish mantillas, accompanied a statue of the Virgin, and the children made flower offerings, and young men carried pyramids of bread. Oh, there was great excitement. The whole village was out, a big crowd, and I lost Kate and Donna in the crush, but I wasn't worried. There was music everywhere, folk bands with tambourines and bagpipes, and I knew we'd find each other eventually at one of the dances. So I ran behind the procession with all the village children and their flowers, and I could see the Virgin ahead, swaying above the heads of all the Spanish women. I remember thinking what it might be to live in the village and to love one of the young Spanish men with their pyramids of bread!' Our mam laughed. 'I was a very romantic young woman. Oh, what a silly girl I was then!

'We were crushed in the village square and I stood on my tippy toes, trying to take a photograph, and that's when your daddy stepped on me. He turned around and apologised in English.'

She paused as Maeve giggled, and Aisling took another biscuit.

'Your daddy had spent the whole summer in Spain and he was as tanned as a Spanish man, so swarthy and strong from fruit picking, but his accent was buttermilk and bread, and his eyes were the colour of home. Gabriel, he told me his name was, and I laughed, puzzling him. Gabriel, I thought to myself, are you an angel come into my life to ward off my dark imaginings, to keep my tread light?'

I didn't know what my mammy meant then – I was too little to understand – when she talked about her dark imaginings, but I think Aisling might have because she looked fearful as she bit into her biscuit.

'What are you doing here? I asked him,' my mam continued, acting out the parts. 'On my way to Compostela, he replied. I asked him if he was walking the whole way and he said yes, the whole way. I looked at his feet, strong toes, smooth brown skin in his sandals, like Jesus.

'And you? he asked. What are you doing here? And what did I say, girls?'

Our mam opened up her hands, waiting for our answer.

'DANCING!' we all shouted in unison.

My mam leapt up from the kitchen table and clicked her fingers, stamped her feet, and we followed her lead. We had no music, but we didn't need it. Even Aisling threw down her biscuit and the four of us danced around the table, our heads filled with the pure romance of our parents meeting in such an exotic place as Spain. Sometimes Daddy would arrive home in the midst of it all, and he wasn't the father I know now. He would be laughing – yes, dear diary, there would be joy on his face at the sight of his dancing wife and daughters. He'd pick Maeve up and swing her in the air as she squealed for joy, while Mammy held hands with me and Aisling. We were the fair, and Daddy and Maeve were the dark. But together we fit. All of us together.

In my head as I walked, I saw the story of my mother and my father. The two of them young and in love, dancing down a dusty track. They were framed by orange groves, in the lap of the hills, with the golden magical light of Spain filling their hearts.

Ah, I was walking down the main street in Listowel, but I was lost in my Spanish dream. I was there at the night-time fiesta of dance and music, fire and passion sparking young love. I imagined I was walking through a Spanish village by the sea, wearing one of my mother's Spanish dresses rather than my shorts, and I had big gold hoops in my ears, and silver rings on my fingers. It wasn't English I was hearing being shouted out from the jammed pubs, nor Irish music, but Spanish, and the sounds were those of flamenco guitarists and dancers, the clickety clack of the castanets, and the stamp of their feet. I stopped in the street and raised my arms, taking the stance I had seen my mother take in the room with her dancing friends Kate and Donna when I was a little girl. The second of stillness before they broke into the dance, the edge of tension in the body before it flowed. Maybe, maybe I could go to Spain. If I didn't have the airfare for America, then what was stopping me from hitching up to Dublin and taking the boat to England, another to France, and hitching all the way to Spain? I could sing for my supper on the streets. Why not? I could find that little village in Spain which my mother had loved and go and join the fiesta procession. I could dance with other girls and women just as my mother had done. I could find out who she had been when she'd first met my father and they had both been happy. I could find that part of my mother which was sunshine, before the Irish rain had drowned her joy, before the lake had swallowed her up.

Lost in my reverie, I glanced blindly down a side street, almost expecting it to turn into a Spanish alleyway, but to my astonishment what I saw shattered my dream completely. For there right before my eyes was Conrad Maguire, kissing my sister Maeve. She was up against the wall and he had her face cupped in his hands. Her eyes were closed as they snogged, but as if sensing my presence, he turned to look at me – as he shifted my sister! It was totally creepy and I broke into a run. What the hell was he playing at? Ten days ago, he told me of his undying love for me, before that he was dating Aisling – and now Maeve!

Well, I knew by the way he had looked at me as he stuck his tongue down my sister's throat that he wanted me to see him do it. That's what he was at. He was trying to make me jealous. What a complete bastard! Maeve had betrayed me so many times, and honestly she deserved to have her heart broken, but there was something about the way she leaned into him, her complete submission, which disturbed me.

'Oh shit,' I murmured to myself. My sister was crazy about Conrad. I had noticed she fancied him but I didn't realise she had it this bad. 'Shit, shit,' I kept saying, all the way back to the campsite. I unzipped the tent the three of us were sharing. Aisling was already in her sleeping bag and I was unsure if she was asleep. Should I wake her up? Tell her about Conrad and

Maeve? But a part of me didn't want to hurt her, too. She had been going out with him, and things were bad enough between Aisling and Maeve. By God, Conrad Maguire was a dirty bastard. I felt a wave of fury pass through me, at myself more than anything, because I had been deceived by him. There was nothing for it. I would have to warn Maeve.

CHAPTER NINETEEN

IRIS

Iris couldn't move her body. It felt as if she had been plunged into an ice-cold bath and she was frozen solid. There was a heavy weight upon her chest, and she imagined she could feel an icy finger pressed in the centre of her forehead, right where her yoga teacher had said the third eye was located. She struggled to emerge from the oppressiveness of her dream, which was all sensation and no content. *Breathe.* She could hear her mother's voice. *Take a breath.*

She inhaled deeply and sighed. The icy finger on her forehead dissipated. She breathed again and was able to wriggle her toes and fingertips. She took another inhalation, followed by a long exhale. The fug of the dream and the weight upon her chest began to lift, and she shifted her body under the covers. She opened her eyes. The room was a swirl of shadows and light, and she sensed it was morning. She sat up and got out of the bed. Her body felt heavy and rigid and there was still an overpowering oppression in the bedroom. Pulling back the curtains, she flooded the room with wintry sunlight, casting away the dark dream and the cloying sense of fear it had filled her with. The day gleamed before her, the grass tipped with frost, and a thin glaze of ice upon Lough Bawn. The sky was the same blue as her Virgin Mary necklace. She walked over to the dressing table and picked up the medallion her Aunt Maeve had given her. Turned it over in her hands. She had been wearing it Virgin side out to please her aunt, but now she looked at the side with the etching of the swan on it. She slipped it over her head, making sure the swan was facing out.

Iris picked up her watch. It was nine o'clock already, and Ruairi had said he would pick her up at ten. She pulled on a sweater and slipped out into the hall, switching on the immersion heater in the airing cupboard, hoping it would heat enough water so she could have a small bath. The house hummed slightly around her. She could hear Uncle Conrad whistling to the dogs, the door opening and closing, and then silence. Her aunt was probably already out with the horses. She was beginning to feel a little more at home in Swan Hall. She liked the fact that her aunt and uncle didn't wait on her. Ever since she had found Nuala's diary, she was obsessed with making pictures of the past inside her head. The three Kelly sisters eating together, playing music together, arguing, separating, coming together again to swim at the lake. She had returned to looking at the photograph albums which her Aunt Maeve had shown her on the first day, and examining the pictures of her mother as a child and young woman. She saw the older woman she was to become in the tip of her chin, or the look in her eyes.

After her bath, Iris dressed hurriedly. All her clothes needed a wash. Spontaneously, she flung open her mother's old wardrobe, and pulled out the purple paisley shirt. It smelled a bit musty, but it was clean. She put it on. It was a little bit big for her, but the colour was beautiful – the deep violet contrasting with her green eyes. She sprayed herself with Chanel, which she'd brought with her (a gift from the Monettis for her mom last Christmas), before pulling on her jeans, and then a big cardigan which her Aunt Maeve had lent her. It was dark green, and contrasted with the purple of the shirt and matched her eyes. These colours of purple and green made her feel Irish. She wasn't sure quite why – maybe because the land was so green, and much of it was covered in purple heathers? They were not colours she wore back home in New York. Just as she was leaving her bedroom, she checked the contents of her purse. There in the bottom was the small pot of the leftover ashes of her mom. She still hadn't decided where to spread them.

As she was coming down the stairs, she heard the scrunch of wheels on the gravel drive. She glanced out of the window, seeing Ruairi pulling up – not in the garda car, thank goodness, but in an old Land Rover. In the passenger seat next to him sat a glossy brown spaniel, which grew very excited when Aed, Conn and Fiacra appeared round the corner, barking. Iris raced down the rest of the stairs, feeling a little twist of excitement in her belly. She grabbed two apples from the bowl on the kitchen table on her way out the door. As she emerged from the back of the house, she nearly banged into her Uncle Conrad.

'What's that guard Ruairi Caffrey doing here?' he asked, looking bothered. 'How do you know him?'

'We met in the pub on Christmas Eve, remember,' Iris said, skipping their first meeting when she'd been driving on the wrong side of the road.

Conrad frowned. 'You should know that the gardaí are not welcome at Swan Hall,' he said to her, while Ruairi waved from the Land Rover.

'Oh, but why?' Iris asked.

'They made all sorts of allegations when Nuala drowned,' he said. 'It was upsetting for the family.'

'What sort of allegations?' Iris pushed.

Conrad huffed.

'It's all over and done with now,' he said. 'No need to rake it up. It's just... Well, they're a sly bunch, that's all, not to be trusted.'

Iris didn't quite know what to say in response. Did her uncle want her to turn Ruairi away? Well, she wasn't going to do that! Besides, her uncle's comments had pricked her interest. She was going to ask Ruairi more about these allegations that were made when her Aunt Nuala disappeared in the lake.

'Can you let Aunt Maeve know I'm out for the day?' she said to her uncle.

'Ah sure, she's up in Dublin anyway,' Conrad said grumpily. 'At one of her Youth Defence protests. Left me to get my own dinner.'

Iris had no idea what Youth Defence was, but she was anxious to get going. Besides, her Uncle Conrad turned on his heel, whistling to the dogs before disappearing around the side of the house.

Iris felt a little unsettled by her uncle's words, but she was desperate for a day out, to get away from the oppressive energy of the house. Besides, Ruairi was cute, and she was enjoying the flirtation. Apart from Freddie, who had used her, she hadn't been on a proper date since Berkeley.

'I see Conrad Maguire's in his morning mood,' Ruairi said, grinning at her as she got in the Land Rover, the spaniel jumping into the back as she did so.

'Yes, sorry,' Iris said, not knowing how else to explain her uncle's rudeness. It was best to change the subject. 'What's your dog called?'

'Maisie,' he said. 'And she's a right terror, aren't you, Maisie?'

The spaniel, excited by the sound of her name, jumped back into the front of the Land Rover, her muddy paws landing on Iris's lap as she licked her face.

'Oh, she's so gorgeous.' Iris giggled.

'She's a handful, that's what she is,' Ruairi said, turning the Land Rover and driving them out of Swan Hall. 'I found Maisie just after Mam died. She's a stray. Come on now, Maisie, get in the back.'

'It's okay, I'm happy with her sitting on me.'

Ruairi gave her a sideways glance, warmth in his eyes. 'Grand, so,' he said.

They drove out of the entrance of Swan Hall and onto the main road, heading in the opposite direction to town. The winter sun shimmered on the frosted fields, and there were no other cars on the road.

'It's so peaceful,' Iris commented.

'A bit different from New York, then?'

'Oh yes,' Iris said. 'But sometimes we took a bus upstate to visit friends of my mom near Poughkeepsie. It's very quiet up there, with lots of nature. Sometimes I saw deer.'

'We'll mostly see cows, and sheep, on the way west. But you might catch sight of a fox or a hare, although they are usually burrowed away at this time of year. We also have a lot of badgers, but they're very shy.'

'Oh wow, I'd love to see a real badger,' Iris said. 'It must be so great to live somewhere with so much space, and nature.'

'Yeah, most of the time.' Ruairi paused. 'But it can get lonely. I'd love to go to travelling, especially experience cities like Paris or New York sometime.'

'It can be lonely in a city too.'

'I am sure it can.'

Neither of them spoke for a while, but it was an easy silence. Ruairi turned on the radio, and the news came on. One of the items was about protest marches in Dublin to do with abortion. Two sides were clashing – pro-choice and those against. Iris picked up the name 'Youth Defence', which she remembered her uncle mentioning earlier.

'What's Youth Defence?' Iris asked Ruairi, thinking of her

Aunt Maeve up in Dublin, although after the news report she now had a suspicion.

'They're a pro-life movement,' Ruairi said.

'Anti-abortion? Is it a big deal here?'

'You could say that!' Ruairi whistled. 'A very political hot potato.'

'Abortion is a big deal in the US too,' she said. 'I just thought it was like the UK here and abortion is a private matter for a woman?'

'Not in Ireland,' Ruairi said. 'The right to life of the unborn child is written as equal to the right to life of the mother in the constitution.'

'So does that mean abortion is illegal in Ireland?' Iris asked.

'Yes, it is,' Ruairi said. 'People get very emotional about the whole thing.'

Iris thought about her Aunt Maeve on the pro-life protest up in Dublin. She guessed it wasn't that much of a surprise because she was very religious, but how different she was from Iris's mom and her godmother, Trina, campaigning for women's rights all over the world. Ruairi said no more on the matter, and she sensed he didn't want to. It was, after all, a heavy topic to begin their date with.

As they drove towards the coast, Iris saw the silhouette of a distinctive hill in the distance. It had a dramatic cliff edge with a flat top.

'That's Ben Bulben,' Ruairi explained.

'Are we going to climb it?' Iris said a little nervously, glancing down at her Keds sneakers.

'No, don't worry,' Ruairi reassured her. 'I thought you might like to see the Atlantic Ocean and walk up to Maeve's Cairn. That's a very easy climb.'

'Maeve's Cairn as in my Aunt Maeve?'

'Yes, Maeve was the Queen of Connacht in the old legends of Ireland.'

'I remember now; my mom would read me some of the stories,' Iris said. 'Didn't she start the Cattle Raid of Cooley?'

'That's right, she was the enemy of the King of Ulster and decided to steal his prize bull to show off to her husband.'

Iris remembered her mom telling her the story about Maeve having three husbands, that she was as fierce and proud a queen as any male king.

'It started a whole war – she was a very unpopular queen because of the suffering the people endured under her reign,' Ruairi told her.

The Land Rover spun along the windy coast road. Iris pushed her fingers into Maisie's soft fur as she lay on her lap.

'If you climb to the top of her cairn, there's great views,' Ruairi continued. 'And it's said that she was buried standing up and facing her enemies.'

Ruairi turned off the main road and drove through a small town. Iris saw the name Strandhill on the sign. He rounded a corner and there was the sea. Waves crashed upon the beach as he manoeuvred the Land Rover and parked facing the sea. The sky was filled with furious grey clouds as the ocean rolled upon the shore.

'It's a little windy,' Ruairi commented. 'But I think it's fine to go up the cairn.'

They got out of the Land Rover, and Maisie ran ahead in excitement.

'She's been before; I go here quite often,' he said. 'We have to walk for a while through the sand dunes to get to the walk up the cairn. Is that okay?'

'Oh yeah, sure, it's great to see some of Ireland.'

'Have your aunt and uncle not been showing you around?'

'Not really, Aunt Maeve is so busy with milking the cows, and then looking after the horses, and I am not sure what my uncle does. I guess help my aunt,' Iris said vaguely, remembering her uncle's warning. But she didn't think Ruairi was sly at all. He offered her his hand as they climbed up the cairn and she couldn't imagine Freddie doing such a thoughtful thing. No, he would run up ahead of her, and then shout down that she was a slowpoke when she couldn't keep up with him. But Ruairi matched her pace, and they clambered up the stony cairn together.

At the top, Ruairi kept a hold of her hand. They turned to face the sea. Iris could see the curvature of the ocean against the leaden sky, a white line of light between the dark sky and the stormy sea. As the clouds shifted, sunlight shot out, illuminating patches of the sea.

The wind made it too hard to speak so they stood together in silence, and for a moment all the questions in Iris's head were silent too. She took in the wild western edge of Ireland and felt a deep sense of belonging. *This is where I am from*, a voice said to her. *Here are my roots.* Her mother had never got to go home, nor see the place she loved ever again. Iris felt so sad for her mom and regretted not having asked her to bring her to Ireland. She regretted not having asked her more about what had happened that had made her run away, and more than anything she regretted not having let her mother tell her who her father was.

'Are you okay?' Ruairi asked.

Mortified, Iris realised she was crying. Tears trailed down her cheeks and dripped off her chin.

'Sorry, I was thinking about my mom.'

'Hey, don't be sorry,' Ruairi said. 'I come here to think about my mam too.'

He put his arm around her and before she could stop herself, Iris sobbed into his chest. She felt his other hand upon her head, stroking her hair. He didn't say anything to try to make her feel better because he knew how empty the words would feel. After a while she managed to regain control and pulled back. She took a tissue from her pocket and wiped her eyes.

'I just wish she was here,' she said in a shaky voice.

'It's tough when we feel like our mams went before their time.'

'I feel so guilty all the time,' Iris said.

'About what?'

'I should have listened. Let her talk to me about her past in Ireland. I think she wanted to share it with me, especially about my dad, but I told her I wasn't interested and now I really, really wish we'd had those conversations.'

Ruairi took her hand in his. 'It's so normal to feel guilty when our loved one dies. I feel guilty about my mam.' He paused. 'She always wanted to go to Paris, and my dad hates travelling. I promised I would bring her but I never got around to it.' His voice cracked with emotion and Iris turned to look at him, saw his eyes glazed with tears. 'Then it was too late.'

She squeezed his hand.

'Well now,' Ruairi said, shaking himself. 'Our walk has taken rather a maudlin turn so it has. Come on, let's change it up!'

With Ruairi still holding her hand, they began to run down the shaley hill. She was a little afraid of slipping in her sneakers, but Ruairi held her steady. Maisie ran on ahead and as they gathered speed Iris felt a sense of relief, as if crying out her grief had lifted a weight. They tumbled down the hill together and she found herself laughing, especially at the antics of Maisie running in circles.

They walked along by the sea and Ruairi shared his love of surfing and told her that the beach in Strandhill was one of the best in Europe for surfers.

'Although at this time of year the waves are so huge, it can be very dangerous!'

He also told her how he loved making things out of wood.

'From trees that have already fallen down,' he clarified. 'My friend Ben is a tree surgeon and gives me discarded wood.'

'What do you make?'

'I started small with bird boxes, but last week I just made a coffee table. I find it very relaxing, and it helps me deal with all the feelings... about my mam.'

'Does your father live round here?'

'No, they never station guards where they're from so they're not having to arrest old schoolfriends. I grew up in County Louth in the north-east of Ireland, but my parents were from County Clare in the south-west. I loved going west as a kid, so it was great to get posted to Roscommon – on the way to the west, so to speak.'

Iris looked at Ruairi as they walked along by the sea. The wind swept through his dark hair, and he looked like he belonged by the ocean. She could see him collecting wood and carving it into beautiful things. He didn't belong in a garda uniform.

'And how about you? What are you studying at college?'

'I'm taking an arts degree,' Iris said, omitting the fact she had dropped out. 'At Berkeley in California.'

'That's amazing! Wow,' Ruairi said. 'And what do you want to do afterwards?'

Iris blushed. She had never told anyone her dream, but then Ruairi had shared his love of carpentry with her. Here in this wild and beautiful place with no other people around to compare herself to, it didn't seem so stupid.

'I want to be a writer,' she said.

'What kind of writer?' Ruairi asked, looking really interested.

'Novels,' Iris said simply.

'Have you written a novel?'

Iris thought of the boxes under her desk at home filled with notebooks. She'd tried writing about four different novels and had finished none of them.

'I haven't finished any,' she said.

Ruairi took her hand again. 'But you will, I am sure of it! You're brave to come here and I think you need that kind of courage to do anything artistic.'

It began to rain, a bitter cold wind suddenly sweeping in from the mountains and pushing them towards the sea.

'We'd better get back before we get soaked,' Ruairi said.

'Wait up a minute,' Iris said, opening her purse and pulling out the small pot containing her mom's ashes. It was nestling next to the little glass swan. She took out the pot, and made sure she was standing in the right place. She could feel the wind behind her, urging her. She knew instinctively this was the moment to release her mom. She took the lid off the pot and shook it, and watched as a stream of ashes like a small swarm of grey flecks flew up into the air and dissipated within seconds. Ruairi looked at her, his eyes filled with compassion. He didn't need to say anything.

He took her hand and they ran back to the Land Rover, Maisie bounding ahead of them. They clambered inside the vehicle, soaked through. Iris was shivering with the cold. Ruairi rubbed her hands between his, and before she could think about it, he leaned down and kissed her gently on the lips. He pulled back, looking at her with questioning eyes. She leaned forward and kissed him back. He wrapped his arms around her and they kissed again. Iris felt like she was dropping into a deep well of comfort. Ruairi's kiss was so soft and tender, and so different from Freddie, who would always immediately thrust his tongue in her mouth. Maisie began to bark at them, and she squirmed her way between them, making them fall apart laughing.

'Well, Maisie is having none of it!' Ruairi said, smiling. His cheeks were flushed and the way he was looking into Iris's eyes made her want to throw all her inhibitions away.

But clearly Ruairi was a gentleman, because he put the key in the ignition.

'Come on, let's find a cosy pub and have a bowl of soup. I'm starving,' he said.

'Do you want an apple?' she offered, handing him one of the apples she had picked up in the kitchen at Swan Hall. Part of her was a little piqued they hadn't taken things further, but another part of her was impressed. Ruairi couldn't be more different from Freddie.

'Sure, thanks,' he said, taking the offering of an apple and biting into it, before resting it on the dashboard so he could reverse out of the space.

Iris bit into her own apple, and sweet juice filled her mouth. She stared at the lashing rain, driving in across the ocean, but in the distance she could see a streak of golden light as the sun strove to reclaim the winter sky. It was the best she had felt for a long time.

CHAPTER TWENTY

NUALA

25 AUGUST 1972

Of course, we won our category! The Kelly sisters – Aisling, Maeve and Nuala – reigned supreme!

But best of all, I came first in Gaelic singing with 'Mná na hÉireann'. Maybe what happened with C and the fact my heart has been broken infused my voice with even more feeling. I think so, dear diary, I do, for even I wanted to bawl with the emotion of it. Afterwards, I felt depleted, like an empty shell. To my surprise, Aisling appeared by my side. She handed me a glass of Coke. It was warm, and slightly flat, but sugary enough to pick me up.

'Are you okay?' she asked.

I nodded. I wanted so badly to tell her about my secret love affair, but could I trust her? I wanted to tell her that I had seen Maeve kissing Conrad in the alley, but it would only make matters worse between her and Maeve. How could two sisters be so different? I thought again of the old folk song – the 'Binnorie' – about the fair sister and the dark sister. Aisling was the fair one, although older, and Maeve the dark, and I guess Conrad was sweet William. Would they tear each other apart over him? Which one of them would drown and then turn into a swan? It all felt a bit sinister, especially because of our home – Swan Hall – and its situation, right on the edge of a lake.

'You look very pale,' Aisling commented. 'Do you want to get some air?'

I looked at her and she was all fuzzy. The air was thick between us, and I was hot and sweaty, and yet a chill ran down my spine. A memory of my mam came to me. I imagined her in Aisling's place, proud of my achievement. Aisling was so like her – a tall young woman with long fair hair in a red dress. I saw her standing by the side of the lake. But unlike Aisling, my mam was shouting at me.

'Leave me alone, Nuala,' she said, and her eyes were filled with tears.

I had yellow and purple irises in my hands and I was thrusting them at her, but my mam snatched them and threw them onto the muddy bank.

'Go away,' she said.

The clouds rolled in over the lake, and the water slapped against the stony shore as if to banish me. My mother was up to her ankles in the cold water and she looked at me as if I was the source of all her sorrows. And so I did go away. My ten-year-old self ran all the way back to Swan Hall, angry and hurt.

'What is it, Nuala?' my sister Aisling said to me now, echoing the same words she'd said all those years ago as I came panting through the back door, tears stinging my eyes.

I reached out and grabbed Aisling's hand in mine. Her fingers were cool to my touch.

'Why did she do it?' I whispered, looking into her eyes.

She jerked her hands away, flinching as if I had hit her. Knowing exactly what I was talking about.

'Stop it, Nuala,' she hissed.

'But why? What did we do?'

I remember Aisling looking out of the window that dark afternoon in Swan Hall. Her hand to her mouth, a small shocked 'Oh,' and then she was running out the door. I watched her from the open doorway of Swan Hall, running through the wet grass, falling, getting up again, and running to the lake. I heard her screaming, 'Mammy, no!' But her voice was drowning in the summer storm as the clouds burst and torrential rain fell. I saw a flash of red and then nothing.

'Why do you have to bring Mammy into everything?' Aisling turned on me. 'Can you not just let her go?'

'Of course not! She was our mother, Aisling. Don't you miss her?'

Aisling looked at me, incredulous. 'We can't talk about this here, Nuala.'

'But don't you?' I pushed.

'How can you say such a thing to me?' she said. 'You don't remember what it was like... You were too young...'

'But why? What do you mean?'

She cut over me.

'We were too much for her, Nuala.' Her eyes hardened. '*You* were too much for her.'

She swung around, leaving me gasping, the warm glass of Coke shaking in my hand.

I don't understand Aisling. One moment kindness, the next cruelty. At least Maeve is consistently mean.

She stalked off and I drank down the glass of Coke as deep-seated rage at my eldest sister took root within me. I wished Trina were there. She was the only one who loved me, and I wanted to be gone from this desperate island, far, far away from my miserable family. My heart ached for freedom.

I wandered outside the town hall where the competitions

were being held, and into the sunshine. The streets of Listowel were packed. On every corner was a musician, as well as little stages with small groups playing instruments. There at the end of the street was a small crowd, and as I pushed through it, I saw Conrad playing his bodhrán. His head was bent over the small drum, his long red hair concealing his face as his hand gripped the bodhrán stick, beating fast upon its surface. Of course, my sister Maeve was by his side, placing her fiddle under her chin. She was watching Conrad for a sign, a way into the music. But he kept on playing his own tune, and she was left waiting, until at last he paused, and looked up at her. I searched the expression on his face. Was he in love with her? I couldn't see it. But Maeve – it was clear she was enthralled with him. My heart sank.

I watched them play for a while, and then I got fed up waiting for them to finish. Conrad was lapping up all the attention. I started walking back towards the campsite. On the way, I passed Aisling in a telephone box. She was thrusting coins into the machine and had a desperate look on her face. I wondered who she was calling from a phone box that she couldn't call once we got back home. She didn't see me, and the last thing I wanted was her accusing me of spying, so I kept on going. On the way, I stopped at a shop and bought a postcard with a picture of Listowel's church and town square on the front and a packet of Tayto crisps.

Back at the campsite, I sat down and wrote Trina a postcard as I munched through my crisps.

Wish you were here! It's weird without you. Did you get my letter? I have to get out of HERE! Tell me about New York. Love Nuala.

I began packing up the tent. We had to get back that night because Aisling was working in the shop the next day and I had a shift in the restaurant. I was nearly done when Maeve arrived back.

'Where's Conrad?' I asked. 'I saw you playing together.'

'Did you?' Maeve said. Her cheeks were flushed and I had never seen her look so happy. 'It was so great,' she said.

'Be careful, Maeve,' I said in a low voice.

She flushed even deeper. 'What do you mean?' she said, not meeting my eye.

'I saw you and Conrad last night.'

'You're such a sneak, Nuala,' she said haughtily.

'All I am saying is Conrad Maguire is not to be trusted. I mean, he was going out with Aisling only a few weeks ago.'

'She's not interested in him any more,' Maeve said defensively.

'And...' I stammered, not quite sure if I should tell her or if she would believe me. 'Only ten days ago he professed undying love to me and wanted to marry me.'

Maeve burst out laughing. 'Ah for God's sake, Nuala, you're pathetic. Just because you fancy him too and can't stand for me to have something you want—'

'No, that's not...'

But I couldn't finish my sentence because Aisling had turned up.

'What are you two talking about?' she asked.

'Nothing,' I mumbled.

'Where's Conrad?'

'He was meeting with some friends from Belfast,' Maeve said.

'Typical of him not to help pack up. Lazy bastard,' Aisling commented.

Maeve looked over at me as if to say – *See, I told you Aisling is not into him.*

But I knew that already. It was more the worry of Conrad Maguire thinking he *could* court the three of us. What was he playing at? And even though Maeve could be a bitch, she was my sister. I didn't want any boy to make a fool of her.

Though there was also another voice in my head saying, *What do you care, Nuala Kelly? You're out of here soon and you're never coming back. Leave them to their secrets and lies.*

CHAPTER TWENTY-ONE

IRIS

31 DECEMBER 1991

Nothing about the memorial gave a sense of her mom. But Iris tried not to let it bother her. It was for her Aunt Maeve, and anyone else in the community who had known her. To her surprise, the church was packed. A sea of faces looking at her, scrutinising her grief, while she didn't have an idea who any of them were. Ruairi had apologised, telling her he was on duty and although she'd only known him a week, she missed his grounding presence. Father Francis was clearly in his element. Iris tried not to listen to his sermon because when she did, she found it offensive. He painted a picture of her mom as a victim with a sad life, running away from home and never making it back. It wasn't true! He glanced at Iris when he mentioned praying for her daughter, and she could see what he was thinking in his head – *Illegitimate bastard who ruined her mother's life.* Everyone was staring at her, and she could hear the whispers again...

Sure she's the spit of Nuala. Nuala who? Sure, don't you remember the third sister? Drowned in the lake just like her mother, nearly twenty years ago. Ah God, guess it broke poor old Gabriel's heart. Sure, glad he's not alive to see another child gone.

It made her feel sick, and now she wished she'd put her foot down and told her Aunt Maeve no about the memorial. She was ashamed of herself for not standing up and giving a eulogy. She should be telling the whole town what an amazing mother she had had. How she had worked hard and given Iris the best start in life, and that it was only Iris who had screwed it up now. Nothing to do with her brilliant mother, who had always believed in her. But she didn't have the courage to leave the pew or go up and speak, and the priest hadn't even asked her if she wanted to say the eulogy. Aunt Maeve hadn't offered to, nor her Uncle Conrad, and so it was up to Father Francis to speak about her mother as if she was a charity case. Nausea swept through Iris and she wanted to run out of the church, keep going all the way out of this dark, gossipy town and back to the big city of New York where she could be anonymous again.

She wondered: was one of the men in the congregation in fact her father? If it wasn't her Uncle Conrad, then who else could it be? Reading Nuala's diary, she'd had a sense her mom was involved with someone other than Conrad – because who had she been calling from the telephone box in Listowel?

Again, she was coerced into taking communion, and afterwards as she knelt down in her pew, she watched the rest of the congregation going up to take the host. She examined each of the men. Was one of them her secret father? Did he even know?

At last, the masquerade of a memorial was over, and they were released into the wet windy day to walk up the town to Creighton's for soup and sandwiches. She was forced to sit at a corner table with her Aunt Maeve on one side, her Uncle Conrad on the other, and Father Francis opposite her. She was hemmed in on all sides, and the pub was hot and smoky. She and her aunt had glasses of lemonade, while Conrad and the priest were digging into pints of Guinness. The girl behind the bar brought over platters of sandwiches, and Iris recognized her as Lizzie, who she'd met walking on Christmas Day. Lizzie gave her a sympathetic smile as she put the platters down on the table. Iris ate a couple of sandwiches, and then made her excuses to go to the restrooms. Next to the Ladies', there was a back door out of the pub and she went outside. It was spitting rain and freezing, but she didn't care.

'Oh, hi there.'

Iris turned around to see Lizzie standing behind her, leaning against the pub wall smoking a cigarette.

'Want one?' she offered.

Iris nodded, taking the cigarette between her fingers.

'How was the memorial?' Lizzie asked, handing Iris her lighter.

'Bad,' Iris said, taking a drag. 'The whole town showed up and I don't know anyone.'

'Sorry I didn't come,' Lizzie said. 'Me and my dad don't go to church. We're not Catholic,' she clarified. 'And even if I were, I wouldn't want to listen to that old pervert priest.' She sighed. 'The town is rife with rumours about him, and teenage girls in the confessional box. I don't know how he gets away with it.'

'Oh God, that's gross,' Iris said. 'I don't think I can look at him if that's true.'

'It could just be rumours!' Lizzie said. 'Sorry, I didn't mean to freak you out.'

They smoked in silence, and Iris felt Lizzie scrutinising her.

'So, how old are you?' Lizzie asked at last.

'Eighteen. And you?'

'Just seventeen. Last year in school. Once I'm done, we're moving back to Germany. Though I'd like to go to college in London. Have you been to London?'

'No, this is my first time in Europe.'

They smoked in silence again. Iris felt the shadow of a bird pass overhead. She looked up at the rain-speckled sky and saw a large black crow swooping above.

'Looking for scraps,' Lizzie said. She put out her cigarette. 'I'd better go back in.' She turned, and then paused on the threshold. 'Wait here a second,' she said, rushing in the door.

Iris stood uncertainly, smoking the rest of her cigarette. Lizzie re-emerged with a napkin and handed it to Iris. On it was her name and number, written in biro.

'That's the number in our cottage. We live on the other side of the woods where we met. My dad's still away, so you know, if you want to come over any time, you're welcome,' she offered.

'Oh, that's real nice,' Iris said. 'But I'm leaving in a couple of days.'

'Yeah, no problem,' Lizzie said, blushing, and Iris felt a little bad. It had been so generous of her to offer.

'But you know, I am sure I have time to visit before I leave,' she added.

Lizzie smiled at her. Iris felt a genuine connection with this girl, and she wondered if they might become friends. She'd always found it hard to make friends. Riley back at Berkeley had always been more of a roommate. They'd had fun together for sure, and they'd had some heart-to-hearts, but Iris hadn't heard from Riley since she'd told her to get a new roommate. It had been a fleeting kind of friendship.

'And you know, you don't even have to ring. If things get too much at Swan Hall, just come on over. All you need to do is go through the woods, and my house is the first stone cottage you come to. Blue door.'

'Lizzie, where are you?' a man called from inside the pub.

'Okay, duty calls, pints need filling,' Lizzie said, giving her a last smile. 'So I mean it, just come over,' she said, patting Iris's arm.

Lizzie went back inside and Iris shoved the napkin in her

pocket. There was something about Lizzie. A natural warmth, an openness which reminded her of her godmother, Trina.

Back inside the pub, her Uncle Conrad was playing his bodhrán, joined by a fiddler and another man on a tin whistle. Her Aunt Maeve sat poker straight watching the music. Iris remembered listening to the three sisters on the tape in her mother's old tape deck. She sat down next to her, and something about the tortured expression, the longing on her Aunt Maeve's face, made her feel sorry for her.

'Do you still play the violin?' she found herself asking.

'No,' Maeve snapped.

'Oh, sorry,' Iris said, a little hurt by her tone.

'Sorry,' Maeve said, gathering herself. 'But we stopped playing music when Nuala died. Well, that is, Aisling and I stopped.'

Iris remembered the day her mother had played the piano at the Monettis' when Iris had been about twelve. How she had danced and danced around the big apartment in her socks, slipping and sliding on the floor she and her mom had just polished. She remembered the tears glistening in her mother's eyes, and now she understood. It must have been the first time she had played the piano since her sister had died, and how like her Iris must have looked.

'Conrad did the opposite.' Maeve's voice was laden with sarcasm. 'He can't stop playing. He can't stop drinking. All in all, he just can't stop himself.'

CHAPTER TWENTY-TWO

NUALA

31 AUGUST 1972

I have to get out of here, now. The shit has hit the fan! I'm up in my bedroom and I've put a chair up against the door, but Daddy could break that down easily. I can hear him ranting and raving downstairs, and Maeve trying to calm him down, but sure she stoked his fire in the first place because she told him about C! I don't know where Aisling is and I really wish she was here because she would have stood up for me.

I said to Daddy – 'What does it matter now? It's all over with.'

But he was as if possessed.

'You're unnatural,' he said. 'It's a sin and damnable to Hell.'

'I'd rather be off to Hell, than anywhere near your bigoted Heaven,' I said, losing my temper. 'Besides, who says it's true anyway?' I challenged him.

'You disgust me,' he hissed, not answering my question. 'I always knew Catrina Finlay was depraved and now I'm proven right.'

I tried a different tack.

'It's just stupid gossip, Daddy,' I said to him. 'Trina and I are friends, that's all.'

'You were seen,' he hissed. 'The two of you cavorting together, naked, doing things to each other!'

He roared. For a moment his outrage made me want to laugh, but I kept silent, looking down at the ground. I felt Maeve's judgemental gaze upon me. Had she told Daddy in revenge for my warning against Conrad?

My father towered over me.

'Father Francis has promised to take you under his wing. You're to visit him in the morning, make your confession and ask for penance.'

I couldn't help but snort.

'No way,' I protested, because everyone knew about Father Fuck Off and his confessional box groping. He liked to sit face-to-face, no antiquated talking through the grille, but a nice cosy spilling of all the beans between priest and penitent. When you did something especially sinful, he always put his hand on your knee to console you.

'You will do as you're told,' my father bellowed. 'Moreover, I am sending you to Sacred Heart convent boarding school next year.'

'Well, Daddy, if you want to fuel my lesbian tendencies that's one sure-fire way to do it,' I gave back cheek.

My father swung his arm and slapped me hard across the face. He wasn't even drunk, but God he was in a foul humour. I staggered back, my ears ringing.

'Daddy!' Maeve gasped. 'I am sure Nuala was led astray by Catrina and will never do it again – promise, Nuala?'

I didn't want her trying to help because I despised Maeve for pandering to my father and telling on me in the first place.

'I will promise no such thing. I have every intention of fulfilling my destiny as a dyke!'

Maeve winced. 'Nuala, please!'

My father came and shook my shoulders. 'You're corrupt through and through, just like your whore of a mother.'

His words ignited me, and I wriggled free, before punching him in the belly. My father doubled over in shock. Maeve came between us.

'Nuala, dear God, stop it now,' she said. 'You've done enough. Apologise to Daddy.'

'I will not,' I seethed. 'Just stay out of it, you two-faced bitch. You're up to as much sin as me...'

She went very still then, and shook her head at me, her eyes pleading.

But I was on fire, and I wanted to destroy everything around me.

'Your darling Maeve is at it too, Daddy! I saw her and Conrad Maguire together, doing *it*!' I lied, because maybe they had fucked anyway and Conrad Maguire was the son of Daddy's best friend and crony Peadar Maguire. I wanted to hurt Daddy as much as he had hurt me.

My father straightened up and looked at Maeve, who was frozen to the spot in horror, and then turned to me.

'Is this true, Maeve?'

'I... Conrad and I are in love...' she squeaked. 'Nothing has happened. Nuala is lying.'

Our father lashed out and slapped Maeve on the cheek.

'Daddy!' she cried out in shock, tears filling her eyes.

I thought it would make me feel better to see my father hit Maeve for once but it didn't. Nor did it deflect his rage from me.

'The shame!' he roared. 'The two of you are sinful girls.'

'But it's Aisling who's staying out all night, it's not me, Daddy, no, I promise, Conrad and I are chaste,' Maeve sobbed through her tears.

I shook my head at my sister in disgust. Why did she have to say stupid lies about Aisling? Daddy was hard enough on her.

'You're such a rat, Maeve,' I hissed at her.

'At least your sister shows some repentance but you, girl, you're an evil, twisted thing expelled from your witch of a mother,' my father rounded on me. 'I wish you'd never been born.'

'So do I!' I yelled back and I meant it.

I walked, head held high, out of the room, not caring if he hit Maeve again. Let her take it because she deserved it after betraying Aisling.

But now an hour later I am sitting on my bed, and I feel bad. I shouldn't have landed Maeve in the same trouble as me. She would never have told Daddy about Aisling if I hadn't said about her and Conrad. What will happen to Aisling when she gets back? What will Daddy do to her? It's unlikely he won't believe Maeve because Daddy hates women, and always thinks the worst of us. The man is cursed with three daughters and though he tries to make Maeve as much like a son as he can, our gender taunts him. We exist to hurt him. That's what my daddy thinks. He can never forgive our mother for leaving him. He takes it as a betrayal. She was supposed to stand by his side through thick and thin. Give him sons, cook for him, clean for him, and be his loyal, submissive wife. A good Irish Catholic woman covering her golden tresses with a black lace headscarf for Mass. But Mammy wasn't like that. She needed to dance. He knew that when he married her so why did he try to cage her in Swan Hall?

I took out my tape deck and put on Tami Lynn singing 'I'm Gonna Run Away from You', which usually makes me feel better. I sat on my bed and I drew up my knees. Tami Lynn was not making me feel better at all and in fact I began to shake after the shock of the argument, and my father's rage. Then I let myself cry where no one could see me. I cried for my lost mother, how lonely she must have been, I cried for my poor sisters, and I even cried for my father, because he hasn't always been this way. Not when we were little. We were the apples of his eye. It wasn't a dream, it was real that the furious bull of a man downstairs was once a gentle giant letting us clamber all over him, and giving our mam a rest while he took all three of us fishing on the lake. What happened to him? The tears have soaked my shirt, and I can't stop shaking, and I can't stop crying because most of all I am crying for myself, dear diary. I know the time has come. I have to leave before my tears drown me and I will be lost just like my mother before me.

CHAPTER TWENTY-THREE

IRIS

31 DECEMBER 1991

Last New Year's Eve, Iris and her mom had celebrated with takeout – Chinese noodles and fortune cookies – and bottles of beer. They had clinked bottles at the stroke of midnight, watching the Times Square buzz on the TV. By half twelve they had both gone to bed. Her mom was always so tired. But Iris's New Year's Eve hadn't ended then. As soon as she'd sensed her mom had dropped off to sleep, she'd slipped out of the apartment. Managing to grab a taxi by a miracle, she had gone to the club in SoHo where Freddie had said he'd be with his friends. He had wanted her to be with him on New Year's Eve – well, the early hours of New Year's Day – and she had gone running, like the fool she was. But it had been a good night. They'd drunk margaritas and danced and danced until she'd felt like her feet would fall off. At some point in the night, Freddie had followed her into the girls' restroom and they had fucked. Despite the fact she had just told him her New Year's resolution was to give him up.

Praying that her mom didn't hear her, she'd snuck back into the apartment at around 4 a.m. and collapsed in her bed, her body humming from the drinking, the dancing and the sex. She felt guilty about deceiving her mom. It wasn't even that her mom didn't allow her to have boyfriends over. When she'd been dating Freddie, he'd stayed over all the time. But they'd broken up, and she had cried all over her mom about how he'd cheated on her. The truth was, she'd been embarrassed that she'd let him into her life again. Ashamed that her mom would be disappointed in her daughter and think she was weak. Why couldn't she resist Freddie? There was something about him, or something he did to her, which made her fall for his lies every time.

No more: she had finally got free of Freddie and her mom would be glad, Iris thought now, as she sat at the dinner table with her aunt and uncle over the New Year's Eve dinner. To her surprise, Conrad had cooked: Beef Wellington with a rich gravy, roast potatoes and carrots. She had been touched by the effort he had gone to and it was one of the best pastries she'd ever eaten.

'This is delicious, real good,' she enthused, as her Uncle Conrad filled his and her wine glasses to the brim. Maeve sipped on her glass of water.

'I have many hidden talents, don't I, Maeve?' Conrad said, winking at his wife, as he knocked back his glass of wine in one and refilled it immediately.

Maeve looked unamused as she speared one of her potatoes with a fork.

'It's been so wonderful getting to know you, Iris,' Conrad enthused. 'About time, eh?'

Maeve looked pained because he didn't have to say the words. It had taken the death of Iris's mother for her relatives to reach out to her. They were such a strange couple, Maeve and Conrad. Her aunt was so reserved, and seemingly moral, with her church-going and anti-abortion marches, whereas her uncle appeared to be rather a free spirit, playing impromptu sessions in the pub, and drinking too much. There was also the mystery of those shifty-looking men he had been talking with in the pub on Christmas Eve and after Mass on Sunday.

'When did you want to head home, Iris?' Maeve asked her. 'We only booked the ticket over, because we want to offer you the opportunity to stay with us as long as you like. We don't want you to feel forced to leave. That's why we haven't booked the return ticket yet.'

'Oh, you haven't?' Iris asked, confused. She had assumed she was going home in a couple of days. She thought that was what she'd told her aunt when she'd arranged the plane ticket.

'She'll have to go when the next semester starts up at Berkeley,' Conrad said. 'When's that now, Iris?'

'I can't remember, exactly,' she said vaguely.

'How do you feel about staying a little longer, until the semester starts?' Maeve asked her.

'Yes, it's great to have some young energy about the place,' Conrad said, winking at her again.

Iris took a sip of her wine. She wasn't sure if she wanted to stay, but then the idea of seeing Ruairi again flickered in her mind. She really liked him. And she thought he liked her too. Although she wasn't sure, because he hadn't come on too strong. Was that good? If she played hard to get, would he like her more?

'Maybe,' Iris said, a little uncertainly.

'I could show you a little more of the farm, explain what I do.' Maeve paused. 'Because of course, after me and Conrad are gone, this place will be yours.'

'Mine!' Iris exclaimed in astonishment. It hadn't even occurred to her.

'Well now, don't be getting any ideas and knocking us off!'

Conrad joked, pouring more wine into their glasses, and then filling one for his wife. It sploshed over the edge of the glass, staining the linen tablecloth.

'I don't want any, Conrad,' Maeve said in an acid voice.

'Of course you don't, darling,' he said evenly, raising his glass to Iris. 'To the heiress of Swan Hall!'

It sounded so far-fetched, as if she were a character in an Irish version of *The Great Gatsby*, that Iris found herself giggling as she joined him in the toast, lifting her glass and taking a big gulp of wine. Her Aunt Maeve frowned.

'Be careful you don't drink too much, Iris.'

Her aunt's words annoyed her and her giggles dissipated. She wasn't a child any more; besides, Maeve wasn't her mom. She was also annoyed Maeve hadn't booked her flight home, plus she was thrown by the knowledge that one day this big spooky house would be hers. All the land, and the woods the other side of the lake. She didn't want it. Not any of it. She would exchange all of it for five more minutes with her mom. What she wanted was for her aunt to talk to her, and let her in. But the woman was so buttoned up, it was impossible to break through. She had seen glimmers the day they had gone horse riding, but since her mom's memorial, her aunt had been even more distant and preoccupied.

Aunt Maeve got up, screeching back her chair.

'I'm going to bed. I have to get up early to do the milking. I could do with some help, Conrad?'

'I think you're quite capable on your own, darling, I mean it's New Year's Eve after all,' Conrad said, rolling his eyes at Iris. 'It's not even midnight yet – are you not going to see the New Year in with your husband and your niece?'

Maeve glanced at Iris. 'Do you mind if I go to bed, Iris?'

'No,' Iris said, although she was a little disappointed. She wanted just one night with her aunt when she might let her hair down, tell her more about her mom when she was younger, but it seemed the only person who wanted to hang out with her was her drunk uncle. She wished that Ruairi wasn't on duty and she might have an excuse to go into town to the pub. But her Uncle Conrad didn't want to go out, and besides they had both drunk too much to drive.

Iris and Conrad moved into the sitting room, where the dogs were lying in front of the fire. Conrad threw on more wood, giving it a poke, before ambling over to the drinks cabinet and drawing out a bottle of whiskey.

'Seeing as it's New Year's Eve, we should see in the New Year in style. I've been saving this bottle of malt for a special occasion. Got it in Scotland when I was over visiting friends for a Celtic match a few years back.'

He brought the bottle over to the coffee table and then gathered a couple of tumblers from the cabinet.

'Are you happy to drink it neat? I've no mixer.'

'Ah yes, sure,' Iris said.

She had never had much tolerance for hard liquor. But it was New Year's Eve and the next year – 1992 – would be the first she had to face without her mom. She wanted to dull the edge of the grief inside her, even if it was just for one night.

They drank the whole bottle between them. Conrad turned on the radio and they danced around the sitting room to old rock music from the Seventies – the Rolling Stones, T. Rex and Led Zeppelin. Her uncle was fun and he didn't care what she thought of him, so she didn't care what he thought of her either. They jumped around making silly faces, and she found herself laughing. It was as if he understood how it felt to lose someone you really loved. Of course he did. Because she was reading Nuala's diary, and Conrad had told Nuala he was in love with her.

The grandfather clock in the hall struck midnight at the same time as the DJ on the radio called it. Uncle Conrad and Iris crossed arms and held hands, singing along to 'Auld Lang Syne'.

They collapsed on the couch. Iris's head was swimming. Her uncle handed her another glass of Scotch. She nursed it while watching Conrad pull out his guitar.

'I've a song for you,' he said, tuning the guitar as he spoke. 'I wrote it myself.'

Iris couldn't believe he was able to still play the guitar, he was so drunk.

'It's called "The Golden Girl", just like you!' he slurred. 'Just like you, Nuala,' he said.

'It's Iris...'

But he wasn't listening to her. He'd gone into his own world as he began playing:

'Come winter there's two swans drifting on the lake
Together, then apart.
Weaving in between the icy eddies, nesting and
departing
Wings spread wide as they take flight.
Come summer there's two souls floating on the water
Me and the girl of my dreams.
She is the golden hour of the day
Golden hair falling into my open palms
We are in love, oh, our hearts beat together
The clock ticks, the days lengthen,
The clock ticks, the days shorten,
And the long hot summer is over.'

He continued to sing. It was sad ballad, a doomed love story about a fairy girl with golden hair and a boy from the real world who could only be together one summer on the lake, and in the winter they turned into swans. Conrad sang with such feeling and Iris felt tears fill her eyes. She could feel how deeply he must have loved Nuala – but she hadn't loved him back, that much was clear from her diary, and that was sad. Was it why he'd married her sister?

Finally, the song came to an end, and Conrad sat back, with the guitar resting on his lap, his eyes closed. Iris wasn't sure if he'd fallen asleep. She should get up, go to bed, but she feared she wasn't able to stand up or walk straight. She hauled herself up from the couch, lurching forwards before righting herself. Everything was spinning, but she managed to stagger towards the door. All she wanted to do now was collapse on her bed. As she passed Conrad, his arm shot out and he grabbed her hand. She gave a little scream of surprise. She had thought he'd passed out. But when she looked at him, his eyes were open, and he was gazing at her with a begging expression.

'Please, Nuala, please,' he whimpered.

'It's me, Uncle Conrad, I'm Iris, not Nuala,' she said shakily.

He tugged on her, and she lost her balance, falling backwards, knocking his guitar to the floor and landing on the couch on top of him. Before she knew it, her uncle's hands were on her, touching her breasts as he moaned, 'Nuala...'

'No!' She pushed him away and tumbled off the couch. Her situation making her suddenly sober, she ran out of the room, stumbling down the hall and up the stairs to her mom's bedroom. Once inside, she pulled a chair in front of the door, knowing in her heart that her uncle didn't have the capability to get up the stairs, let alone accost her in her bedroom. But she was freaked out. He had been touching her up, thinking she was Nuala. She opened the door to the wardrobe and looked in the mirror. She stared at her reflection, and everything seemed hazy. She did look different, not herself. The air felt thick all around her and she shivered, feeling that oppressive weight upon her shoulders she'd felt the other day.

She fell into bed, dragging the covers over her head, and closed her eyes. But she couldn't sleep. Her head was a mess, and she could hear Nuala's voice from her diary, clear as a bell. She was singing, and it wasn't a lullaby. It was a call for help.

CHAPTER TWENTY-FOUR

NUALA

31 AUGUST 1972

Once I heard Daddy drive off to meet up with Peadar Maguire and his cronies in Flanagan's pub, I escaped down to the lake, weaving through the long coarse grasses as they scratched my skin. The sunset was a ball of fire in the seamless blue sky. The moorhens and coots paddled in the brackish water, insects buzzed and whirred around me, and I felt such a deep longing for rain.

When will this long summer end? But then, do I really want it to be over? Because all my money is gone, and it looks like I am going to be sent to a convent boarding school to turn me straight. I HAVE to get to America because now it's all out in the open I want to be with C, with Trina, with Catrina. I love her. I do. So think, Nuala, think. How can you get the money together for the ticket?

I was sitting in the cracked reed beds, hiding among the stalks of reeds, when I saw Conrad strolling along the edge of the shore, guitar slung over his shoulder. He is good-looking, granted, the way his long red hair falls just below his shoulders, his brown eyes big puppy-dog pools of 'save me'. Well, he's pulled on the heartstrings of both my sisters so effectively with his tortured soul routine. It doesn't fool me! As you know, dear diary, Conrad is not my type.

He sat down on a rock by the lake and began to play the guitar, his hair cascading over his face. I watched his fingers moving along the fretboard with agility. It was a beautiful ballad that he'd clearly written himself about two swans taking flight from the lake, and summertime, and being in love with a girl with golden hair.

It was a love song, of course, and as he sang it really did sound as if he was completely in love with the girl in the song. But who was she, this girl with golden hair? Maeve had brown hair. Was he singing about Aisling? Or worse – was it me?

I emerged from my hiding place, and Conrad started in surprise, immediately stopping playing. He stared at me as I walked over towards him. I drew strength from my feet, firmly rooted on the earth, the lap of the water behind me, and the sinking sun illuminating my path towards him. I was angry.

'Nuala,' he said in a soft voice, his brown eyes entreating. But they didn't work on me as they did on my sisters. I stood over him, hands on hips.

'Did you write that song, Conrad Maguire?'

He nodded, looking at me as if in awe – what a loser!

'Who is the song about?' I demanded. 'Because last thing I knew, you were going out with Maeve and she has *brown* hair.'

At least he blushed; at least he looked a little chastised.

'Ah no, that was just a kiss at the Fleadh, I'm not into Maeve.'

'But she is crazy about you, Conrad Maguire, so what are you going to do about that?'

'Oh,' he said, looking nervous.

'Is the song about Aisling?' I continued. 'Because you've screwed her around enough…'

'Course not, sure everyone knows Aisling's seeing Stefan, that is apart from you and Maeve!'

'Stefan?' I repeated, feeling a blush creeping across my face, and remembering Maeve had told our father Aisling was out every night. 'Stefan who works in Lough Bawn Forest Park restaurant with me?'

'That's the one,' Conrad said, looking a little pleased with himself, as it was obvious I had no idea.

Now it made total sense. I had seen Stefan enough times going into Aisling's shop and chatting with her; I had just been too wrapped up in my own world to notice their friendship was more than platonic.

'The song is about you, Nuala,' Conrad said in a quiet voice. I shook my head.

'Why would you write a song about me?' I blurted out.

'Because you're so beautiful, Nuala. I told you before, I'm mad about you...' He stood up, placing his guitar to one side.

'Stop it now, Conrad, just stop it.' I sighed in frustration. 'I've no interest in you, and even if I had, I'd never do that to Maeve.'

'She doesn't own me,' he said crossly. 'She keeps following me about – I didn't ask her to.'

'And she made you kiss her, right?' I said in a sarcastic voice.

'Well, kind of, you know... I closed my eyes and thought of you.'

'That's disgusting,' I said, furious. 'Conrad, will you not get it into your thick skull that I'm in love with someone else!'

Conrad bristled. 'Who?' he snapped.

'Sure you'll hear it soon enough when my dad confides in your father,' I told him. 'It's Trina, I'm in love with her.'

Conrad looked confused. 'But she's a girl!'

'Yes that's right, ten out of ten for observation.'

He took a step towards me, shaking his head. 'But you can't be into Trina, you're making it up. I've seen the way you look at me sometimes, Nuala. Don't deny you were flirting with me at Listowel? I only got off with Maeve to get you jealous!'

'Christ, Conrad, you're unbelievable!' I said, exasperated.

'I can't stop thinking about how it would feel to kiss you,' he said. And then, taking me off guard, he pulled me towards him and kissed me on the lips. I jerked my head back and pushed him away. Too late, for behind Conrad, to my horror, I saw the back of Maeve, running into the woods. Oh fuck! Had she been watching all this time? What had she heard us say?

Conrad was staggering backwards, a stupid grin on his face.

'Go after her!' I told him, pointing at Maeve as she disappeared into the trees.

'You felt something, didn't you?' he asked, triumphant.

'No, Conrad, no I didn't. I don't fancy you, right? Now, go after my sister! She clearly saw you kissing me and has the wrong idea.'

I turned on my heel and ran back to the house, wiping the taste of Conrad Maguire from my lips with the back of my hand.

The air feels heavy and loaded, and my skin is itchy, which always happens when a storm is on the way. I long for release from the pressure building up in the land around us. It is so humid and oppressive, I crave to be able to stand in the downpour of rain and wash away all the secrets and lies in my family. I long to be borne away by the storm. I have to get away. But how?

CHAPTER TWENTY-FIVE

IRIS

Iris just made it in time to the bathroom before she emptied the contents of her stomach into the toilet. There wasn't much left at this stage. She had spent the whole of yesterday – New Year's Day – either in bed or throwing up in the bathroom. By midday, her Aunt Maeve had knocked on the door.

'Iris, can I come in?'

'Yes,' she'd croaked, shivering under the bed covers.

Her aunt stood over her, shadowy in the dim room.

'Are you okay?' she asked.

'I think I have a stomach bug,' Iris said weakly.

'Mmm,' Maeve responded, her eyes creasing in mild amusement. 'I believe it's more likely Conrad persuaded you to drink too much last night.' She gazed down at Iris in sympathy. 'Years ago, I tried to keep up with his drinking. It didn't do me much good, and when Daddy died I stopped drinking altogether.' She patted the bedclothes. 'I did try to warn you to be careful. My husband is always on the lookout for a drinking pal.'

Iris winced at the memory of what had happened last night.

Had she led her uncle on? Was it her fault that he'd tried to touch her up? Oh God, it was mortifying.

'I'll bring you up some tea and toast; that will make you feel better,' Maeve offered.

When she came back with the breakfast, Maeve sat on the end of Iris's bed while she nibbled on the toast. It did in fact make her feel a whole lot better, and she gratefully drank all the tea. Her throat was so dry. Maeve had also brought up a jug of water and a glass.

'Make sure to drink all of this; you'll feel better,' she said. 'As I said, I used to drink an awful lot too, but I saw what it did to my father, and my husband, so that's why I promised my father I would stop.'

'I'm sorry,' Iris mumbled. 'I didn't mean to drink so much...'

'I don't blame you. I should have stayed up, kept an eye on Conrad.'

If only she had, Iris couldn't help thinking. The night had got chaotic. Her head still felt a mess.

'Well, I did want to show you around the estate,' Maeve said. 'Maybe we should wait until tomorrow to do that?'

'Right,' Iris said. 'Yes, sure.'

She remembered now what Maeve had said to her last night. One day she would inherit this house, the farm and all the land. What would her mother think of that? All the years of scrimping and saving. But the inheritance felt like a weight hanging over Iris. She wasn't sure she ever wanted to come back to the heavy presence of the house, the gloomy lake and dark woods ever again, let alone live here one day. *Just sell it, Iris*, a voice inside her counselled. But that seemed like the ultimate betrayal to her mom and her mom's sisters.

After her Aunt Maeve left, Iris pulled the covers back over her pounding head, trying to push her concerns away. She didn't have to think about it now. That was all years off in the future, and who knows, maybe she'd want to be in Ireland.

Thoughts of Ruairi came into her head, and she began to fanta-
sise about being married to the Irish guard. He would give up
being a cop, and together they'd run the farm, but it would be
for crops, not animals. They'd make their own cheese, and ride
horses together at sunset on the shore of the lake. She would
give him a baby boy and then a girl and they would live happily
ever after, the four of them dancing in a ring in a meadow full of
fragrant bluebells. It was a grand and lovely dream and Iris lost
herself in it for a while until she drifted off to sleep.

When she woke up again, her aunt had left her more food.
A tray laden with a big slab of sponge cake and a pot of tea,
scones and jam. Iris was touched by her consideration, as if
Maeve knew her niece wanted to hide away in her room. She
was dreading seeing Conrad again, although she hoped he had
been so drunk he'd forgotten what had happened.

The day fell away into night, and she felt a little better for a
while, but as soon as she woke up the following morning, waves
of nausea assaulted her again. She sat back on her heels in the
bathroom, feeling green in the face. She had never had such a
bad hangover, and she'd been drunker the New Year's Eve
before. She got off the bathroom floor and sprayed her face with
water, before shakily walking back to the bedroom. She felt
terrible. And then it occurred to her, in one second of dreadful
realisation. She'd not had her period since just before her mom's
funeral, and that had been at the end of October. She had been
so buried in her grief, she hadn't kept track of her cycle, and part
of her had just thought the shock of losing her mom had
disrupted things. But now...

'Oh, crap!'

As soon as she had the thought, she knew it. Even though
they'd used condoms, somehow Freddie had got her pregnant.
She tried to convince herself it couldn't be possible, that she was
imagining things, but her instincts were suddenly wide awake.
How had she not noticed before? She should never have come

to Ireland, because now she had to deal with this crisis on the other side of the world. One thing she knew for certain was there was no way she could have a baby. It would tie her to Freddie for the rest of her life, and she had just gotten over him. Her mom was gone, and she'd have to deal with it all on her own. She'd seen how her mom had sacrificed her life for her, and Iris knew she wasn't as strong as her mom. All of a sudden, she felt a wave of nostalgia for Berkeley. She had been so lucky. She had to get back to college no matter what, and finish her degree, not just to honour her mom but also for herself. Iris gave a deep sigh. Okay, first things first. She had to get hold of a pregnancy test and check if she was pregnant. Then she needed to get home and deal with it.

She clutched her hands in her lap, took some deep breaths.

'It will be okay,' she told herself, but now more than anything she wished her mom were with her to help her. She was all alone in this.

Downstairs, the kitchen was empty, but a pot of tea was still warm on the table. Iris poured herself a cup and forced down a slice of soda bread with jam. She felt a little better after eating. In the hall, the keys to the VW Golf which her aunt had lent her were lying on the table. She picked them up and slipped out the back door. She felt the house watching her in silent judgement as she got in the car and started it up. Maeve was most likely out on the farm, but what about Conrad? Was he spying on her? It was all getting too freaky. Her crisis had pushed her over the edge. Whatever the test said, she wanted to go home now.

Iris kept driving through the town and out the other end. She needed to find a pharmacy in a place no one knew her. She kept going, driving for another hour, through several towns. She was heading towards Dublin, in the opposite direction to which

Ruairi had taken her the other day. Tears sprang to her eyes when she thought about Ruairi. If she was positive, she was going to head home as soon as she could so she could sort herself out. Most likely she'd never see him again. It was just too bad, because there had been something between them; she wasn't making it up in her head. She'd really liked him.

Eventually, she felt she'd gone far enough and pulled into the car park in a shopping centre in a place called Mullingar. She walked around until she found a pharmacy and went inside, her legs feeling like wood. Standing in the Irish pharmacy, looking for pregnancy tests, Iris felt more self-conscious than she'd ever felt back home. She'd bought pregnancy tests before, of course, who hadn't? But she'd never been pregnant, always lucky. This time, though, something told her she wouldn't be lucky, because already her body felt different. She grabbed two tests, just in case she screwed up the first one, and went to the counter, her cheeks crimson. The sales assistant took her time, eyes disapproving behind her spectacles. But at least she put the tests in a brown paper bag before handing it back to Iris. She fled the pharmacy, running all the way back to the car and bursting into tears once she was behind the wheel again.

Her whole life was a complete mess. Her mom was gone, she had fucked up her degree, and now this! So, she'd found her relatives in Ireland, might one day inherit a big pile of land and a falling-down house, but it wasn't what she wanted or needed. No, what she craved right now was to be on the beach with her college roommate, Riley, with not a care in the world. Watching some hot guys as they played volleyball and sharing secrets. She missed her roommate and wished so much she'd been more open with her, gone to hers for Thanksgiving when she'd offered – and God, how she wished she'd gone to hers for Christmas. But she'd never let herself get close to Riley. She'd always wanted a sister, but now she realised friends were just as important, more so sometimes. Look at her godmother, Trina, and her mother, who had fallen out with her own sister Maeve for years. And now here Iris was, trying to make up with her. But did Maeve deserve it? Iris had come all this way to discover her mother's family was even more dysfunctional than she could ever have imagined. No wonder her mom had never talked about them. All she'd found out by reading Nuala's diary was that her mom was miserable, and now possibly her father was some random boy called Stefan whose second name she didn't know. She couldn't ask Maeve or Conrad about him because she didn't want them to know she'd found and read Nuala's diary. Moreover, how had Nuala died? Had it really been an accident? She was now certain it hadn't been suicide.

Iris's mind raced as she drove the miles back to Swan Hall. *Please, please don't let me be pregnant*, she begged. *I'll believe in you, God, I'll go to church with my Aunt Maeve, but please don't let it be true!* She felt the Virgin Mary medallion against her chest. *Please, Mary, mother of God, have mercy on me! I can't be pregnant, I just can't.*

She made it up to the bathroom without seeing either her aunt or uncle. She ripped open the packet of the first pregnancy test and took a deep breath. The moment of truth had arrived.

Downstairs, her aunt was in the kitchen making dinner.

'How are you feeling?' she said, giving Iris a wan smile as she turned around from chopping carrots.

'Better,' Iris lied, standing awkwardly in the doorway.

'Well, dinner won't be long. Would you like to lay the table?'

'Sure,' Iris said, glad to have something to do. She took the knives and forks out of the top drawer in the dresser.

Iris cleared her throat nervously as she placed the cutlery on the table. 'Aunt Maeve, remember we were talking about my ticket home? Would you mind booking it for tomorrow, or the next day at the latest?'

'Tomorrow!' her aunt said, knife aloft and staring at her in astonishment. 'But that's so soon.'

'Yes, but I need to get back to college, see…'

'Surely next semester doesn't start for a few more days? It would be ideal if I could show you around the farm a little more, spend some time together, just us two.' She sighed, turned back to her chopping. 'I am sorry if you've found me a little aloof, Iris. It takes me a while to warm up, and I've lost so many loved ones over the years that I am a little wary of opening up to new people. But I would really like to make up for all the lost years…' She paused. 'I even thought we could take a little trip – just the two of us – to Galway. We could stay in a hotel, have spa treatments, that sort of thing. My treat.' She turned around, beaming at Iris.

'Oh,' Iris said, feeling terrible. 'That's so lovely, but—'

'So you'll stay?' Maeve pushed.

'Sure,' Iris heard herself saying, because she couldn't think of a good reason to say no. And she knew the one person she could *not* tell about her pregnancy was her Aunt Maeve, the staunch pro-lifer.

She put the glasses out and the plates. *Come on, Iris, it's just another week.* But when she counted the weeks in her head, panic started to flood her. She knew from talking with girlfriends at college that things were so much simpler if you had an abortion up to ten weeks. You could get pills and there was no need for surgical intervention. It was going to be so much harder, and more expensive – she had no idea where she'd get the money from – if she couldn't take the pills.

'Iris? Iris?' Maeve was talking to her, and she'd gone off in a trance. 'Are you okay? You look very pale.'

'Yes, I'm fine,' she said.

'Well, will you go and tell Conrad dinner is ready? He's in the sitting room.'

Oh, crap. The last thing she needed was to have to face her sleazy uncle. She still felt so guilty about what had happened on New Year's Eve, no matter how many times she tried to tell herself it was not her fault.

'Iris!' Her uncle stood up as she came into the sitting room, the book he had been reading falling to the floor. 'How are you? Maeve said you've been sick.'

'I'm better now,' Iris said, trying not to catch his eye.

'Iris.' Conrad paused. 'I am so very sorry about the other night – I mean, it's a bit of a haze – but I have a feeling I was very out of order.'

'It's okay,' Iris said, desperate to get out of the room.

Her uncle walked towards her.

'Please believe me, I am appalled at my behaviour. All I can say is the drink got a hold of me, but that's no excuse of course...' He paused. 'It's just you look so like Nuala, and well, in a way, you're rather like her in personality too.'

Iris jerked her head up. She'd read Nuala's diary and she didn't think she was like her one bit. Nuala was brave and ballsy and said exactly what she thought. Nuala would not have let her uncle grope her and then feel guilty about it. And Nuala would not have let herself get caught out by a douchebag like Freddie. Nuala all together was magnificent, in Iris's opinion, whereas she was a complete mess.

'No, I'm not, Uncle Conrad,' Iris said. 'I believe I am a very different person.'

'Yes, yes, of course. But you see, I adored Nuala and, well, I have never really got over her.'

Iris wanted to say, *She didn't love you!* but then she'd let on that she'd read the diary, and the last thing she wanted was to share her discovery.

'Well anyway, dinner's ready,' she said, looking away from the burning look in her uncle's eyes.

Her Uncle Conrad reached out and touched her arm. 'Is everything all right, Iris? If there's anything I can do?'

She pulled her arm away, heart racing. 'No, no, I'm fine,' she said tightly.

'I can tell something's wrong.' He paused. 'And I know how my wife can be cold and a little insensitive. What's happened?'

Iris looked up at Conrad. Everything about him gave her the creeps, but she was desperate and there was no one else who could help her. 'I need to get back to New York urgently. Could you lend me the money for the ticket?'

He raised his eyebrows in surprise. 'But didn't Maeve agree to pay for the ticket?'

'She wants me to stay another week, but you see I can't...'

'All our money is tied up in the farm. Most of our income is from selling cream and milk and Maeve is in charge of our bank account. It would be hard for me to buy you a ticket without her noticing.'

Iris shook her head, her heart plunging with despair. 'It's okay, don't worry.'

'But what is so urgent that you need to go tomorrow?'

This man was the last person she wanted to confide in. Iris was unnerved by her Uncle Conrad's obsession with her likeness to Nuala and his seedy behaviour. But she was so desperately lonely, it was all beginning to feel too much. She needed to confide in someone, she needed help, and Conrad was her only option.

'I'm pregnant,' she whispered, eyes on the floor.

'Oh!' Uncle Conrad took a step back. 'Goodness. Have you told your aunt?'

'No, no, because I need to get home; I need to get an abortion.'

'I see,' Conrad said.

Iris looked up, and her Uncle Conrad was staring at her. She wasn't sure what at all he was thinking. She'd made a terrible mistake. She should never have told him.

But then he reached out his hand and took hers in it.

'It will be all right,' he said kindly. 'I will help you.'

CHAPTER TWENTY-SIX

NUALA

1 SEPTEMBER 1972

The animals were restless as I walked past the fields. The cows were lying down – a sure sign of rain – and the sheep were jittery, staring at me with crazy Devil eyes. I could see Daddy driving the tractor into the barn, and I crept around the back of the house, careful to make sure he couldn't see me.

Aisling didn't come home last night.

Had she got wind of the fury she would face once she walked in the door because Maeve had told Daddy she stayed out all night? I was a little worried about her. I couldn't help it, although she clearly didn't care too much about me if she hadn't come home. Maybe she'd finally done a runner with Stefan and was never coming back. I climbed the stairs to the first floor and walked along the corridor, knocking on Aisling's door. No answer. I opened it and peered into the room. There was a pile of clothes on the bed, and all her things on the dressing table. I felt a little stab of relief, and then guilt because the truthful reason I was glad she hadn't gone was because Aisling is the buffer between me and Daddy.

I went in and sat down on the bed, chewing my nails. I was still thinking about how I could get the money to buy a flight to America. We have nothing of value in the house. It is a big empty pile of a house, like a shipwreck which has lost its treasure. Over the years my father has sold anything of value to keep the farm going (and himself on the whiskey). He keeps saying we are lucky to have the land that we have. That one day we'll be millionaires because of it, but the land takes too much from us to make it worth it. It took my mother away, that's for sure.

Sitting on her bed, I remembered the last time Aisling and I had spoken at any length at the Fleadh. She had said some very hurtful things to me about how I had been too much for our mother. How can she imply it's my fault our mam drowned herself? It was a wicked mean thing to say.

My eyes landed on a coffee tin on Aisling's beside table. Why would she have a coffee tin in her bedroom? I went over and unscrewed the lid of the tin. Inside was a huge roll of notes. I pulled it out, and more notes were underneath the roll. It had to be all of Aisling's wages – apart from what she gave Daddy monthly – from the whole year in the shop. I counted the notes, and it was more than enough to buy my plane ticket to America, even if they are so expensive. I stared at the money. No, I should put it back. It's Aisling's. But what does she need it for? She isn't going anywhere. I can borrow it, so I can, and send the money back to her as soon as I have made enough in New York. Excitement flooded through me. I miss Trina so much. The idea of her touch upon me in a matter of a few days sent a thrill through me. My freedom is so close, I can taste it on my lips!

But I need to be clever about it. I can't take the money right now because Aisling will be home soon to change her clothes at least, and she'll notice. I have to wait until she is gone on her next morning shift. Then take the money. That gives me all day to pack and get the bus up to Dublin. Go to the passport office to get my passport, and then straight to the airport and buy the plane ticket. I have my birth certificate, found in the kitchen dresser months ago when Trina and I first decided to leave, and if needs be I am totally capable of forging my father's signature.

My heart has lifted at the idea of getting away from Swan Hall. I know if I don't go, I will go mad or drown like my mother. Surely Aisling will understand that one day? She isn't as unstable as me. She is a solid sort of girl and she will be fine. The way she deals with Daddy and his anger is evidence of this. I will drive him to murder one day, I am sure of it. It is better for my family if I leave. After all, Aisling told me I was too much. So, I will go to somewhere where I can be as much as I want to be.

CHAPTER TWENTY-SEVEN

IRIS

3 JANUARY 1992

'Is there something you want to talk to me about?' Aunt Maeve said to Iris, as they sat over breakfast, just the two of them. Uncle Conrad was nowhere to be seen.

'Er, no,' Iris said, trying to quell the morning sickness by biting into a slice of jam-laden soda bread.

'Are you sure?' Maeve said, before putting the empty pregnancy test box on the table between them.

Iris froze. *Crap.* She had so carefully disposed of the test in multiple plastic bags and put it in the bins outside, but she'd forgotten about the box.

'I found it down the back of the bathroom cabinet, and it's certainly not mine or Conrad's.'

'Did he tell you?'

'Tell me what?' Maeve raised her eyebrows.

'Uncle Conrad, he said he'd help me.'

Maeve looked astonished. 'You went to your Uncle Conrad for advice on pregnancy?' She shook her head. 'Iris, you picked the wrong person for sure.'

'He was kind, he understood...'

'I doubt it,' she said crisply, two spots of crimson on her cheeks. 'So, are you pregnant, Iris?'

'I don't think that is any of your business,' Iris said defensively. 'And I would like you to book me a flight home, right now!'

'I will take that as a yes.' Maeve's voice softened. 'Do you really want to go through this alone? Let me help you—'

'I don't want it,' Iris interrupted, her voice sharp. 'I'm getting an abortion.'

'Oh,' Maeve responded, eyes widening.

Iris got up from the table, because she didn't want to hear any of her aunt's pro-life lecturing. Maeve was not her mother, and Iris was an adult so her aunt had no say in what she decided to do with her own body.

'Where's Uncle Conrad?' Iris asked.

'He's gone out.'

'What? But...' Iris was confused by his disappearance. Her uncle had said he would help her, but where was he now? Why couldn't he speak up for her in front of her aunt?

'I can't believe you told him you were pregnant, Iris,' Maeve said in a low voice. 'Oh, my Lord.'

She got up from the table and went towards Iris, arms outstretched, but Iris pushed her away, hard, and her aunt stumbled back against the kitchen counter.

'You're not a nice person, Aunt Maeve. I've read Nuala's diary and I know what you did...'

Her aunt's face went white and she shook her head. 'What do you mean? What did Conrad tell you?'

'Just stay away from me,' Iris said, running out the kitchen and upstairs.

In the bedroom she grabbed her case, and piled clothes into it. She opened the bedside table drawer to get her passport, but it was gone. Iris hunted around the room, looked in her bag, but it was nowhere to be seen.

She stormed back downstairs. Aunt Maeve was still in the kitchen, her back to her, staring out of the window at the lake.

'Where is it? Where's my passport?' Iris demanded. 'Give it back immediately.'

Her aunt turned around slowly. Her eyes were red-rimmed and she had clearly been crying, but Iris didn't care about her. She was a horrible woman.

'You can't stop me! You can't keep me here; give it back!'

'Oh Iris, you should never have told Conrad,' Maeve said in a whisper. 'But look, sit down with me. We'll work this out.'

'I am not having a baby!' Iris said to her. She just knew in her heart and soul that being pregnant would push her over the edge. She couldn't cope, and what then?

'Come on now, just take a breath. Please sit down.' Maeve reached out to her, but Iris flapped her away.

'No, I told you, I'm not having a baby, so just leave me alone.'

Iris ran out of the kitchen, out the back door and across the lawn. It was pouring with rain, and she could barely see where she was going. She slipped and slid on the wet grass, and her feet squelched in mud as found herself standing on the edge of Lough Bawn. The rain drove across the surface of the lake, creating ruffles of white waves and the illusion that she was by the sea. The wind tore through the trees, and it sounded like her rage. Iris was so angry. How could her mom have done this to her? Leave her alone when she needed her most. The lake surged towards her, slopping over her wet feet, drenching her sneakers, and once again Iris felt pulled towards it. A part of her wanted to walk into the lake and keep going. Walk until her feet couldn't touch the bottom and water closed over her head. Then all the fear, all the pain and confusion would be over. There would be sweet nothing. There would be peace.

Iris took another step forwards as the lake now splashed over her ankles. She waded in deeper, soaking her jeans and plastering them to her legs.

Was this what Nuala had done? Followed her mother's fate into the deep lake? But no, Iris knew that wasn't true. Nuala hadn't chosen to drown. But Iris could... She could. Iris pushed out further into the churning lake and beneath her feet she felt it suddenly drop so that now the water was over her knees, inching up her thighs. And still she went on as a voice inside her urged her forwards. The wind whipped her hair across her face and she could feel herself slipping away, lost in misery.

'Iris?'

The voice was faint against the wind and rain, and for a moment it sounded as if it had come from the depths of the lake.

'Iris?'

But when Iris raised her eyes from the hypnotising batter of the waves upon her legs, she saw a figure in a yellow mackintosh waving at her from the other side of the lake, and by its side, a little white dog.

Iris couldn't bring herself to wave back. She willed Lizzie to go away, leave her alone in her desolation. She moved forward in the water, and it slapped against the tops of her thighs.

'Iris!'

The water was at her waist now, but before she could go further in, she could hear barking. Lizzie's voice was closer. Urgent.

'Iris, don't move, just stay where you are!'

The water was freezing, and all her limbs were trembling with the effort of standing. There was a part of her that wanted to get out of the water, but the other part just couldn't find the will. The next minute, Lizzie was beside her in the lake. She was shorter than Iris, and the water was up to her chest, slapping against her yellow mac.

'Come on.' She tugged on Iris. 'We'll get swept in.'

She spoke so calmly, as if the fact they were both submerged in the choppy lake on a freezing cold winter's day was a normal event. Iris looked at Lizzie in a daze, her eyes watering, and noticed the other girl's nose had gone blue, and her hands were purple. Suddenly she realised just how cold she was, so cold she couldn't speak.

'Hold onto my coat,' Lizzie instructed.

The little dog, Rascal, was on the shore barking in terror to see his mistress in the dangerous lake, but though Lizzie might not have been tall, she was strong. Raising her arms above the water level, she began wading back to shore, as Iris clung onto her coat. Fortunately, the water was surging towards the shore, pushing them out to land as if it spurned them.

They were both drenched and shivering, the rain bucketing down.

'We need to get dry now,' Lizzie said through chattering teeth.

Still unable to form words, Iris took Lizzie's shaking hand and pulled her towards Swan Hall, Rascal at their heels. They staggered up the lawn, their clothes heavy with lake water. Iris pushed the back door open and they clattered inside, Rascal behind them. Her aunt came running in the back door after them. Her hair was plastered to her face from the rain, and her coat sprayed water onto the ground where puddles were gathering underneath Lizzie and Iris's feet.

She took in the situation and pushed the girls forward. 'Into the bathroom, quick,' she said. 'Take off your clothes,' she ordered the shivering girls. Iris looked at Lizzie and the other girl's eyes were warm with encouragement, although her teeth were chattering.

They stripped off, and Lizzie got in the hot shower while Iris clambered into a steaming bath as her aunt turned the hot tap on full. Slowly, some sensation started coming back into her body as the room filled with warmth. Maeve brought in some towels, and some of Iris's clothes for them – sweatpants and sweatshirts.

'I've put the fire on in the sitting room,' she said. 'Come in when you're ready and have a hot toddy.'

Lizzie got out of the shower first and dried herself off. Iris couldn't bear to look at her. She was so ashamed of herself. Lizzie handed her a towel. Iris looked up and took it, while Lizzie turned her back so she could get out of the bath.

As they got dressed, they caught each other's eyes in the mirror.

'Are you okay now?' Lizzie asked.

Iris looked at Lizzie in the mirror, and she felt tears blooming in her eyes. She didn't feel any better at all, just even more desperate because she'd not had the courage to go through with it. In fact, she'd nearly caused another person to drown instead.

'What is it, Iris?' Lizzie said.

She hardly knew the girl, but Lizzie was looking at her with such compassion, and there was that feeling she had with her again, as if they'd always known each other.

'I'm pregnant,' she whispered.

'Oh, shit,' Lizzie said immediately.

'I want to go back home to New York but my aunt won't buy the ticket... and she's taken my passport.'

'Right.'

'I need to get an abortion,' Iris said. 'But I've no money and my aunt won't help me...' Her voice trembled and she began crying again.

Lizzie put her arm around Iris's shoulder. She smelt of the citrus shower gel and her skin was soft.

'It's okay, I'll help you, Iris,' she consoled her. 'A friend at school was in the same position not long ago and I helped her.'

Iris looked up. 'You did?'

'Yeah,' Lizzie said. 'You can go to London. I know of a place. Do you have a driving licence with you?'

Iris nodded.

'That's enough to get to England. We can take the ferry. I'll drive you.'

Iris looked in wonder at Lizzie. 'You'd do that for me?'

'Of course, I'd do it for any girl in Ireland in the same position as you, Iris,' she said fiercely, her eyes blazing. 'Just don't tell your aunt what the plan is, okay?'

They padded down the chill corridor in their bare feet. Iris's body felt so alive now after the shock of the cold water, and the comfort of the hot bath. Lizzie's words of support flooded through her being and she already felt stronger.

Inside the sitting room, her aunt had the fire roaring in the grate, and had made two mugs of hot whiskey, lemon and sugar. Rascal the dog was already set up by the fireside.

'What was all that about?' Maeve asked as they sat down with their drinks. 'Iris, what were you doing going into the lake?' Her aunt's voice was shaking and she looked as shocked as Iris still felt.

'It was an accident. We both slipped and fell in,' Lizzie intervened.

Maeve frowned. 'I went looking for you,' she said. 'But the rain was so heavy, I didn't think you'd go all the way to the lake'.

'I'm sorry,' Iris said in a small voice.

'I'm just relieved you're okay,' she said. 'I've put your things to dry in the laundry room, Lizzie. Girls, go upstairs and get some socks on your feet. I forgot to bring them into the bathroom for you.'

They drank up their hot toddies and Iris felt a little better. She took Lizzie up to her room and lent her a pair of her white slouch socks.

'I've never been inside Swan Hall,' Lizzie commented,

looking out of Iris's bedroom window at the driving rain. She shivered. 'It's a bit eerie, isn't it? It looks so grand from the outside, but inside—'

'It's a shambles,' Iris interrupted.

'Well, yes.' She laughed. 'Sorry, I don't mean to be rude.'

As they finished speaking, a car pulled up outside, and Iris heard the noise of Aed, Conn and Fiacra barking as they came in. Rascal lifted up his ears and stood to attention.

'It's okay, Rascal,' Lizzie said, picking up her little white dog.

'That's probably Uncle Conrad. I'll tell him my aunt has hidden my passport and he'll get her to give it to me.'

Lizzie was looking at her in a queer way, her head on one side. 'I think the best thing is if we just go now to avoid a confrontation.'

'But my Uncle Conrad said he'd help me. He might have money for me too...'

Iris wasn't so sure how reliable her uncle would be, but at least he wasn't a fanatical religious freak like her aunt. He was inappropriate, weird, and drank too much, but he had also said he would help her. Surely he would back her up when she demanded her aunt give her back her passport?

Outside the sitting room door, Lizzie put her hand on Iris's elbow.

'Are you sure about this? Don't you think we should just go?'

'I will not run away,' Iris said indignantly. 'Uncle Conrad said he would help me, so I will make him keep his word.'

'But...'

Iris opened the door into the sitting room before Lizzie could say any more. There were her uncle and aunt sitting either side of the fire, mugs of tea in hand. But to her surprise there was a third party in the room. Old Father Francis, balancing a mug of tea on his lap, and devouring a piece of cake.

'Ah, there she is!' he said, a patronising smile on his face.

'Oh, shit,' Iris heard Lizzie whisper behind her. She turned to look at her new friend, who was holding little Rascal to her chest, and shaking her head at Iris.

'What's he doing here?' Iris turned back to Uncle Conrad, ignoring the priest. 'Why did you bring him here?'

Her Uncle Conrad looked different. He had combed his hair for a start and was wearing a clean shirt. Around his neck was a cross, which he held with one hand.

'I've brought Father Francis here to talk to you about your options.'

Iris looked wildly at her uncle, and then back to Aunt Maeve, whose expression was impassive.

'Are you fucking serious?' Iris said, her voice going up several decibels.

She felt Lizzie's hand on her shoulder, and she was so glad she was with her.

'With all respect, Mr and Mrs Maguire, and Father Francis, I believe Iris doesn't want to talk about it with you.'

Aunt Maeve looked at Lizzie in surprise.

'So you know?' she asked.

'Yes, Iris told me,' Lizzie said. 'She's my friend.'

At Lizzie's words, Iris felt a warmth inside her which she'd not experienced since coming to Ireland.

'Well, this is a family matter, young lady, and we would appreciate it if you kept your nose out of it,' Uncle Conrad said. 'Good day to you!' He got up and opened the door.

Lizzie turned to Uncle Conrad, Rascal still in her arms. The dog was growling, which didn't improve matters. But Lizzie remained calm and looked up at the man towering over her. 'I will only leave if Iris asks me to,' she said.

'Who do you think you are, interfering in our family business?' Conrad stormed. 'You're a disgrace to our country, girls.' He turned to the priest, speaking as if he were the victim in the situation. 'As an Irish nationalist and a Catholic, I never want to see the day when there are abortion clinics in every market town in Ireland. But what am I to do if my kin is willing to murder their own baby?'

'Let's not bicker amongst ourselves,' Father Francis said in a lighter tone of voice. 'Come and sit down, my poor girl,' he entreated Iris.

'No,' she said, bristling at being called a poor girl.

The priest sighed.

'Ah, I remember your mother, Aisling, in exactly the same position just over eighteen years ago when she was pregnant with you, Iris,' Father Francis said. 'Would you have wanted her to have an abortion then?'

'That's different. She had no options,' Iris said, anger beginning to inch through her numbed, shocked body. 'She told me that you and her father tried to make her have the baby adopted anyway. You were going to take me away from her!'

'Indeed yes, and if you don't want your baby, Iris, we can arrange an adoption, because there's plenty of Catholic couples with good homes who are desperate to provide a loving and secure upbringing for an unwanted baby,' Father Francis said. 'But, child, don't think you will ever get over having an abortion. It will be hard to live with yourself, knowing you took the life of an innocent unborn.'

Next to her, Lizzie dug her fingers into Rascal's fur, and Iris could see her jaw twitching, but she remained silent. Iris looked at her Uncle Conrad, and he was nodding in agreement with the priest. Shock swept through her as she realised her Uncle Conrad was never going to help her. She had got him all wrong. She looked to her Aunt Maeve in desperation, but she said nothing, though her expression appeared tortured.

'Your mother never had to run away in shame like she did – like you're planning to do, Iris,' Father Francis continued. 'Because Maeve did the right thing by telling their father that her sister was pregnant. We were able to offer Aisling help. But she turned her back on her family and on her faith. She ended up all alone and lost. Do you want the same fate, Iris?'

'You don't know who I am or who my mother was! She wasn't alone and lost, she was happy!' Iris replied, while she turned to look at her Aunt Maeve in disgust. Having read most of Nuala's diary, Iris could only imagine how her mother's father must have exploded at her when Maeve had told him Aisling was pregnant. 'How could you have betrayed your own sister? It's your fault my mom had to run away!'

Maeve's eyes filled with tears. 'It was because of Nuala...' Maeve whispered weakly.

But what had her mother being pregnant got to do with Nuala? Iris had had enough. Her family were despicable and she never wanted to see them again. She turned to Lizzie.

'Shall we go?'

'Definitely,' Lizzie said, looking relieved.

They walked out of the sitting room, heads held high, although Iris heard her uncle calling after her. 'You can't go anywhere, girl! I've your passport, you've no money...'

'Come on,' Lizzie said. 'Let's go before they try to barricade you in!'

'I need to get my things first.'

They went back up the creaking stairs of Swan Hall. The walls of the house felt as if they were closing in on them, and Iris thought of Nuala and her desperation to get away from its oppressiveness. In Iris's mother's old bedroom, Lizzie helped her finish off the packing she had started earlier in the day.

'Take a look in there.' Iris pointed at the wardrobe.

'Oh, wow!' Lizzie said as she opened the door and saw the colourful array of Iris's mother's clothes from the past. 'This stuff is amazing.'

'I want to bring it with me.'

'Here, you can use this old rucksack,' Lizzie said, reaching into the wardrobe.

They pulled all her mom's old clothes off the hangers and pushed them into the musty rucksack. Every single thing, including the go-go boots and the cassette player with the box of tapes.

'You know what, I'm going to change my clothes,' Iris declared, pulling off her sweatpants and sweatshirt and retrieving Nuala's apple-green maxi dress which she had put on the other day.

She instantly felt better, especially when she put on the platform suede boots as well.

'I think we should get going,' Lizzie said, an anxious tone to her voice.

Iris made sure to put Nuala's diary in her purse as well as picking her mom's little glass swan off the bedside table to put it in her bag as well.

'Come on, let's go,' Lizzie said.

As she spoke, the bedroom door opened, and Aunt Maeve burst into the room. As soon as she saw Iris in Nuala's dress and boots, she gave a little cry, bringing her hand to her mouth in shock.

'Oh my God,' she breathed out. 'Nuala!'

Tears filled her Aunt Maeve's eyes, but they just made Iris feel even colder towards her.

'Get out of my way, Maeve,' she said.

'Iris, please don't leave,' Maeve begged her. 'I'm so sorry about Conrad and the priest. I didn't know he'd gone to get him.'

'Then why didn't you speak up for me?' Iris raged at her. 'You betrayed my mom and you're an awful person for doing that. And now you've betrayed me! Who knows what you did to Nuala?'

Maeve visibly blanched. 'How can you say such a thing?' she said in a hoarse whisper. 'It's not that simple...'

'I don't care any more,' Iris said. 'You can't keep me prisoner here. I'm leaving.'

Iris lifted her case and Lizzie took the rucksack. They walked across the room, but Maeve reached out and grabbed Iris's arm.

'Please, Iris, please don't leave me...'

'Get out of our way,' Iris said, shaking Maeve off her.

'Lizzie.' Maeve turned in desperation. 'Please, make her listen to me.'

'I'm sorry, Mrs Maguire,' Lizzie said. 'I'm here to support Iris.'

'Iris, you must listen to me, I need to explain...' her aunt begged.

But Iris didn't wait to hear any more. She followed Lizzie and Rascal out the bedroom door, and down the stairs. She walked past the closed door of the sitting room where she could hear the low murmur of the men's voices. She raised a finger to the closed door. Fuck them. They had no right to have an opinion on, let alone decide the fate of her life and her body. Her Irish family were not good people – the ones left alive, anyway. Iris planned never to return to Swan Hall. As they stepped outside it had stopped raining, and the wind had dropped. The sky was stretched palest grey over the soaked landscape. Lizzie took her hand, and for the first time since her mother died Iris didn't feel so alone. Lizzie was a stranger, and yet she had done more for Iris than any of her family.

CHAPTER TWENTY-EIGHT

NUALA

2 SEPTEMBER 1972

This is it! I'm ready! Up at first light, and all packed. I'm only taking my harp, my flute, and a small suitcase with me and leaving most of my stuff because I'll get new clothes in New York. I've written two letters: one for Aisling and one for Maeve. Daddy doesn't deserve one. This morning I feel very sad about how it is to have a monster as a father. It's easier when I am angry with him. But there had to be something in him which made my mam love him. I can see a shadow of the young man in Spain who met my dancing mother at the fiesta by the sea. I think the monster, in all honesty, is the drink. My father has long gone, his heart and soul drowned in whiskey and beer, just like my mam drowned at the bottom of the lake. And that makes me very sad, dear diary, because I am grieving for both my parents. But still, I remind myself. He's a grown man, and he should have some control. He deserved what we did to him last night because of the beatings – well, when the Devil possesses him so to speak – he is responsible for that. We got him back for the bruises on my arm, and the cut lip he gave Aisling last night.

He was waiting for her – hours it must have been, because me and Maeve had long gone to bed. I wanted a good night's sleep before my early start today. But I was woken up by the storm, or maybe it was my father's roaring. I caught the odd word rising up the stairs. *Whore. Dirty. Shame.* Then a crack of lightning and a low roll of thunder as I got out of bed. I opened my door, listening down the little stairwell. The other door opened and Maeve stood on its threshold. I hadn't seen her since the incident with Conrad the day before. She stared at me coldly, and my heart sank: Conrad had clearly not explained things properly. Should I even bother trying to talk to her, because she seemed set against me – although she had seen me with Trina, too, and told Daddy about us in the first place! A streak of lightning lit up the contempt upon her face and another clap of thunder as we stared at each other across the tiny landing.

She cocked her head on one side. 'So, are you bisexual now, Nuala?' she asked me in an icy tone.

I could have tried to explain how if most of us were truly honest with ourselves we would accept that our sexualities don't need to be narrowed to being either straight or gay. There are so many nuances in between. I guess strictly speaking, you could say I am bisexual, which is even more unheard of than being a lesbian in Ireland in 1972. But I have always been attracted to a person irrespective of gender. It used to confuse me at first. In Fifth class at national school, I had a big crush on Dolores O'Connell, but by Sixth class I was mad about Martin Molloy. Once I was in post-primary school, I focused more on boys, of course, because that's what I was expected to do. I dated four boys in a row (I always had plenty to choose from), but I always lost interest. And yes, I shifted those boys too, and unlike Maeve, who I am pretty sure is still a virgin, I had sex last summer with a boy from Dublin called Gerald, who was visiting one of my friends from school, Alison. A big gang of us

met up on the shores of Lough Bawn in the Forest Park for a
bonfire and to drink cans, and me and Gerald snuck off into the
woods for a short while. It was okay. I was glad to get it over
with, as well as impressed he had a condom. But I quickly lost
interest, and never answered the postcard he sent me when he
got back to Dublin. When I got together with Catrina, it was
the first time I had felt anything like that. We had been friends
for years, but when we first kissed one afternoon as we were
listening to music together, sitting on my bed, well, it was like
peeling another layer off our relationship. We went in deep, so
fast, and it felt so very right in a way that it never had with boys.
Well, all of these things I could have explained to my sister
Maeve, but it would have been wasted on her because she is
insensitive to real feelings, and stuck in traditional concepts of
what she should be. Honestly, I feel sad for her. So what I said
to her was:

'None of your business.'

'Well, it is my business, if I catch you shifting my
boyfriend!'

Another flash of lightning, and then a crack of thunder fast
upon its tail, which meant the eye of the storm must be very
close. And yet it wasn't raining – not yet. The landing felt
charged with electricity, hot and oppressive.

'Conrad's not your boyfriend,' I said to Maeve.

Why was I being so mean? What did it matter if Maeve
thought Conrad Maguire was her boyfriend – because I didn't
want him, that was for sure! But there's something in me which
can't lie. The truth according to Nuala Kelly, no matter how
much it hurts, has to be told.

'We're going out, as well you know it; you saw us at the
Fleadh, remember?' Maeve continued. 'It's real, unlike you and
Trina which is – well – wrong and unnatural. What you do
with her is a sin, Nuala!'

'Conrad told me he's not interested in you, Maeve,' I

snapped back, flaring up. 'Tell me, has he ever written a song about you? Because he wrote one about me; it's quite beautiful.'

She couldn't help but take a little gasp of shock as if I had poured cold water over her head. Before she could hit back, though, we heard a loud bang downstairs, and Daddy roaring more. Unlike me, Aisling never shouted back. She just tried to get away from him as she tried to get away from all her family.

Me and Maeve looked at each other.

'Do you think she's all right?'

'Why would you care, Maeve? It's all your fault because you told Daddy about Aisling sneaking out at night.'

'I was upset,' she whimpered.

'Just go back to bed; you're pathetic,' I said and began going down the stairs. Thunder boomed overhead, accompanying the sounds of our father's rage down below.

'You'll only make it worse,' she called after me.

I couldn't help it, though. I was planning on stealing all of Aisling's money once she'd gone to work in the morning and the least I could do was stand up for her now.

I walked into the kitchen in the nick of time. Daddy was standing over Aisling as she was backed against the wall, her hands on her belly.

'You're a dirty little whore,' my father roared. 'A waste of space just like your mother, living off the back of me, sitting on her arse all day while I slaved away to put food on the table.'

Aisling was saying nothing, although she was looking at our father fiercely, tears in her eyes.

'Leave her alone,' I said, pulling the heavy pan off the stove. 'Leave us all alone, Daddy, or I'll brain you!'

My father turned around, taking in his diminutive daughter holding the pan aloft, and laughed at me. It made me furious, so I went for him with the pan but he caught my wrist, twisting it, so the pan dropped onto the floor. I thought for a moment he was going to break my arm and that would be no good at all because I needed to be able to carry my case the next day. But Daddy understood the extremities of pain; he was an expert at taking us to the edge, and then letting us go just before a bone would snap, or the skin would break. I fell to the floor off balance, and then I felt his boot kicking me in the back. It hurt like hell. Lightning lit up the room as I tried to get back up off my knees.

'Leave her be!'

I looked up, shielding my face with my hands, ready for more blows, to see my sister Aisling launch herself from the wall, and land on Daddy's back. If it weren't so awful it would have been funny, as he twirled around the room like a crazy bear and she hung on. All the while lightning flashed, and thunder boomed. Of course, he was too strong for her and prised her off, and she landed hard on the floor next to me, making a squeaky sound. We looked at each other, my sister and I, and we understood with no need for words. We wanted to end it tonight, for good. Out of the corner of my eye, I saw Maeve watching from the hall doorway in horror. But she wasn't a part of the bond I now shared with Aisling. The tables had turned and Maeve was the outsider, not me.

Aisling and I both shot up from the floor at the same time. I grabbed the kitchen knife, and Aisling sprang up and pushed our daddy back into his chair. He was so surprised, he fell into it. You'd think we'd rehearsed it, we were so synchronised. Aisling took the scarf from her neck and pulled it around our daddy's throat, and I brandished the knife at him. Dear God, I could have plunged it into his lily-white neck, as easy as if I were cutting up chicken for the dinner.

'You are never going to touch Nuala again,' Aisling said to Daddy, as the lights flashed on and off in the storm. 'Nor me, nor even think about Maeve. Because if you do, you'll never have a good night's rest again, because one night when you've passed out like a pig from the drink, we'll slit your throat.'

I looked at Aisling in stunned awe as she spoke. I had never heard her retaliate or speak back to our father before. She had always taken silent beatings and then run away. But tonight, her eyes were wild with fury. My heart surged with admiration at her courage. Another crash of thunder, and then we heard the heavens opening above as rain beat down upon the roof of Swan Hall.

'Stop it! Leave him be!' Maeve ran into the kitchen, standing between Daddy and the knife.

'We have to make him stop, Maeve,' Aisling responded. 'Otherwise, he will kill one of us.'

'No, he doesn't mean it,' Maeve sobbed. Behind her, rain battered against the windowpanes, and the night was as dark as death without. 'He's not well. What Mammy did to him... what she did, sure it would break any man.'

'It doesn't mean he can terrorise us,' Aisling said, but she released the scarf as my father sputtered. He looked at me with frightened eyes, and he reminded me of one of the bullocks out in the field. Stupid and spooked.

'Heed what Aisling's said, Daddy, because I will cut you up next time,' I said to him. I dropped the knife on the kitchen floor in disgust. My whole body began to shake with shock.

My father lowered his head. Sorrowful now. 'Dear God forgive me, girls, I don't know what gets into me.'

I heard a distant roll of thunder as the storm began to move away, though the rain kept lashing down. I could hear rivers of it running down the gutters outside and burbling in the drains in the yard.

'It's okay, Daddy, come on, I'll make some coffee. It will be okay,' Maeve coaxed the old bastard.

'What your mother did, abandoning us all...'

'We don't want to hear it, not again,' Aisling said coldly, before stalking out of the room. I followed her up the stairs and a part of me ached to tap her on the shoulder. To ask her if she was okay. There was something about the way her body moved that was different. She paused at the end of the corridor, her hand on the doorknob, and turned. I ached to run to her and demand an embrace. Beg her to help me escape. Did I really need to steal from her? Maybe we could go together. But there was only enough money for one ticket, and I *had* to have it.

'Good night, Nuala,' Aisling said in a dull voice, before opening her door and slipping inside the bedroom. I stood for a while on the landing, listening to the rain hammering upon the roof of Swan Hall, wondering if she might come out again, but she didn't.

'Goodbye, Aisling,' I whispered back.

So much has been left unsaid. The story of my mother is, for me, partly untold. What made our father the way he was? I will never know because, dear diary, today I am leaving.

Too restless to sleep, I sat up in my bed, listening to the sounds of Swan Hall. The house moaned and creaked as if it were an old beast in agony. At last, I heard Aisling leaving for work – she was on the usual 6 a.m. shift in the shop. I got out of bed and looked out of my window, saw her get in her car and drive off. I crept out of my bedroom, down the stairs, and across the landing. I could hear Daddy's deep snores, thank goodness. I know from habit that he won't emerge until the afternoon, and then he'll be extremely penitent for the next couple of days until he drinks again. But I'm not going to be around for that.

I put my hand on Aisling's doorknob and though none of us have keys, for a moment I imagined she had somehow found one and locked her door. But to my relief, the door clicked open. I tiptoed over to her dressing table and there was the coffee tin. I opened it up and pulled out all the money. Dear diary, I felt just terrible doing it, but honestly, it was a matter of life and death. My father will kill me, or more likely I will kill him if I stay at Swan Hall.

I crept out of the room and back upstairs, thrusting the money into my handbag.

I have just taken a slow spin around my attic bedroom, my place of retreat over all these years. I remember the beginning of the summer, so full of promise, when I danced flamenco for Trina. Soon we will be together again, and my heart races at the thought of it.

I write these last lines gazing out of the window in my attic bedroom, taking one last look at the lake. Ah, the scene is so heavenly. There's no trace of last night's storm, and the world appears rosy and gentle again. Soft orange light emanates from the risen sun and reflects upon the pale blue lake water. How can such a place look so divine, and feel like Hell on earth? Already I can feel the heat of the day rising, despite the storm clearing the air. The bus up to Dublin doesn't leave town until ten and I have plenty of time to walk to the stop.

I am staring at Lough Bawn, drinking in the last sight of it as if it were the well of my mother's love, the source of all my suffering, and yet the place of my ease and joy, the place where me and Trina first made love. Dear diary, I feel an overwhelming urge to touch the lake's cool water right now and submerge beneath it as if to bless me for my hot journey today. As if I am baptising myself into my new life. I ache to take another memory with me all the way to America. The lake is shimmering Madonna blue with the white swans upon it gliding serenely. Its sanctuary calls to me one last time.

CHAPTER TWENTY-NINE

IRIS

3 JANUARY 1992

Lizzie's cottage couldn't have been more different from Swan Hall. They reached it by walking through the woods and out the other side. Clambering over a stone wall, which was a bit of an effort in Iris's case, though Lizzie managed the rucksack easily, they then walked through a field and gate into the back garden. They passed some outhouses which looked renovated, with big double doors, and round to the front of a grey stone cottage with latticed windows.

'It used to be one of the houses that the estate workers lived in,' Lizzie explained as she opened the door.

Inside, it was as warm and snug as Swan Hall had been cold and unwelcoming. Lizzie took Iris into the kitchen where there was a large range. She opened its door and threw in some peat. The walls of the kitchen were painted warm terracotta, and there was a big table in the middle of the room. Upon it was an open sketch pad, beside which were watercolours and a bottle of ink. Lizzie went to close the sketch pad, but not before Iris caught sight of the beginnings of a drawing. It reminded her a little of the Jim FitzPatrick picture she'd taken from her Aunt Nuala's room, with a border of Celtic design, but the image was a landscape rather than a figure such as the goddess Macha. She also caught sight of what looked like an ancient stone edifice, a little like the stones at Stonehenge she'd seen pictures of in history books at college.

'Are you an artist?' Iris asked.

'Studying,' Lizzie explained. 'I'm planning on going to art college in London next year.'

'Right,' Iris said.

Lizzie took a breath. 'I'm going to put the kettle on and then we'll get everything organised.'

'Thanks,' Iris said, sitting down at the table. She appreciated Lizzie's complete support. She seemed so grown up, but she was younger than Iris, only seventeen. Not once had Lizzie questioned Iris's decision or asked her to think about it. Iris had doubts, of course. In another fantasy universe, there she was, married to Freddie, faithful now, and living in a house with a white picket fence and a chubby baby on her hip. But it was not her reality. In her heart, she knew that would be a miserable life path. She was eighteen and this crisis had made her realise how much she wanted to get back to college. Not waste all the sacrifices her mom had made for her.

It took just over twenty-four hours and several phone calls for Lizzie to organise their trip to the abortion clinic in London. They were due to leave early the next morning. Lizzie was going with Iris, she had insisted.

'You're not doing that trip alone,' she said, making them both a cup of herbal tea. 'We'll go in my car. Take the ferry.'

'But don't I need my passport?'

'No, a driving licence is fine for the ferry,' Lizzie assured her.

Iris was overwhelmed by her kindness and generosity. She didn't know quite what to say. It was as if this girl was an angel her mom had sent to help her.

The whole day, Iris had waited for her Aunt Maeve or Uncle Conrad to call her or even to turn up at Lizzie's place, but there wasn't a peep from either of them. Iris was relieved, although a little surprised.

'I can't believe they got a priest to try and stop me having an abortion,' Iris said to Lizzie, as she curled up on the couch with her cup of peppermint tea. 'I mean, how dare they!'

'As far as they're concerned, they view abortion as a criminal act, akin to murder.'

'But that's just crazy!'

'It's an extremely divisive issue in this country,' Lizzie said.

Iris remembered talking to Ruairi about it the day they'd gone to Queen Maeve's Cairn, and how he'd told her that in the Irish constitution the mother's life was of equal value to the life of the unborn. She wondered what he would think about her decision. He had seemed so liberal and open-minded. But Lizzie assured her you just never knew.

'So, say you knew your baby wasn't going to live, and it put your life at risk to carry it, you still can't have an abortion?' Iris asked Lizzie now.

'That's right. If the baby has a heartbeat, then they won't abort it.'

'But it's crazy, the mother could die!'

Lizzie looked down at her hands. 'I know. My mam died of sepsis, because of a fatal abnormality with the foetus.'

'Oh my God, I'm so sorry,' Iris said in horror.

'It was over fifteen years ago, but it's still happening now,' Lizzie said in a bitter voice. 'Hundreds of Irish women and girls are forced into unwanted pregnancies, or the ones that can afford them end up having to travel to England for an abortion, frightened and traumatised.'

'It's so wrong.'

'Ireland might look modern – and don't get me wrong, I do love Ireland, it's my home,' Lizzie said. 'But it's still run by men like your Uncle Conrad – religious, nationalist pro-lifers.'

It dawned on Iris just how nasty her Uncle Conrad was. 'I thought he was shady but not that dangerous,' she said.

'He's involved in all sorts, Iris,' Lizzie said. 'There's been rumours he's linked somehow with the IRA, just like your grandfather was. Did you not know you're from a big Republican family?'

Iris looked at Lizzie in shock. 'No, it's never been mentioned.'

'There's been a few run-ins with the local gardaí over the years,' Lizzie told her.

Iris remembered her Uncle Conrad's hostility towards Ruairi because he was a garda. Now she understood why.

'Your uncle is associated with a dangerous bunch of men, Iris,' Lizzie said. 'These men are extremely pro-life, too. View themselves as devout Catholics.'

Iris felt sick. Not only was her Uncle Conrad a creep, harassing her because she looked like Nuala, but he was also involved in some really dark stuff. She had been so stupid to ask for his help.

'And what about my Aunt Maeve?'

'Who knows!' Lizzie said. 'Although she must be aware of Conrad's goings-on.'

They finished off their tea, and Lizzie showed Iris into the guest bedroom.

Iris didn't sleep for a long time, imagining any moment her relatives would come banging on the door to drag her away. Lock her up in Swan Hall and force her to have the baby.

. . .

The next morning, they were up while it was still dark. Lizzie brought in a cup of tea and a couple of cookies. Iris had nodded off at some point, but she'd woken up feeling sicker than ever.

'Eat the biscuits, you'll feel better,' Lizzie advised. 'Take your time.'

Iris forced them down and to her surprise, the nausea lifted slightly. She hoped the crossing on the ferry would be smooth because any hint of a roll would flip her stomach over again. She felt hot and sweaty with nerves, and she was angry too, mainly with Freddie. He had no idea of what she was going through, and it was partly his fault she was in this predicament. She picked up Nuala's diary where she had left it on her bed last night. She had now finished all of Nuala's entries. After Nuala had described her plans to go for one last swim in the lake, there was just blank page after blank page. Iris had turned them over, hoping for some kind of clue as to what had happened to her. That last swim must have been when Nuala drowned.

Had it been an accident? It was clear Nuala hadn't been suicidal, but both her sisters had had reason to be angry with her, hadn't they? Maeve over Conrad, and Iris's mom over the money Nuala had stolen from her. She remembered Ruairi telling her that he'd been told all three sisters had been at the lake together that morning. That didn't make sense, because Nuala wrote about Iris's mom driving off to work at 6 a.m. She could have come back, though, right? Anyway, Iris knew with all her heart and soul her mom would never have done anything bad. So then, was it Maeve?

Iris sighed, taking another biscuit to quell the morning sickness. She was desperate to find out what had happened to Nuala, but she also needed to let it go for now. She had enough to contend with her unplanned pregnancy. When she got back from London with Lizzie, she would give Ruairi a call. See if he wanted to meet up again, and she could question him further on the mystery surrounding Nuala's drowning. In any case, she would ask him in his capacity as a guard for help in getting her passport back from her relatives. It would be the perfect excuse to see him again, too, before she headed home to the States.

The sun was just beginning to rise as they packed Lizzie's car with their bags.

'I've booked you into a good clinic in Hammersmith.'

'But the money...'

'It's okay, my dad is paying.'

'Your dad!'

'He took my friend when she needed help, although her parents turned their backs on her. My dad's special, he's on our side.' Lizzie cocked her head and smiled at her. 'He's offered, so don't turn it down.'

Iris shook her head, mortified that Lizzie's father, a man she'd never met, knew her personal circumstances – but what could she do otherwise?

'Please tell him thank you.'

'Of course. Right, we'd better get going,' Lizzie said, getting into the driver's seat.

Iris strapped herself in and took a deep breath. In a few days, this part of the nightmare would be over. Then she just had to get her passport back and get home.

They were just pulling out the drive when Iris heard a siren – the sound incongruous in the rural setting – and saw the flashing lights of a garda car. It came whizzing down the lane and blocked their exit.

'Fuck!' Lizzie said under her breath, turning off the car engine.

Two guards got out of the vehicle, and to Iris's dismay one of them was Ruairi. They walked over to their car and as Iris stared at Ruairi, he looked directly away from her, at Lizzie. The other guard was Eamon, whom Iris had met at the pub on Christmas Eve.

'Under Article 40.3.3 of the Constitution of Ireland, we're

here to take Miss Iris Kelly into custody to prevent her from having the illegal procedure of an abortion.'

'Are you kidding me, Eamon?' Lizzie exploded. 'We're leaving the Irish State, so we're not doing anything illegal in Ireland.'

'But it's breaking Irish law to have an abortion and since we know this is your intention, we can stop you from travelling,' Eamon came back.

'I don't believe it!'

'Let me say it again,' Eamon said icily. 'Abortion is illegal in this country, and we can't knowingly let you travel to England for an abortion.'

'But we all know that women travel to England for abortions, it goes on all the time!' Lizzie exclaimed, exasperated.

Iris watched in horror as the altercation between Lizzie and the guard Eamon continued while Ruairi looked at his feet. Why wasn't he intervening? The whole situation was unreal. They were treating them as if they were criminals, and more than that, it was humiliating. She didn't want these men to know about her private life, especially Ruairi.

'Get out of the car, Miss Kelly,' Eamon ordered her.

'Don't,' Lizzie said, putting her hand on Iris's knee.

'If you don't get out of the car, we'll have to arrest and charge both you and Miss Weber,' Eamon continued.

'With what?' Lizzie exclaimed, raising her arms to heaven. 'I am sure this is in contravention of our human rights in Europe. Ireland is a member of the European community, despite people like you wanting to drag us back into the dark ages.'

'All I know is that I have my orders to stop you from breaking Irish law by travelling to Britain to obtain an abortion.' Eamon said, refusing to back down. 'Miss Kelly, you're under arrest!'

'What for?' she protested, her voice breaking free, still not understanding how it could be legal for them to stop her from travelling. She looked over at Ruairi, hoping for him to step in, but he looked at the ground, his cheeks burning crimson.

'As I have already stated, you are breaking Irish law by intending to procure an abortion.'

Iris gave a laugh at the craziness of the situation. How could this be a modern civilised country, when its police could do such a thing to half the population?

'This is no laughing matter, Miss Kelly. This is murder we're talking about, here,' Eamon said in a harsh voice.

'It's no such thing,' Lizzie declared hotly. 'It's your cruel laws which are causing the deaths of innocent women. My mam was murdered by the Irish constitution!'

'Enough!' Iris exclaimed, worried Lizzie was going to go off the deep end. She didn't want Lizzie to get into trouble – this was her own mess, so she opened the door.

Lizzie squeezed her knee, and gave her a searching look. 'Don't get out,' she said.

'I can't let you get arrested, because you live here all the time,' Iris said, sounding braver than she felt. 'Besides, I'm American. They can't make me abide by their rules.'

'I think they can!' Lizzie warned.

'Thank you, Lizzie, honestly, it will be fine,' Iris said. 'I'll call my godmother, Trina, and she'll sort it out.'

Iris got out of the car and stood facing Ruairi. His face was scarlet as he led her to the garda car, and opened the back door for her to get in.

'Don't worry, Iris,' Lizzie called to her from the open driver's window of her car. 'I'll be right behind you.'

'Ruairi, please can you explain to your colleague how crazy this is?' Iris said, once they had started driving away from Lizzie's cottage.

But Ruairi didn't answer. It was as if she wasn't there.

'Ruairi, come on, this is my own private affair, it's got

nothing to do with you guys,' Iris tried again, but Ruairi didn't answer her.

'Please refrain from speaking to Garda Caffrey, Miss Kelly,' Eamon turned around and addressed her. He gave her a look as if she was a complete slut, and every part of her wanted to scream at him, but she held herself back. *Stay cool*, she told herself. She knew once she contacted Trina things would be all right. Her godmother had faced down far worse adversaries in her quest for equal rights for women over the years, in all sorts of dangerous locations.

In the meantime, Iris sat in stunned silence, wondering where the lovely boy Ruairi had gone. Who was this judgemental young man in his place? How could she have got someone so wrong?

At the police station, Eamon insisted on putting her in a cell.

'Is that necessary?' she heard Ruairi challenge him. 'She should be allowed to call someone.'

'I'm the sergeant in charge here, and you'll not question my decisions. She can wait a bit longer for her phone call.'

She sat on the cold bench in shock, frightened and confused. She couldn't even cry, although she was forced to throw up twice in the bucket in the corner of the cell.

After what felt like hours, the door opened, and Ruairi stood there. For the first time, he looked into her face.

'You're free to go,' he said, his eyes filled with apology.

'No charges?'

'No,' he softly. 'I'm so sorry, Iris.' His cheeks burned with shame. 'But my hands were tied. Eamon is my superior officer.'

She pushed past him now, anger replacing the fear she'd been in for the past hours as she had wondered how this country could force her to carry a baby against her will. Did it really happen to the women of Ireland? Were they banned from taking a boat to another place where they had no family nor friends to get the help their own country should be giving them? It was barbaric, that's what it was.

He caught hold of her arm.

'Iris, please, I persuaded Eamon to drop it in the end.' He paused, licked his lips, and gave her a nervous look. 'I'm so sorry.'

'And you want me to say *thank you*?' she flared up at him. 'Thank you for giving me back my human rights? Have you any idea what you've just put me through?'

He looked shocked at her response. 'Your arrest came at the express command of some very dangerous people, Iris. We had to be careful there were no repercussions.'

'Who are these dangerous people who think it's their business to interfere in the personal life of a young foreign woman? My Uncle Conrad, right, and his cronies?'

'It doesn't matter who now, Iris, all that matters is that you're free to go.' He paused, and lowered his voice. 'And do whatever it is you choose.'

'Oh well, thank you so much, Guard, now I have your permission, that's just fine!'

Iris barged past Ruairi, and stormed out into the lobby of the police station. Lizzie was sitting on a chair waiting.

'Are you okay?' she asked, standing up.

Iris nodded. 'I just want to get out of here,' she said.

'Come on then,' she said, leading her out of the station. 'I've changed the ferry tickets for tomorrow, and the appointment for the next day. We can stay at a friend's place in Dublin tonight to make sure no one else interferes with our plans.'

'Okay,' Iris said. 'But I want to call into Swan Hall on the way.'

Lizzie shot her a look. 'Are you sure?'

'Yes, I need my passport back.'

'They might not give it to you – they might try to stop you from going again,' Lizzie said.

'The truth is, I also want to ask my aunt what happened to Nuala,' Iris admitted. 'I feel it's part of everything, as if it's a sort of curse I need to lift.'

'Well, I'm coming with you then,' Lizzie said. 'Just in case.'

Iris didn't protest because she was glad of Lizzie's support. She thought of Riley, and how she had pushed her roommate away when her mom had died. She wasn't going to make the same mistake with Lizzie.

'Thanks,' Iris said, linking arms with Lizzie. 'That would be great.'

CHAPTER THIRTY

AISLING

21 OCTOBER 1991

Aisling dreamed about the last morning of her sister Nuala's life all the time. Whenever she was particularly anxious or stressed, especially about Iris, she would return to Swan Hall and its lake in her slumber. It was just as it was all those years ago. A beautiful golden morning in early September, the air fresh after the storm the previous night. The grass was lush with morning dew, the birds were a cacophony of sound, the air around her bursting with bright, joyous song. She had driven back to the house because she had forgotten the keys to the shop. When she walked back into her bedroom, she had seen immediately that the coffee tin was empty, rolling on its side on the floor. Nuala hadn't even tried to hide her betrayal.

Aisling went down to the lake in her bare feet. In her dream, she was looking for Nuala, not angry as she had been the day she died, but to tell her she was sorry, to ask for her forgiveness, to tell her the truth. She had blamed her little sister her whole life for the death of their mother, and it hadn't been fair. But hunt as much as she could, sometimes on her own, sometimes with Maeve, and even Conrad in tow, she never found Nuala. She would call and call for her. Beg her to come back. But Nuala was gone to the bottom of the lake, like a stone. She was gone to their mother and she was never coming back.

Sometimes when she had these dreams, Aisling would wake, her face wet with tears, and then she would get out of bed, her heart racing with terror. She'd open the door to Iris's bedroom and check her daughter was still safely tucked up in bed. She would sit in the chair next to the bed and watch the gentle rise and fall of Iris's chest and wonder how it was she was given a child in the image of her dead sister. Was it a sign of forgiveness? Or was it a curse of sorts? That for the rest of her days, she would fret about her own daughter's safety.

She had meant to tell Iris about Nuala as she got older, and about her childhood at Swan Hall, but it was all so painful. Her sister Maeve blamed her for what had happened, and maybe she was right, maybe it had been her fault in the end, because she had once promised their mother that she would look after Maeve and Nuala. She had let them down. She had run away and never come back.

The guilt gnawed away at her, and as Iris got older, it became worse. She sensed her daughter was lost. Unhappy. How had she not noticed that awful boy Freddie inveigling his way into her daughter's heart, just as Conrad had weaselled his way into Maeve's life? She fretted about Iris all the time, all the way over in California. She was too far away. Why hadn't she encouraged Iris to apply for college upstate, or even in Boston?

She had called Iris last night and she had been able to tell her daughter didn't want to speak to her. When she'd asked her about her assignments, or any of the course content, Iris's answers had been monosyllabic. They'd only been speaking for a few minutes when she'd cut her off – Aisling had been telling a long story about one of her clients' dogs messing up her freshly polished floor – and granted it had been a bit boring, but she'd been hurt that Iris couldn't even spare her the time to listen to her day.

'I'll call you tomorrow if you have to go right now, Iris,' she'd said.

'But we're finished, Mom, you don't have to call tomorrow. I'm out.'

'I wanted to ask you about Thanksgiving. You're coming home, right?'

'Actually, I don't think so.'

'What do you mean, you don't think so? It's Thanksgiving! I'm expecting you.'

'I can't get into this right now, Mom, I told you I'm going out.'

'But where're you going?'

'Just out with Riley.'

She heard Iris's frustrated sigh, and Aisling felt a mixture of shame and hurt. She was that awful, interfering mother she'd used to judge when she had been a teenager – well, maybe had been jealous of, as she'd lost her mother so dramatically when she was fifteen. And then she'd had to be a mother to her sisters. She hadn't wanted to, and she'd used to mock those micro-managing mothers of her sisters' friends, like Trina's mam. But now, God, now she understood. It was her penance to love her daughter so much that sometimes she could hardly breathe. There was no room for anyone else in her life. Although she'd had plenty of boyfriends over the years, all of them, in the end, were jealous of Iris. The only person who understood was Trina, because she had loved Nuala more than anyone. Aisling had never told Trina the full story of what had happened at the lake that day, and her friend had never asked. Trina had been Nuala's legacy, and Aisling treasured her for her sister's sake.

Aisling sighed. It was time to get up. She was exhausted, and today was full-on. She had three houses to clean, plus she'd a full shift in the bar this evening. Well, she'd no choice: Iris's college fees were partly covered by a scholarship, but the last thing she wanted was her daughter coming out with loads of debt. That meant she had to work her arse off. Once Iris was through college, she could relax. She had a dream of moving upstate to where her friends lived and renting a cottage, getting dogs, and having a beautiful big garden which deer could wander into.

In the bathroom, as she brushed her teeth, Aisling suddenly remembered the end of the dream she'd had the night before. It had been different from her usual dreams about searching for Nuala. In this dream, it was the night before her sister was lost, and lightning was cracking the sky open. Her mother was walking on the lake like Jesus walking on water, but with a face like the Devil, full of fury. Aisling had never seen her like this when she was alive. Her mother's face was white, all hard angles, and she bared her teeth. Her hands were on the small mound of her belly. She was shouting at Aisling: 'Give me back my daughter. Give me my daughter. She's mine.'

She wanted Iris, that was who she had come to get. Aisling was saying, 'No, Mammy, she's mine, my girl, not yours.'

'Her name is Iris Kelly of Swan Hall, and she belongs here with me.'

'No, Mammy, Iris's home is with me.'

But her mam was having none of it. She roared at Aisling, and she said, 'You bring me my girl, Aisling!' And as she spoke, she spread her arms, and they turned into two big white wings, and her neck arched and lengthened. She shapeshifted into a swan, shimmering with strength and certitude.

Aisling stepped upon the water, beseeching her, 'Mammy, Iris is mine.'

And as she did so, as the water lapped around her, something quite wonderful happened. Aisling felt her body transform, fear falling away. Feathers breaking from her flesh, spine curving, toes webbing, wings spreading wide, neck lengthening.

She saw the lake through the eyes of a swan and it was no longer a place of death, no indeed, it was a haven.

Aisling knew, then. She was in her mother, her mother was in her, and Iris was within them both, as was Nuala – as was Maeve, even, the dark sister. Together they took flight, mother and daughter, two swan sisters lifting off Lough Bawn, the sound of their wings whipping through the wind with the power to mend hearts.

CHAPTER THIRTY-ONE

IRIS

Iris's aunt was in the kitchen, the kettle whistling on the range as she stared out of the window at the lake. As Iris and Lizzie came through the door, and the three black Labradors greeted them enthusiastically, Maeve turned around. Iris saw a wave of relief wash over her face.

'Oh, thank goodness they didn't lock you up,' she said. 'I've been so worried.'

'But you told the guards, you and Uncle Conrad and the fucking priest,' Iris accused, anger shooting through her. 'It was none of your business—'

'It wasn't me!' Maeve defended herself. 'I tried to stop Conrad but... but... I am sorry, Iris.'

Iris looked at her aunt in disgust. She was pathetic. The act of the tough farming woman was just that. In the end, she was an obedient wife going on her fanatical pro-life marches and doing just what her husband demanded.

'I want my passport back,' Iris said coldly. 'And then we're out of here.'

'I have it,' Maeve said, pulling the passport out of her pocket and handing it to Iris. 'I found it hidden in the back of the drinks cabinet.' She gave a bitter laugh. 'No surprises, he put it the place he treasures most.'

'He's foul,' Iris said, clutching her passport. 'Why don't you leave him?'

'It's complicated,' Maeve said. 'Look, let's just sit down for a minute and talk before you leave.' She looked at Lizzie. 'Thank you, Lizzie, for helping Iris. I truly mean it, and if there's anything I can do – money, drive you...'

'Are you now saying you're going to help us go to England?' Iris asked, furious her aunt had denied her the support she needed before.

'Yes, yes,' Maeve said, and then she sighed. 'My mother might still be alive if she'd been allowed to choose. Then none of these terrible things would have happened to us – the Kelly sisters – I truly believe that.'

'What do you mean?' Iris asked, curious to hear more, despite her anger.

'Please, girls, let's go in the other room, just sit down for a minute. I need to explain myself,' Maeve said.

Iris shrugged and looked at Lizzie.

'I think it might be a good idea,' Lizzie suggested. 'You said you wanted to know what happened to Nuala.'

The fire had been lit in the sitting room and it emanated warmth into the chilly room. The three dogs immediately splayed out on the rug in front of the crackling wood while Maeve brought in a pot of tea and cups, along with scones. Iris was starving. She hadn't eaten all day and she'd been feeling nauseous for hours. While Maeve poured the tea, Iris grabbed a scone and slathered it in jam and cream before sitting down next to Lizzie on the couch. Maeve took the armchair next to fire, placing her cup of tea on the little table by her side.

'Where's Uncle Conrad?' Iris asked, anxious she would have to face him again.

'He's gone to the pub. He's been there for two days. We had a big argument after you left and he's been out drinking ever since.'

'Why do you put up with him?' Iris blurted out.

'I told you, it's complicated,' Maeve said. 'But first I want to explain that I don't hold the same opinions as my husband. You see, my mother is dead because abortion is illegal in Ireland. When she became pregnant again, I was twelve, Aisling was fifteen, and Nuala was ten. My mother begged our father to take her to England for an abortion, but of course he was horrified she would even suggest it. My mother had got very sick after Nuala was born, not physically, but mentally. There had been a few incidents when she'd left Nuala outside or down by the lake, and gone off into the woods. She was never right after she had Nuala, and as we got older it was up to Aisling to keep an eye on our mother, make sure Nuala was okay. I was only little myself, so not much help.' Maeve sighed, her eyes full of sadness. 'As Nuala grew up, she became so demanding, and our mother was exhausted all the time. Maybe Aisling and I resented our younger sister for that, I am ashamed to say.'

Maeve paused, sweeping her hand across her brow, as her dark hair fell in waves about her face. She looked older than her years, and tired. Iris couldn't help feeling a tug of compassion for her, despite how angry she still was with her.

'When our mam was pregnant again ten years after she had Nuala, she became desperately depressed,' Maeve continued. 'We would find her sobbing in the rain and staring into the lake. She said it was calling to her.' Maeve's voice cracked. 'We should have known...'

Maeve paused, took a breath. Neither Iris nor Lizzie spoke.

The fire crackled in the grate, and the clock ticked in the hall. They waited for Maeve to speak again.

'So that is why I am not pro-life,' Maeve clarified. 'My own mother took her life because she wasn't allowed an abortion.'

'But you went on a pro-life demonstration in Dublin! Uncle Conrad told me,' Iris said with indignation.

'That's what I told *him*, but I was demonstrating for pro-choice,' Maeve said, giving a wan smile.

'Then why didn't you help me?' Iris threw at her.

'Because your Uncle Conrad has something on me,' Maeve said, her hand shaking as she attempted to take a sip of her tea. 'Something I've done – to do with Nuala...' she stumbled. 'And he's bribed his way into my life with it all these years.'

Iris felt the cold finger on her forehead again. The air in the room thick, and a weight upon her chest. She shivered and glanced at Lizzie. Her new friend was staring intently at Iris's Aunt Maeve, her big eyes fixed on the older woman.

'I go to the lake every day, no matter what the weather,' Aunt Maeve said as she placed her teacup back in its saucer. 'What I seek, what I need, is solace. If I can stand on the stony contours of the lake on my land and watch every tiny thing...' She paused, closing her eyes for a moment. 'If I can consider the small – a hawthorn twig, a strand of green algae stuck to a rock, a tiny sheep's bone – for a fleeting second, then the forgiveness I crave fades.' Maeve sighed and Iris could hear the ache in her voice. 'But then I hear Nuala's singing in my head. Remember her cartwheeling along the lake shores, and I am wracked with guilt again. You see, it's my fault Nuala died,' Maeve said, spreading her arms wide.

Iris held her breath, waited for Maeve to continue her story. At last, she was going to find out what had happened to Nuala. But did she really want to know now?

'It was the first time Daddy had ever hit me, and I was so angry with Nuala because she had told Daddy that Conrad and

I were having sex, and it wasn't true!' Maeve gave a little cough of embarrassment. 'I was still a virgin, unlike her! Oh, she was so... so... well, she sucked all the air out of the room. There was only space for her – the one magnificent Kelly sister. Nuala eclipsed both me and Aisling.' Maeve shook her head.

'I hadn't slept. I lay there until first light, my eyes itching, and my jaw was still sore from where Daddy had smacked me the night before last. I heard Nuala's door open and close just after Aisling drove off to work. I got up and looked out my window. I saw her carrying a suitcase, her little Celtic harp, and her flute bag. I knew what she was up to. She was running away and leaving me to deal with Daddy's wrath.' Maeve clasped her hands in her lap as if she were making her confession. 'She hid her things behind a tree, and then she walked down towards the lake. I thought she was taking one last look, but she pulled off her dress and got in. She began to swim out into the lake.'

Maeve stood up abruptly and walked over to the tall sash window which overlooked the lake. She stared out at the view, while Iris and Lizzie exchanged looks, waiting for her to continue.

'I wasn't thinking straight because I was still so angry,' Maeve said, turning around to face the girls. 'Nuala had betrayed me to Daddy and she had tried to steal Conrad away from me. I wasn't stupid. It was clear to me that he was besotted with my sister. What if she had persuaded him to run away with her? The thought of it was too much to bear. She was so mean, you have no idea, and I knew she wasn't even serious about him because I had seen her with Catrina. Nuala was deserting us all and leaving a great big mess behind.'

Iris could still hear traces of bitterness in her aunt's voice.

'I ran out of my room and down the stairs, still in my pyjamas. Out the door and across the garden in my bare feet, sliding on the wet grass. She was already swimming too far out when I got there. Graceful, languid strokes, her golden hair piled on top of her head. When she saw me, she waved, and actually smiled!'

Maeve clasped her hands again, her eyes shining with emotion. 'That made me even more furious,' she confessed. 'I waded out into the lake and she started to laugh. I remember she mocked me for getting into the lake with my pyjamas on. I swam towards her, not quite knowing why or what I would say to her. But when I reached her she was smiling at me, bobbing up and down in the water. She told me she had something to tell me.'

Iris held her breath, waiting for her aunt to tell her what happened next.

'She was treading water, effortlessly part of the lake, and I was out of breath from the effort of swimming so far. Nuala looked at me with those eyes of hers and told me that what I had seen the day before – her kissing Conrad – had been an accident. She told me that Conrad had forced a kiss on her.'

Maeve brought her hands to her chest as if her heart were breaking.

'Oh, her words made me even more angry. She couldn't even own up to the fact she had been shifting my boyfriend. She didn't say sorry, no, instead she told me that Conrad was a complete shit, those were her words. She said – *Maeve, he doesn't care about you.* She said – *Maeve, you deserve better.'*

Maeve gave a jagged sigh and shook her head again. Her eyes were loaded with tears.

'She was right, of course, but I didn't believe her. No, girls, I just saw red. I told her to shut up and I told her I hated her.'

Maeve put her hands to her throat as if she wished to take back her cruel words from all those years ago.

'Nuala looked shocked at my rage, which made me angrier. How presumptuous of her to think I would agree with her! I remember she said something, *you're really thick*, or something like that and I just had a gut reaction. I kicked out with my leg. I could feel my foot hit her chest, and she let out a gasp. I swivelled in the water to swim back to shore and saw Aisling emerge from the house with a face like thunder.'

Maeve closed her eyes again. Her face was drained of any colour and Iris thought she looked like she might faint.

'Nuala called after me. She said she was only trying to help me and I was a fool. I spun around again in the lake, pure, undiluted rage coursing through my body, and I kicked Nuala again, really hard. My foot missed her chest but whacked her in the face. Blood began to pour from her nose, and she looked a little dazed. I was shocked at the force of my rage, and part of me faltered, but she deserved to be hurt because she had hurt me.'

Maeve gave a low, tortured sigh as she opened her eyes again.

'I remember she just said *Oh* and put her hand to her head. But she was bobbing up and down in the water and I thought she was fine, so I swam back to shore. Meanwhile, Aisling was running towards the lake and she was yelling at Nuala that she was a bitch and to give her back her money. She clearly hadn't seen me kick our sister because she had been too far away, but as I waded out of the lake in my dripping pyjamas, I had never seen Aisling as angry before. She was cursing Nuala and demanding she swim back in and give her the money. She didn't even seem to notice I had got into the lake in my nightclothes. I had never seen her so worked up. I remember she told me that Nuala had stolen all her savings. I remember she said – *I really need it.*'

Maeve lowered her arms and they hung by her sides as tears began to trail down her cheeks.

'I told your mother that Nuala was running away, and she'd hidden her things in the trees. I reckoned Aisling's money was in Nuala's bag. I had my back to the lake, and Aisling was facing it. I will never forget what she said next... *Nuala, stop that and come up. Stop hiding!'*

Aunt Maeve paused in the telling of her story. She sat back down in her chair, her hand pressed to her chest, as if struggling for breath.

'It was when I heard Aisling call out those words to Nuala, I knew something wasn't quite right. I could just feel it. I turned around and saw the lake's surface rippling where Nuala had gone underwater. *Where is she?* I asked Aisling, slightly panicked. *Nuala does this all the time*, Aisling said. *She can hold her breath for ages. She'll bob up in a minute. I just saw her treading water.* I thought of the kick I had given Nuala to the head. I turned to Aisling, and I asked her to swim out with me. *Maybe we should go and check on her.*

'But your mother thought Nuala was just being difficult and doing what she did all the time. Hiding under the water until we left her alone. She didn't know what I had done to her and I didn't tell her. So she stalked off towards the trees to get her money back. I should have told Aisling I had kicked Nuala in the head, but I didn't. I stared at the lake and willed my sister to reappear. One minute went by, two, and still she didn't surface. I called to her again and again, begged her to stop messing about, but still she didn't reappear, so I waded back into the lake. I was really panicking now as I plunged back into the cold water and began to swim out. I went under the water, my eyes wide open, but all I could see were the swaying reeds at the bottom of the lake, shoals of fish shimmering by. I came to the surface and a flock of birds took off like tiny pieces of tin foil in the sky.'

Maeve paused again, and her face was tight with the pain of the memory of the last day she had seen her sister in the lake. Iris shivered again, and despite the fire crackling away in the grate, she felt cold right down to her bones.

'I was screaming her name, *Nuala, Nuala*, spinning around in the water. *Nuala! Nuala!* But there was no reply. My sister was gone.'

Maeve paused, her breath heavy and laboured, tears dripping off her chin. Lizzie got up and handed her a tissue, but Iris couldn't move because it was hard to believe what she was hearing. She had never met Nuala, and yet she felt as though she had through the pages of her diary, and she had loved her lost aunt. She felt a mixture of anger for what had happened to Nuala, and pity for her sobbing aunt who had lived with the guilt of killing her sister for decades.

'And that's when I saw Conrad. On the other side of the lake, he was watching me. He had seen the whole thing.' Maeve sniffed, wiping her eyes with the tissue Lizzie had given her. 'It's my fault Nuala died,' she said, in a trembling voice. 'If I hadn't kicked her then she wouldn't have drowned in the lake.' She shook her head from side to side. 'I've lived with the guilt and the pain for years. No matter how much I ask God for forgiveness, I just can't give it to myself. If only I could go back in time, I would tell Nuala she was right about Conrad. I have lived with the agony of this truth all my life.'

Maeve squeezed the wet tissue in her hands. 'And it tore me and Aisling apart, too, because I couldn't face the blame on my own. I turned on Aisling. I accused her of knowing that Nuala was in trouble and walking away. Oh, God,' Maeve said, beginning to cry again. 'In front of Daddy, after the search for our little sister's body was called off, I screamed at Aisling that at least I was trying to help Nuala by going back in the lake and swimming out to look for her, but Aisling was more interested in getting back her money than her little sister's life. And then our father turned on her and he said Aisling let Nuala drown, just like she let our mother drown.'

Maeve looked down at her lap, unable to hold Iris's gaze.

'I am so ashamed of what I did to your mother, Iris,' she said. 'But it made it easier to blame her, rather than myself, at the time. It made it easier to make myself out as the one who had tried to save her sister rather than the one who walked away. I never told her that I kicked Nuala. But now I accept what I did, and I am asking for your forgiveness, for your mother. It was me who was responsible for Nuala's death.'

Iris didn't know what to say to her aunt. Her revelation had been so shocking, and Nuala's vibrant sixteen-year-old voice was still spinning around in Iris's head. Moreover, Maeve had blamed Iris's mom and made it impossible for her to return to Ireland. And yet, Iris wasn't angry with her Aunt Maeve. She felt incredibly sorry for her and deep down she wanted somehow to comfort the poor tortured woman. She searched for the right words to say, but before she could speak there was a sound at the door which had been ajar while they spoke. Suddenly it was pushed open and there was her Uncle Conrad. He swayed in the doorway, holding a bottle of whiskey in his hand.

'What a pathetic, spineless woman you are, Maeve! Sobbing away and looking for sympathy. *Oh, I killed Nuala, it's my fault, forgive me.* But, dear wife, your story is not true.'

Conrad's eyes glittered dangerously as he came into the room. Iris wondered how long he'd been listening at the door. Her uncle turned to her, and she could see how bloodshot his eyes were, the menace in the curl of his lips.

'It's not what happened, is it, Nuala?'

'She's not Nuala, she's Iris, our niece,' Maeve hissed. 'And I don't want you anywhere near her. In fact, I should have done this years ago – but I want you to leave. Get out!'

Conrad didn't move – instead, he smiled, but it was mirthless. 'But aren't you afraid I'll go tell on you, Maeve, that I saw you kill your sister?'

'It was an accident.' Maeve stood up, gathering up her height to face her husband. 'And haven't you made me pay for it? I married you knowing you didn't love me so you could have half of the house and land, use it for you and your IRA pals to hide guns or God knows what!' she said in a trembling voice.

'Well, I don't care any more. I don't care who you tell now; I just want you gone.'

Conrad slowly clapped his hands. 'At last, you've finally got some backbone, Maeve. Well done.' He collapsed into the armchair, the bottle of whiskey still in hand, and pulled out his cigarettes. 'But I am not going anywhere,' he said, lighting a cigarette. Then he leant forward, staring at Iris. 'Will you tell her or will I, Nuala?'

'My name is Iris,' Iris said, standing up as well. 'Come on.' She turned to Lizzie. 'Let's go.'

She walked past her uncle, his head swaying, the stink of cigarettes and booze off him making her want to throw up. Her aunt stood motionless in the centre of the room, a tortured expression on her face. Iris paused, and then she reached out her hand to her aunt. Maeve looked at her with doleful eyes.

'It was an accident,' she said to her aunt. 'You didn't mean for Nuala to die.'

'But it wasn't, not really,' Conrad sputtered. 'You see, Nuala never drowned.'

All three women turned to look at him in astonishment.

'What did you say?' Maeve said, her voice a husk.

'While you were diving down to the bottom of the lake, looking for Nuala, she had already swum to the other side, over to me. She was a strong swimmer, remember? And yes, she had a bloody nose, but that was all.'

Conrad looked almost gleeful at the shocking impact of his words on the rest of them.

'Nuala was alive?' Maeve whispered in shock.

Conrad closed his eyes as if in a dream, a smile upon his face.

'She walked out of the lake, in her underwear, and she was like some kind of goddess. Like Áine with the golden hair, who lives on the bottom of the lakebed. I just wanted a little piece of her for myself. Just one kiss.'

He opened his eyes up again, smile gone.

'But when she saw me, she laughed at me, and called me a Peeping Tom. She denigrated my feelings for her.' Conrad's voice hardened, his eyes narrowing into slits. 'I only wanted one kiss, but she wouldn't let me – she was such a tease – pretending she was all wholesome on the outside, but she was black inside. A little slut, right, Nuala?' He leered at Iris.

'What did you do to my sister?' Maeve's voice was shaking, as horror swept across her face.

'Nuala was a nympho, you know that, right? She slept around, and all I asked for was one kiss! She made such a fuss.' Conrad pulled on his cigarette, but Iris could see his hand shaking slightly as he did so. 'She pushed me first, you know. So I just pushed her back.' He paused, took a swig from his whiskey bottle. 'And then she fell.'

'What do you mean, she fell?' Maeve asked, her voice rising to a hysterical pitch.

'Exactly that. One push, that's all, and she fell backwards. She hit her head on a stone.' Conrad paused, a cruel smile on his face. 'God, I've enjoyed watching you torture yourself with guilt for years, Maeve. But I guess it's only fair that one day I told you the truth. I killed Nuala. Though, of course, I didn't mean to, but then it was done. She was gone. All because she didn't want to give me a kiss. What a tragedy, eh?'

Maeve shrieked, clutching her hand to her chest as if she couldn't breathe. Iris and Lizzie stared at each other in horror.

'It was a waste of a life to be sure, and maybe she didn't deserve it, not like the others,' Conrad said, his tone so casual it was hard to believe he was talking about Nuala's death.

'What do you mean, the others?' Lizzie spoke up.

'This land' – Conrad narrowed his eyes – 'is full of bodies.'

'What? Who?' Maeve gasped, as her fingers dug into Iris's hand.

'The disappeared, traitors, those who snitched on the IRA,

that's who,' Conrad said. 'Did you really think our fathers were out badger baiting all those years ago? They were true Republicans.' Conrad sneered at Maeve. 'And to your father, I was the son he never had. Someone to be proud of and help the cause that he and my dad believed in. He never trusted you girls, not even you, Maeve.'

Iris didn't know what Conrad meant by 'the disappeared', but clearly Lizzie did. She marched towards the door, speaking to Iris's Aunt Maeve as she did so.

'Let's get out of here now, and go straight to the guards. Yer man and his cronies have been burying victims of the Troubles on this land! He needs to be locked up...'

'Good luck with that,' Conrad mocked her. 'I've friends in places of influence, don't you know. What I suggest, girls, is that you get going before I give Donovan and the lads a call.'

'Where's Nuala's body? What did you do with her?' Maeve's back and shoulders were arching with anger and pain.

'She's in the lake all right, Maeve. I made sure to put her back in, weighted with stones. She's with her mam. God rest their souls,' he said, crossing himself with fake decorum.

'You're a monster.' Maeve let go of Iris's hand and ran over to the fireplace, picking up the poker.

'No, Maeve, no,' Iris called out, and Lizzie ran to pull back Maeve's arm. Made her drop the poker.

'He's not worth it,' she said to Maeve.

Conrad was laughing so much that he spilled his bottle of whiskey all over himself. His eyes were half-closed, he was so drunk.

'Go on and fuck off, Maeve, you barren bitch,' he mocked.

Iris took a hold of her aunt's arm and between her and Lizzie they got her to leave the room. Maeve was still shaking, and Iris wasn't sure if her aunt was angry or broken-hearted by her husband's brutal revelations. In the doorway, Maeve paused and whistled to the dogs. They immediately got up from in front of the fire and trotted over to her.

'He's not having Aed, Fiacra and Conn like everything else I have,' she said between gritted teeth as she walked out the door, her loyal dogs at her heels. But Conrad was so drunk, he didn't seem to care.

Looking over her shoulder, Iris saw her uncle slouch in the armchair, fag still between his fingers, bottle in the other hand.

'Ah, Nuala,' he said to her, his eyes black as coals. 'You asked for it. You know you did.'

CHAPTER THIRTY-TWO

NUALA

The lake is the well of our sorrows. Filled with the tears of all the women of Ireland who did not get to sing their song. You can hear us if you listen hard. Our sighs in the gentle lap of water upon land, our chagrin in the wild waves the wind whips up.

I dwell in the Lake of Birds, which has existed since the time of gods and goddesses, when mere mortals walked among the divine. When to be divine was touchable, not the precinct of priest and papacy. When to be divine was within the feminine and our solace was through quiet reflection in all beings, no matter gender.

Here I am with mother, with daughter, sister to myself. And we spin together the old legends of Ireland with the silken threads of our wet hair, and we sing them from our hearts so that on a mist-laden night you see through the veil to the world of the fey. Hear the echo of our calls. We are what has passed, what is to come, what is present.

Our goddess is Áine and she lives at the bottom of the lake, combing her golden hair with a golden comb. But do not be deceived by her benign appearance, for she is as much a warrior as Queen Maeve. If you come to the lakeshore at night and tell her your wrongs, she will see you right. For she has brought down kings that dared to defile her. She will be your champion, and when your voice is taken from you, Áine speaks for you. She never gives up on justice for the abused. She brings down retribution on those who deserve it. She tells me –*Rest now. Be easy. Float within my depths, for all will be as it should.*

I am Nuala of the Lake of Birds. My spirit free in the flight of wild swans, and my truth sown into the destiny of my descendants. As raindrop is to lake, so we are a part of each other, each of our souls a glint of gold. Together, we can become the sun of a new dawn and burst the dark clouds of patriarchy. Listen, can you hear our morning chorus? Sing with us.

CHAPTER THIRTY-THREE

IRIS

5 JANUARY 1992

Inside Lizzie's cottage, it felt as if the dust was settling after an explosion. Finally, Iris had learned the dreadful truth about what happened to Nuala. She felt awful for her mom. After Nuala had disappeared, her mom had probably blamed herself for not trying to save her little sister. Iris couldn't find it in her heart to be angry with her Aunt Maeve for letting everyone think so badly of her mother, because the poor woman was clearly in a lot of distress and wracked with guilt herself.

'Let's have some hot sweet tea,' Lizzie said, putting on the kettle as Iris and her aunt sat down at her kitchen table.

'I just can't believe it,' Maeve whispered. 'All these years, I never knew the truth about Nuala.'

'We need to tell the guards about what Mr Maguire is up to, right?' Lizzie asked, looking at Maeve anxiously.

'Yes, of course. I won't stop until I get him out of my house,' Maeve said, gathering herself. 'But I'll do it after you girls have left tomorrow. We don't want any more drama before then.'

Iris clasped her hands under the table. Tomorrow, she and

Lizzie were heading off to London so she could get an abortion. Now she had her passport back, she could go back to New York and sort it all out there. But even though she'd only known Lizzie a short time, it felt so much better not to have to go through the experience of the abortion alone. She wanted it to be over so badly and at the same time she was dreading the long journey. Would the other passengers be looking at her and Lizzie and thinking one of them was an Irish girl in trouble? Would they judge her when they got to the clinic? What if there were pro-life protestors outside it? She was so scared, but at the same time, very sure that she was doing the right thing for her and that she would have Lizzie by her side. She just wished it could have been more private. It felt like so many people, even Lizzie's father, who she had never met, knew about her crisis.

As the three of them drank their tea in stunned silence, Iris heard a car pull up outside. Both she and her Aunt Maeve stiffened, but Lizzie jumped up from the table and looked out of the window.

'It's okay, it's my dad,' she said, glancing at Iris and giving her a peculiar look. 'I didn't know he'd be back today, sorry.' She looked uncomfortable. 'I thought I'd have more time to explain—'

Her sentence was cut off as the door swung open, and in walked a tall man with fair hair and beard, wearing a pair of round spectacles. He had on a big red sweater and faded jeans.

'Dad!' Lizzie ran over and hugged her father, and Iris felt a little twinge of envy.

'Hello, there,' Lizzie's father said, looking over at Iris and her aunt.

'Hello, Mr Weber,' Maeve said. 'I am so sorry to barge in on you like this, but—'

'Dad, *so* much has been going on,' Lizzie interrupted in excitement. 'We found out what happened to Nuala Kelly!'

Mr Weber's gaze fell on Iris. 'You must be Iris,' he said,

really looking at her, as if he was searching for something in her face. 'I am sure your aunt has told you how like Nuala you look.'

Maeve looked up at Mr Weber in surprise. 'Did you know Nuala?' she asked him.

'A little,' he said, a blush creeping up his neck. 'I spent one summer working at Lough Bawn Forest Park in the restaurant. But when I went back home to Germany, I missed Ireland so much that I returned a few months later, and I've stayed ever since. Set up my glass-blowing business here.'

'I had no idea,' Maeve said, looking at Mr Weber curiously.

'Yes, I never met you, Maeve,' he said. 'You didn't work at Lough Bawn Forest Park, did you?'

'No,' she said. 'But both Nuala and Aisling did.'

Iris began to feel her heart quicken. Was it just possible... No, it was too much to believe, not after all the revelations of the day.

'Did you know my mother, Aisling?'

Mr Weber blinked at her and gave a slight nod. 'Yes I did, Iris, and I am so sorry for your loss,' he said, sounding like he really meant it.

'Tell her, Dad,' Lizzie said in a quiet voice by his side.

Lizzie's father paled, all the while looking intently at Iris. She felt as if a wave of emotion was passing through her, making her a little dizzy.

Lizzie walked over to the kitchen dresser, and pushing aside a vase full of wild rushes, she revealed a small glass swan exactly like the one Iris possessed – but instead of shades of blue and violet, the body of this swan was red and green.

'My dad makes these swans, and you have one, don't you?' Lizzie nodded at her encouragingly.

Iris opened her purse and took out the swan, placing it on her palm.

It gleamed in the dusky light.

'Did you give this to my mom?'

'Yes, Iris,' Mr Weber said.

Iris stood up, her legs shaking.

'Oh, my goodness!' Maeve exclaimed, putting two and two together.

'Are you my father?' Iris whispered, looking up at tall Mr Weber.

'Yes, yes, he is!' Lizzie called out joyfully. 'He's been looking for you for years!'

Hours later, Iris was lying in one of the twin beds in the spare bedroom, listening to her aunt snoring and trying to go to sleep. But it was impossible. The events of the whole day had been too overwhelming. Lizzie's father was her father too! He was the mysterious German boy, Stefan, who had fallen in love with her mother in the summer of 1972. But Stefan had gone home to Germany before her mother had discovered she was pregnant.

'There was a missed call for me one day,' he had told Iris as they sat around the kitchen table in the cottage, eating vegetable soup which Lizzie had made for them all. 'My mother said it was an Irish girl, and I knew it must be Aisling, but I didn't have a number to ring her back on.' He shook his head with regret. 'We were so young, I just thought that was it, you know, but I did receive a letter from her eventually. It had been sent to the wrong city in Germany by mistake and had taken weeks to get to me. In the letter, she told me she was pregnant, and she asked for my help. She told me she wanted to keep the baby, but things were difficult at home.

'I went back to Ireland immediately, but by then it was November,' he explained. 'Aisling was gone, and Swan Hall was shrouded in this tragedy about Nuala. I decided to stay in the locality, hoping that Aisling might come back, but weeks went by. I eventually went to see her father.'

'I bet that didn't go down too well,' Maeve said, raising her eyebrows.

'He sent me packing, said he had no idea where Aisling was and if he saw me on his property again he'd put a bullet to my head, to be exact.' Stefan gave a wry smile.

'That sounds like Daddy all right,' Maeve said.

'I waited some more, hoped Aisling might come home, but time went on, and then I met Lizzie's mam. I fell in love again,' he said, simply.

'He always told me about you,' Lizzie said to Iris.

'There's enough dark secrets in Ireland,' Stefan said. 'I didn't want to hide anything from my daughter.'

'I'm sorry,' Iris said. 'But my mom never told me anything about you.'

Stefan looked disappointed.

'But I think she didn't want me to get hurt when I was little, in case we couldn't find you, or you didn't want to know me,' she said. 'And then when I was older, I didn't want her to tell me. I thought I was better off not knowing.'

'I've always felt you out there.' Lizzie spoke up, her eyes shining. 'I've always known I had a big sister, and I've longed for you. I just knew it when I saw you in the woods with Maeve Maguire. But I didn't know how to tell you.'

Iris placed her hands on her heart as it thumped in her chest. She had lost her mom, and would never get her back. It was so hard to accept that. But she'd found something quite unexpected here in her mother's homeland. A father and a sister, who both wanted her, had always wanted her.

Iris rolled over in the bed. Try as she could, sleep evaded her. The more she thought about how important it was she got some rest before the long trip tomorrow, the more awake she felt. Her stomach swirled with nerves about what the next day would bring. She pulled off the bed covers and tiptoed out of the bedroom so as not to disturb her Aunt Maeve. She made her way down the stairs as quietly as she could. Inside the cottage living room, the embers from the fire were still smouldering in the wood stove, and a small lamp was lit, casting a warm glow around the room. She felt safe and protected here in her father's cottage, in a way she never had in the big draughty spaces of Swan Hall.

Iris walked over to a door leading into a small glass conservatory where the dogs were sleeping. The night wasn't as dark as she'd expected. In fact, the whole sky was lit up a deep umber orange, as if the sun was still setting. Iris stared at the sky, watching the dark shapes of birds rising from the woods at Swan Hall and flying off in a flock as if in panic. She went back into the cottage sitting room and looked at the clock on the mantelpiece over the fire. It was well after two o'clock in the morning, and the moon was waning. Where was the orange light coming from? Iris went back into the conservatory and unlocked the door, disturbing the three black Labradors, although Lizzie's little dog, Rascal, slept on.

As soon as she stepped outside, she could smell burning. She ran to the end of the cottage garden, dogs alongside her, and climbed over the gate, up the rise of land towards the woods. Even before she could see what was happening, she knew it. Aed, Conn and Fiacra began to whine in unison. They knew it too. At the top of the cottage garden was a view of the woods, the lake and Swan Hall. She gasped as she saw flames leaping from the downstairs windows of the old house, and smoke pluming up into the sky. Iris and the dogs ran back down the field, the three of them barking in alarm. She hurled herself over the gate, and into the conservatory as the dogs continued to bark, joined by Rascal, who had now woken up. She tore up the stairs of the cottage, banging on the bedroom doors. First to emerge was Stefan, looking blurry-eyed and confused.

'There's a fire!'

'What!' he said, immediately awake and looking around him in confusion.

'No, not here, at Swan Hall,' Iris said, as Lizzie emerged on the landing.

Iris stormed into the spare bedroom, turning on the light. 'Aunt Maeve, wake up!'

'What is it, Iris?' her aunt said, sitting up in the bed, her eyes heavy with sleep.

'Swan Hall's on fire!'

Her aunt leapt out of the bed immediately. 'The horses!' she gasped.

While Lizzie rang the fire brigade, and stayed behind with the dogs, Iris, her Aunt Maeve and Stefan got in Stefan's car, speeding down the lane to Swan Hall. Iris gasped as they bumped down the drive. Up close, it was even worse than in the distance. The whole house was aflame now. Iris thought of her Uncle Conrad. Was he still inside the house somewhere? Or had he set Swan Hall on fire as some kind of sick revenge, and was long gone?

They left the car at the top of the drive and ran towards the house. Iris could hear the sound of the fire within splintering wood as black smoke churned out of the windows.

'Is your husband inside, Maeve?' Stefan shouted at her over the roar of the fire.

'I don't know!' she said, and then, catching sight of Conrad's VW Golf in the stable yard, she nodded.

Stefan ran towards the back door, but the heat from the house was too intense and he was pushed back.

'I'm sorry,' he told her. 'We'll have to wait for the firefighters to get inside.'

'We'll get the horses,' Maeve called to Stefan and Iris as they turned towards the stables. Sparks from the fire were landing all around them, the air churning with smoke, and Iris could hear the panicked whinnying of Merlin and Pixie.

'You take Pixie,' Maeve ordered Iris. 'Stefan and I will manage Merlin. He's terrified of fire.'

Iris caught sight of her aunt's black stallion rearing on his hind legs as Maeve and Stefan tried to guide him out of his stall. Pixie, in comparison, was rooted to the spot, whinnying in terror and looking at Iris with terrified eyes.

'It's okay,' she clucked, pulling a bridle over the pony's head. She took her scarf from around her neck and tied it over Pixie's eyes as she saw Maeve blindfold Merlin with her own scarf. 'Come on, you can do it.' But the pony stood firm and wouldn't budge. Panic began to mount inside Iris as she watched Maeve and Stefan gradually move Merlin out of the stable.

'Are you okay?' Stefan turned to her. 'Shall I help you?'

But Iris could see her aunt couldn't manage Merlin on her own. The horse was rearing and bucking in terror.

'I've got this,' she said, with as much confidence as she could muster.

'Get out quick, Iris,' Stefan said, his eyes blazing with concern. 'If the pony won't move, you'll have to leave him.'

'No.' Iris gritted her teeth. 'No, come on, Pixie.'

Maybe the pony sensed she wasn't going to give up, because all of a sudden he lurched forward. Carefully, Iris coaxed Pixie out of the stables, ignoring the burning smell, the air spinning with embers and ashes. She had never felt so frightened and brave all at the same time.

Outside on the cobbles, they led the horses out through the stable yard and onto the lawn. At the same time, they heard the fire engine coming down the drive.

'Oh my God,' Aunt Maeve groaned as she watched her ancestral home disintegrating into fire. 'Conrad...'

'Maybe he got out before it took hold?' Stefan said.

'But where is he, then?' Maeve said, her voice cracking. 'His car is still here. Oh Jesus, Conrad!'

Her aunt brought her hands to her face while Stefan put his arm around her. Iris watched on, praying the firefighters could rescue her uncle, much as she loathed him. She remembered the last sight she had had of her Uncle Conrad, slumped in the armchair, full of whiskey and with a lit cigarette hanging between his fingers.

She couldn't say anything. It was too shocking. All Iris could do was stroke Pixie as the horse shook beside her, and watch the firemen attempt to put out the blazing house. The fire had turned the sky orange, and in front of Swan Hall, the lake reflected red as if it were made of blood, not water.

CHAPTER THIRTY-FOUR

IRIS

5 AUGUST 1993

NEW YORK

Iris plumped up the cushion on the couch for what felt like the hundredth time.

'Relax, would you, Iris?' Trina teased. 'You're acting like they're the royal family.'

'But it's important,' Iris said, feeling jittery with nerves. 'It's Lizzie and Stefan's first visit to New York and I want them to love everything about the apartment.'

'Of course they will,' her Aunt Maeve said, joining Iris and Trina in the living room. 'Aisling made a beautiful home here,' she said, looking a little sad. 'I knew she would.'

'Remember, Maeve, we've talked about this,' Trina said to Maeve. 'No regrets. Guilt is not a useful emotion to share with the world.'

'I'm trying,' Maeve said, sitting down on the couch and looking out of the window at the view of Brooklyn Bridge. 'But there's a lot to feel bad about.'

Iris still couldn't get used to her Irish aunt spending so much time in her mom's apartment in Brooklyn. But after the fire at Swan Hall, when Maeve's whole world had come crashing down and she'd lost everything – her home, her livelihood, and her husband – Iris had invited her to come out to New York for a while. She had never expected her to stay, but Maeve had in fact hung out for three months with Iris that first time, even flying out to California with her and visiting her college. She'd come back the following Christmas and met Trina again, her fear of flying long gone. Despite the fact they'd never liked each other as teenagers, Maeve and Trina, as older women hit it off immediately. Maeve had even got involved helping Trina with her welfare work, although her heart was with animal rights rather than human rights. On this visit, Maeve had announced she'd turned vegan, which was quite a turnaround from someone who had once made their living from dairy farming.

They didn't talk about Swan Hall often. It was too painful for all of them. After the fire, the remains of Conrad's body had been found in the house. Maeve had told the guards about all the IRA activity on the property, and they had begun digging up the land around the lake. Bodies had been found of those who had gone missing and had been suspected as being executed by the IRA as traitors as far back as the early Seventies. It was a gruesome history to the house, and Iris had no desire to ever return there. There was no need to. Her aunt had used the money from the house insurance and selling off the land to buy an apartment in Dublin. Lizzie had moved to London to study art, and Stefan had sold his cottage and moved back to Germany.

The intercom buzzed and Iris jumped up in excitement. 'It's them!'

'So go and let them in, dummy.' Trina laughed.

Iris ran out to the hall and pressed the intercom. 'Hey!'

'We're here!' Lizzie's voice sang down the line, lifting her spirits instantly.

Iris flung the door of the apartment open. She couldn't wait a moment longer to see her sister. She bounded down the stairs, floor after floor, until she saw Lizzie's bouncing fair hair moving towards her. In Lizzie's wake was Stefan, their father. Iris was pleased he was such a nice man, though a little sad for her mom, that she had never got to meet him again. But if Iris was honest, it was Lizzie she wanted to see the most. They had a special bond. One which would last their whole lives. Iris thought about her mom and her sisters, the lost Nuala and the estranged Maeve, and she promised herself no matter what, she and Lizzie would never fall out.

Iris and Lizzie fell into each other's arms, laughing and hugging. It was as if they had seen each other the day before, although it had been nearly a year since Iris had visited Lizzie in London. That was how it was with true sisterhood, whether blood or not, because Iris knew in her heart, Lizzie had been a sister to her from the moment she had pulled her out of the lake at Swan Hall.

CHAPTER THIRTY-FIVE

RUAIRI

IRELAND

Ruairi watched his daughter, Carrie, charge up Queen Maeve's Cairn. She was angry. Not with him, but with what was happening back home in the States. She had ranted all the way in the car on their drive to Strandhill. They were on a visit back to Ireland, to see his father and stepmother, who had recently moved from County Louth to the west of Ireland. When Ruairi had told Carrie the story behind Queen Maeve, she'd been keen to come with him. She loved hearing about all the Irish Celtic warrior queens. Besides, her obsession with what was happening back home was causing a little friction with Ruairi's father, who couldn't understand why his grand-daughter was so enraged by the overturning of Roe v. Wade by the American Supreme Court and its impact on abortion rights. Ruairi had suggested he take Carrie over to Strandhill for the day while his father and stepmother went off to visit friends.

Carrie scrambled up the cairn, and even though Ruairi had longer legs, he found it hard to keep up.

'What next? They'll be after marriage equality! Trans rights!' Carrie gave out as they stood on the top of Queen Maeve's Cairn.

Ruairi didn't reply. Of course he agreed, but he knew his twenty-one-year-old daughter needed to voice her rage and frustration rather than listen to any platitudes.

Ruairi gazed at the view, and the deep blue of the Atlantic Ocean drew out memories of another time he had stood on top of Queen Maeve's Cairn. He was surprised by the ache in his heart as it flooded with shame and regret.

'We're going back in time!' Carrie said. 'They're saying that they're going to try to stop women from states where abortion is now illegal from travelling to other states to get an abortion – can you believe it, Daddy?'

Carrie looked up at her father, and Ruairi felt such admiration for his daughter. She had red hair like her mother but possessed his brown eyes, though hers were even bigger and framed by long, thick eyelashes. Having a daughter had changed his life from the moment he had held her in his arms. He would lay down his life for her, and he wanted to fight her battles for her. But today, she was so possessed with rage over the ruling by the Supreme Court that had led to trigger laws meaning that in many American states it was now illegal to have an abortion. At first, he had tried not to listen, because it was a subject which always stirred up so much guilt for him. But Carrie had made him comprehend why abortion rights were vital for women's rights.

'The ones who will suffer will be the marginalised,' Carrie said. 'If you're rich and white, then you can travel to another state, go private, get help, but it's the most vulnerable that will suffer. Women trapped in abusive marriages, rape victims...'

Tears were glistening in his daughter's eyes, and Ruairi was shocked by how upset she was. It occurred to him – had his daughter ever had an abortion? He knew in that instant, as the wind pushed into him, that he would fight with all the force he could to protect her right to choose.

'Daddy, what was it like living in Ireland when abortion was illegal?' Carrie turned to face him. 'Did you know any girls that had to travel to England?'

His daughter's question, so out of the blue, gave him a fright, and Ruairi felt the blood drain from his face.

'No, no one,' he said, looking away quickly. 'Come on, let's go down and get a coffee.'

Her daughter slipped her hand into his as they walked down the cairn, and he imagined, as he sometimes liked to do, that she was still his little girl. For most of her life, he had been trying to make up for the fact that he and her mom had broken up when she was eight years old. He was proud of the fact they had both put Carrie first and dealt with their differences respectfully and in private. His ex was now remarried, and he liked her new husband. They had even all gone out to dinner together on Carrie's twenty-first birthday. Today of all days, he'd wanted to bring Carrie to see Queen Maeve's Cairn. He had never brought his wife here.

'I can't believe you were once a cop, Daddy,' Carrie said as she took a sip of her hot chocolate. No sooner had they taken a window seat in the seaside café than it had begun to rain, dramatic curtains of it, sweeping in from the sea. 'I can't imagine you arresting someone or reading them their rights. You're so gentle!'

'Being a guard in rural Ireland is slightly different from being a New York cop, Carrie,' Ruairi said. 'But it's true, honey, it never felt like the right thing for me.'

Ruairi placed his hands on the wooden armrests of his chair.

It felt good to connect with the smooth wood and made him feel a little better. Ever since they had come down from Queen Maeve's Cairn, he'd had a headache. But touching wood, making his furniture, and being near trees made him feel himself again. That was why he'd moved to Washington State, not too far from Seattle, to be close to old-growth forests.

'I just can't believe the Supreme Court ruling,' Carrie began again, tears in her eyes. 'It feels like such an assault on my rights as a young woman.'

Ruairi looked at his daughter, so bereft at the news of the loss of abortion rights in her home country, and he believed he understood exactly how she felt. Again, deep shame overwhelmed him at his behaviour all those years ago. He could never tell Carrie about what he had done to Iris. Why had he not stood up to Eamon and told him that he wasn't going to arrest Iris? But at that time, it was as if everyone he knew had thought abortion was murder. He had got swept up in the self-righteousness of his colleague, who had been pushed to detain Iris by Father Francis and Conrad Maguire. If Ruairi was truthful, though, he had also been angry with Iris. He had really fallen for her that day they had climbed Queen Maeve's Cairn. When he had found out she was pregnant by someone else – obviously before she'd met him, but still, she should have told him – he had felt she'd played him somehow. He had been hurt and he'd wanted to see her suffer.

'What's wrong, Daddy?' Carrie interrupted his thoughts.

'Oh nothing, darling,' he said.

'But you look so sad,' she said, placing her hand on his. 'Is it hard coming back here after all this time?'

His daughter was so empathic sometimes, it took him by surprise.

'I'm just thinking about someone I once knew,' he said, surprised by his need to share.

'A girl?'

He nodded.

'Ah, well, what was her name?' Carrie looked pleased to be taken into her father's confidence.

'Iris,' Ruairi said, again feeling a stab to his heart.

He had tried to make it right, but when he had called to Stefan Weber's cottage, Iris had already left for the ferry with Lizzie Weber. The fire at Swan Hall had created a big local drama, especially when it was found out that the IRA had been using it to dump the bodies of those they considered traitors. He had been pulled into the investigation, supporting all the guards and special branch who came down from Dublin. Conrad Maguire had been killed in the fire, and when the investigators had finished at the scene it had been discovered that the fire had been an accident, started by a dropped cigarette.

By the time Ruairi had managed to call out again to Mr Weber, he had been told that Iris and her Aunt Maeve had left for New York. At first Lizzie had refused to give him Iris's address, but when he'd explained he wanted to write and apologise, she had finally given in.

Not long afterwards, Ruairi had resigned from the Garda Síochána, and gone travelling. He had headed for South America, but always on his radar was New York, and a year later he had found himself standing outside Iris's apartment in Brooklyn. He had been so close to ringing the buzzer to the apartment, but every time he'd tried to do so, he had been consumed by guilt and shame. How could she ever forgive him or trust him? He had walked away, persuading himself she would have been in California at college anyway, and not long afterwards he had met Carrie's mom and decided to leave Ireland, Iris and his past behind.

But the past was coming back to him now. He had found himself dreaming of the west of Ireland with such a deep longing, and now he was here, with his daughter, he did feel like he was home.

On the way back to his father and stepmother's house, Ruairi took Carrie on a detour. Without even planning it, he found himself driving up the laneway to Swan Hall. A battered *For Sale* sign was shoved in the ground next to the gateposts bearing the two stone swans, one of which had its beak broken off.

'Where's this?' Carrie asked, as it stopped raining, though clouds still loomed overhead. 'It looks real spooky.'

The land had taken over. Trees pushed in from the woods to create a dark tunnel which they drove through, the lane bumpy with rocks, potholes and thistles. As Ruairi turned the corner, Swan Hall loomed into view. It was a ruin. The roof had caved in during the fire, and you could still see the charred innards of the old house. He pulled in and stopped the car.

'This house belonged to Iris,' Ruairi told his daughter.

'The one that got away?' Carrie said, giving her dad's arm a squeeze.

He shrugged, slightly embarrassed by his daughter's questioning as they both got out of the hire car. They walked towards the derelict house. There was a *Danger* sign on the door, but Ruairi had no intention of going inside Swan Hall.

'What happened to the house?' Carrie asked her father.

'There was a fire,' he said.

'It's such a shame,' she said. 'What a waste!'

As they walked around the corner of the house, the garden was a jungle of high grasses and weeds, but also filled with wildflowers, buzzing with bees, the air alive with fluttering butterflies.

'It's so beautiful,' Carrie said. 'Oh, look, do you see the lake?'

They walked down to the water, the high grasses soaking their jeans. To Ruairi's eyes, the lake appeared so much smaller than how he remembered it. The sky was reflected upon its still surface and he watched the clouds racing upon it. Beneath, he could see a tangle of green weeds and algae, as little insects buzzed and hopped above. When his father talked about the legend of Swan Hall, he spoke of the three sisters who could find neither peace nor harmony, as if they were the Morrígan in the old Irish myths, primed for conflict and war. Or else his stepmother spoke in whispers of the horrors the IRA had done to their own inside its dark woods. But for Ruairi, Swan Hall was Iris, the girl with golden hair who had stolen his heart that winter in Ireland.

'Look, Daddy, see the swans!' Carrie pointed.

Two white swans were gliding on the choked waters of Lough Bawn. Ruairi wondered how many years they had come to nest at Swan Hall.

As they turned back towards the car, Carrie linked her arm through Ruairi's. 'So where is this Iris now?' she asked her father.

He could lie to his daughter and tell her he didn't know, but the truth was he had been following Iris Kelly all his life. He had bought all twelve of her novels and devoured them because he could hear her voice in their words and feel the beat of her heart in their tales of loss and longing. He had read in articles that she had been married, had two children and was now divorced.

'She lives in Vancouver. She's a writer.'

'But Dad, you're only down the road in Seattle,' Carrie said. 'Go find her.'

'It's too late now,' Ruairi said, but maybe it wasn't. Maybe Iris thought about him too. He realised he had to find out. Even if it meant she slammed the door in his face. But maybe she might see how he had changed and that he understood a little now how it was for a woman. His daughter had made him see that. Maybe Iris would open her door and forgive him. That was all he could ask for, right now.

A LETTER FROM NOELLE

I want to say a huge thank you for choosing to read *The Last Summer in Ireland*. If you did enjoy it, and want to keep up to date with all my latest releases, just sign up at the following link. Your email address will never be shared and you can unsubscribe at any time.

www.bookouture.com/noelle-harrison

Every family has secrets. *The Last Summer in Ireland* aims to unearth the complicated lives, loves, betrayals and loyalties of the three Kelly sisters of Swan Hall in the west of Ireland. Here lies a lake with hidden depths and the darkest of secrets lost within its watery kingdom. Is the truth worth the day of reckoning it will bring?

The Last Summer in Ireland is about sisterhood and the bonds between women. Having lived in Ireland during a time when abortion was illegal, I have always wanted to write a story which raised this issue, but have been a little fearful of its impact. However now, in the light of recent events concerning women's rights, particularly in America, I feel this story set in the Seventies and early Nineties in Ireland has powerful resonance for the present. Within the very real-life dramas which Iris, our young American heroine, faces, she seeks the truth about her mother and her sisters. Finding solace in the myths and music of Ireland, Iris learns about the true courage of the women of Ireland and through that, finds her own voice again.

I hope you loved *The Last Summer in Ireland*, and if you did, I would be very grateful if you could write a review. I'd love to hear what you think, and it makes such a difference helping new readers to discover one of my books for the first time.

I love hearing from my readers – you can get in touch on my Facebook page, through Instagram, Twitter, Goodreads or my website.

Thanks,

Noelle Harrison

www.noelleharrison.com

 facebook.com/NoelleCBHarrison

 twitter.com/NoelleHarrison

 instagram.com/noelle.harrison5

ACKNOWLEDGEMENTS

Thank you to my fabulous agent, Marianne Gunn O'Connor, my wonderful editor, Lydia Vassar-Smith, and the great team at Bookouture.

I am so grateful for all my family and friends who have supported me as a writer and believed in me. Thank you to Lizzie McGhee, Kate Bootle and Donna Ansley for the parts they have played in inspiring this novel. Thank you also to Becky Sweeney, Bex Hunt, Charley Drover, El Lam, Monica McInerney, Sinead Moriarty, Caroline Byrne and Sandra Ireland and all my other wonderful friends from all over the world. Thank you to my son, Corey, and my daughter, Helena, and all my cherished family. Finally, thank you, dear reader, for taking time to immerse yourself in my story. I hope it brought you on a journey worth taking.

CPSIA information can be obtained
at www.ICGtesting.com
Printed in the USA
LVHW040922301222
736152LV00003B/252